THEIR FIRST NOEL

Celebrate the holidays with these four heartwarming Christmas stories about the joy of love and the miracle of birth!

LEIGH GREENWOOD
"Father Christmas"

"Leigh Greenwood's love stories will warm your heart and soul!" *—Romantic Times*

BOBBY HUTCHINSON
"Lantern In The Window"

"Ms. Hutchinson portrays the often heartrending travails of the human spirit with skill." *—Romantic Times*

CONNIE MASON
"A Christmas Miracle"

Connie Mason writes "the stuff fantasies are made of!" *—Romantic Times*

THERESA SCOTT
"The Treasure"

"Theresa Scott's captivating writing brings you to a wondrous time and shows you that love itself is timeless!" *—Affaire de Coeur*

THEIR FIRST NOEL

Leigh GREENWOOD
Bobby HUTCHINSON
Connie MASON
Theresa SCOTT

LEISURE BOOKS NEW YORK CITY

A LEISURE BOOK®

November 1995

Published by

Dorchester Publishing Co., Inc.
276 Fifth Avenue
New York, NY 10001

Leigh GREENWOOD

FATHER CHRISTMAS

For Brandon, who never got to celebrate Christmas

Chapter One

"I've got to be a fool to come here. I should be headed for California, where nobody would ever find me."

Joe Ryan glanced over at his dog, Samson. The big, yellow, short-haired mongrel was sniffing among some rocks, a growl in his throat, the hair on his back standing up.

"Stop looking for coyotes and listen to me."

The dog looked up but almost immediately turned back to the tangle of boulders and desert broom.

"You keep poking your nose into every pile of rocks you pass, and you're going to find a wolf one of these days. Maybe you can talk to him," Joe said to his horse, General Burnside. "He never listens to me."

Joe rode through the Arizona desert with care. He kept away from the flat valley floor, where a man could be seen for miles. Rather than stop for water at the cottonwood-lined San Pedro River, he looked for springs and seeps. He had shaken the posse before he left Colorado, but the law would soon figure out where he was. He planned to be gone by then.

"I can't imagine why Pete wanted a ranch in this country," Joe said aloud. "Even a coyote would have a hard time making a living."

He had fallen into the habit of talking to his dog and horse just to hear the sound of a human voice. He'd seen few people since he broke out of a Colorado jail a month earlier.

Sometime after midday, Joe pulled up just short of the crest of a small ridge. He paused to light a cigarette and let his gaze wander over every part of the landscape. When he was satisfied that there was no movement, he started forward. Using the cover of juniper thickets, scattered mesquite, and greasewood, he crossed the ridge and rode into a basin.

Pete Wilson's ranch lay below.

Joe studied the land closely as he rode in. It was good land. It would be hot in summer, but there was plenty of food for cattle. A small creek passed close to the house. He was surprised Pete had had enough sense to choose such a good spot. His former partner hadn't struck him as a far-sighted man. Impatient and bad-tempered was a better description. But then, a shrewish wife could ruin any man. And from what Pete had said, Mary Wilson was a thoroughgoing harridan.

Well, it didn't matter to Joe. He meant to find the gold, clear his name, and be on his way. It wasn't cold for December, but he was looking forward to the warm breezes of California.

"Come on, Samson. Let's get it over with."

Pressing his heels into the flanks of his lanky, mouse-gray gelding, Joe started toward the ranch.

Mary Wilson struggled to sit up. The room spun violently before her eyes. She closed them and concentrated hard. She had to get up. She was too weak to stay here any longer.

"Get the horse," she said to the blond child who watched her with anxious eyes. "Don't try to saddle him. Just put a halter on him and bring him to the porch."

"He won't come to me," Sarah Wilson said.

"Offer him some oats. I'll be outside in a moment."

The child left reluctantly. Mary didn't like forcing Sarah to fetch the animal, but she had no choice. She wasn't even sure she was strong enough to make the twenty-two-mile trip into town. She didn't know how she could be so weak without being ill. She had felt fine until two days ago. Then her strength had just vanished. Taking a firm grip on the bedpost, she pulled herself to her feet. The room spun more rapidly than ever. Gasping from the effort, Mary refused to let go of the bedpost. She *would* stand up. She *would* make it to town. She had thought she had more time. The baby wasn't due for another month.

She attempted to take a step, but her swollen stomach unbalanced her. She used a chair to steady herself. No sooner had she regained her equilibrium than she heard Sarah scream. Fear gave Mary the strength she lacked. She stumbled across the room to the rifle she kept on the wall next to the door. She took it down and managed to open the door about a foot. Leaning against the door jamb, she pushed herself forward until she could see into the ranch yard.

Sarah came flying up the steps. She almost knocked Mary down as she buried herself in Mary's skirts. Mary's gaze found and locked on the rider who had reached the corral. What she saw frightened her.

A stranger dressed in buckskin and denim, astride a huge gray horse and accompanied by a large dog, was riding into the yard. A big man with very broad shoulders, he wore a gun belt and carried a rifle. His hat was tilted too low to allow her to see much of his face, but his chin and cheeks were covered by several weeks' growth of dark blond beard. He rode right up to the porch.

Sarah tightened her grip on Mary's skirts. Mary's grip on the doorway began to give way. She leaned her shoulder against the wood to keep from falling.

The man came to a stop at the steps. He didn't dismount, just pushed his hat back from his forehead and stared hard at Mary. Mary found herself looking into the coldest blue eyes she'd ever seen.

"This Pete Wilson's place?" the man asked.

His voice was deep and rough. It didn't sound threatening, but it sounded far away. The ringing in Mary's ears distracted her. She felt her muscles begin to relax, and she tightened her grip on the rifle. "Yes," Mary said.

"You his wife?"

"I'm his widow. What can I do for you?"

The man's face seemed to go out of focus for a moment. Then it started to spin very slowly. One moment he was right side up, the next upside down. Mary fought to still the revolving image, but it only moved faster.

Then she saw nothing at all.

Joe wasn't surprised when Mary Wilson met him at the door with a rifle. He *was* surprised to see she was pregnant. He was even more surprised when she fainted. Damn! Now he'd have to take care of her. He knew absolutely nothing about the care and handling of extremely pregnant women.

Still, he was out of the saddle and up the front steps almost before her body had settled on the floor. He scooped up the unconscious woman. Despite her condition, she weighed very little. She looked white, totally drained of color. That wasn't good.

He kicked open the door and entered the small stone cabin. Looking around, he saw a rope bed in the corner. He carried her to the bed and eased her down. She rolled on her side. He put his hand on her forehead. She didn't feel hot. If anything, she seemed too cool. She looked more exhausted than anything else. Thin in the face. Almost gaunt. Maybe the baby was taking everything she ate. She looked big enough to be carrying a colt.

He pulled the blanket over her. Pete had lied. She was a pretty woman. There was nothing harsh or shrewish about her face. He'd never seen any female who could look that pretty without painting herself and putting on a fancy dress. She reminded him of some kind of fragile bird—but one with the heart of an eagle—standing guard over her chick.

She lay there, helpless. He wanted to touch her again—her skin had felt so soft under his hand—but the sight of the child cowering in the corner behind the bed caused him to back away.

"Is she sick?" he asked.

The child just stared at him, her eyes wide with fear. She pressed close to Mary but well out of his reach.

"Speak up, girl. I'm not going to hurt you. I want to know if she's sick or if she faints all the time."

The child cringed and practically buried herself in the crack between the bed and the wall. He noticed that her eyes kept going toward the doorway. He turned. Samson had followed him inside and flopped down a few feet from the door.

"Outside," Joe ordered, with a wave of his hand. "You're scaring the kid."

The dog whined in protest.

"Maybe later, but right now you're not welcome. Out."

With a protesting woof, the dog got up and ambled outside. He lay down directly in front of the open door, where Joe would have to step over him to get out.

Joe closed the door on Samson. "Nosy brute. I guess I spoiled him. I don't suppose you have a name," he said to the girl, "something I can call you?"

The child continued to stare.

"I didn't think so. You got anything to eat around here? I'm hungry. I haven't had a decent meal since I went to jail."

Still no answer. Joe was confused about the child. Pete had talked about his wife a lot—that was how he'd conned Joe into teaming up with him—but he hadn't said a word about a daughter. Was this kid Pete's or Mary's?

"What does your ma like to eat?"

No answer.

"How about you?"

It was clear that the child wasn't going to say anything, so Joe decided to look around for himself. He found a little coffee, sugar, salt, some tea, beans, bacon, and flour. Some canned goods lined a shelf against the wall. He glanced back at Mary. She looked as if she needed something sustaining. "Do you have any milk?" Joe asked the child.

She continued to stare.

"Look, I'm not going to hurt you. I'm going to fix something to eat, but I need a little help here. Your ma's looking right run down. You want her to get better, don't you?"

The child nodded, and Joe felt a little of the tension inside him relax. It wasn't much progress, but it was a beginning.

"Do you have any milk?"

The child shook her head.

Hell, he thought, every ranch or farm kept a milk

cow. What was she going to feed the baby if her milk ran dry? "How about eggs?" Come to think of it, he hadn't seen any chickens when he rode up. What kind of place was this, anyhow?

The child didn't say anything, but she cautiously left her corner, approached the door, and opened it a crack. With a sharp intake of breath, she jumped back.

Joe crossed the room in a few strides. "Dammit, Samson, I told you to get out of here." The dog got up and moved off the porch. "Go on. Find me a rabbit or something for supper."

Samson disappeared behind the house. After peeping around the corner to make sure the dog wasn't waiting to attack her, the kid headed toward a shed that seemed to serve as a barn and chicken coop. Joe figured he'd better stay outside just in case Samson came back. He stuck his head inside, but Mary hadn't moved. When he turned back, the child was out of sight.

Hell! He was on the run from the law, and he had a pregnant woman and a child who wouldn't talk on his hands. He hadn't been around a respectable woman in years and didn't know what to do with one.

The kid emerged from the shed, cast a worried look around for Samson, and ran across the yard toward the house. She slowed and came reluctantly up the steps. Looking up, she held out her hands. She had an egg in each.

If it hadn't been for the long hair, Joe wouldn't have been able to tell if she was a boy or a girl. She wore a red-checked flannel shirt and black pants. Her shoes looked more like boots several sizes too large. There was nothing feminine or appealing about the child.

"Put them on the table," Joe said. "I've got to get a

few things from my saddlebags." He should unsaddle General Burnside and give him a good rubdown, but that would have to wait. He unstrapped his saddlebags. He had started back up the steps before he turned back for his rifle. He didn't think there was anybody within twenty miles of this place, but he'd feel better if he had his rifle with him.

The kid had retreated to her position behind the bed. Joe placed his rifle against the wall and tossed his saddlebags on the table. For now he'd have to use his own supplies. He had plenty of beef jerky. He didn't know anything like it for building up a person who was weak.

"Water," he called out to the child. "I need water." When he heard nothing, he turned around. She was pointing to a bucket. He looked inside. It was half full. It was also tepid.

"Fresh water." Joe held out the bucket.

Reluctantly the child came forward, took the bucket, and headed outside again.

Joe hadn't had time to pay attention to his surroundings. Only now did he notice the dozens of drawings covering the walls, all of them black ink on white paper. There were drawings of a town somewhere in the East, of the ranch and surrounding countryside, of the child, of Pete. Even of the stone cabin.

The winter scenes were the most incredible. Even in black and white, they had the power to evoke memories of winters back home in the foothills of North Carolina. The snow weighing heavily on pine boughs, icicles hanging from the roof of a wood frame house, a woman leaning over the porch rail, barnyards made pristine by a blanket of snow.

Joe pushed the recollections aside. Not even a mantle of snow could turn his past into a happy memory.

He moved along the wall, studying each picture in detail, until he stumbled over a bunch of twigs. "What the hell!" he muttered. He had knocked over a bundle of hackberry branches tied together. A few red berries showed among the dense green foliage. Each branch ended in a sharp, strong thorn.

A muffled cry from the doorway caused him to turn. The kid dropped the bucket and threw herself at the bundle of twigs. The water spilled out and quickly disappeared down the cracks between the floor boards. Joe watched, unbelieving, as the kid set the bundle of twigs back in the corner.

"That's Sarah's Christmas tree," Mary informed him in a weak, hesitant voice.

Joe hadn't realized Mary was conscious. He drew close to the bed, scrutinizing her. She seemed okay, but he intended to make sure she stayed in bed.

"That's a bunch of hackberry branches, for God's sake," he said, unable to understand why the kid continued to fuss over them, pulling and twisting the branches until she had arranged them to her satisfaction. "They ought to be tossed on the fire. She could kill herself on those thorns."

"Sarah is determined to have a Christmas tree, and that's the best she could do."

"Why didn't she look for a Jojoba? At least it doesn't have thorns."

"She wanted the red berries. Her mother used to tell her about decorating for Christmas with holly."

"You should have stopped her."

"Who are you?" Mary Wilson asked, changing the subject. "What are you doing here?"

"I'm Pete's old partner."

She started to throw back the covers.

"Lie still."

Joe's peremptory order stilled Mary's hand in mid-

17

air. He pushed her arm down to her side and jerked the blanket back in place.

For a moment she seemed on the verge of defying him. Probably learning he was Pete's partner wasn't enough to make her trust him. But if she was afraid, she didn't show it. More likely she'd show her talons.

"I'm about to fix me something to eat. I need that water," Joe reminded the kid. She reluctantly left her tree to pick up the bucket and go back outside.

"Does the kid talk?" he asked.

"Yes."

"She got a name?"

"Sarah."

"Who is she?"

"Pete's daughter. Her mother died. I was his second wife."

Sarah entered the cabin with the fresh water. Joe took the bucket over to the work table. "Make sure your ma doesn't get up," he said over his shoulder. "Maybe if you sing to her, she'll go back to sleep."

"I can't . . . You shouldn't . . ." Mary began.

"Probably, but I'm doing it anyway," Joe said. "Sing!" he commanded the child.

Turning away from the two females watching him in open-mouthed bewilderment, Joe opened his saddlebags and began to lay out their contents. He was surprised when he heard a very soft voice begin to sing. He knew just enough to know the kid was singing in French.

He wondered what had made Pete Wilson leave such a family—a daughter who was petrified of dogs, wouldn't talk, and sang lullabies in French; a beautiful young wife who was so weak she couldn't stand up and was going to have a baby any minute if he could judge from the size of her.

Memories he thought he'd forgotten came rushing back. Damn! He hadn't thought of Flora in five years.

He didn't know why he should now. The two women had nothing in common.

Flora had been vibrantly, noisily alive. She laughed, sang, cried, shouted, always at the top of her voice. He had been wildly in love with her, but she hadn't been willing to settle down. She had liked flash, excitement, money, action—all the things Joe had learned to avoid.

Mary was nothing like that. She was fair, thin, faded, and extremely pregnant. Despite that, she had a feminine allure. Soft skin, thick eyebrows and lashes, generous lips, the curve of her cheek, the expanse of her brow—all combined to give her an appearance of lushness completely at variance with her condition.

This woman would never want flash or excitement. She would work hard to build the kind of home that nurtured a man, that he would shed his blood to defend.

She'd be the kind of woman his grandmother almost was.

After Joe's father disappeared and his grandfather died, his grandmother had raised him. Sometimes when she spoke of her husband there was a light in her eye, a softening in her voice and touch, that spoke of a time when she had been happy and content. But most often she was harsh and demanding, the kind of woman she had become to survive on her own, to hide her grief over the kind of woman her daughter had become.

Joe was sure Mary would never be like that. She had the kind of strength, the kind of staying power, that it took to endure ill fortune.

Pete Wilson was a fool.

The sound of soft singing gently drew Mary out of the darkness that clutched at her. She opened her

19

eyes. She must have fainted again. Sarah knelt by the bed, her hand gripping Mary's, as she softly sang one of the French lullabies her mother had taught her.

A noise caught Mary's attention, and she remembered the man. Pete's partner. He was at the stove. Then she realized that the cabin was warm. She hadn't been able to cut wood for a week. She had done her last cooking with twigs Sarah had gathered.

It was tempting to lie back and let him take care of everything. She was so tired. She couldn't tell what he was doing at the stove, but he moved with quiet confidence. Then she caught the delicious aroma of coffee.

He was cooking!

Her stomach immediately cramped, and saliva flooded her mouth. It had been almost two days since she had eaten a full meal.

"You never did tell me your name," she said.

The man turned. "Joe Ryan. Stay put," he ordered when she attempted to sit up. "The cornbread's not ready yet."

"I can't lie here while you fix supper."

"Why not? You couldn't do anything if you did get up."

Mary had never seen a man cook. She'd never even seen one in the kitchen except to eat. A good woman didn't get sick. There was no time. She remembered that. She'd heard it all her life, especially after her mother died and she'd had to take over managing the household.

"You don't have to take care of me."

Joe looked at her as if she were talking nonsense. "I considered leaving you lying in the doorway, but I figured I'd get tired of stepping over you."

"What did you fix?" Mary asked.

"Beef and cornbread. It's not fancy, but it's good."

"I appreciate your feeding Sarah. It's been a while since I've been able to fix her a decent meal."

"Or eaten one yourself," Joe said as he began to ladle the stew into two plates. "I don't suppose you have any butter?"

"No. I haven't been able to catch the cow."

"I guess the kid will have to drink water. Do you like molasses?"

"We both do," Mary answered. "I always did have a sweet tooth."

Joe opened the oven and took out a pan of cornbread. "I made it soft. That's the way my grandma used to make it."

He hadn't had cornbread this way in years.

He scooped cornbread out of the pan and put some on each plate. He covered each portion with a generous helping of molasses. "Get your water if you want it," he said to Sarah. He moved a chair next to the bed.

"I can get up," Mary said.

"I told you to stay put."

"I'm not an invalid."

"Then why did you faint twice today?"

"I'm sorry."

"I don't mind that," Joe said. "I just mind you acting like you're well. It's not sensible. I don't like it when people don't act sensible."

"Then what is the *sensible* thing to do?" Mary asked, slightly put out.

"Lie back and let me feed you. Then go to sleep until supper. You're worn down. I'm surprised you didn't faint before you reached the door."

She would have if it hadn't been for Sarah's scream. Only fear for the child had gotten her that far. She had passed out the minute she realized Joe didn't mean them any harm. She watched as he picked up the table and moved it next to the chair.

Then he placed both plates on the table. He placed a spoon beside one. He pulled up a second chair, and Sarah slid into it.

"Eat," he said to Sarah.

"Go on," Mary said when the child hesitated. "I'm sure it's as good as anything I could make."

"I'm a good cook," Joe said. "You sure you can sit up?"

"Of course." Mary managed to pull herself into a sitting position. She hoped he didn't know how close she was to fainting again.

"Lean forward."

She couldn't. He lifted her up and placed the pillows behind her.

"You're weak as a damned kitten."

"I was on my way to town when you got here."

"You wouldn't have made it out of the damned yard."

She would have loved to disagree with him, but she doubted she would have made it out of the house. "I would appreciate it if you would watch your language in front of Sarah."

"She's heard worse if Pete's her pa."

"Not since I've been here."

"You stopped Pete's cussing?"

"No, but he did make an effort to curb his tongue."

He looked as if he was considering her in a new light. Mary wasn't at all certain it was a flattering one.

"Open up. Your dinner's getting cold."

Mary half hoped she'd be able to tell him how truly awful it was, but the first taste confirmed his opinion of himself. He was a fine cook. It was all she could do to wait until he brought a second spoonful to her mouth.

"Eat a little cornbread. I put two eggs in it. As soon as I can find that cow, we'll have some butter. Beef's good for building a body up, but nothing works like eggs and butter."

Sarah looked up at Joe, glanced at Mary, then back at Joe. Mary was delighted to see her plate already empty.

"Get yourself some more if you want, kid," Joe said.

Sarah filled half her plate with stew, the rest with cornbread.

"For a little thing, she sure can eat." Joe put a spoonful of stew into Mary's mouth. "For a woman who was about to meet her maker, you sure talk frisky."

"I'm afraid any frisk I had disappeared long ago," Mary said, feeling a little as if she'd been chastised, "but I do have a sharp tongue. That's been a problem all my life." She swallowed another spoonful of stew. Her stomach didn't hurt anymore. Much to her surprise, she was beginning to feel full. She leaned back on the pillows.

"You haven't told me a thing about yourself," she said. "I don't even know why you're here."

"That can wait. All you have to do now is eat and sleep. It would help, though, if you could convince the kid to talk to me."

"The *kid* is named Sarah."

"Maybe, but she doesn't answer to that either."

"Talk to the gentleman, Sarah. It would be rude to remain silent, especially after he's been kind enough to cook our dinner."

"I'm not kind, and I'm not a gentleman," Joe said. "At least, no one ever thought so before."

"Maybe you never gave them reason, but you have me. Thank you."

"The only thanks I want is to see you eat up every bit of this food."

"I'm feeling rather full."

23

"That's because your stomach has shrunk to nothing. Eat a little more. Then we'll let you rest until supper."

By the time Mary managed to eat everything on the plate, she was exhausted. She was also hardly able to keep her eyes open. The hot food, the warmth in the cabin, and the knowledge that she was safe combined to overcome her desire to stay awake and question this unusual man.

"You must tell me what you're doing here," she said as she slipped back down in the bed. Joe adjusted the pillows under her head and pulled the covers up to her chin.

"Later. I'm going outside now so you can get some rest." He picked up his saddlebags and headed toward the door. He turned back. "Tell the kid she doesn't have to be afraid of Samson. He never did more than growl at a kid in his life."

"I'll explain it to *Sarah*," Mary replied.

Joe disappeared through the door. A moment later she heard him start to whistle.

Mary nestled down in the bed, but she couldn't sleep. She had never met a man in the least like Joe Ryan. She couldn't imagine him being Pete's partner.

Mary had disliked her husband. She was ashamed to admit it, but now that he was dead, it seemed pointless to continue pretending. He'd been mean, thoughtless, frequently brutal. She had never been able to imagine why her uncle had thought his stepson would make her a good husband. Not even her uncle's affection for his wife could blind him to the fact that her son was a cruel, selfish man. Her father should have protected her, but he was eager to get her out of the house. One less mouth to feed. Mary had been relieved when Pete left to prospect for gold in Colorado. Not even learning she was pregnant had made her wish for his return.

"Look out the window and see what he's doing," Mary said to Sarah.

"He's just looking," Sarah told her.

"At what?"

"Everything."

"The horse?"

"Yes."

"What's he doing now?"

"Looking in the shed."

"Anything else?"

"He's digging a hole next to the shed."

That made Mary uneasy. Any partner of Pete's was likely to be of poor character. Stealing horses from a helpless woman would probably be a small thing to him.

"Bring me the pistol," she said to Sarah. The child got the pistol from its place in the dresser drawer and brought it to Mary.

Mary checked to see that it was loaded. "Tell Mr. Ryan I would like to see him."

Chapter Two

Joe rubbed the last of the dried sweat off General Burnside with a handful of straw. "I shouldn't have left you standing this long," he apologized to his mount, "but I had to dig a few holes first. No gold buried next to the shed."

He tossed the straw aside. They both contemplated the corral. "I suppose you might stay in that if you'd been ridden so hard you were wobbly in the knees." He pushed on a rotten rail. It broke into two pieces and fell to the ground. "I guess I'll have to hobble you."

Samson trotted up from his round of inspection. "Did you find any likely places to bury gold?" he asked the dog as he put hobbles on General Burnside. "I hope you didn't eat any of those chickens. Apparently the coyotes consider them their own personal property." He shook his head at the gaping holes in the chicken fence.

He walked to the shed, a large structure open in

the front and the back. In between was a room entered through a door from the house side. Much to his surprise, Joe found wire for the chicken yard and a large number of rails for the corral. From the dust on them, they had been there a long time. Apparently Pete hadn't lacked the money or the materials to keep up the ranch, only the will to use them. Joe looked around, but saw no likely place to hide a strongbox. He'd look under the floorboards, but he doubted he'd find anything. Too obvious.

"I don't know why Pete thought panning for gold was easier than fixing a few fences now and then," Joe said. All the tools anybody would ever need were scattered around the shed. "It's a hell of a lot harder to build a sluice box and defend it from some rascal who'd rather shoot you than build his own."

He walked back out into the December sun, pulling his hat lower over his eyes. He glanced toward the house. The gold had to be there, but was it inside or out? He'd have to make a thorough search.

He could see the kid watching him through the window. Funny little kid. Odd she should be afraid of dogs. It was almost as if she was afraid of him, too. Her mother wasn't. In fact, she'd sent the kid to tell him she wanted to see him. He'd obey the summons once he'd finished in the yard.

"Don't know why Pete left a woman like that," Joe said to Samson, who followed at his heels. "She's got a bit of an edge to her, but she's got standards. A woman ought to have standards. Gives a man something to live up to." He tested the poles in the chicken yard. They needed bracing. "I can't believe Pete was such a lazy skunk."

The broken fence irritated him. It was such a little job, so easy. But it wasn't his responsibility. He looked up into the hills beyond the ranch house. If the gold was up there, he'd probably never find it.

He didn't think Pete had told his wife about it. The place didn't look like five dollars had been spent on it, certainly not twenty thousand. No, Pete had buried it here because he didn't have time to bury it anyplace else before he was killed in a card game over a pot worth less than two hundred dollars. Only a fool like Pete would do something like that when he had twenty thousand buried.

His irritation made it even harder to ignore the broken fence. "Oh hell, I might as well fix it. Why should the coyotes have all those chickens?"

He was silent while he braced the corner poles and replaced others that looked ready to break. Then he cut out the broken sections of wire, leaving clean sections to be replaced. "Can't say I look forward to catching all these chickens," he said to Samson as he wired a new piece of fence into place. "But she'll need eggs to get back on her feet. After the baby comes, she won't have time to be chasing them down."

He finished one section of wire and began cutting a piece to fit the next gap.

"Can't figure why a woman like that would marry Pete, the lazy son-of-a-bitch. She wasn't brought up out here. You can tell that from her voice. It's soft, sort of gives the words a little squeeze before she says them. You know, leaves off a few letters here and there. Virginia or Carolina. After bringing her all this way, why did Pete run off and leave her, especially with a baby coming? It's a terrible thing for a woman to be alone."

He finished the last piece of wire, tested his work, and found it strong enough to withstand coyotes and wolves.

"A lot of good work was done on this place some time ago, Samson. The man who built that cabin knew what he was doing. This shed, too. But everything is in bad need of work now."

Joe hadn't been on a farm since he was sixteen. He'd thought he hated it. But as he had grown older, he'd come to treasure his memories of the years he'd spent with his grandmother. But that kind of life needed a family, and he'd had none since she died. He'd never found a woman who made him want to stop drifting. He'd never found the right kind of place. Despite the sagging corral, the missing shingles in the roof, loose hinges, broken windows, this place seemed the right kind, Mary the right kind of woman.

No use letting those thoughts take root in his mind. He'd be gone in a few days. This place needed a man here day after day, a man who loved it as much as the man who built it. Maybe Mary Wilson could find her a better husband this time. She sure was pretty enough. Dainty and feminine. She was the kind of woman to mess up a man's thinking, start him to doing things he didn't want to do.

Like fixing a chicken yard.

Joe went into the shed and started tossing out fence posts and corral rails until he got down to the floorboards. They came up easily. The ground didn't look as if it had ever been disturbed, but he took a shovel to it anyway. Half an hour later, he knew Pete hadn't buried the gold under the shed. He replaced the floorboards, but balked at dragging all those posts and rails back inside.

"Hell! As long as I've got everything out, I may as well fix the corral. I'm going to need someplace to put that damned cow once I find her."

Joe picked up the poles and started for the first gap in the rails. He wasn't able to get thoughts of Mary out of his mind. Nor of the farm he hadn't seen in seventeen years. In his mind they just naturally seemed to go together.

*   *   *

Mary woke up feeling better than she had in days. She was strongly tempted to get up and have some more of the stew. But she resisted. She was going to tell him to leave. She couldn't have a stranger of unknown character hanging about the place.

"He's coming!" Fear sounded in Sarah's voice and showed in her eyes. She bolted from the window into the corner between the bed and the wall.

Mary felt tension mount within her. It was a lot easier to plan to tell Joe to leave than actually do it. The sound of his footsteps on the porch made her flinch. The grating sound of the door frayed her nerves.

He entered with a plucked chicken in his hand.

"I figured the coyotes could do without this cockerel," he said as he walked over to the table and laid the chicken down. He poured part of the water into a pot, the rest into a basin.

"More water," he said to Sarah, holding out the bucket.

Sarah glanced at Mary. Mary nodded her head, and Sarah inched forward to take the bucket. However, she froze when she opened the door.

"Your dog," Mary said.

"We've got to do something about that."

Joe sent his dog to keep his horse company. At least that was what he told him to do. Mary doubted the animal would actually obey.

"Do you want this chicken cooked any special way?" Joe asked, going back to the table and beginning to prepare the chicken for cooking.

"No." She had meant to tell him to go at once, but he had taken the wind out of her sails. She was acutely aware of his overpowering male presence. Just watching him move about the cabin in those tight pants caused something inside her to warm and soften. The feeling unnerved her. She found Mr. Ryan very attractive. Stranger or not.

"You never did tell me how you and Pete came to be partners, or why you decided to come here now."

She shouldn't be asking questions. It would just postpone the inevitable. She decided to sit up. It was impossible to talk to this man lying down. She felt at such a disadvantage. Unlike her attempt earlier, Mary was able to sit up and position the pillows behind her.

"It was more an accident than anything else." Joe spoke without facing her as he worked over the chicken. "We had claims next to each other. A mining camp is a dangerous place. Men who find color sometimes disappear or turn up dead. I watched Joe's back, and he watched mine. When our claims played out, it made sense to take what gold we'd found and hire on to guard a shipment of gold to Denver."

He started cutting up the chicken and dropping the pieces into the pot.

"I don't remember anything after the first mile."

Joe had paused before the last sentence. He went back to work, cutting through the joints with short, powerful thrusts of the knife.

"I woke up in my bedroll with the sheriff standing over me and the empty gold sacks on the ground next to me. I was convicted and sent to jail."

He finished cutting up the chicken, wiped his hands, and set the pot on the stove. He looked straight at Mary. "Pete set me up. He stole that gold. When I found out he was dead and the gold never found, I broke out and came here. This must be where he hid it."

Mary was too stunned to speak. He couldn't possibly expect her to believe that. She had never thought much of her husband's honesty, but she couldn't believe Pete was a common thief.

She started but discarded several responses. "That's absurd," she finally said. "Pete didn't steal any gold. He didn't hide anything here."

"He did both. I mean to find it and clear my name. Besides, part of that gold is mine. Some is yours."

Mary wondered how much gold was hers. She needed to hire someone to help with the ranch. There was so much she couldn't do, especially with a baby. Of course, he might not be telling the truth. She wasn't going to get excited about the money until she saw it.

Joe started a fire under the chicken. When he was satisfied that it was well caught, he opened the window and tossed out the dirty water.

Sarah entered with the fresh water. Joe placed the bucket on the table, and Sarah retreated to her place in the corner.

"You don't have to hide from me," he said.

Mary thought he sounded as if his feelings were hurt.

"Why don't you rummage around on those shelves and see if you can find some canned fruit or vegetables," he told Sarah. He took out some coffee beans and put them in a pan to roast on the stove. Next he measured out rice and set it on the edge of the stove. Then he cleaned the table and set out plates.

Mary didn't know what to do. Her hands closed over the gun under the covers. She had to tell him to leave. It was out of the question to let him stay. He had to go now. It would soon be night.

"I find it hard to believe Pete did what you said. But if he did, I'm truly sorry." She didn't know how to say there were times she had come close to hating her husband. "It was very kind of you to fix us something to eat, but you needn't stay any longer.

I'm much stronger now. I'm sure you'll want to make it to town in time to get a room in the hotel."

Joe looked at her. She felt a flush burn her cheeks. She would swear he was laughing at her. Inside, of course. His expression didn't change.

"If you're trying to get rid of me, you're wasting your time. As soon as I find the gold, I'll head out for California, but not one day before. As for a hotel, I don't dare go near town. Somebody might recognize me."

"There's no gold here. Pete was home only one night after he came back from Colorado. He went off again the next day and got himself shot."

"Don't worry, I don't mean to stay any longer than I have to. And if you're worried about your reputation, your condition is protection enough." He directed a frankly amused look at her. "I wish you'd put that pistol back where it belongs. It's not a good idea to sleep with a loaded gun."

Mary didn't know why she brought the pistol out from under the covers. Maybe it was the fact that he seemed to be able to read her mind. Maybe she felt she ought to do something and nothing else had worked. Whatever the reason, she found herself pointing the pistol at Joe.

"If you're going to shoot me, get on your feet first. I'd hate to have it known I was killed by a woman so weak she couldn't stand up."

"I can stand up," Mary insisted. To prove her point, she threw back the covers and started to get to her feet. Immediately she felt faint.

Joe caught her before she fell.

"I never met such a foolish woman in my life. Stay in that bed, or I'll tie you down. You can shoot me when you feel better. Meantime, you'd better give me this." He took the pistol from her slackened grasp. "Next thing you know, you'll drop it and put a hole through the chicken pot. I'm not chasing down another rooster."

Mary started to laugh. The whole situation was too absurd. Nothing like this happened to ordinary people. She was ordinary, so it shouldn't be happening to her.

She certainly shouldn't be experiencing this odd feeling. It almost felt as if she wanted to cry. But she didn't feel at all sad. She felt bemused and bewildered. Her brain was numb. Here she was, completely helpless, and she had tried to shoot the only human who had come along to help her.

She must be losing her mind. This man, this stranger, had taken the gun from her hands, put her to bed, then gone back to fixing her supper. And he planned to stay until he found the gold he insisted Pete had hidden here.

He was always ahead of her. That was a new experience for Mary. She had never known a man to act intelligently. She wasn't even sure she thought men could be intelligent, but Joe was. He was kind, too, despite his gruff manner.

"The kid has found some peaches," Joe announced. "I hope that's all right with you."

"I like peaches," Mary said. The aroma of roasting coffee beans permeated the cabin. The smell made her mouth water.

"Supper will be ready in less than an hour. Time for a nap. You can dream of ways to spend your share of the gold when I find it."

Again he had read her mind. The first thing she intended to buy was a dress for Sarah.

"Dinner was delicious. You could make a living as a cook."

"Don't much like cooking."

"But you're so good at it."

"If I have to eat it, I want it to taste good. Just put those dishes in the sink, kid. If you cover them with water, most of the stuff will soak off by itself."

"Why won't you call Sarah by her name?"

"Why won't she speak to me?"

"I don't know."

"Neither do I."

"I thought a man like you would have an answer for everything."

"Hell, there's more I don't know than I'll ever be able to figure out."

"That doesn't bother you?"

"I know what I need. The rest would just clutter up my head."

The clatter of plates caught his attention. "Well, I think I'll see about fixing up a bed for myself."

Mary figured she must have looked startled.

"Don't worry about me crowding in here. Samson and I will bed down outside. I don't like being closed in, in case somebody comes looking for me."

He stood and stretched. "I've had me a full day. I imagine I'll sleep tight. Leave the chicken and coffee right where they are, kid. All they need is a little heat, and they'll be just as good tomorrow. Don't worry about locking the door. With Samson around, nothing's going to come near the house."

Mary wondered how he knew she was planning to lock herself in.

Joe backed into Sarah's tree and knocked it over. Uttering a sharp oath, he bent to set it up. Sarah was there before him. She cast him a glance that was at once fearful and accusatory.

"I asked you to watch your language," Mary reminded him.

"I did," Joe said, looking aggrieved. "I could have said much worse." He rubbed a spot on his leg. "That damned tree stuck me."

"I appreciate your restraint."

"No, you don't. You're like every other woman God ever made. You smile and mumble about restraint, but you keep after a man until you get exactly what you want. I had a grandmother just like you. Sorry about your tree, kid."

"She has a name."

"And I'll use it when she talks to me. 'Night, ma'am."

When the door closed behind him, Mary felt the strength go out of her body just like water from a sink when the plug was pulled. The man energized everything around him. Now that he had gone, she felt exhausted. Being full of hot food didn't help.

"Leave the dishes in the water, Sarah. I ought to be able to get up tomorrow. We can do them then."

"I'll do them now," the child replied. "He wouldn't leave them."

No, he wasn't the kind of man to leave things undone. He seemed methodical, capable, dependable, yet he was drifting through life, able to do any job required of him, but never stopping to put down roots.

Mary had decided not to marry again. Her father and Pete had taught her that a bad husband could destroy all the love and comfort around him. But if she ever changed her mind, she meant to find a man she could depend on to stay in one place year after year. That wasn't Joe. Yet somehow she kept thinking about him.

"Is he really going to sleep in the shed?" Sarah asked.

"That's what he said."

"Is he going to be here tomorrow?"

"Why do you ask?"

"I like him. He's nice."

"Then why don't you speak to him?"

"Pa never liked it when I talked. He said girls ought to keep quiet because they have nothing to say."

"Your father didn't think much of women. It seems to be quite the opposite with Mr. Ryan. I've never in my life seen a man pay so much attention to a woman's comfort."

"Do you think he'll stay?"

"He said he would stay until I was stronger."

"I mean all the time."

That warm feeling flooded through Mary. "He means to go to California. He's only staying out of politeness."

"I wish his dog would go to California."

"I'm sure he won't hurt you."

"He so big."

"So is Mr. Ryan, but you're not afraid of him, are you?"

"I don't think so."

Mary felt a silent chuckle inside. "I don't think I am either. Now it's time to go to sleep. I have a feeling Mr. Ryan will be up early in the morning."

"That's one beautiful woman," Joe said to Samson. He took a last puff on his cigarette and rubbed it out. "A man like me ought not stay around here too long. I should head for California as soon as she can get out of bed without falling over."

The night had turned cold. Millions of stars glimmered in a cloudless sky. The saguaro cactus cast black shadows against the horizon. The spidery arms of an ocotillo contrasted with the broom-like arms of the paloverde, the more dense ironwood and mesquite. An owl hooted. Some field mouse wouldn't be around to see the dawn.

This place made him uneasy. It was like a home, the kind that folded itself around a man and made him want to stay put. It made him think of his mother and the time he saw her last. He was just sixteen when she threw him out for the man she was living with. Five months later she was dead.

"There are two kinds of women," Joe said to Samson as they walked across the ranch yard. "There's the kind that's hot to get married but doesn't like men the way they are. They pretend they do, but as soon as the preacher says a few words over them, they set about changing their husbands into something they like better than what they got. Stay away from them. They'll either drive you to drink or drive you out of the house."

Joe untied his bedroll. He climbed into the loft and spread it over the straw. Samson looked up as if he were waiting for Joe to invite him in, but Joe didn't.

"Then there's the other kind, the kind that use men and let men use them. They destroy themselves. Like Flora. Nothing was ever enough. She always had to have more. Until one day she just burned herself out."

Samson sat down on his haunches. Joe leaned back on the straw and smiled. It sure beat his rock-and-sand bed from last night.

"Of course Mary is different from either one of them. She's pretty enough to make a man forget his responsibilities. She's so delicate and fragile, you want to protect her. You saw me. I couldn't wait to cook her dinner and fix up her chicken yard.

"But she's strong. She's got staying power. Once she picks out a man, she won't throw him out no matter how much work he needs. She'd even have made something of Pete if the fool had stayed."

Joe told himself he should have been looking for gold instead of mending fences and chasing chickens. This woman was going to get him into trouble yet. He turned over, didn't like his position, turned back again.

38

"Of course she tried to be brave, to pretend she wasn't scared to death. She could hardly hold the gun. I doubt she'd have had the strength to pull the trigger if a wolf had been coming through the door. Makes you want to hold her close and tell her nothing's ever going to hurt her again."

Joe sat up and glared at Samson.

"And that's how they get you," he said. "You got to keep alert. Because if that's not enough, they throw in babies and little girls. That Mary Wilson has got a quiver full of arrows. The first man who sets foot on this place won't have a chance. He'll be Mr. Wilson before the dust settles."

Joe flopped back down. He was the first man on the place.

"That's why I'm heading out to California the minute I find the gold."

Some time in the night Joe awoke to the sound of a crescendo of growls. Then he heard a yip cut off in mid-cry.

"Samson, I sure wish you could smell gold as quick as you can coyotes," he commented before he turned over and went back to sleep.

Chapter Three

Joe wondered if Mary and the kid always slept this soundly. Mary had locked the door, but it had been a simple matter to enter through the window. He'd searched almost every corner of the cabin, and neither of them had awakened. He would have liked to think this trusting slumber was due to his presence, but if it was, it would vanish the minute they found out what he had done.

Joe didn't like going through Mary's things. It made him feel like a sneak, but he had to search every part of the cabin. It was stupid to let scruples stop him now. Still, he was uncomfortable when he opened a drawer to find it filled with undergarments. He almost closed it again. It hardly looked big enough to hide one bag of gold. He closed his eyes and ran his hands under the neat piles of garments to the bottom and back of the drawer.

Nothing.

He felt his body relax. He hadn't realized he was

so edgy. Nor did he know why. Mary was a virtual stranger. Searching her home shouldn't bother him at all. But seeing and touching her clothes produced a feeling of intimacy he didn't welcome. It made him acutely aware of her physical presence. His body's response embarrassed him. He was a decent man. He shouldn't feel this way about a pregnant woman.

He quickly finished the wardrobe and turned his attention to the trunk. It wasn't locked. The top shelf needed no search to see there was nothing there. He had his hands deep among the dresses and blankets underneath when he heard a pistol click. He turned to see Mary sitting up in the bed, the cocked pistol aimed at him.

"What do you think you're doing?" she asked.

"Searching for the gold." He didn't think she would shoot him, but he couldn't be sure. He boldly finished running his hand along the bottom of the trunk.

"I told you I knew nothing of the gold," Mary said.

"I had to make sure for myself."

"I ought to shoot you."

"You'd have trouble getting rid of the body. And if you didn't kill me, you'd have to take care of me."

The kid woke up. She was frightened to find Joe in the house, Mary holding a pistol on him.

"I ought to turn you in to the sheriff."

"I'd be gone before he could get here. And I'd come back."

Mary kept the pistol pointed at Joe a moment longer, then slowly lowered it. He felt the tension in his muscles ease.

"You really think Pete stole that gold and buried it here, don't you?"

Joe began to put Mary's things back in order. "There's no other explanation for what happened. He came here right after the trial. It hasn't turned up anywhere else, and it wasn't on him when he was killed."

"He certainly didn't give it to me."

Joe closed the trunk and got to his feet. "I can see that, unless you're the kind who can sit on a fortune for six months and not spend a penny."

Mary looked him in the eye. "I could sit on it for a lifetime. I won't touch stolen money."

He believed her. There was a quality about her that said she would have nothing to do with a dishonest man.

Joe went to the woodbox and started picking up pieces of wood to start a fire in the stove. "Well, it's not inside the cabin, so you don't have to worry about me going through your things again."

"Despite your actions, I think you're honest."

Joe laid the fire carefully. Her response was unexpected. At best, he'd supposed she would only tolerate him. What else could she do? She was alone, down in bed, twenty-two miles from town, with no one to help her but a six-year-old kid. But to decide he was honorable! She must be up to something.

"No need to go flattering me. I know what I am. I never pretended to be anything else."

"And just what are you, Mr. Ryan?"

Joe lighted the coal oil-soaked stick he had placed at the center of the wood. A pale yellow flame illuminated the inside of the stove, casting flickering shadows on its sooty walls.

He had avoided that question for years. He wanted to think he was like everybody else—worthy of dreams, worthy of success. But Flora said he was nothing but a two-bit drifter, a poor and overly serious one at that.

"Nothing much, ma'am. I guess you could say I'm drifting along looking for a reason to stay put. Kid, I need some eggs for breakfast. See what you can find." He poured water into the coffeepot and put it on to heat.

"Where is your dog?" Mary asked. "You know she's afraid of it."

He went to the door and looked outside. "He's gone," he said to Sarah. "Scram."

The child stuck her head out the door, looked around, then darted outside.

"Don't you want to be something else?" Mary asked after Sarah had gone.

He poured out a handful of coffee beans and dumped them into a grinder.

"I want my name cleared," he said over the noise of the grinder. "Once a man is branded a thief, it doesn't matter what else he is. People can't see anything else."

"Isn't there anybody who can speak for you?"

"It won't do any good. I broke jail. As long as the gold is missing, nothing else matters." He poured the freshly ground coffee into a pot.

"Then I hope you find it."

"Enough to help?" He unwrapped the bacon and began to cut thick slices from it.

"I don't know anything."

"You can try to remember everything he did while he was here, every movement, every word he spoke. Even his expression, his mood." He pulled the curtain across the alcove where Mary slept. "You'd better get dressed. Breakfast will be ready in half an hour."

"What was that noise last night?" Mary asked.

She was seated at the table, a cup of coffee in front of her, waiting for Joe to finish filling her plate. He had tried to keep her in bed, but she had been determined to get up. He had insisted on helping her walk. She didn't need his help, but it was nice of him

43

Leigh Greenwood

to offer. The least she could do was lean on him.

"It was Samson," Joe said, setting down a plate with bacon, one egg, and a thick slice of bread in front of Sarah and another in front of Mary. "You won't be troubled by coyotes any more. Give him a month, and there won't be one within ten miles."

"It's a shame you can't leave him here when you go to California. We could sure use him."

"Can't do that. If Samson stays, so do I."

The statement had been made in jest—at least Mary thought so—but the effect on each of them was electric. Mary realized that she had practically issued Joe an invitation to remain at the ranch indefinitely. Judging from his expression, he had considered accepting it. What shocked Mary even more was the realization that she wanted him to stay. She didn't know what kind of arrangement they might be able to work out, but the idea of having Joe Ryan around all the time was a pleasant one.

"Eat your breakfast," Joe said. "There's nothing much worse than cold eggs." He glanced over at Sarah. "We're going to have to do something about that cow. A kid like you should be drinking milk. You're nothing but skin and bones."

"Sarah has always been thin," Mary said.

"Thin is okay. Skinny as a stick isn't," Joe said. "You know where that cow got to?"

Sarah nodded.

"As soon as we clean up, you show me. I refuse to let an old cow turn her nose up at me."

Mary watched him clear away the breakfast things, talking to a mute Sarah as if they were old friends. He didn't act like any man she'd ever known. In some ways he was just as dictatorial, just as unconcerned with her feelings as Pete had been. In other ways, he was the kindest, most thoughtful man she'd ever met. He was certainly the most helpful.

44

He must be up to something.

After Pete was killed, Mary had realized that she had never been able to trust men or depend on them. She had looked toward this Christmas as the beginning of her new life—just her, Sarah, and the baby.

Then Joe had showed up and she had started to question her decision. She found herself thinking *if all men were like Joe,* or *if I could find a husband like Joe.* . . . The fact that he was an escaped criminal, a man on the run, didn't seem to weigh with her emotions. It didn't even weigh much with her mind.

She tried to tell herself to be sensible, but she couldn't. Maybe it was the baby. Her mother used to say pregnant women were prone to being emotional and sentimental. Her mother also said love nourished life. Nobody had ever nourished Mary like Joe. Whatever the reason, she liked him. She didn't want him to go away.

Joe had reached the conclusion that six months in jail had made him crazy. There was no other way to explain why he was leading a milk cow and talking to a six-year-old girl who wouldn't say a word to him. He ought to be turning the place inside out. Failing that, he ought to be on his way to California. Some U.S. marshal was sure to be on his trail by now.

But here he was, walking through the desert with a cow and a kid as if he didn't have a care in the world. Yep, he was crazy.

"You got to be firm with a cow," he said as they reached the yard. "They're real stubborn, especially if you're little. My grandma had an old black-and-yellow cow who used to chase me until I beat her with a stick. Never had any trouble after that. Get me that bucket I left on the porch."

"You got to tie the cow's head close to the post," he said when Sarah returned with the bucket he had washed and set out on the porch earlier. "That way they can't turn around. Won't fight so much if they can't see. Now fetch me the stool."

Joe felt silly sitting on the tiny stool, but he had to show the kid what to do. After that, she could do all the sitting.

"You got to watch her at first," Joe said. "She's been on her own and won't like being milked." The cow kicked at Joe when he started to wash her teats. Joe slapped her on the hip. "Let her know you won't put up with any nonsense." He pushed on the cow's hip, but she wouldn't move her leg back. "Keep pushing on her until she moves that leg," he told Sarah. "It's easier to milk her that way."

Joe pulled on a teat. A stream of warm milk hit the bucket. He jerked the pail out of the way just as the cow kicked at him. He smacked her on the hip again.

"She'll do that a few more times before she figures out you mean business. Cows are stubborn, but they're not dumb. Has she got a name?"

The kid shook her head.

"She's got to have a name. How will she know when you're talking to her?" Joe thought a moment. "How about Queen Charlotte? She acts like a queen, and she's just as ugly as the real one."

Sarah nodded her agreement.

"Good. Now it's your turn."

Sarah looked reluctant.

"You can't let her know you're afraid, kid, or she'll keep on kicking until you give up. Come on, sit down."

Sarah sat. She reached out a tentative hand.

"Don't be timid. You're the boss."

Sarah squeezed the teat three times before the cow kicked the bucket over.

Joe smacked Queen Charlotte on the hip and moved her back into milking position. "Now try again." Seconds later the cow kicked again. Sarah stood up.

"Here, let me show you," Joe said, taking his place on the stool. "I haven't done this in nearly fifteen years, but it's something you don't forget. Move over, Queen Charlotte," he said to the cow. "You're about to get the milking of your life. You kick this bucket one more time, and I'll feed you to Samson piece by piece."

Sarah giggled.

Through the window, Mary watched, bemused, as Joe milked the cow, talking to Sarah and the cow equally. When Samson wandered up, Joe included him in his conversation, introducing him to Sarah just as if he was an equal.

The man fascinated Mary. The more she saw of him, the more she wanted to know about him. She was drawn to him in a way that defied her notions about the feelings that could exist between a man and a woman. He touched a part of her that had lain silent all these years, the loving and longing part that Pete had nearly killed. She wanted to reach out and touch him, as though physical contact would recapture the youthful dreams she'd nearly forgotten.

She found herself looking at his body, admiring the shape of his thighs, the curve of his backside, the power of his shoulders. She had never felt this way about Pete. She had never looked forward to their nights in bed, nor did she miss them after he had gone. But Joe touched something deeper in her, far beyond anything Pete had touched. She found herself blushing, wondering what it would be like to sleep with Joe.

Samson tried to lick Sarah's face. The child was still frightened of the huge dog, but Joe made her hold out her hand for Samson to smell. Then she had to pat him on the head. Sarah was still wary, but Joe had broken the back of her fear.

Joe laughed, and the sound sent a frisson of pleasure racing through Mary. It was a deep, rolling sound, a sound that promised something very special to the person who could find the source and tap into it.

She picked up her pad and began to draw. In a few moments, she had preserved forever some of the magic of this morning.

Joe looked over Mary's shoulder as she drew a picture of Queen Charlotte and General Burnside staked out in the meadow beyond the barn, mountains in the distance.

"It's incredible," Joe marveled. "I don't see how you do it. You put a few squiggly lines here, a few more there, and you have a picture. All I'd have would be a bunch of squiggly lines."

Mary laughed, pleased with the compliment. Pete had never liked her drawings. He had considered them a waste of time. "It's not very hard. You just have to practice."

"Hell, I could—Sorry, I can't seem to control my tongue. It doesn't hardly know how to talk without cussing."

"That will come with practice, too."

"Maybe. What do you do with all those pictures?"

"What should I do with them?"

Joe looked at the drawing again. "Sell them. I know hundreds of miners who'd pay plenty to have something like that to brighten up their walls. You could make more money than you can running cows on this place."

"I'm perfectly content to stay here running cows. Besides, I like to do drawings for people I know. I ought to be doing some for Sarah. She wants to decorate the house for Christmas."

"If that pathetic tree is any example," he said, indicating Sarah's bundle of thorns, "she ought to give up the idea."

"If you understood about her mother, you'd understand why it's so important to her."

"Then tell me. I won't figure it out otherwise."

"Sarah's mother died when Sarah was four. I don't know why Pete married her. He seems to have hated everything about her. He got rid of everything that belonged to her or reminded him of her. According to Sarah, her mother loved Christmas and would spend weeks getting ready for it. She used to spend hours singing to Sarah, telling her stories about *Père Noel*. Last Christmas was Sarah's first since her mother's death. Pete wouldn't let her decorate, have a tree, or do anything for Christmas. To Sarah, that was like taking away the last link with her mother. She likes me, but she adored her mother. Christmas is all she has left of her. It's terribly important to her."

"Pete was a real bastard," Joe said. "Why in hell did you marry him?"

Mary ignored the curses. "Pete's stepfather was my uncle. He thought Pete would make a good husband for me. My father was anxious to get me out of the house. One less mouth to feed; one less female to contend with. I guess I was tired of waiting for a man who didn't exist."

Joe gave her the strangest look. Mary badly wanted to know what he was thinking. She wondered if he'd ever been in love, if he'd found his perfect woman. He seemed light-hearted, but beneath that she detected a cynical streak. He didn't believe in goodness. That was odd, considering he had so much of it in him.

"If she's hoping that ratty old tree will attract her

Père Noel, she's looking down an empty chute."

"Please don't tell her that." Mary looked to where Sarah sat churning cream for butter. "She thinks if she believes hard enough, *Père Noel* will find her."

Joe shrugged and headed toward the door. "I don't know anything about *Père Noel*, but I do know about horses and cows. I'd better do some work on that corral."

"You don't have to do that."

"If I don't, you won't have any milk after I leave. It'll never hold Queen Charlotte the way it is now."

Still amused by his habit of bestowing fanciful names on his animals, Mary asked, "When are you leaving?" She was stunned to realize that she had known this man less than twenty-four hours, but she no longer thought in terms of his leaving.

The baby kicked, and her hand went to her swollen stomach.

She liked him. He might be a criminal, but she liked him.

No. He was an escaped convict, but she couldn't believe he was a criminal. He'd fixed three meals for them, perfect strangers he owed nothing, especially if Pete had set him up. He had spent hours helping Sarah, even though the child wouldn't speak to him. He had even praised Mary's drawings.

He was rugged, curt, and given to cursing, but underneath all that roughness he had a generous nature. He showed a wonderful understanding of her and Sarah. On top of that, he took better care of her than any man she'd ever known, including her father. Why shouldn't she fall in love with him? He was exactly the kind of man she'd always hoped to find.

No, she had to be mistaken.

She couldn't love him. She was letting his kindness go to her head. Maybe it was being pregnant. Her mother had warned her that pregnancy could do strange things to a woman.

Mary redirected her attention to her drawing pad. She needed more Christmas pictures for Sarah. Drawing would give her something to do and keep her mind off Joe and the foolish notion that she might be falling in love with him.

That evening after dinner, Mary tacked up the drawings she had done during the day. She wondered if they would mean anything to Sarah. The child had never known anything but the desert. To Mary, nothing about the desert spoke of Christmas. She had done a few drawings of the surrounding hills and mountains, but she had been in Arizona only eleven months. Christmas to her was the snow-covered pines and oaks of her native Virginia, magnolia, and bright holly berries.

It sounded strange to hear rain on the roof—it had been raining since late afternoon. Even more strange to Mary, everything would look the same tomorrow. In this land, rain didn't bring the green she longed for.

"It's a shame you don't have any paints," Joe said, inspecting a drawing before he handed it to her to put on the wall. "It just doesn't look like Christmas without color."

"Pete would never buy me any. No paper either. This is my last pad."

Pete used to get angry when she drew. But when she was drawing, she could pretend he didn't exist. Joe was a part of her drawings. He was already in several.

He liked to watch her. He said it pleased him to see the lines come to life, capturing a living scene. Her pleasure increased because of his. He would laugh and point to a cactus or a ridge that had just come into being. For a few minutes, it would seem

51

he almost forgot the gold and the sentence hanging over his head.

At times like that, it was terribly hard to remember he'd soon be gone.

"Would you mind heating some water so Sarah can have a bath?" she asked.

Joe gave Sarah an appraising glance. "The kid *is* rather dirty."

Taking a bath was not a simple operation. A fire had to be lighted in the stove and water brought in from outside and heated in every available pot and pail. The tub had to be cleaned out and brought in from the shed. Last of all, the water had to be poured into the tub. Mary hadn't been able to do this for months. Cloth baths just weren't the same as soaking in a tub of hot water.

"What about you?" Joe asked.

"I'll take cloth baths until after the baby comes," Mary said. "I hate to ask you, but you'll have to go outside until Sarah is finished."

"I do all the work, then I'm the one who gets to sit shivering on the front porch?"

"I'm sorry, but it wouldn't seem right to—"

"Never mind. I need to dig a few more holes anyway."

The door opened with a protesting squeak. Joe reminded himself to put some bacon grease on it in the morning.

"You can take the bathtub out now," Mary said.

She was framed in the doorway, golden light behind her. Joe thought he'd never seen anyone so beautiful. Her thick, dark hair—very sensibly done up at the back of her head with a few curls loose to soften the look—seemed jet black in the dark, her skin nearly white by comparison. Her eyes glistened luminous and wide in a face that seemed too delicate for a land known to be hard on women.

Joe got up off the porch steps. His joints felt stiff. It had stopped raining, and the stars had come out, but the night was too cold for sitting on stone steps. He was surprised to see the kid still in pants. "Why isn't she wearing a dress? Girls ought to be clean and sweet smelling, all curls and ruffles and bows. She still looks like a boy."

"She doesn't have any dresses," Mary said.

"Why not?" Joe asked. He'd never heard of a girl having no dresses. It didn't seem right.

"Pete wouldn't buy her any. He said she'd only tear them up and have to wear pants anyway."

"I wish I'd known. I'd have beaten the hell out of Pete when I had the chance." He caught Mary's stern look. "I'm sorry, but it's enough to make a man cuss to see a little girl as pretty as the kid have to look like a boy because her bobcat-mean pa wouldn't buy her a dress."

Mary brushed Sarah's long auburn hair to help it dry faster. "I mean to do something about it as soon as I'm able."

Joe decided they ought to do something about it now. "You got some ribbon?"

"Yes."

"How about some good-smelling powder?"

Mary smiled. "Yes. What do you want it for?"

"I want you to put the powder on the kid, the ribbon in her hair."

"Open the trunk and hand me the round box on the top. And a piece of red ribbon if I have any."

Joe found the box easily. The ribbon was another matter. He found a tangle of red, but it was too narrow for Sarah's hair. He chose a yellow ribbon instead. "You can use the red to make bows for the tree," he said. His grandmother used to do that when he was a little boy. He handed the yellow ribbon to

Mary, then turned to the tree. It was a pathetic mess. He couldn't put bows on that. His grandmother would rise out of the grave and come after him.

"We've got to have a better tree than that," he said aloud. "That's a disgrace. Are there any pines or junipers nearby?" he asked Mary.

"There're some up in the hills."

"After breakfast tomorrow I'll see what I can find." He turned to see Sarah, staring at him, eyes wide. The yellow ribbon was just the right shade to set off her hair. "See, I knew you were a pretty little thing. Pretty enough to have little boys giving each other black eyes over you." He squatted in front of her. "Would you like a real tree?"

Sarah nodded her head vigorously.

Mary had dusted Sarah's shoulders with white powder. Joe bent over and took a sniff.

"Pretty as a picture, and you smell good, too. I know your mama would be proud as a peacock to see you. Now all you need is—"

Sarah threw her arms around Joe and hugged him until he thought she was going to cut off his air. Slowly he let his arms slide around her. Her body seemed much too slight for such intense feeling. He didn't know how to react. In his whole life, he'd never had a child hug him.

For a while he thought she wasn't ever going to let go. Then, quite as suddenly, she unclasped him and hid herself behind Mary.

"I was going to say all you need is a dress," he said, "but you're pretty enough without it." He stood up. His muscles felt as strange as his voice. "I guess it's time I get myself over to the shed. Samson doesn't like to go hunting unless he knows I'm tucked up tight."

*   *   *

Joe needed some time alone. He was feeling at sixes and sevens. He was strongly attracted to Mary. That he understood, that he knew how to combat. But this business with the kid hugging him until she nearly choked him had caught him off guard. Mary had weakened him, and the kid had closed in for the kill.

Not kill exactly, but he was down and sinking fast.

He no longer thought Mary had anything to do with Pete's thievery. If she found the gold, he was certain she would hand it over to him. She hadn't even been interested enough to ask how much of it was hers.

Despite the way he'd forced himself into her life, she had been gracious. She hadn't been pleased when she found him going through her things, but she seemed to understand why he'd had to do it. That was a hell of a lot more than he'd expected. Flora would have screamed like a wildcat. His mother would have hit him up beside the head. Mary had accepted his explanation and put her gun away.

No woman had ever taken his word for anything. Except his grandmother.

Mary had every reason to throw him out, but she greeted him with a smile sweeter than a spring sunrise. She talked to him about little things, things you talked about with people you felt comfortable around.

But now the kid had hugged him and his comfort had fled. There was something about a kid hugging you that was unlike anything else in the world. There must be a special soft spot in every man reserved for little girls. He had seen men who wouldn't hesitate to commit almost any evil reduced to tears by the plight of a child, but he'd never suspected that he was similarly susceptible. But he was, and the kid had scored a bull's eye on her first throw. He wanted to march right back in there, give her a hug, and promise her that Christmas was going to be just as wonderful as she hoped.

But he couldn't. He had to find the gold and be gone before then. The longer he stayed, the greater the danger that the law would find him. He was foolishly letting Mary and the kid distract him from his goal. He'd spent no more than an hour looking for the gold today.

He dropped to his bed in the straw and pulled his bedroll around him. He'd start checking beneath all the stones in the yard tomorrow. After he and the kid found a decent Christmas tree. He couldn't stand the thought of her pinning all her hopes on that bundle of twigs.

And Mary and her baby?

That was a tough one.

Chapter Four

The kid was helping Joe fix the chimney when he heard Mary mutter something under her breath. He looked around the corner of the cabin to where she sat on the porch.

"The preacher and his sister are coming," she said, "Brother Samuel and Sister Rachel Hawkins."

Joe hadn't intended to fix the chimney this morning, or any other morning. He had been inspecting the cabin to see if any stones showed signs of having been removed recently. A few stones in the chimney were loose.

Once he realized that there was nothing behind them but more stones, his excitement had died down, to be replaced by a dull fear that he would never find the gold. Then he decided to reset the stones properly rather than just shove them back into place.

He had almost finished the job when Brother Samuel and Sister Rachel drove into the yard. Joe could tell at a glance that he wasn't going to like them.

From the look of things, they weren't going to like him any better. Brother Samuel frowned as though he'd just come upon a condemned sinner and didn't like the smell. Sister Rachel looked as if she'd never had any fun in her life and was determined that nobody else would have any either. They were both dressed in black.

Joe didn't like black. It depressed him. Seemed it had depressed Brother and Sister Hawkins, too.

Samson had been lying next to Mary's chair. When the Hawkinses got down from their buggy, he rose to his feet, a growl deep in his throat.

"Good morning," Mary said, greeting the pair without getting up. She patted Samson until the growls stopped. "It's awfully kind of you to drive so far to see me."

"It didn't seem so far," Brother Samuel said. "The morning is brisk, the sun heartening."

"I've been expecting to see you in town," Sister Rachel said. "You know my brother can't think of you out here alone without becoming distressed." Brother Samuel helped his sister mount the porch steps. She walked around Samson to take the chair Mary offered her. Brother Samuel chose to stand.

"I know I look as big as a cow, but I've got another month," Mary told her. "Besides, if all goes well, I mean to have the baby here."

"Surely you don't mean to have it by yourself."

"Oh, no. I'll hire someone to stay with me."

"I'd feel so much better if you would move to town now," Brother Samuel said. "I'm most concerned about you."

"I can't afford the cost of putting Sarah and myself up in a hotel for a month."

"I'm sure the ladies of Pine Flat would be glad to offer you and Sarah places to stay."

Joe wondered why neither brother nor sister offered to take Sarah and Mary into their own home.

"I couldn't be separated from Sarah," Mary replied, "not after her losing both her mother and her father. Neither could I settle myself on anyone. I won't have a friend in the world if I start doing that."

"You'll have a friend in us no matter what you do."

"We'd offer to keep you with us," Sister Rachel said, "but we're away from home nearly all the time."

"Nonetheless, you can stay with us if it will convince you to come to town."

Joe noticed that Sister Rachel didn't look quite so enthusiastic as her brother. He guessed Brother Samuel was in the habit of offering haven to people and leaving Sister Rachel to do all the work.

"I didn't know you had hired a man to work for you," Brother Samuel said, eying Joe.

"Oh, he's not a hired hand. He's Pete's old partner. . . ."

Mary's lips formed Joe's name, but she didn't say it.

Brother Samuel didn't come down the steps to shake hands with Joe. The inclination of his head was the only acknowledgment he made of their introduction.

"Pete's been dead six months. What's he doing here now?" Sister Rachel asked.

"He's here to . . ." Mary's voice trailed off.

". . . to settle a partnership," Joe said, leaving his work and coming around the corner.

"Then why are you fixing the chimney?" Sister Rachel demanded.

"It needed fixing."

"It's not suitable!"

"I'm not a stone mason, but I think it'll hold up for a while."

"My sister means it's not suitable for you to be

59

staying with a single woman without proper chaperonage."

"I should think her belly and the kid are chaperons enough."

Joe's answer was mild enough, but he felt anger boiling up inside him. Who the hell was this man to come in here and stick his nose in their business? Joe had read the Bible, and he didn't remember anything giving preachers permission to interfere in other people's affairs. Sister Rachel's shocked response to his answer amused him. The old biddie would probably fall down dead if a man so much as kissed her.

"In that case, I don't imagine you'll be staying long," Brother Samuel said. He didn't appear to be quite as shocked as his sister. He seemed angry. Joe suddenly wondered if the Reverend Brother had designs on Mary for himself. She was certainly pretty enough to tempt a man, even a cold fish like the Reverend Brother.

"I probably won't be here longer than a couple more days," Joe said. "Mary was a little run-down when I arrived. I'd like to be sure she's back on her feet before I leave."

"Why didn't you tell us you were unwell?" Sister Rachel asked. "I'd have come right away. In fact, I'll stay with you now. Samuel will just have to do without me for a few days."

"That's not necessary," Mary hastened to assure them. "I'm feeling much like my old self. I know your brother depends quite heavily on you, especially during the Christmas season. No, I'm fine now."

"If you're sure."

Joe would have sworn Sister Rachel was disappointed. Maybe she would have appreciated some relief from the heavy duties of the season.

"Will you be stopping by town when you leave?"

Brother Samuel inquired of Joe.

"Probably," Joe replied. "I imagine I'll need to pick up a few things."

"We have other calls to make, so we'd better be on our way," Brother Samuel said to Mary as he helped his sister down the steps. "I'll be looking for you in town in a day or two," he said to Joe. "I know you wouldn't do anything that might damage Mrs. Wilson's reputation, but you can't be too careful. People will talk."

"They'd better not within my hearing," Joe answered.

Brother Samuel looked as though he hadn't expected that answer. His smile was uncertain.

"We'll be expecting you and Sarah in town to stay right after the New Year," Sister Rachel said to Mary. "If not, I'm coming to stay until after the baby arrives."

"I'll let you know," Mary said. She got to her feet, but didn't go down the steps.

Joe went back to his work. But he kept watch until Brother Samuel and Sister Rachel had disappeared over the ridge. "I wonder where Sister Rachel left her broomstick?" he said to no one in particular. "Bound to be faster than that old buggy."

Mary laughed, then tried to pretend she hadn't.

Mary eased down on the bed and leaned against the mound of pillows. She had to do some serious thinking. She couldn't have Brother Samuel thinking she would become his wife. He had never asked her, but she couldn't fail to notice the look in his eye.

She had been given no opportunity to dispel his illusions, but she would never marry him. She felt lucky to have survived her marriage to Pete, and she had no intention of putting herself in that trap again.

She wanted a quiet, stable life, not one manipulated by a man.

Yet she didn't want Joe to leave. She had felt her heart lurch when he said he'd see Brother Samuel in town in a couple of days. Already she had come to depend on him, to look forward to his company.

It was impossible not to compare the two men. Brother Samuel was an ardent man, even a passionate one, but his passion had nothing to do with the flesh. Being around Joe had made Mary very aware of her physical nature. It was impossible to look at him and not feel the magnetism of his presence. He was simply the kind of man who made a woman achingly aware of her femininity. Even pregnant, he made her feel desirable.

Mary decided that was a dangerous situation. It would undoubtedly be safer if Joe did meet Brother Samuel in town and then continued on to California. But she knew her life would be very empty if he left.

Her mother had warned her she wouldn't always be able to find love where she wanted it. Was she looking for it with Joe?

Joe was jealous. There was no point in denying it. From the moment that man drove into the yard, he had felt it gnawing at his insides. He hadn't recognized it at first, but he did now.

He was jealous of the Reverend Brother Samuel Hawkins.

He looked around. There was nothing that could remotely be considered a Christmas tree. Sarah rode behind him, the little pinto struggling to keep up with his big gelding. Samson loped ahead on the lookout for coyotes. The low hills were covered with a scattering of vegetation—mesquite, catclaw, and ironwood all looking much alike; ocotillo and prickly pear cactus; spiky agave with their tall blooming stalks; assorted grasses and bushes.

But no pines or junipers.

They would have to go higher if they were to find a Christmas tree.

Could he be falling in love? He couldn't allow that to happen. But wasn't that what being jealous meant? He'd only loved two women, and both of them had sent him away. Mary had tried—even held a gun on him. He didn't know if she had changed her mind, but he knew he wasn't the kind of man she wanted or the kind who would be good for her. She'd send him away in the end.

"What do you think of that tree?" he asked Sarah. It was a pitiful excuse for a tree, but it was a pine.

She shook her head.

"Look, if I'm going to traipse all over this mountain looking for a tree, you're going to have to talk to me."

The kid watched him out of silent eyes.

"You ought to know by now I won't hurt you. Even Samson likes you."

She still didn't speak.

"Okay, let's go back."

Before he could turn General Burnside around, she said, "It's not pretty," just as if she'd been talking all along. "Let's go higher."

As they wound their way up the mountainside, Joe decided that women got the hang of being female at an early age. Boys didn't figure out what it meant to be a man until much later. By the time they started courting, the girls had a ten-year head start. It was like shooting fish in a pond.

He headed General Burnside up a slope toward a patch of green about a mile away. Samson disappeared down a canyon.

He was letting himself get distracted. A dangerous thing. It was time he went back to looking for the gold and got out of here. He was getting too settled.

He was starting to like where he was.

He'd forgotten what being on a farm was like. For years he'd thought only of his mother and the man she threw him out for. But being here reminded him of the things he had liked about the farm. It seemed strange to him now, but he liked the way he was living. He didn't even mind the chores. He was beginning to get ideas about how to improve things, ideas about what Mary ought to do come spring. He'd enjoyed teaching Sarah how to milk Queen Charlotte. Hell, he'd sworn he'd never milk another cow after he left the farm. But there was something solid and comfortable about their big brown bodies. And it sure as hell was nice to have butter to put on his biscuits.

"Do you like that man?" Sarah asked.

"What man?"

"The one who came to the house this morning."

"No reason to dislike him."

"I don't like him. He makes Mary sad."

"How's that?"

"She gets all jumpy whenever he comes. She mumbles a lot after he's gone. I think she's afraid of that woman."

"I think your ma is just afraid they'll try to take too much care of her."

"Mary doesn't need anybody to take care of her. She has me."

Joe thought it was a nice thing for a little girl to say, but Sarah had no idea just how much a woman needed someone to take care of her. He didn't see how Mary was going to make out by herself.

"Do you always call your ma Mary?"

"Mary says she loves me like a mama, but she knows I have a real mama who's gone to Heaven and is waiting for me there."

That would teach him to stick his nose in where it didn't belong.

"I bet she'd like it though. She won't think you're forgetting your real ma, but women like to be called Ma. It's just not the same when you call her Mary."

"If you were married to her, would you want me to call you Pa?"

That nearly knocked him out of his saddle. No messing around. The kid had cut to the heart of the matter.

Joe wanted to marry Mary. He had fallen in love with her when she fainted pointing a rifle at him. He'd just been dancing around the issue since then, trying to fool himself and everybody else.

"Yes. If I were married to Mary, I'd want you to call me Pa. I'd like having a little girl like you. I know Pete's your real pa, but I'd want you to call me Pa because that's how I'd feel about you."

Joe realized that he'd stayed away from women because he didn't believe in love. He'd never felt it. His mother and Flora talked about it all the time, but he didn't want any part of the destructive emotion they felt.

Mary and Sarah loved each other in an entirely different way. Wasn't it possible they could love him as well?

Don't be a fool. You're on the run. You can't stay here or anywhere else.

"Let's look up there," Sarah said, pointing to a clump of green even more distant than the one he had picked out.

Samson climbed out of the canyon and came to join them.

"Why is Christmas so important to you?" Joe asked.

"Mama told me she was going to die," Sarah began. She looked up at Joe. "But she said she wouldn't really be gone. She said she was going to stay with *Père Noel*, far away where I couldn't see her. She said *Père Noel* brought things from mommies to their little girls so they would know they hadn't forgotten them. She said she would send me something every Christmas."

Sarah looked away.

"Last year Papa said we couldn't have Christmas. He said it was foolish. He said *Père Noel* was a lie and Mama was just telling me a story so I wouldn't cry. He said she was gone away and I'd never hear from her again. He wouldn't even let me put a ribbon on the door so *Père Noel* could find our house."

She looked up at Joe once more.

"He didn't come. I put out my shoes, but there was nothing in them. Do you think Papa was right?"

Joe decided that if anybody'd ever deserved to die by slow torture, it was Pete Wilson. "No. *Père Noel* probably couldn't find you among all these cactus. I'm sure he's got all your presents saved up. He's going to look extra special hard this year to make sure he doesn't miss you again. We'll put an extra big bow on the door. We can leave a light in the window, too. We're a long way from town, you know."

"You really think he'll come?"

"I'm sure of it. Now we'd better find that tree and get back home, or we'll never get it decorated."

They had climbed several thousand feet. There were pines and junipers all around to choose from.

Sarah stopped and pointed to a ledge fifty feet above their heads. "There, that's the tree I want."

Mary saw them when they topped the ridge a mile away. Joe on his big gelding, a big man silhouetted against the landscape; Sarah on the pinto, a little girl who looked even smaller next to Joe; Samson sniffing rocks in his never-ending quest for coyotes. And the tree. It was tied to Sarah's pony. It almost enveloped the child.

The baby turned over. Mary put her hand on her stomach. She was feeling funny today. The baby seemed to have moved lower in her body. It caused her to waddle like a duck. Just the thing to make a man like Joe look on her with approval.

She had given up pretending she didn't like him. Watching him riding patiently with Sarah conjured up even warmer emotions.

She loved Joe Ryan.

She still found it hard to believe a man like him existed. All the other men in her life had ended up being pretty much alike—rotten. She had given up hoping to find anybody different. Then, just when she felt she could carry on alone, Joe Ryan had come into her life and upset everything. He was exactly the kind of man she wanted.

But she couldn't have him.

If she were a sensible woman, she would marry Brother Samuel. He wasn't a warm man, but he was a kind one. He would prove to be stubborn in many ways, but a clever woman could probably handle him quite easily. And she was a clever woman.

But she didn't want Brother Samuel, even if he hadn't been a preacher, even if Sister Rachel hadn't been his sister. She wanted an escaped convict who was on the run. That made her real clever.

They stopped. Apparently Joe had to readjust the tree. She wondered where they'd found it. They had been gone for most of the day. It was nearly eight o'clock. The sun had dipped beyond the western hills, leaving streaks of orange, mauve, and a deep purply-black across the sky. She had become worried about them. She had been sitting on the porch for nearly two hours.

The fire in the stove would have gone out. Dinner

would be cold. But that didn't matter now. Joe would be home in a little while. She could warm everything up.

Yes, Joe was coming home. This was where he belonged, where she felt he wanted to be, where she wanted him to be. But the world outside wouldn't let him stay.

She picked up her pen and began, with swift, sure strokes, to create a picture of Sarah and Joe silhouetted against the evening sky.

While she waited, she had tried to think of what she might do to help him. She had racked her brain for any possible clue to where Pete had hidden the gold. She had even thought of hiding Joe. There were miles of hills in which a man could lose himself. But she knew Joe wouldn't agree to that. He had come here to clear his name. He would never consider marrying her until he had.

And she wanted to marry Joe. She wanted him to be her husband, her lover, the father of the child she carried, the other children she hoped to have. She didn't know what she could do, but she made up her mind not to give up hope. She'd never thought a man like Joe existed, but he did. There had to be a way to keep him.

She flipped the page and began a second picture as Joe and Sarah rode into the yard.

Sarah seemed hardly able to contain her excitement. She flitted around the cabin, talking enough to make up for several months of silence.

"I bet it's the biggest Christmas tree in Arizona," she said.

Joe leaned the tree against the wall, then made a stand for it. It almost reached the ceiling. The branches spread out three feet on either side of the trunk.

"I'm sure it is," Mary agreed.

"We found dozens of other trees," Joe told her, "but she wouldn't be satisfied with any of them. She had to have the one growing on the highest ledge."

"It was the prettiest."

"You should have seen me clambering up the rocks like a mountain goat," Joe said. "Nearly broke my neck."

"It's beautiful," Mary said, "but a smaller one would have been nice. There's hardly enough room left for us."

"You can put lots of pictures on it," Sarah said, "lots more than that other old tree."

That other old tree had been shoved into the stove, its existence forgotten and unlamented.

"Joe said we could put ribbons all over it," Sarah told Mary. "I can't reach the top. Will you lift me, Joe?"

"If you don't stop dancing about, he's liable to hang you from the ceiling," Mary said.

"No, he won't. He said he'd like having a little girl like me. He said if he was married to you, he'd want me to call him Papa."

The escalation of tension was tangible. Joe kept his eyes on his work. He laid the tree on its side and measured the stand to make sure it fit. "Any marrying man would like a kid like Sarah," he said as he drove a nail through the stand into the bottom of the tree. "She rides like she was born to it." He drove in a second nail. "She'll probably learn to rope cows before she's ten."

"Will you teach me?"

The tension increased another notch.

Joe nailed one of the braces, turned the tree over, and nailed the second. "It's like Brother Samuel said, it's not proper to have a man like me hanging around." He nailed another brace. "I should have left

69

by now." He nailed the last brace. He stood the tree up before he dared glance at Mary. "Some men just aren't born to settle down."

Joe set the tree in the corner.

Sarah's face broke into an ear-to-ear grin, and she jumped up and down, clapping her hands in her excitement. "It will be the most beautiful tree in Arizona. I know it will."

"We'll certainly do our best," Mary said, coming out of her trance. "I'll make the bows. You and Joe can tie them on."

"Give me one. Give me one," Sarah begged, too excited to be silent.

Mary quickly made a bow and handed it to the child.

"Lift me up," Sarah said to Joe. "Lift me high."

Mary's fingers flew, cutting ribbon and making bows as fast as she could, but nearly every other fiber of her being was focused on Joe. Time and time again he lifted Sarah as if she weighed nothing, good-naturedly joining in her excitement, talking to her as though she was the most important person in his life.

The child blossomed under his attention. It was hard to remember the scared, silent, hollow-eyed child she'd found when she became Pete's wife. Joe might think he wasn't meant to settle down, but he had the key to Sarah's heart.

And her own. She watched those powerful arms lift the child and longed to feel them wrapped around her. She saw his smile, felt the warmth of his caring. His presence transformed everything around him—her, Sarah, the cramped and cold cabin. Mary felt warm and protected. She felt happy and content. She felt a longing so intense that it blocked out the pain in her back.

"That's all the ribbon," she said. "It's time for the

pictures. Make sure you tie them on the tips of the branches so they'll hang right."

"You can do that," Joe said.

"I think I'll watch."

Sarah took her hand and pulled. "Please, you help, too."

Mary started to get up, but the pain in her back grew worse.

"I'd better sit down. I think I did too much today."

"I told you I'd fix dinner when I got home," Joe said, worry clouding his eyes.

"You've done that often enough. Besides, I thought you'd like something warm after a long, cold ride. Only then I let it get cold."

"We came home too late."

Home! He'd said it. He couldn't be as untouched as he acted. He might not think he was a family man, but that was probably because things hadn't worked out for him in the past. That didn't mean he couldn't be a family man now.

The ugly fact of his uncompleted prison term reared its head, but Mary pushed it aside. Given time, they could find an answer to that. The real problem was how Joe felt.

She shifted position to ease the pain in her back. She wished the baby hadn't settled so low. It made it easier for her to breathe, but it put extra pressure on her spine.

Almost instinctively she reached for her drawing pad. Of all the scenes she had rendered with her pen, this was the most important. She regretted having no colors. Without them, there was no way to capture the golden quality of the light that illuminated the cabin. It was impossible to show the drab, ordinary nature of Joe's clothes in contrast to the vibrant love of life that glowed in his eyes. It was impossible

Leigh Greenwood

to show the transformation that had taken place in Sarah.

Most important of all, it was impossible to show the difference he had made in her life. Black and white had been all she needed before. That was how she'd viewed the world. But Joe had changed all that. He had brought spirit and passion into her life. He had brought love.

It was impossible to show that without color.

She looked down at her drawing. She hadn't missed anything—the cabin, the tree, Sarah, even herself in the corner. But Joe was at the heart of the picture. Without him, this would have been just one more in a long string of dismal evenings.

"Your mother is drawing again," Joe said to Sarah. "Let's see what she's doing this time."

Mary turned the page over quickly. "I'm trying to get you two and the Christmas tree in the same picture. That one didn't turn out the way I expected. Stop trying to look over my shoulder. I can't concentrate when you do that."

"I can't help it," Joe said. "I can't get over the way you make a picture appear—like magic."

Nothing like the magic you've wrought, Mary thought.

But as Mary turned her attention to her drawing, she realized that there was something missing.

There were no presents under the tree.

Joe thought about the presents, too. He imagined Mary had something hidden away for Sarah, but it couldn't be much. She hadn't been able to get to town, and Christmas was only three days off.

He paused on his walk to the barn. The night was radiant. The full moon flooded the landscape with light. It wasn't the warm light of the day, and it was too weak to vanquish the shadows, but it was beautiful nonetheless. There was a ghostly stillness that was comforting, as though all the trouble of the world were held at a safe distance by some almighty hand. Countless stars winked in the dark canopy of the sky, their tiny lights friendly and cheerful.

Samson trotted up. "Are you taking the night off?" Samson licked Joe's hand. "Don't come oiling up to me. I know you like Mary better than me. I can't say I blame you, but I'm not going to forgive you either. I know she's prettier than I am, but we've been together for six years. I even rescued you from that drunken old squatter. I was planning on taking you to California, and look at the thanks I get."

The dog gamboled around him, wagging his tail and barking playfully. "Don't think you're going to talk me into letting you share my bed. You'll just get me up in an hour to let you out."

Fifteen minutes later, settled into his bedroll with Samson nestled beside him, Joe thought about the presents that weren't under that tree. He knew Sarah didn't expect much, but that wasn't the point. Presents would mean that *Père Noel* had come. Presents would mean her mother still remembered her, still loved her.

Either he was going to have to be Father Christmas, or Sarah would be disappointed again.

Then there was Mary. She probably didn't want anything. She certainly didn't expect anything, but for her, Christmas would be a new beginning. Especially with the baby. He wanted to give her something to celebrate that new beginning, but he couldn't think what. He certainly didn't have anything in his saddlebags. Even if he could find her share of the gold, that wouldn't be it either. What he wanted to give her couldn't be found under any tree, but he didn't allow himself to dwell on that.

He would go into town tomorrow and hope no one recognized him.

* * *

"Are you sure you have to go?" Mary asked next morning when he told her he was going into town.

"I've got a few things I need to buy before I leave. And I told Brother Samuel I'd see him in a couple of days. He's liable to come out here again if I don't show up."

She didn't care about Brother Samuel. She could put up with a hundred of his visits as long as Joe was here. She was afraid he meant to ride out and never come back. She was afraid that going to town was only a ruse to cover his leaving forever.

"You've got to hurry back," Sarah said. "You don't want to miss Christmas."

"That's not for two days," Joe said. "That's enough time to go to Tucson and back."

"I don't want you to go to Tucson," Sarah said.

"I won't. Now be sure to milk Queen Charlotte, gather the eggs, and take care of your ma. She's not feeling too well."

Joe had noticed the moment he walked in the door. He always noticed.

"I'll leave Samson here to take care of you. Now I've got to be on my way. If I don't leave soon, I won't get back before midnight."

Mary felt some of the anxiety leave her. He wouldn't go off and leave his dog. He had to be coming back. But she didn't feel entirely reassured. She wouldn't be until she saw him riding back over the ridge.

Chapter Five

Pine Flat wasn't much of a town. There weren't any pines in it either. The town had been thrown up on a flat piece of desert between mountains. A dry wash ran along the base of the near ridge. The unpainted, weathered wood of the buildings stood out in stark contrast to the backdrop of orange-grey rock, pale-green cactus, and sapphire-blue sky.

Joe pulled the brim of his hat low over his face. He rode down the single street quietly and slowly. He didn't want to attract attention. It was after twelve o'clock. He'd timed it that way, hoping most people would be eating their midday meal. The fewer who saw him, the less chance there was of anyone recognizing him.

He stopped in front of Jones Emporium because it was the largest store in town. He wasn't sure what he wanted to buy. He didn't have much money. He had plenty in a bank in Denver, but he couldn't touch that. He wouldn't have any now if he hadn't been in the habit of keeping a little gold dust back every time he made a shipment. After breaking out of jail, he'd made a quick trip to his claim to dig up the gold before heading south.

He hoped the law still thought he was hiding somewhere in the Colorado mountains.

"Wish me luck," he said to General Burnside as he dismounted, "and keep your eyes open. If you see the law, go to bucking and whinnying for all you're worth. If they catch me now, they'll be auctioning you off before the month's out. No telling what kind of sidewinder might buy you."

Inside the store, four oil lamps suspended from the ceiling couldn't dispel a gloom made worse by dark wood and no windows. "Do you have any dresses for a six-year-old girl?" Joe asked a young female clerk.

"How big is she?"

Joe held his hand barely above his waist. "About this high."

"Over here," the young woman said, leading him to a table covered with dresses. She showed him three of the correct size, a blue serge, a yellow party frock, and a dark blue dress with a white pinafore.

Joe bought all three.

"You got anything to make a house look like Christmas?" he asked. "Red ribbon and stuff like that?"

"Not much," the girl said.

Joe bought ribbon, colored paper, and streamers of colored crepe paper to wrap around the tree.

That was when he found the set of paints.

"This all you got?" he asked. He opened the box. Inside were sixteen little compartments containing a rainbow of colors.

"It's the last one," the salesgirl said.

"I need some drawing paper."

He was in luck. They had several pads. He bought

them all. He also bought a baby's rattle, a white dress the girl said could be used for a christening, and a thick blanket. His grandmother used to say all babies caught cold in the winter. He didn't want Mary's baby catching anything.

He also bought some canned fruit, a jar of jelly, a ham, a side of bacon, and a sack of flour. He bought Sarah a box of bath powder and a mirror; he bought Mary a box of scented soap and a small cameo pin.

He also bought himself a coat. It would be a long, cold trip to California.

"You got quite a haul there," the man behind the counter said when Joe had added stick candy and a small box of chocolates to his pile.

"I don't get home much," Joe said. "Almost missed Christmas."

"They'll sure be glad to see you this time," the man said as he sorted Joe's purchases and added up the prices. "You'll want this wrapped up?"

"Good and tight," Joe said. "I'm on horseback."

"Better be a strong horse," the clerk said as he gave Joe the total.

Joe took out a small bag of gold dust. "Got some scales?"

"I'll have to get Mr. Jones," the clerk said.

Joe fidgeted while the clerk found the proprietor. He forced himself to remain outwardly calm while Hiram Jones peppered him with questions as he weighed out the proper amount of gold.

Joe was anxious to get out of town. He had drawn too much attention to himself by the amount of his purchases and paying in gold. He wanted to be gone before Mr. Jones and his clerks had a chance to spread the story.

He cussed aloud when, just as he had loaded his purchases and mounted up, Brother Samuel Hawkins came striding down the boardwalk. The man eyed Joe's bundles with suspicion.

"That seems like a lot to be carrying all the way to California," Brother Samuel observed.

"It's mostly Christmas presents for Mary and the kid," Joe said, damning Brother Samuel for his nosiness. "I decided I couldn't leave just now. Nobody likes to be alone at Christmas. Besides, with the baby coming, Mary hasn't been able to get to town to buy anything for the kid."

"*Mrs. Wilson* needed only to ask my sister or myself. We would have been more than happy to make any purchases for her."

Joe gathered up the reins and started General Burnside walking down the street. If the Reverend Brother Samuel wanted to talk to him, he was going to have to keep up.

"She probably didn't want to bother anybody. She'll most likely be mad enough to chew splinters when she sees what I've done. But I couldn't do anything else. Sort of in Pete's memory, you know."

The Reverend Brother looked as though he didn't like the answer but didn't know quite how to punch a hole in it. "My sister and I were planning to visit on Christmas."

"You come right ahead. I'm sure she'll be glad to see you. Now I gotta be going. General Burnside here is getting impatient to be home before dark."

"I believe my sister and I will come out this afternoon."

Joe pulled General Burnside to a halt and leveled a stony glance at Brother Samuel. "Now why would you be wanting to do a thing like that? You were just out there."

Brother Samuel didn't look quite so self-assured now. "I tried to explain how important it is to be scrupulous with Mrs. Wilson's reputation."

Joe could feel cold anger start to build in him.

"There's nobody I know of doubting Mary except you."

"I don't doubt Mrs. Wilson!" Brother Samuel exclaimed.

"Sounds like it to me. I thought preachers were supposed to have faith in good people."

"Not everybody is so high-minded."

"Then I wouldn't care a whit about what they thought."

"I have to care," Brother Samuel announced. "I intend to ask Mrs. Wilson to marry me. My wife's reputation must be above reproach."

Joe glared at the preacher. He was a little beetle of a man, an insect dressed in black. How dared he think of touching Mary, much less marrying her. She was too good for him. He would be too stupid to know what he had found. He'd try to hedge her in with restrictions and rules and protocol and everything else he could think of to squeeze the life and soul out of her.

Joe didn't want Brother Samuel to marry Mary because he wanted to marry her himself.

"Mary's reputation is good enough for you or anybody else," Joe said, his anger rising. "I'll break the neck of any man who says otherwise."

"I said nothing like that! I merely said—"

"You've said too much. You'd better go home to your midday meal. Hunger is making you sound out of temper."

Joe turned his horse and nearly rode into the sheriff.

"Howdy," the sheriff said. "You're new in town, aren't you?"

It took Joe a moment to calm his anger enough to answer in an even voice. "Just passing through."

"You've got quite a load for a traveling man."

"Christmas," Joe said. "For friends."

Brother Samuel started to introduce the two men. The sheriff's name was Howells. "I just realized I don't know your name," Brother Samuel said to Joe.

"Hank Frazier," Joe said. "I used to be Pete Wilson's partner. Just stopped off to give my respects to his widow on my way to California."

"It's a sad thing to happen to a new bride," Sheriff Howells commented. "She hardly got here before her husband was killed. Then to find herself expecting a baby."

"The Reverend here seems to think he's the one to lend her a helping hand," Joe said.

"She could do worse," Sheriff Howells said. "Much worse."

"Well that's none of my concern," Joe said. "Nice to meet you, Sheriff, but I got to be on my way."

Joe pulled his hat a little lower on his head and walked General Burnside out of town. He couldn't decide which worried him more, the possibility that Mary might marry Brother Samuel or the chance that the sheriff had recognized him.

"This is what comes from getting hooked up with a woman," he told General Burnside. "Normally I wouldn't care who a pregnant woman married. Never cared two hoots about kids, especially little girls. Now look at me. I've spent nearly half my money, I still haven't found the gold, and I'm running around town talking to a sheriff who probably has my picture on his wall. Worst of all, I'm jealous of some beak-nosed fool who calls himself Brother Samuel Hawkins."

Joe rode for a few miles in silence.

"I can't marry her. Everything was against it from the start. It's done nothing but get worse since. Besides, who's to say she would have me? Any sensible woman would choose the Reverend Brother Samuel over me. Now that's a lowering thought. Samson would be laughing out of both sides of his mouth."

Of course women preferred almost any kind of man to an ex-convict. You couldn't get much lower than that without killing a man. And if Joe could have gotten his hands on Pete right after the conviction, he might have done that.

Joe was late getting back. Mary had expected him by mid-afternoon. It was dusk now, and there was still no sign of him. She knew she shouldn't try to milk the cow, but she needed to keep busy. It helped keep her mind off Joe's absence. And she needed to be outside, away from all the Christmas decorations.

"You sure he's coming back?" Sarah asked for the dozenth time. She was more worried about Joe than Mary was.

"Absolutely," Mary said. "Now help me down these steps. Queen Charlotte is probably in a fret to be milked by now."

Mary paused on her way across the yard to let a pain in her back pass. The pains had been getting worse all day. She had started to worry that something was wrong with the baby. It wasn't supposed to come for another month. Between worry about Joe and the baby and trying to reassure Sarah that Joe would be back, she was nearly frantic.

"He wouldn't leave Samson," she said to Sarah. "Now stop fretting and fetch the cow."

But when Mary reached the shed, she turned to the room where Joe slept. She stepped into the shadowy interior. She could see his bedroll spread out over the deep straw. She felt even closer to him here.

Without warning, a pain wrapped itself around her and squeezed until she was sure she would faint. Clutching her belly, she fell to her knees. The pain let up long enough for her to call for Sarah before it struck again. It was blinding in its intensity. She couldn't move. She couldn't think. She could only sink to the straw.

The baby was coming!

"Joe will be home soon," she told Sarah as the frightened child hovered over her. "Everything will be all right then."

By the time the cabin came into view, Joe had made up his mind to leave the next day. He had given up any hope of finding the gold. Maybe he could come back, but for now, his time had run out. Sooner or later people would forget him.

Even Mary.

He was surprised not to see a light in the cabin. It was only dusk, but it would be dark inside. It seemed unlikely that both Mary and Sarah would be taking a nap at this time of day.

He urged General Burnside into a trot. The packages bounced noisily, but he didn't slow down. He urged his horse into a canter when he saw the cow standing in front of the shed, lowing in distress.

Something was wrong. He was headed toward the house when he saw Sarah emerge from the shed.

"Where's Mary?" he called as he slid from the saddle.

"In the shed," Sarah said. The child looked badly frightened.

"What's wrong?" Joe said, heading toward the barn at a run.

"She fell down and can't get up again," Sarah said. "She said the baby's coming."

Inside the shed, Joe dropped to his knees next to Mary. He could hardly see her in the dim interior. "What are you doing here?"

"I can't move."

"I've got to get you inside. You can't have this child in a cow shed." Joe slid his arms under her. "Brother

82

Samuel would have apoplexy."

Mary groaned when he picked her up. She groaned even louder when a pain struck.

"You had no business leaving the house," Joe said as he carried her across the yard. "Open the door, Sarah. And turn back the bed covers."

Mary moaned, but she seemed relieved to be inside.

"How long have you been in pain?"

"The really bad ones started this afternoon, but my back has been hurting ever since last night."

"You mean you were getting ready to have this baby this morning and you didn't tell me?"

"I didn't know. It's not due for another month. I thought I had a backache."

"How long is having a baby supposed to take?"

"It depends. Maybe five or six hours."

"You mean I don't have time to go back to town for Sister Rachel?"

"No," Mary said. The word was changed into a howl by the pain. "You're going to have to help."

"Me!"

"You and Sarah."

"But I don't know anything about having babies."

Mary tried to smile. "It pretty much happens by itself. All you have to do is keep telling me it will soon be over and that it'll all be worth it because I'll have a beautiful baby to show for it."

"Shouldn't I get hot water and things like that?"

"You won't need water until time to clean up."

Joe decided the baby had *better* come pretty much by itself. He was too dumbfounded to do anything but stand around wringing his hands. Mary was equally helpless as one pain after another gripped her in its coils.

"You're going to have to catch the baby," Mary managed to tell him between gasping breaths.

"In what?"

"Your hands."

Joe looked down at his hands as if he'd never seen them before and didn't know what they were for.

"Sarah will help you."

But Sarah was even more upset than he was. The poor child didn't know what was happening. He couldn't help her. He didn't know what was happening, either.

Instinctively he reached out to take Mary's hand. She took hold of him as if he were a lifeline and she a drowning sailor. He had no idea a woman could be so strong. When the pain hit her and she squeezed his fingers, he expected to come away with a collection of broken bones.

He directed Sarah to gather towels, put water on to heat, and find the extra blankets. But each time the pain hit Mary, Sarah would stop, her gaze shifting between Joe and Mary. Only when the pain had passed and Mary's face was once again reasonably calm would she move.

Joe had never felt more helpless in his life. It was even worse than watching himself be convicted for a crime he hadn't committed. Then he had had his anger to sustain him, his plans for what he would do to Pete Wilson when he got out. Now he easily understood why men got drunk and left birthing babies to the women. Joe wasn't a drinking man, but he wished he had a drink right now. As Mary's pains got worse, he found himself wanting a whole bottle.

"Help me sit up a little," Mary said. "I need a pillow under my back."

Just as Joe slid his arms around Mary, she screamed in pain.

"What!" he said, jumping back. Sarah was hitting and kicking and scratching him for all she was worth.

Joe decided they had both gone mad.

"No!" Mary managed to say as the pain started to recede. "He's not hurting me."

Sarah didn't stop until Joe took her by the shoulder and pushed her away from him. Even then she would have bitten him if he hadn't jerked his hand back when he saw her go for him with bared teeth.

"It's all right," Mary said, reaching out to pull the child to her. "He's not hurting me. It's the baby."

"You mean she thinks I did that?" Joe asked.

"Her father used to hit her mother. I saw him hit Sarah once. I told him if he ever hit her again, or me, I'd kill him."

Joe looked at Sarah and felt anger surge through him. He wasn't proud of a lot of things he'd done, but he'd never hurt a child. "Why the hell did you think I'd hurt Mary?" he demanded.

"She doesn't," Mary assured him. "She's just frightened. She doesn't know what to think."

"Do I look like I'm beating her?" Joe demanded, his own worry finding release in anger.

Sarah stared up at him, frightened.

"I'm trying to help her have this baby," Joe said, "and I don't know what the hell I'm doing. I can't figure it out if I've got you biting and scratching like a bobcat."

"She won't," Mary said, hugging the child to her. "You won't, Sarah. I'm going to scream a lot more. Joe's helping. You've got to help too."

As though to prove her words, Mary went rigid and cried out. Joe jumped to her side, holding her hand, supporting her until the pain released its grip.

"The baby is almost here," Mary said. "See if its head is showing."

"Huh?" Joe said, stunned.

"See if it's showing. If it is, you've got to get ready for it."

"Can't Sarah do it?"

"No."

Joe had never been shy around women, but this was different. He felt that in some way he was violating Mary, and that went against his grain.

"What am I supposed to look for?"

"The muscles have to relax to allow the baby to pass. If you can see the top of its head, you know it will be born soon."

It was easy for Joe to clear his head of coherent thoughts. He didn't have any. To pretend he wasn't doing what he *was* doing was more difficult.

"I see it," he said, so excited he forgot his embarrassment. "I can see almost the whole top."

"Good," Mary said. "Then I might not die before it's born."

Another excruciating pain caused her to cry out.

"Hold her hand," Joe told Sarah. "I think it's getting ready to come."

It seemed to Joe that the pains came one right after another, giving Mary no time to rest or recover in between. Then it was all over, and he held a baby girl in his hands. He stared down at the child, unable to believe he had just witnessed the birth of another human being, the beginning of a brand-new life. He had looked like this once. So had Mary, Pete, and Sarah. Someday this baby would be a grown woman and have her own children.

It was amazing, incredible, unbelievable.

The baby's cry brought Joe out of his daze. "It's a girl," he said, handing the infant to her mother. "And she looks like you."

Mary was exhausted, but she managed a smile. "She doesn't look like anybody yet. But she's beautiful just the same."

"She's all messed up," Sarah said.

Mary laughed. "Yes, she is. Why don't you help Joe clean her up."

"Me!" Joe was counting himself lucky to have done nothing wrong so far. "I'll bring the water to you," he said. "I don't know a thing about washing babies."

"It's simple."

"Maybe, when I'm not shaking so much." He held his hand up in front of him. It was quivering.

Mary managed a weak smile. "Maybe you'd better let Sarah bring me the water."

Joe turned away from the bed and came up short. Samson sat by the door, his gaze following every movement. Outside, General Burnside and the cow stood with their noses to the window, their breath fogging the panes. They looked as if they had been watching the entire proceedings. "I forgot all about them," he said, turning to Mary. "The presents are still tied to the saddle, and Queen Charlotte hasn't been milked."

"Then you'd better take care of them," Mary said. "Sarah and I will try to have everything cleaned up by the time you get back."

Joe stumbled out the door, too dazed by the events of the last few hours to be aware of the cold or that Samson had followed him. Like a man in a trance, he caught up General Burnside's reins. Queen Charlotte followed on her own.

"Did you see what just happened?" he asked the animals. "Mary had a baby. It's a tiny little thing, so tiny you can hardly imagine it growing up into a real person."

He began to untie the ropes that held the packages to General Burnside's back.

"One minute there were just three of us. Next minute, there were four. A brand new person, just like that." He snapped his fingers.

Samson was sniffing the packages with particular

attention to the ones containing the ham and bacon.

"She's got little tufts of black hair all over her head. She's all wrinkled up from being squeezed inside Mary. Can't be too much room inside a little woman like that, even for a tiny baby. Leave that alone," Joe spoke sharply to Samson. "That's Christmas dinner."

He put all the packages inside the shed and closed the door on Samson. He unsaddled General Burnside and turned him into the corral.

"Okay, it's your turn, Queen Charlotte." He patted her side as he settled himself on the milking stool. He looked again, then ran his hand carefully along her side. "Looks like you'll be having a little one come spring," he said, the streams of milk beginning to hit the pail with rhythmic smoothness. As the milk filled the pail, the high ping thickened until it more closely resembled a rip in a piece of fabric.

"You get busy on those coyotes," he said to Samson. "We can't leave any hanging around. We don't want Queen Charlotte here to lose another calf. And no telling what they might do to a baby girl. No, sir, you get up off your haunches and get going."

Almost on cue, a coyote yip-yipped somewhere in the hills close by. A second answered.

"See, I told you there was work to be done." But Samson had already disappeared into the night on silent feet, a growl deep in his throat.

Joe finished milking the cow and let her into the corral. He looked toward the house, at the light shining brightly through the window in the dark night, and felt a wonderful sense of peace. The horse and cow were in the corral, the chickens were safe in their pen, and it was warm and secure inside the house where Mary, Sarah, and the baby awaited his return. Everything he'd ever wanted was right here.

Only he had to leave.

But he couldn't, not until he was sure Mary and

the baby were all right. He was worried about her. She looked so worn out. Sister Rachel was coming on Christmas. He couldn't leave until then.

Tomorrow was Christmas Eve. He had to help Sarah make a bow for the front door. And he wanted to see her open her presents on Christmas morning. He wanted her to have some pretty dresses, but the biggest reason for staying was to scc the expression on her face when she unwrapped them.

He wanted her to know her mother still remembered her.

He'd stay until Christmas. Then he'd go.

Chapter Six

Mary had never felt so happy or content. She held her daughter in her arms, the infant nursing contentedly. Sarah bustled about helping Joe fix breakfast for all three of them. Nothing more was needed to make Mary's life complete. It was all here in this small cabin.

She loved Joe. She was comfortable with that now. It would never change. But she knew he couldn't stay. It would mean capture and return to prison with very little chance that he would get out for a long time.

"Have you been thinking of a name for her?" Joe asked.

"I had several in mind."

"Like what?"

"Elizabeth. Anne. Ruth."

"They're such sober names. Don't you think a greedy little puss like her ought to have a different kind of name?"

The baby nursed with noisy, slurping sounds. "What did you have in mind?"

"I haven't known many good women, but I think Holly's okay."

"Holly," Mary said half to herself. "It is a nice name. It makes her sound strong, bright-eyed, and ready to fight if she needs to."

"Like right now."

Mary was changing Holly to the other side, and the infant screamed her anger at having her meal interrupted.

"I think Holly is a fine name," Mary said. "I'll always think of you when I call her name."

The silence that fell made them both painfully aware that their time together was drawing to a close.

"You haven't found the gold."

"No."

"What are you going to do?"

"Go to California. Somewhere else if I have to. Maybe after a while I can come back and look for it again."

She knew he wouldn't. If he didn't find it now, he would never come back.

"When do you have to go?" She didn't want to know the answer, but she had to ask.

"Christmas. I got a few presents in town."

Her eyes filled with tears. Her husband had caused him to be sent to jail. She had caused him to risk being caught. Still he had taken the time to buy presents for them. How could anybody believe he'd stolen that gold? "You didn't have to do that."

"It's not much, just some little things."

The baby finished eating. She rewarded Mary with an enormous burp. "That's what you get for eating too fast," Mary said, but her smile and tone turned her censure into words of love. "Here, why don't you hold her while I eat?"

"Me?" Joe said.

Mary smiled. He always seemed to be saying that, like there were things he'd never considered he could do. "She's a lot nicer to hold now than she was last night."

"I don't—"

"All you have to do is put her in the crook of your arm. Come here, and I'll show you."

Joe approached reluctantly.

"Put your arm across your chest," Mary said.

He did, and she placed the baby in his arm. He immediately clamped her against his chest with his other arm. He was certain he would drop her before he made it to the chair so he could sit down. Holly looked up at him with the biggest black eyes he'd ever seen.

Joe walked to the chair with small, stiff-legged steps. He felt as if he'd never walked before, as if his legs had forgotten how. He practically fell into the chair. Holly continued to look at him with her big eyes.

"She ought to go to sleep in a few minutes," Mary said as she prepared to get up.

"Stay in that bed." Joe's order was so sharp that Holly started to cry. He held her a little closer and, miraculously, she stopped. "You're too weak to get up," he said in a hushed voice. "Sarah can bring your breakfast to you."

"I feel fine. I—"

"You can get up this afternoon. For now, you stay where you are."

Satisfied that Mary would remain in bed, Joe turned his attention back to Holly. Mary had dressed her in a soft flannel gown that was twice her size. She looked too small to be real. He rubbed her cheek with his callused finger. It was incredibly soft. She opened her mouth wide and yawned. She took hold of his finger with her hand. It looked absurdly small, too small to encircle his finger.

She closed her eyes but continued to hold on to his finger. He thought her pug nose was cute. He supposed it would grow to look like her mother's, but it was just the right kind of nose for a baby. He compared her fingers to his own. She had the same number of joints, the same wrinkles at the knuckles, fingernails—everything he had, only so much smaller.

She was asleep in his arms. It almost made him want to cry, and she wasn't even his kid.

Something turned over inside Joe. This was what he wanted—Mary, Sarah, and Holly. He wouldn't ask anything more of life if he could have that much. He understood love now. He could trust his feeling for Mary and hers for him. Holly had made him understand that he could love and be loved.

"You better give her to me," Mary said. "You need to find that gold."

Joe's gaze locked with hers. "If I do?"

"Then you won't have to leave."

Joe couldn't speak for a few minutes. "Are you sure? I've never had a family. I might not be good at it. I'll always be an ex-con."

"I don't care. I never met a man like you, Joe. I didn't think there was one. I don't know why you should be so different from Pete, my father, and all the other men I've known, but you are. Sarah knows it. Even Holly. Look at her sleeping. She knows she's safe as long as you're holding her."

Joe hadn't thought about it that way, but he knew there wasn't much he wouldn't do to protect this child. He managed to lever himself out of the chair without waking Holly. He handed her over to Mary.

"I'm going to make her a cradle. She ought to have a bed of her own. Then I'm going to turn this place inside out. I've still got twenty-four hours to look for the gold."

"Is Joe going to leave?" Sarah asked.

"I hope not," Mary said.

"Why can't he stay?"

Mary was reluctant to tell Sarah the truth, but she knew she would have to learn it some day. "Pete stole some gold and blamed Joe for it. They put him in jail. He broke out so he could find the gold and prove he didn't steal it. Pete buried the gold here, but Joe can't find it. He has to leave, or they will put him back in jail."

"Can't we go with him?"

Mary felt excitement leap within her. Why hadn't she thought of that? It was so simple, so obvious. "Would you want to go with him?"

"Joe's nice. I want him to be my papa. He said he would like having a little girl like me."

"I'm not sure he would let us go. Joe's a very proud man. He'd probably feel he couldn't share his name with us if he couldn't do it without fear of being put back in jail. If he could just find the gold, everything would be all right. Can you remember anything unusual Pete did when he came home?"

Sarah shook her head.

"I know you were afraid of him, but please try to remember. Anything might help Joe. Now you'd better finish cleaning up. I'm going to take a nap. I promised I'll be strong enough to help with dinner."

But Mary's thoughts weren't on dinner or getting stronger. She was trying to think of some way to convince Joe to take her and the children with him.

* * *

Joe had never built a cradle, but it wasn't a difficult task. There were tools for everything in the shed. He bet Pete had never used half of them. "We can't have Holly sleeping on Mary's bed," he said to Samson. The big dog sat watching everything he did. "She's pretty quiet now, but she won't be for long. She could roll right out of that bed."

He tested the bed. "The runner isn't smooth enough," he told Samson. "You can't expect a baby to go to sleep when you're bouncing it all to bits." He turned the cradle over and started to file down some of the ridges. "Of course she can't stay in this cradle forever. As soon as she's able to pull up, she'll have to have a crib. We don't want her falling out on her head."

Samson yawned.

"I know this isn't as exciting as hunting coyotes, but you don't have to be rude. Go talk to General Burnside if you're so bored."

But Samson just yawned again, rested his head on his paws, and continued to watch Joe.

"I think that'll do it," Joe said when the cradle finally rocked smoothly. "It doesn't look very fancy, but it'll give her a place to sleep." Joe picked up the cradle and started toward the cabin. "Well come on," he said to Samson when the dog didn't move. "I don't think Sarah's scared of you anymore. At least, she won't be if you behave yourself. Just go inside, lie down, and keep quiet."

Samson followed Joe into the house. Sarah did look a little apprehensive, but when the big dog lay down, she looked relieved.

"It didn't seem a good thing, the three of you sleeping in that bed together," Joe said as he set the cradle on the floor next to the bed. "Somebody could roll over on that baby and never know it."

Tears pooled in Mary's eyes. "That was very thoughtful of you, Joe."

"You want me to fix it for her now?"

"No, I'd rather hold her."

"Well, I'll be outside taking the place apart if you need me," Joe said as he backed out of the room. "Just give a yell if you need anything."

"Now, Samson," Joe said once they were outside, "I want you to put coyotes completely out of your mind and concentrate on gold. Unless you want to wear out your feet trotting all the way to California, we got to find it before nightfall."

The hours of the afternoon stretched longer and longer. Mary could hear Joe as he moved about the ranch, digging, sounding for hollow spaces, cursing when another idea proved to be as useless as all the previous ones. She found herself praying that he would find the gold. She knew she would never find another man like Joe. She could never love anyone else the way she loved him.

She marveled to herself. She had known him less than a week, yet it seemed they had always known each other. It was as if they were the missing halves of each other. Now that they were together, it was as though they had never been apart.

She looked down at Holly. She wanted more babies—Joe's babies.

"Did you find anything?" Mary asked Joe when he came in, a full milk pail in hand, to begin supper. She knew the answer, but she kept hoping he would say something to give her hope. She couldn't give up yet.

"No, but I got a few more places to look."

"It'll soon be dark."

"I can use a lantern."

"You're never going to find it, Joe. You know that."

"There's always a chance that—"

"If you haven't found it by now, you won't. You might as well accept it."

"I can't."

"Why?"

"Because it means I'll have to leave you."

"You could take us with you."

Joe turned sharply. "No."

"I wouldn't mind."

"I would. I couldn't have you following me all over the country, wondering if the law was going to catch up with me one day or the next."

"It would be better than never seeing you again. I love you, Joe Ryan. I never thought it would be possible to love anybody like I love you."

Joe fell down beside the bed, took Mary in his arms, and kissed her. "I love you. Too much to turn you into a vagabond."

"I won't mind."

"I know you'd try. You might even succeed, but you'd never like it. You long for stability, permanence, a feeling things will be the same tomorrow and the day after. It wouldn't be fair to Sarah and Holly, or any children we might have. I've been wandering since I was sixteen. It was hard for me even then."

"Then you've got to keep coming back until you do find the gold. Sarah and I will help look. You can't give up."

"Where is Sarah?" Joe asked.

"I don't know. I thought she was with you."

"I haven't seen her all afternoon. When did she leave?"

"While I was taking a nap."

"That was more than six hours ago."

"Did she take the pinto?"

Joe looked out the window. "He's not in the corral. I can't believe I didn't hear her leave."

"You were concentrating on finding the gold."

"I was wasting my time," Joe said. He turned to the stove. "If she isn't back by the time supper's ready, I'll go look for her. It's getting cold. Wouldn't be surprised if it freezes tonight."

Sarah returned before supper, but all she would say in response to where she'd been was, "I was looking for some branches to make a Christmas wreath."

"You have no business being gone by yourself so long," Joe said. "You nearly scared your mother out of a year's growth."

"Did I scare you out of a year's growth, too?"

Joe decided that things turning over inside him was going to be a regular occurrence as long as he was around Mary and Sarah. "You scared me out of two years," he said. "Look here," he said, pointing to the hair at his temples, "I'll bet you can see gray hairs."

Sarah looked. "No."

"Well, you will if you do anything like that again."

"I won't."

"Promise?"

"Promise."

They spent the rest of the evening decorating. Joe cut the crepe paper into thin strips and ringed the tree with them. Sarah made big bows out of the ribbon. Joe helped her tack these up on the windows. Then they made a wreath, wired several pine cones in it, tied a huge bow to the bottom, and attached it to the front door. Mary cut out scenes in colored paper, and they pasted them on the windows. By the time they finished, there was hardly a part of the cabin that didn't have some sign of Christmas.

"There's nothing left to do but put a lantern in the window, go to bed, and wait for Christmas morning,"

Joe said, rubbing his hands together.

"Are you sure *Père Noel* will find us?" Sarah asked anxiously.

"Sure," Joe said. "With that wreath on the door and the lantern in the window, he can't miss." Joe looked at Mary. She was putting an extra blanket over Holly. The baby slept soundly in the cradle.

"I guess it's about time I said good night," he said.

Mary straightened up. "I don't want you to go."

"Mary, I already told you I can't—"

"I mean tonight. I don't want you to go tonight."

"But I can't sleep here. Brother Samuel would be horrified."

"The Devil take Brother Samuel."

"We can only hope," Joe murmured.

"If this is to be your last night, I want you to spend it with us."

Joe stood still. He'd been thrown out of many places in his life. People had turned their backs on him, but he'd never been invited in. He ought to go. If they came for him in the night, he'd be trapped here. Worse still, Mary's reputation would be ruined.

But he wanted to stay. More than anything in his whole life, he wanted to stay in this room with these people. If tonight was all he was to be granted, then he would take it.

"I'll put my bedroll by the door. That way—"

"I want you to sleep here," Mary said, patting the bed, "with Sarah and me."

"But you've just had . . . Sarah won't . . . Sister Rachel would fall down in a dead faint if she knew."

"I'm not asking for anything more than to be near you."

"Are you sure?"

"Absolutely."

"Okay, but I'll sleep on top of the covers."

Joe was prey to so many conflicting emotions, he

hardly knew what he felt. He had never slept with a woman without touching her. He vowed he'd cut off his right hand before he touched Mary. She'd just had a baby, for God's sake. Besides, he was leaving tomorrow. He couldn't make love to her, then walk out of her life. Maybe other men could, but he couldn't.

And he knew he wouldn't be back. He would never find the gold. He accepted that now. Without the gold, he could never ask Mary to be his wife. He couldn't accept that. Something inside wouldn't let him give up. Maybe he could look again in the morning. Maybe he could come back in a few months.

Maybe.

But all he had—all he might ever have—was this night. He moved closer to Mary, reached out, and took her hand in his. He felt as if he was fighting for his share of her attention. Holly wouldn't settle down. Finally he released Mary's hand, put his arm around her, and pulled her to him. Holly settled between her breasts and went to sleep. Sarah reached up to take hold of the hand Joe had around Mary's shoulder. In moments she was asleep as well.

"This wasn't what I had in mind," Mary whispered as she clasped Joe's free hand.

"Me, either," Joe whispered back. He kissed her hair. "But I wouldn't trade it for anything in the world."

It was far more than he had expected. So much less than he wanted. He told himself to concentrate on the moment. It was warm and wonderful. It just might be enough to last him for a lifetime.

Mary woke when Holly began to stir. She fed the baby before her cries woke Joe or Sarah. Even in sleep, Sarah held tightly to Joe's hand. Mary wanted to do the same thing for the rest of her life. Joe had gone to sleep with his head on her shoulder. She felt almost crushed by the love that surrounded her.

And it all came from Joe.

Joe woke at dawn. The cabin was cold. Taking care not to wake Mary, Sarah, or the baby, he eased out of bed. Still in his stockinged feet, he opened the stove and began to lay a fire. "Shut up, Samson," he said when the dog started to whine. "I'll let you out shortly."

In a few minutes he had water on for coffee. He looked outside. The ground was covered with a light dusting of snow. It was closer to a white Christmas than he had ever had growing up. He shoved his feet into his boots, grabbed the milk bucket, and eased the door open on silent hinges he'd oiled two days ago.

The frozen ground crunched under his feet. "Queen Charlotte's just going to love getting milked this morning," he said to Samson, who frisked about, his breath making clouds in the frigid air.

The cow did mind being milked, but Joe milked her under the shed out of the wind. She showed her appreciation by kicking only once. Joe set the milk on the porch. "Let the cream rise to the top and freeze. Used to do that back in Carolina," he told Samson. "Sweetest cream you ever did taste." He fed and watered General Burnside, then got his presents from the shed.

Mary was at the stove slicing bacon when he entered the cabin, loaded with presents. She stopped, her knife suspended in midair. "What have you got there?" she asked.

"Just a few things I thought you and Sarah might like."

Mary put her knife down, went to the trunk, and opened it. She took out a handmade doll and a pair of white shoes. "I couldn't afford to buy anything but the shoes. I was going to make her a dress."

"It doesn't matter. I got her some."

Mary watched as Joe stuffed each of Sarah's shoes as full as he could get with powder, a mirror, candy, ribbons, and all the little things the girl in Jones Emporium assured him a little girl would want. "So that's why you risked going to town."

"No, it isn't. I—"

Mary put her hands on his shoulders, stood on tiptoe, and kissed him hard on the lips, her knife dangerously close to his jugular.

"Don't tell lies, not even little ones. It's Christmas."

The word worked its magic, and Sarah and Holly woke up at the same time.

Sarah's gaze went straight to the tree. She rubbed her eyes, looked, and rubbed them again. "*Père Noel* really did come," Sarah said, staring at her shoes.

"I told you he wouldn't miss the light in the window," Joe said. "Now you can't open anything until after breakfast. I'll take that while you feed the baby," Joe said, removing the knife from Mary's hand. "Sarah, you can set the table."

Joe tried not to think that this was the last time he would sit down to eat with Mary and her family. He tried to tell himself this was the high point of his stay. He would concentrate on enjoying it. He would have more than enough time to think about what he would be missing.

Joe gave Mary the rattle, dress, and blanket for Holly. Sarah emptied her shoes, exclaiming over everything she found. But when she opened the package Joe handed her with the three dresses inside, she shrieked so loudly that he thought she didn't like them. She bounded up, threw herself across the room, and hugged him until he thought he couldn't breathe.

"Every pretty little girl ought to have a dress," Joe said. "I just bought you a couple of spares. Here, put this one on," he said, handing her the party dress. "And don't forget to powder yourself real good," Joe said as Sarah retreated behind the curtain. "I like my little girls to smell good."

"You shouldn't have spent all your money on us," Mary said, her eyes filling with tears.

"I bought myself a coat. I've got plenty left."

"You're telling lies again."

"Enough, then." He reached back into the welter of brown paper and handed Mary the box of scented soaps. While she was thanking him for that, he handed her the books of drawing paper, the pens, and ink. Before she had recovered completely, he handed her the set of colored paints.

She just sat there, her hand over her mouth, tears pouring down her cheeks.

"Next Christmas, I want every one of those drawings to be in color," he said, a huskiness in his voice. He cleared his throat. "Christmas should never lack color, even in Arizona."

"Oh, Joe," Mary said, and threw her arms around him.

Joe found himself hugging Mary and Holly at the same time. Holly objected. Loudly.

"Be quiet, child."

"No, she's right," Joe said, pulling back. "No point pretending. We've got to face up to it. This is the last we'll see of each other for a time."

"Joe," Sarah said.

But Joe didn't answer her. Mary was clinging to him, and he couldn't summon the willpower to let her go. He buried his face in her hair, willing himself to remember this moment forever.

"Why won't you let us go with you? It won't be a hardship, not like it will be living here without you."

"Mary, I already explained why I can't do that."

"Joe," Sarah called.

"Just a minute," Joe said to her. He wanted to memorize the feel of Mary in his arms, the smell of her. "I'll come back, I promise. Maybe by then you can remember something that will help, but I can't take you with me while this stolen gold is hanging over my head."

"Joe."

"What is it?" Joe said, finally turning to Sarah. "Can't you see—" Joe froze. Sarah was dressed in her party dress, a ribbon in her hair, the white shoes on her feet. She was beautiful. She looked like a little angel.

But that wasn't what mesmerized him. She was holding her hands up toward him. In them was a bag of the missing gold.

"Can you stay now? Can you be my papa?"

Chapter Seven

Mary saw them long before they turned into the yard—Brother Samuel and Sister Rachel, accompanied by Sheriff Howells. She wrapped the baby in Joe's blanket, put her in her crib, and put on water for coffee. She threw a heavy woolen shawl, the last of Joe's presents, over her shoulders and met them at the door.

"You poor woman," Sister Rachel exclaimed as soon as she stepped inside, "we came the moment the sheriff told us." She threw her arms around Mary and embraced her.

"To think you've been alone with him all this time," Brother Samuel said.

"Saints preserve us!" Sister Rachel exclaimed, patting Mary's flat stomach. "What happened to the baby?"

"She's asleep in her crib," Mary said. "Apparently I miscalculated when she was due."

"But how . . . who . . . when?"

"Two days ago. Joe and Sarah helped me."

"You let that strange man, that *criminal*, help you!" Brother Samuel exclaimed.

"I didn't have much choice. He found me in the shed unable to get up."

"Poor woman. And all the time you didn't know what he was."

"I know exactly what he is," Mary said, proud, calm, and happy. "He's the man I'm going to marry."

Sister Rachel and Brother Samuel practically threw Mary down in a chair. "Having the child so unexpectedly must have brought on brain fever," Sister Rachel said.

"He's an escaped convict, Mrs. Wilson," Sheriff Howells added.

"Suppose he didn't steal that gold?" Mary asked. "Would you have to take him back?"

"Well, I don't know. He did break jail."

"But he broke out so he could find the gold and prove he didn't steal it. Wouldn't that be reason enough not to send him back?"

"If he can come up with the gold, the transport company would drop the charges. They'd probably give him a reward, too."

"That's a perfectly absurd question," Brother Samuel said. "Of course he has to go back to jail."

"I never trusted him, not from the first," Sister Rachel said.

But Mary wasn't to be sidetracked by Brother Samuel or Sister Rachel.

"So if he can return the gold and prove he didn't steal it, do you promise not to send him back to Colorado?"

"Yes, ma'am, but I can't promise Colorado won't still charge him with breaking jail."

"But why should he be punished for that when he shouldn't have been in jail in the first place?"

"You got a point there, ma'am. I think we could work things out. Of course, he might have to go up there a while later to talk to some people, but I don't imagine they'd hold anything against him. If he can prove he didn't steal that gold, that is."

Mary got to her feet. "How about coffee? I've made a new pot."

Joe had expected to see Brother Samuel's buggy in front of the cabin, but he wasn't surprised to see the sheriff's horse as well. He balanced the strong box across the saddle in front of him. His and Mary's gold was safely stowed in the bottom of his saddlebags.

"How did you know where to find the gold?" he asked Sarah, who rode beside him.

"Papa showed me the cave once. He threatened to put me in it if I was bad."

"Why didn't you tell me last night?"

"I wanted to surprise you."

"You sure did that."

"Are you going to be my papa now?"

"It depends on what the man riding that horse says." Joe pulled up in front of the house. The sheriff and Brother Samuel came out to meet him.

"You want to give me a hand with this box?" Joe asked.

"That the stolen shipment?" the sheriff asked as he came down the steps.

"Yes."

"Where did you find it?"

"I didn't. Sarah did."

"Papa hid it in a cave," Sarah said.

"How did you know?" The sheriff took the box from Joe. Joe dismounted and helped Sarah down.

"Last night Mama said Joe would have to go away if he couldn't find the gold. She told me to try to think of everything Papa did when he was home that time.

That's when I remembered him sneaking out of the house."

Mary came down the steps. "You called me Mama."

Sarah threw her arms around Mary's neck. "Joe said you'd like it."

"I do," Mary said, hugging the little girl tight to her chest. "I like it very much."

"Pete set me up," Joe explained to Sheriff Howells. "But he was killed before he could come back and get the gold. It's all there. See for yourself."

Mary came to stand by Joe, one arm around him, the other resting on Sarah's shoulders. "The sheriff says you won't have to go back to Colorado. He said you can stay here."

"You sure about that?" Joe asked.

"I don't see why not. They've got their money back. The way I see it, they owe you something for being locked up all that time."

"You think I can get that conviction taken off my record? I don't want my kids' pa to have a record."

"Ought to be able to do that, too."

Joe turned to Brother Samuel. "I want you to marry us."

"Right now?" Sister Rachel asked. It was almost a shriek.

"Yes, right now," Mary confirmed.

Brother Samuel looked horrified. "I can't do that."

"Why not?" Joe asked. "You're a preacher, and you have two witnesses."

"You don't have a license."

"Please," Mary asked.

"I can't without a license," Brother Samuel repeated, looking belligerent.

"Mary can't travel into town for a while yet," Joe said. "And I don't intend to set one foot off this ranch until she does. Unless you want me to ruin that reputation you were so worried about, you'll marry us right now."

"It wouldn't be right. I can't—"

"Oh, shut up, Samuel, and marry them," the sheriff said. "We can make out the license when we go into town. I'll bring it out tomorrow. I think we've caused this man enough trouble as it is."

"I still can't believe it," Mary said that evening as she snuggled down next to Joe. "I swore I'd never get married again. Wait until I tell my family."

Holly was asleep in her cradle. Over in the corner, Sarah had burrowed deep into Joe's bedroll. Samson lay next to her. Joe and Mary occupied the bed alone.

"I'm not sure Brother Samuel believes it, and he married us."

"Poor man. I thought he would choke on the words. He looked miserable."

"Not half as miserable as you'd have been if you'd married him."

"I never would."

"Let's forget about Brother Samuel and Sister Rachel. From now on, it's just you and me."

"And Sarah and Holly."

"And General Burnside and Samson."

"And Queen Charlotte and her calf-to-be."

There seemed to be no end to the love that surrounded Joe. But that was the way it ought to be. Love was what Christmas was really about.

LANTERN IN THE WINDOW

For my mother, Bertha Dahl Rothel, who was born eighty-some years ago in the middle of a snowstorm, out on the prairie near Medicine Hat, and whose vivid memories of those pioneer times inspire many of my stories. Thanks, Mom.

Chapter One

February 22, 1886

"She's good and late. Prob'ly hit a blizzard." The garrulous man also awaiting the arrival of the west-bound train tugged his knitted cap closer around his ears and huddled into his woolen overcoat, eyeing Noah's heavy buffalo coat with envy. "That's some coat you got there, mister. You shoot the buffalo yerself?"

Noah nodded, wishing the man would go pester someone else and leave him alone. He wasn't in any mood for small talk this afternoon.

"You a rancher hereabouts?"

Noah nodded again, a curt nod.

"Only just moved out here me'self," the man went on. "Don't know many folks yet, takes time. Name's Morris, Henry Morris." He held out a mittened paw.

"Noah Ferguson." Noah shook the extended hand. Any other day, he'd have welcomed this stranger to the Canadian West, taken time to get to know him, but today he was too distracted.

"Nice meetin' ya, Ferguson. Waitin' on my wife Sadie and the kids, comin' out from the East," Morris confided, then waited expectantly.

When Noah didn't respond, Morris shifted from one foot to the other and then gave up. "Well, no sign of the train, and it looks like we're in fer a real blow, way that wind's pickin' up. Don't know about you, but I'm about freezin'. Why not come along inside the station house with the rest of us? No tellin' how late she'll be."

"Thanks. I'll be along presently." Relieved to be left alone, Noah thumped his mittens together and stamped his booted feet, pulling his scarf up and his weathered Western hat further down, painfully aware of the cold on his newly shaven cheeks and chin.

What the hell had possessed him to shave off his beard this morning? His rugged features might look better without all that wild black hair, but the beard might also have kept his chin from freezing, waiting for this damnable train.

And after all, what did he care how he might appear to her? It wasn't as if he had to court her; the marriage was over, the legal bond established between them. She had insisted on a proxy marriage before she left Toronto on the four-day train journey that was bringing her here to Medicine Hat. Against his better judgment—and the advice of the only lawyer in town—Noah had agreed.

He'd wanted it all over and done with. He'd signed the papers and sent the money for the fare, and now that she was almost here, his gut was churning. He wished to God the train would get here so they could be done with this awful first meeting, he and Annie Tompkins.

Annie Ferguson, he corrected himself. Annie Ferguson, his second wife. Tall, she'd described herself. Thirty-four, on the thin side, and plain, which suited him just fine. He'd been relieved to read her description of herself; after all, this was no love match, far from it.

Instead, it was a practical solution for them both. She was a soldier's wife, widowed in the Rebellion of 1885, a farm woman trapped in the city, working in some dingy factory to support herself and her young daughter while longing for the country life she'd known as a child.

And as for him, this marriage was a desperate measure.

He thought of his cranky, bed-ridden father, being cared for at this moment by a kindly neighbor, then deliberately forced his thoughts back to his new wife.

Redheaded, she'd said, which worried Noah some—was it true, what they said about a redhead's temper? There'd been no sign of it in the eight letters she'd sent during the past months, and Lord only knew he had no experience of women's temper and no desire to learn.

Molly had been the sweetest of women. In their three years of marriage, Noah was hard put to recall times when she'd even come close to losing her temper.

Molly. Without warning, bitter rage at his loss welled up in him, rage so intense that his tall, well-muscled body trembled with the force of it, and he clenched his teeth and knotted his hands into fists inside the blue wool mittens his dead wife had knitted for him.

There were holes worn through one thumb and two fingers. Noah had clumsily mended them.

It had been two years now since Molly and his eighteen-month-old son, Jeremy, had died within

115

hours of one another, victims of typhoid, and in recent months he'd begun to believe this smothering, impotent, choking fury was gone forever, that time had eased the agony of his loss. Instead, here it was back again, as powerful as ever, and now there was this gnawing guilt as well.

I never wanted any woman but you, Molly. Still don't, but I can't do it alone anymore, not since Dad had the stroke—if you'd lived, Molly, I wouldn't be in this damnable position, waiting to meet some stranger. I've had to invite her to share the house we built together, the bed we slept in—damn it all, Molly, how could you do this to me?

He struggled for, and as always, recovered his self-control. He reminded himself with harsh honesty that his new wife would share as well the work of the ranch, the care of his father, the constant, ill-tempered demands of a once sweet-natured man who'd become a tyrant since his stroke.

Noah swallowed hard and the last of the rage subsided, replaced with apprehension. He'd mentioned in his letters to Annie that his father wasn't well, but he'd never really explained exactly what taking care of Zachary involved. Hell, if he had done so, no woman in her right mind would have agreed to come, would she?

Like him, Annie and her young daughter would just have to make the best of this situation. He brushed one hand across his eyes, clearing away the snowflakes that blinded him, and squinted down the track.

Far off down the rails a single headlamp flickered in the driving snowstorm, and over the sound of the wind he could hear the eerie wail of the steam whistle and the sound of an approaching engine. The train was coming.

At last, the waiting was done.

With a screech of brakes and a cloud of steam, the engine groaned to a halt. Outside the passenger car, it was snowing heavily, but through the frosted window Annie could see a small knot of people on the platform, all staring expectantly up at the train.

An old man with a white beard was shoveling frantically to clear a path from the platform to the small wooden station.

"Med—i—c—ine Ha-a-a-t," the conductor called in his sing-song fashion, making his way down the crowded aisle to open the door.

After four endless days riding across empty wilderness, at last they'd arrived. Heart thumping so hard she was certain it would fly out of her chest, Annie tried to adjust the flamboyant hat Elinora had given her as a parting gift, but it wouldn't stay put.

At last, Bets reached out and straightened it, and Annie gave her a grateful smile and a wink, trying to pretend a bravado she was far from feeling. With trembling hands she gathered their bundles together, wrapped Bets's wool shawl tighter around her, and followed the other departing passengers to the door.

Tilting her chin high, Annie lifted her skirts and stepped down into snow on legs that had turned to jelly.

Lordie, it was freezing. She paused and caught her breath as the cold air seared her lungs. Once the first shock was over, however, the icy air felt clean and invigorating after the stuffy train compartment, but it started Bets to coughing again.

Annie twisted her sister's scarf up and over her chin and mouth, and then, feeling sick with nerves, she squinted into the snow and tried to pick out which of the men waiting a short distance away might be Noah Ferguson.

117

Thirty-six years old, he'd written. Tall, dark-haired.

Her eyes skittered past a short, round figure with a cable knit hat pulled down to his eyelids, lingered on a thin, red-faced man with a handlebar moustache and a brimmed cap, and then settled on the giant standing like a statue a little distance from the others, brimmed hat hiding his face, hands thrust deep into the pockets of a huge furry coat. Annie looked, and looked again.

Some sixth sense told her that this was her husband.

His gaze touched her face and flicked past her, to the passenger car where a very fat woman with several children was now being helped down the step. "Sadie," bellowed the man in the knitted hat, racing over and throwing his arms around her.

There were no other passengers getting off. The conductor was closing the door.

The man in the heavy coat looked at Annie again, puzzlement in his frown, and Annie swallowed hard and said a silent, fervent prayer as he moved towards her.

Lordie, he was big. She was tall for a woman, but he towered over her. There was a ruggedness and raw strength about him unfamiliar to Annie, accustomed as she was to city men.

She drew herself up and squared her shoulders, praying that she didn't look as terrified as she felt. She attempted a smile and knew it was a dismal failure.

"How do you do?" Her voice was barely audible.

His face was all angles and planes—a stern, strong, handsome face, clean shaven and unsmiling.

"I'm looking for Miss Annie Tompkins. Rather, Mrs. Annie Ferguson," he corrected. His voice was a deep baritone.

"That's me," she managed to say. She tried again to smile, but her lips felt paralyzed. "I'm Annie, and this is my—this is Bets."

Bets, her wide, feverish blue gaze intent on Noah's face, made a small curtsy and then edged fearfully behind her sister, doing her best to stifle her coughing and not succeeding.

Annie cleared her throat, desperately trying to remember the dignified little speech she'd been preparing every anxious moment since she'd left Toronto. Not one word came to her.

"Hello, Noah Ferguson," she finally managed to stammer. "Pleased to meet you, I'm sure," she choked out, painfully aware that she sounded both weak-minded and simpering.

He didn't respond. Instead, his coal-dark eyes slowly took in her hat, her face, then her figure. He looked her up and down. Annie refused to flinch under his gaze. She clenched her teeth as he stepped around her to stare at Bets before he once again turned his attention to Annie.

"You're considerably younger than you led me to believe, madam. How old *are* you, exactly?" He was scowling down at her, and a shiver ran down her spine that had nothing to do with the snow swirling around them.

Here it was then, the first consequence of all her lying. There was nothing to be done except confront it head on.

"I'm twenty-two." Annie tilted her chin as high as she could and met his coal-dark eyes, but after a long moment under his steady gaze, her bravado crumbled.

"Well, almost twenty-two. I'll be twenty-one this June." At the thunderous look on his face, she hurriedly added, "I know you wanted someone older, Mr. Ferguson. I was afraid if I told the truth, you

wouldn't have me. Us. But I assure you, I feel a lot
older inside than my years. If that's any help."

He actually snorted in disgust. He looked from her
to Bets and back again. "Twenty years old. And with
a fourteen-year-old daughter? That's quite an accomplishment, madam." His voice dripped with sarcasm.

If it weren't so cold, Annie would have sworn this
was hell.

"She's—Bets is my little sister, not my daughter,"
she confessed miserably. "I—I've never been married. I thought you might not—I thought—"

He stared at her until she gulped and was silent.

"You thought I was fair game, and you told me
only what you figured I wanted to hear. I take it most
of what you've told me about yourself is nothing but
a pack of lies. Is that so, madam?"

His voice was quiet, but lethal.

Annie desperately wanted to contradict him, but
couldn't. The fact was, a great deal of what she'd told
him was a pack of lies. There was no denying it.

"Some," she admitted miserably. "The part about
growing up on a farm wasn't exactly honest. But the
part about me and Bets being hard workers, that's
the god-honest truth," she burst out. "We worked
from dawn to dusk in Lazenby's cotton mill—anybody could tell you we were among the best. Just give
us a chance, and we'll prove it to you, Mr. Ferguson,
I promise we will."

"If I'd wanted farmhands, I'd have hired men." He
looked as though he was about to explode, and Annie
steeled herself.

Bets had been choking back her coughing, but
now it took hold of her with a vengeance and she
doubled over, her face purple.

Annie drew the smaller girl close against her side
and felt Bets's whole body trembling. The wind had

picked up and the snow was swirling around them.

Annie had been too distraught to even feel the cold, but now it suddenly thrust icy fingers past the inadequate barrier of her clothing, and she was miserably aware that the soles on her boots were worn through in places, letting the snow in.

"My sister's sick, Mr. Ferguson. She caught the grippe on the train, and we're both freezing cold. Please, couldn't we talk this over at some later time?"

Annie knew the moment had come when he could—probably would—turn his back on them and simply walk away. She knew he'd be well within his rights to do that very thing, leaving them to fend for themselves in a snowstorm in the middle of the wild Canadian west.

Desperation gripped her. If he left them, what in God's name would she do? She had little money left; she knew no one in this barren, savage place. All she'd ever done was work in the cotton mill, and she was pretty certain there were no mills within a thousand miles of here.

She was terrified. She trembled with fear, and her stomach churned. She clutched Bets's arm so tightly that the girl cried out.

Ferguson's eyes held hers for what seemed an eternity, and with her last vestige of courage, Annie stared straight back, willing him—begging him, entreating him—to give her a chance.

Chapter Two

Warm in his heavy coat, utterly furious at being deceived, Noah was suddenly conscious that the woman and her sister were shivering. He noted that their coats were thin, and they were poorly dressed for temperatures below freezing. The ridiculous hat with the bird's nest on it seemed about to blow away in the wind.

Annie was holding on to it with one arm and hugging her sister with the other.

The girl coughed again, hollow and harsh, and the ferocity of it coming from such a skinny little kid shocked him and added to the impotent anger he felt at his proxy bride.

The lying little trollop had saddled him with still another invalid, if the sound of that cough was any indication. The girl sounded as if she might have consumption.

The irony of the situation brought a grim smile. At least he needn't feel guilt any longer about Zachary—

Annie Tompkins had far outdone him in duplicity.

Her lies were grounds for annulling the marriage, he knew that. He need have no qualms about washing his hands of both her and her ailing sister right there and then—no court in the land would say different.

But where would he be then? Noah raged. It would take months to get a response to a new advertisement, and spring wasn't that far off, with its dawn-to-dusk clearing and ploughing and planting of hay. There was his prized herd of cattle to tend to, chores to finish with no time or energy left at the end of the day to prepare meals and do the endless tasks a household seemed to require . . . tasks he had no skill for and despised. And most important of all, worst of all, there was his father, bedridden, needing constant attention and care.

He'd already hired two people in the past six months, one an elderly spinster he'd brought out from Lethbridge and the other a young Englishman, a drifter. Both had quit after only one week of dealing with his father.

It had become all too obvious to Noah that he urgently needed a wife. Wives didn't just quit when things were tough.

But women of any sort were a rare commodity out here on the Canadian prairies, which was why he'd finally advertised in the blasted Toronto newspaper in the first place. And there hadn't been much choice, when it came down to it; the only other woman besides Annie who answered his ad had been the widowed mother of six small children.

It seemed he was well and truly stuck with her. Lies or not, he urgently needed this woman he'd married. At the very least, he'd have to postpone judgment for a few days, perhaps a week.

With great reluctance, he decided he'd take her

and her sister out to the ranch, and if the situation proved truly intolerable, he'd buy them a train ticket back to the city.

His voice was harsh. "Get inside the depot and get yourselves warm while I bring the horse and wagon around. The stationmaster'll give you hot coffee. Is that your luggage over there?" He pointed down the platform, where a single tin trunk and several carpetbags were all that was left of the pile unloaded from the baggage car.

At Annie's timid nod, he turned on his heel and made his way past the depot and down the street to the livery stable, cursing himself for being a soft-hearted fool.

Afterwards, Annie had only fragmented memories of the long, snowy ride to the homestead.

He'd been thoughtful enough—in the back of the wagon, he'd made a cozy nest for them from heavy buffalo robes he'd brought along, placing their trunk so it blocked some of the wind. He'd lifted Bets as if she were as light as a snowflake and plunked her into the wagon.

Annie grabbed her long skirts and started clambering in by herself, but suddenly his hands grasped her waist, and she too was lifted, none too gently, up and over the backboard. He said not a single word. She stowed her hat safely beside her and snuggled down beside her sister amidst the smoky, wild-smelling fur robes. The wagon tilted as he climbed up on the seat and clucked to the horse.

Annie peeked out as they lumbered through the small frontier town, past a building that said Post Office, then a two-story log building with a sign proclaiming "Lansdowne Hotel." The rest of the town was made up of a few frame houses, numerous shacks, and even a dozen tents. They crossed a narrow steel bridge that spanned a river almost covered in ice and finally set off across an expanse of frozen prairie.

For a while, Annie worried about Indians. She knew that the red-coated Mounted Policemen had brought law and order to this barren land several years ago, but she didn't see any around here.

She didn't see any Indians either, so after a while she worried instead about how Noah Ferguson knew which direction to take. The whole flat, bleak landscape looked exactly the same to her in every direction—cold and gray and empty, dreary beyond measure. She'd never imagined this much space with so little in it. She realized after a time that he was more or less following the path of the frozen river.

Slowly, despite the cold wind and the snow whirling around them, Annie's body grew warm beneath the heavy covering. The fatigue of the long train journey coupled with intense relief at not being deserted at the depot combined to make her sleepy.

Bets had already cuddled close beside her beneath the heavy robe. She was sound asleep, and at last Annie too put her head under the covering, pulling it over the two of them until only a small space remained for fresh air.

It was dark inside. It smelled strange, but it was like being safe in a warm cave with a storm raging outside. She slept, an uneasy sleep interrupted by the sound of the wind, the jingle of the harness, and the occasional word of encouragement spoken by Ferguson to his horse.

His voice and the fierce, joyful barking of a dog startled her awake. "Hello there, old Jake," she heard him say. "Good dog, good boy."

She stuck her head out, shocked to discover how dark it had become. The snow seemed to have

125

stopped, but the air was frigid.

The wagon was still moving, but past Noah's shoulder Annie could see a substantial log house directly ahead with light in the windows, and the dark outlines of numerous other buildings scattered nearby. The dog, large and black, was barking madly and running alongside the wagon.

"Quiet, Jake, good dog." At Noah's order, the dog stopped barking, running close beside them with his tail wagging hard.

Bets, too, was awake now. Eyes still heavy with fever, she peered around and then took Annie's mittened hand in her own and squeezed it. Annie gave her a reassuring smile.

The wagon stopped. Noah jumped down and came around, lifting first Annie and then Bets to the snowy ground.

"Go ahead in," he instructed. "Tell Gladys Hopkins I'll take her home right away."

Stiff from the hours in the wagon, Annie staggered up the steps and across the porch to the door, Bets's hand tight in her own. It was thrown open before she could decide whether to knock. Inside was a small, round woman with a neat brown bun on the top of her head, prominent blue eyes, and a wide, welcoming smile. She looked perhaps a dozen years older than Annie. The room behind her was warm and smelled of food cooking.

"Well, so here you are. Welcome to you." Already wrapping herself in a black coat and holding a red checkered shawl, the woman closed the door behind them with a bang. "No sense heatin' the world, I always say. I'm Gladys Hopkins—we're Noah's neighbors west of here. So you're the new Mrs. Ferguson. Noah already said your name was Annie." Her bright eyes were kind and curious. "And who might you be, dearie?" She smiled at Bets.

"This is Betsy Tompkins, my sister," Annie supplied hurriedly. "Pleased to meet you, Mrs. Hopkins."

"You call me Gladys, I'll call you Annie. We're gonna be friends—goodness knows we're the only white women this side of the Hat. Sorry I have to hurry off like this, but it's fixin' to storm, and I got a husband and a daughter waitin' on their supper. I left soup and fresh bread on the warmer over there fcr you."

She gestured to the cookstove against the wall and then tied the red wool scarf over her hair. She leaned close to Annie, whispering in her ear, "The old man in there's had his supper. Didn't eat enough to keep a sparrow alive. He's in a right fair temper, same as always these days. Don't you let him get the best of you now, dearie."

At that moment, the door opened and Noah came in with the tin trunk.

Gladys jumped back and said in a loud, guilty voice, "I'll come visitin' soon as the weather allows. Hope you settle in fine, Annie. My stars, would you look at this snow? Bye-bye, now, Betsy." She went out quickly, closing the door behind her.

Noah thumped the trunk on the floor, returning a moment later with the carpetbags and her hat, which he dumped unceremoniously on top of the trunk.

"Make yourselves right at home," he said, and Annie flushed, recognizing sarcasm when she heard it. "It'll take me at least three hours to get back, and then, madam, I'd say you have some explaining to do."

Before Annie could begin to think of a response, the door slammed shut behind him and she and Bets were alone. She closed her eyes for a moment and breathed a sigh of relief. At least she'd have time to gather her wits about her before she had to face him again. He was downright formidable.

For a few moments, they busied themselves with taking off their coats and shawls and boots. They hung their things on the pegs by the door, then stood side by side, looking wide-eyed around the large, pleasant room, each silently comparing it with the small, cramped space they'd shared in the city.

Noah Ferguson had written that he wasn't well off, but to Annie, this looked like a grand house indeed.

The area was softly lit by a coal-oil lamp that had roses on the glass shade. The lamp was set on a crocheted doily on a high dresser beneath a window.

The room, a very large combination kitchen and living room, had a huge iron cookstove presiding at one end and a wood heater at the other. Both were giving off waves of comforting warmth, and Annie and Bets moved hesitantly to stand by the heater and warm themselves.

There was a square wooden table and four chairs near the cookstove, and a horsehair sofa and a rocking chair at the opposite end of the room where a narrow staircase led to another floor. There were several cross-stitched pillows on the sofa, and a border of hand-embroidered roses trimmed the white fabric of the curtains at the window. The wooden floor had several braided rag rugs, and there was floral wallpaper on the walls. An ornate clock sat on a shelf specially made for it. Also on the walls were several pictures clipped from magazines and carefully mounted on cardboard.

Everywhere Annie looked was the mark of a woman who'd made this house into a cozy home.

Noah Ferguson had told Annie in his first letter that he was a widower, that his wife and baby son had died two years before.

It was obvious that Noah's wife had loved this house, Annie thought uneasily. Her touch was everywhere, although as Annie looked more closely, there was also a general air of neglect. There was a thick layer of dust on the dresser, and the curtains were limp with dirt. Although the wide boards on the floor showed signs of a recent sweeping, it was plain they hadn't been scrubbed in some time.

Near the heater were two doors. One was shut, but the other was ajar, and suddenly, a loud banging came from behind it, as though someone was hammering on the floor with a heavy object.

"Lordie, that scared me." Annie's hand went to her heart. "I forgot there was anybody else here."

Bets's eyes were wide and fearful.

"I think it's Mr. Ferguson's father," Annie indicated. "I will see to him. You warm yourself by the fire."

Hesitantly, she tapped at the door and then pushed it open so she could enter the small room. It was painted blue, and on the wall was a picture of a smiling cherub cuddling a kitten. A chair, a dresser, and the single bed took up most of the space.

"Mr. Ferguson?" Annie said in a hesitant tone, standing beside the bed. "I'm—I'm Annie. I've only just arrived. Is there something you want?"

The white-haired man lying propped on pillows in the disheveled bed held a cane tight in his right fist. When he saw Annie, he lifted it up and brandished it threateningly, making strange guttural noises in his throat.

She cried out and leaped back, certain he was about to strike her.

His face was twisted grotesquely to one side, and it was plain to Annie that his right hand and side were useless. It was also obvious that he was in a furious temper.

Annie stared at him, horrified. Was he a madman? Noah Ferguson had mentioned his father in his letters, but all he'd said was that the older man was "in ill health."

He stopped trying to speak and lay back panting, staring at Annie with the same coal-black, angry look his son had given her earlier.

"Can—can I get you something, sir?" she asked again.

He used the end of the cane to gesture at a water glass and Annie cautiously sidled over and snatched it up.

"Water? I'll bring it directly." She backed out of the room, expecting at any moment that he'd throw the cane at her.

In the outer room, Bets was coughing again, huddled in an exhausted heap on a chair by the fire. Annie went over and felt her head.

"You're burning up. We need to get you to bed, sweets."

She filled the water glass from the pail on the washstand, but before she could take it back into the bedroom, the awful hammering began again.

Annie rolled her eyes and blew her breath out in an exasperated *whoosh*. He was trying her patience, that was certain.

She walked quickly back into the bedroom and over to the bed, holding out the glass. In a firm tone, she said, "Here you go, and I'd be grateful if you'd please stop that banging, Mr. Ferguson."

The old man made a grumbling noise, put the cane on the bed beside him and snatched at the glass with his good hand, but he misjudged and bumped Annie's arm. The glass spilled, sloshing most of the water on the patchwork quilt that covered him.

With a roar of absolute rage, he grabbed the glass and flung it against the blue-painted wall. It smashed into shards, and Annie let out a shriek and ran for the door. Trembling, she closed it firmly behind her, and the now-familiar thumping began again.

She wasn't going back, she told herself. Thirsty or not, he'd have to wait until his son came home and tended to him.

With the constant banging as accompaniment, Annie set out bowls, and she and Bets ate the thick, aromatic soup simmering on the back of the cookstove. A loaf of freshly baked bread stayed warm beneath a snowy napkin, and there was butter in a bowl.

Annie sent Gladys a heartfelt thank-you, but the incessant banging was difficult to ignore, and her hand trembled as she spooned up the soup and spread butter on a slice of the crusty bread.

Bets ate only a spoonful of soup, took several bites of bread, then sank back in her chair, exhausted.

The young girl needed rest, but where would she put Bets to sleep? Hurriedly finishing her meal, Annie lit a candle and peeked into the other ground-floor bedroom. It was obviously Noah's room; his clothing hung on wall pegs, and two pair of immense boots stood side by side on the floor.

Feeling like an intruder, Annie stepped inside, swallowing hard as she looked at the wide double bed. Her mind's eye filled now with the image of the muscular giant who, in name at least, was her husband. Her cheeks grew hot at the thought of climbing into that bed beside him.

"I'd say you have some explaining to do, madam." His parting words echoed in her head. *Well, Mr. Ferguson, you have a bit of explaining to do yourself,* she concluded. *Such as why you didn't tell me the facts about that impossible old man.*

Next she ventured up the staircase with her candle, anticipating an unfinished loft, drafty and primitive. There were two doors, and when she opened the one on the right, her eyes widened and she

131

caught her breath with pleasure.

Here was a cozy little gabled room with a single bed covered with a warm quilt. There was a beautiful old dresser against the wall and a rocking chair beside the window. A wooden chest stood at the foot of the bed, hand-carved in a beautiful pattern of birds and flowers. It was the gnarled pipe and the tin of tobacco resting on top of the chest that told Annie this must have been the old man's room before he became ill.

She looked around again, more carefully this time. In a corner was a box of wood-carving tools and several small blocks of wood, one of them half carved into the rough shape of a bird. She remembered the twisted claw that was his hand, and she felt a stab of compassion for the wild old man trapped in the bedroom downstairs.

She peeked behind the other door before she went down.

It was an unfinished attic, and the candle sent eerie flickers of light over a cradle, a high chair, a box spilling over with toys—sad reminders that a baby had lived in this house not long ago.

Annie loved babies. Her throat grew tight and she quickly shut the door and hurried downstairs.

In front of the heater, she helped Bets take off her clothing. Her sister was exhausted and sick. Annie sponged her down quickly from a basin, rubbing her dry with a clean hessian towel she found in the drawer of the washstand. From their trunk, she took a thick flannel nightdress and fresh underdrawers and bundled her sister into them. She urged Bets up the stairs and then tucked her into bed in the cozy little room, pressing a kiss on her sister's flushed cheek. Bets sighed and was asleep in seconds.

Downstairs, Annie realized that at some point the floor banging had stopped. She tiptoed to the old man's door and peeked in. He was snoring heavily, cane propped beside the bed, damp quilt thrown on the floor. She drew the covers up over him, blew out the lamp, and brought the damp quilt to dry by the heater.

The farmhouse was silent except for the crackling of the flames in the two stoves and the occasional gust of wind outside.

More than anything, Annie wanted a wash, and she'd better hurry, before *he* got back.

She stripped off every scrap of her soiled clothing and lathered a cloth from the bar of yellow soap. Luxuriously, beginning with her face and working downward, she methodically washed and rinsed every inch of herself, glorying in the wonderful sensation of being clean again.

Her bone-thin body ached as if every muscle had been strained to the breaking point, and she longed to be able to lie down somewhere and sleep as Bets was doing, but she didn't dare give in to the bone-crushing weariness. She couldn't even put on a nightdress. She opened her trunk and found a clean dress, underwear, and stockings, and put them on.

She intended to stay alert, because when Noah Ferguson returned, he wasn't going to get the best of her.

She glanced at the room where the old man slept, and shuddered.

Maybe she'd been less than honest in her letters, but it seemed that Noah Ferguson wasn't far behind her when it came to leaving out important details.

Annie's mouth tilted in a rueful grin.

Maybe after all was said and done, the pair of them were made for each other after all.

Chapter Three

The wind had quieted, but it was black-dark and icy cold by the time Noah again drove into his farmyard late that evening.

He was in a foul mood. Gladys Hopkins, kind as she was, talked far too much. All the way to the Hopkins homestead, she'd blathered on and on, all of it about his new wife.

"That red hair of hers is a caution, don't you think, Noah? And she looks mighty frail, poor soul. Makes a body wonder if folks in the city get enough to eat, don't it?"

Noah made an indeterminate noise in his throat and clicked his tongue, flicking the reins so the team would go faster.

Unfortunately, Gladys went right on talking.

"But those eyes, my stars, Noah, I never in all my born days saw eyes that shade of green before. Must be what the books call emerald, wouldn't you say? And big like saucers—they seem to swallow her

134

whole face, don't they? Long eyelashes too. Awful pale complexion, though. Needs some good old farm grub to fatten her up some. Now how old did you say she was, again?"

Fortunately, he hadn't said, and he didn't now. "Old enough to wed," he growled. *Old enough to deceive an honest man.*

Gladys wasn't in the least put out. "Her sister's a quiet little thing, ain't she? Not a single word out of her. Looks to be about the same age as my Rose. Rosie's gonna be over the moon when she hears there's a girl her age over at your place. She'll pester me to death wantin' to visit. Now, Noah, my experience with girls that age is they never stop talking. Just you wait till she gets over her fit of shyness— won't be a quiet moment. I think you did good, the two of them will be a big help with Zachary, that's certain." She paused for a moment, then added in a different tone, "Your poor old dad ain't doin' too good, is he? You sure had your share of trouble, Noah, first Molly and the boy, and now Zachary."

Damnation. With all the goings on, Noah hadn't given a single thought to the inevitable meeting between the two females and his father. He felt a twinge of apprehension and a renewed surge of guilt. He ought to at least have warned Annie.

"How was he today, Gladys?" Noah fervently hoped that Zachary was having one of his rare quiet periods, but Gladys's response settled that idea.

"Contrary. Threw a cup at me, he did," she said with a sigh. "And he banged that infernal cane on the floor most of the day. It beats all how a kind, sweet gentleman like your father was could turn so willful now he's sick," she commented with a shake of her head.

"Mind you, I recollect Harold's aunt, sweetest old thing—"

Noah was relieved beyond measure when at last Gladys was safely inside her own house and he was free to ride home in silence. Trouble was, some of what she'd prattled on about seemed stuck in his head.

Annie did have amazing green eyes, he conceded. And some secret part of him was immensely relieved that she wasn't grossly fat—he preferred a slender woman. He wondered what all that wild, curling hair would be like, loose down her back.

The need for a woman in his bed had been growing more urgent as time blurred the pain of Molly's death. Part of him had been anticipating the bodily pleasure of having a woman beneath him again.

But this woman—well, it wasn't at all certain she'd be staying, he reminded himself. God only knew what the real facts were about her, and until he knew for certain, he'd not be beguiled by the demands of a healthy body.

A horrible thought struck him. Maybe she'd lied about working in the mill. Maybe she'd been a strumpet, a woman of easy virtue.

But reason asserted itself. Surely there was something about her, a kind of innocence, that would be impossible to pretend?

But what was the truth? He was convinced that hardly one single thing she'd said about herself in those damnable letters was the least bit honest. At the thought of her duplicity, he grew angry all over again, and he held firmly to his righteous outrage the rest of the drive home.

Once there, he tended to the horses in the barn, threw hay down for the livestock and, finally, headed for the house. For the first time, he didn't feel his usual pleasure and anticipation about coming home. He was troubled more than he cared to admit about the forthcoming scene with the woman inside.

As he climbed the porch steps and opened the door, he remembered something a friend had said about a neighbor's marital trouble: "Marry in haste, repent at leisure."

Noah's mouth twisted in a bitter smile as he opened the door. It seemed there was a lot of truth to the old saw after all.

He wasn't sure exactly what he expected, but to his immense relief, all was quiet, peaceful, and blessedly warm inside. The room was tidy, and the table was set for his meal.

There was silence from his father's room and no sign of the younger girl. Annie was curled in a ball on the sofa, sound asleep.

The door banged when he closed it. She let out a small cry of alarm and sat bolt upright, sleepy green eyes wide and startled.

She was wearing a clean but rumpled blue checked dress, and her hair was even wilder than before, curling in fiery disarray around her face and neck. She reached up to tidy it, and he couldn't help but notice the slight, delicate curves of her body.

She wasn't wearing shoes or slippers; all she had on her narrow, long feet were white cotton stockings that seemed more mends than fabric. There was a fragility about her that threatened to soften the hardness in his heart if he weren't careful.

"Hello." He bent to remove his boots. He hung his coat and hat up and made his way to the washstand, rolling up shirt and underwear sleeves and lathering his face, neck, and arms thoroughly. He tugged a comb through his thick, tangled hair without so much as a glance in the wavy mirror on the wall above the basin.

He didn't give a damn what she thought about the way he looked, he told himself sternly.

"I put Bets to bed in the room at the top of the

stairs. I hope that's all right," she said.

He nodded. "It was my father's room. I had to move him down when the first housekeeper came. Her legs were bad and she couldn't climb up and down the steps." He didn't add that the little room his father now occupied had once belonged to his baby son. He'd packed the cradle and the tiny clothing, along with Molly's things, up to the attic and never set foot there again.

"You have a lovely house," she said shyly, and added, "Your dinner's waiting."

She'd set a place for him at the table, and now she filled a bowl with hot soup and put sliced bread in front of him. "You want coffee?"

"Yes, please." He'd grown accustomed to serving himself. It was pleasant to have her see to his needs.

She filled a cup from the enamel pot on the back of the stove and set it before him along with a pitcher of milk. When his needs were tended to, she poured herself coffee as well and took the chair opposite him at the table.

"The storm's stopped," she said in a conversational tone.

"Yes, it's died down. Temperature's dropping, though. It'll be a cold night."

Obviously, she'd decided to postpone serious discussion until after he'd eaten, and he was grateful. He was as hungry as a wolf. He spooned in the delicious soup, sopping up the juice with thick slabs of bread. She sipped her coffee and refilled his soup bowl before he could ask, and once she got up and restocked the heater. In spite of himself, he noticed how quick she was, lithe and light on her feet.

When at last he was comfortably full, he sat back with a second mug of coffee, wondering just where to begin, and while he pondered, she bested him.

"I made your father's acquaintance," she said in a

quiet tone. "He wanted water, and when I brought it, he spilled it and threw the glass at me. I didn't clean up the splinters. I was afraid he might take it in his head to hit me with that cane if I ventured back in there. He's not very easy to get on with."

So instead of accusing her the way he'd planned, Noah somehow found himself on the defensive. "My father had a stroke just before Christmas. Before that, he was a strong and independent man."

He'd also been Noah's best friend. "He finds it hard to be bedridden and helpless."

She gave him a level look. "I can understand that. It's a terrible thing to depend on other people for everything. But you didn't tell me how sick he really was, in your letters. You said he was in ill health, but I took that to mean he'd get better. Is he going to?"

He blew out his breath and shook his head, holding her gaze. It was hard to put into words, hard to believe even after all these months, that his father had become the pitiful, angry man in the bed in the other room. The agony in Noah's heart made it hard to speak. "No. This is pretty much how it's going to be, according to Doc Witherspoon."

She nodded slowly, a frown creasing her brow. "And he needs a whole lot of caring for." It wasn't a question.

A muscle in Noah's jaw twitched as he saw the direction this was taking. "Yes, he does." His voice was dangerously quiet. She wasn't about to have this her own way. He took control again, his voice harsh. "And I don't suppose you know any more about taking care of sick folks than you do about farming," he said.

"Matter of fact, I do." She lifted her chin and looked him square in the eye. "My mama was sick for two years before she died, and between us Bets and I cared for her as well as we knew. The last few months, she couldn't get out of bed either."

"And where was your father?" He watched her closely, wondering how he'd even know if she was lying again.

She met his eyes, honest and forthright, and her full lips tightened. Her expression made her look much older suddenly. "He was drunk, mostly. He wasn't mean, like some who drink, just sad and useless. He never could keep a job very long."

Noah knew of men who drank. He enjoyed a whisky now and then, but along with all the other things Zach had taught him was a respect for spirits and what they could do to a man. "How did you live?"

"My mama was a seamstress, a good one. She managed to feed us and pay the rent until she got sick," Annie said. "Then I got the job in the factory, and that helped. But after Mama died, I couldn't manage any more to feed us and pay the rent, so Bets had to start working too." A haunted look came and went on her face. "Bets isn't as strong as me. The air's bad in a factory, and she coughed a lot."

She interpreted the look on his face and added defensively, "She isn't an invalid, honest. All she needs is some fresh air and good food, and she'll be fine again. She hasn't got consumption, or anything bad like that."

He didn't comment, because he had his doubts. Instead, he went doggedly on. "You said in one letter that your father was dead. Is that true?" What if her sop of a n'er-do-well father turned up, looking to Noah to support him? He shuddered. There were aspects to this proxy marriage that Noah had never thought about till now.

But she answered promptly, and unless she was an accomplished actress, Noah was convinced she was being honest.

"Papa's been dead four years now. He fell and hit

his head one night coming from the tavern, and he died the next day."

It was relief to hear it, although naturally Noah didn't say so.

"Who taught you to read and write?" He'd been impressed by her letter-writing ability, and he found himself liking the proper way she talked. She sounded educated, a rare thing in a woman of her background.

"My mama taught both my sister and me," she said proudly. "Her father was a schoolteacher. He taught her. We had books."

"Reading's fine, but do you know how to cook?" He was plain fed up with the meals he was forced to throw together. They'd given him a new respect for good food.

She hesitated. "Some. A little. Plain food, mostly— we never had money for anything fancy. Bets is real good at making soup."

"You said you grew up on a farm," he went on relentlessly. "You talked of making butter, of milking cows, of growing a garden." More lies, he reminded himself again. "How'd you know what to say about those things?"

She looked down at the table, her finger circling a mark on the cloth. "I have a good friend, our landlady, Elinora Potts. Elinora grew up on a farm. She helped me." She raised her eyes and met his accusing gaze with rebellious courage. "See, I'd answered three other advertisements before yours, and I was truthful in them, and not one man wrote back to me."

So he'd been the bottom of the barrel. It wasn't exactly flattering, but somehow it amused him.

"Don't you see, Mr. Ferguson, I just had to get Bets out of there?" she went on, her voice trembling. "She'd have *died*." She leaned her arms on the table and bent towards him, intent on making him understand. "Have you ever been inside a cotton factory, Mr. Ferguson?"

He shook his head no. He was intrigued by the fierce passion in her voice, the fire smoldering in her green eyes. Against his will, he was drawn to her. Whatever else she was, she was wholly alive and very female, this Annie.

She didn't seem to notice that he shifted uncomfortably in his chair.

"Cotton factories aren't healthy. The air's full of lint, it's hot all the time; a shift's twelve hours with only a few minutes for lunch, and you've got to pay close attention every second. Many girls are injured or killed at the machines. Wintertime, you never see daylight at all." She tapped a forefinger against her chest. "Me, I'm tough."

The assertion made Noah want to smile. She sat there, in her washed-out blue dress, her body so thin, it seemed a good wind would blow her away.

"I got used to it. But Bets—" her eyes welled with sudden tears and she brushed them away with her palm. "She's my baby sister, Mr. Ferguson. I promised Mama I'd take care of her." There was a desperate plea in her voice, and Noah couldn't help the flood of sympathy her words aroused.

"When I saw your advertisement, it felt like a last chance to save her. I—I was scared. She was coughing all the time. She's all I have for family. So I"— the rest of the sentence burst out in a flurry of words—"well, that's why I wasn't honest in most of what I told you."

In spite of himself, her story touched him, but he didn't let any of what he felt show on his face. A great deal depended on the next few moments, and he didn't want to make a mistake that would be hard to rectify.

He narrowed his eyes at her, and his voice was deliberately harsh. "The last thing I need is another invalid in this house. Life out here in the West is tough. It takes able-bodied people all their time just to survive. Far as I can see, you didn't give much thought to that when you brought your sister here. There's drought and frost and pestilence, hail storms that can level a man's crops. There's wild animals and Indians that can kill him and his family. There's no one to call on for help. It's a half-day's drive into town and an hour and a half just to get to the Hopkins place. Ranching is backbreaking hard work for everybody. Come spring, I'll be in the fields from sunup to sundown."

"I told you I was a good worker," she pleaded. "I'll prove it if you give me a chance. Just tell me what you need done, and I'll do my best."

"I don't want any misunderstandings about how hard it will be." Noah drew in a breath and let it out again. "You've seen how my father is," he said deliberately. "I'd expect you to take good care of him in spite of his temper. You'd have to tend to all the household chores, the chickens, the garden, the pigs. If I can't get a hired hand, I'll need you to help with haying in the fall. My advice would be to take your sister and hightail it back to the city."

She stared at him, waiting for him to go on. When he didn't she said in a hesitant tone, "You're trying to scare me off, aren't you? You're leaving it for me to decide whether we should stay or go."

Noah nodded. "I am. And now that you know exactly how it would be, seems to me you should give some serious thought to leaving."

She eyed him warily, as if there were a trap here somewhere. "But you're not sending us back?"

He shook his head. "I can't say I'm entirely happy with the way things turned out, but the simple fact is, I need help. I need a wife." It was the raw, honest truth.

She looked into his face, her wide-spaced eyes somber. After a moment she lifted her chin and said firmly, "Then we're staying. I'm used to hard work, like I said. Besides," she added as her eyes dropped to the oilcloth and her voice became suddenly less certain than before, "we—we're married, you and I, before God."

He nodded. "We are that." Something inside him eased, relieved at her words.

"There's one more thing, though." She was agitated, twisting a bit of her skirt between her fingers, unable to look at him now. "There's another thing I didn't tell you that probably will make you—make you change your mind after all. I—I was wrong, not telling you before," she added, and for the first time, there was outright panic in her voice. "You have to know, you'll find out anyway soon enough," she added miserably.

Her expression, the quaver in her voice, told him that this was far more significant than anything else she'd lied about. Noah felt his stomach clench. What terrible thing was she about to reveal?

"It's—it's—ummm, it's my sister, Bets." Now her words tumbled out, one on top of the other. "She's— she's the sweetest girl, and smart as a whip, but— well, she got a fever when she was a baby, not even two years old." She still wasn't meeting his eyes, and he frowned, confused.

He'd expected some damning, shoddy confession about herself, and instead Annie was talking about her sister? Puzzlement furrowed his brow.

"After it left her—the fever, I mean—well, she— she couldn't—she didn't—she was—" her eyes were enormous as they met to his. "Bets didn't hear us anymore." Her breath came out in a quavering sigh. "It affected her ears. What I didn't tell you was that my sister is stone deaf, Mr. Ferguson."

144

Chapter Four

A log fell in the stove, and from the bedroom came the muffled sound of Zachary snoring.

Noah stared across the table at this woman he'd married, feeling the strangest mixture of compassion, impatience, desire—and outrage.

What miserable kind of man did she take him for, to think that her sister's affliction was something he couldn't accept? The other things she'd lied about—her knowledge of farming life, for instance—those things were serious, they would mean he'd have to take precious time to teach her all the things he'd thought she already knew. But deafness . . .

"Having a deaf sister seems to me to be a fact of life and nothing to feel shame over," he said, and his reward was the astonished relief that slowly mirrored itself on her mobile features.

"There are practical matters to consider, of course," he added. "Does she talk?"

Annie shook her head. "She makes sounds, but

they're hard to understand. She lip-reads well, and we have hand signals that mean different things. They're not hard to learn," she assured him eagerly. "I can easily teach you, if you want to learn."

He nodded. "I do. I want there to be good understanding between me and the girl."

Annie suddenly seemed to droop, like a candle burning down. Her shoulders, held high and tense, relaxed now, and her hands fell to her lap. Her full lips parted, and the small, worried crease between her delicate brows smoothed away.

"I do thank you, Mr. Ferguson," she breathed, her voice husky and low. "I truly think you are a kind, good man."

Noah's face reddened at her compliment, and he cleared his throat, embarrassed. "Enough of this calling me Mr. Ferguson," he said gruffly. "It makes me feel old and downright doddery. Call me Noah."

"All right, Noah," she said with a quick, almost mischievous grin.

"Annie," he responded formally, trying the feel of it on his tongue and lips.

Annie, his wedded wife.

They sat in silence for several long, charged minutes, each realizing that what had passed between them just now was a commitment, a true beginning to their life together.

Whatever the future held, they would face it united.

Not with bonds of love, Noah assured himself—never that, never again—but instead, those of responsibility, of mutual commitment to the common purpose of making a decent life for themselves in a difficult land.

The clock chimed eleven and Noah stood up, uncomfortably aware that although they'd crossed one dangerous abyss, another yawned right in front of them.

"Time for bed." He did his best to make it casual, but there was a tension in his tone he couldn't seem to hide. There was also tension in his body, anticipating the act he'd missed so sorely for so long.

She nodded and rose, and he could see the flush that crept from the demure neck of her gown all the way to her hairline. Her eyes slid toward the door of his bedroom and away.

New questions sprang into his mind, questions he couldn't ask. Earlier, he'd suspected her of being a whore. Now it crossed his mind that perhaps she was a virgin.

"You go in." He handed her a candle and motioned to the door of his bedroom. "I'll douse the lamps and stoke the heater," he said.

He waited until the door closed behind her, then turned the wick down on the lamp and filled the wash basin with warm water from the kettle. In the dim glow, he shucked off his shirt, pants, woolen socks, and long underwear and swiftly, thoroughly, washed himself from top to toe. He'd shaved that morning, but now he drew the straight razor over his jaw and neck again.

It was a habit he'd grown away from since Molly's death, this ritual grooming every night before he went to bed. It was a legacy from his father.

Before his wedding to Molly, Zachary had talked with Noah about women and their ways, and part of his practical advice had been always to go to the marriage bed washed clean of sweat and clean shaven.

Unbidden came the image of Molly, wrapped in his arms, her nose buried in his neck, her shy whisper tickling his ear.

Dearest Noah, you always smell so good—

He thrust the memory away as he toweled himself dry, dumped the basin in the slop bucket, and after a moment's indecision, tugged his pants on again. He took a deep breath, willing his thoughts away from the quicksand of remembrance as he opened the bedroom door.

She was already in bed. Only the high, ruffled neckline of her white flannel gown showed above the patchwork comforter. She tried for a smile when he came into the room but didn't quite succeed. After a single, startled glance at his uncovered chest with its mat of dark hair, she looked away.

He took the candle from the dresser and carried it to the small bench beside the bed. He blew it out, removed his pants, and climbed in naked under the covers. His weight made the mattress sag, bringing her closer toward him.

For long moments, he lay perfectly still, aware of her light breathing, the smell of the soap they'd both used, wondering if she could hear the way his heart was hammering against the wall of his chest. At last, he propped himself on an elbow and reached out and gently drew her closer, one hand on her shoulder, the other on a narrow flannel-covered hip.

She was trembling, and he was conscious of how delicate she was, how big he must seem to her. "Are you afraid of me, Annie?" he whispered. "I won't hurt you, I promise."

"I—I've never done this before." Her choked whisper was so soft, he had to lean close to hear it.

"I'll try to make it as easy as I can for you." She didn't answer, and for long moments he stroked her shoulder and arm with his fingertips, and when she began to relax, he unfastened only the top buttons of her gown so he could slip his fingers in and touch the velvety skin of her neck.

Soft. She was so soft—he'd forgotten the delightful

softness of a woman's body—Molly's body—

Ruthlessly, he slammed the top on the treacherous box of memory and nailed it tightly shut, forcing himself to think only of here and now.

This wasn't love, he reminded himself ruthlessly. This was seduction, but it wasn't love. As long as he kept them separate—

He bent down and put his mouth over hers in a light, feathery kiss. He took his time, savoring the sweet taste of her skin, the warmth and softness of her neck. Her lips were soft and full, closed until his tongue teased them open. Her breath, the taste of her mouth, was pleasing. He felt her catch her breath as the kiss deepened.

"You taste good," he murmured to her.

Tentatively, her chapped hand came up and lightly rested on his bare arm, and he could feel the tips of her small breasts against his chest, the supple and surprising strength of her long, narrow frame teasing him through the maddening fabric of her gown.

His starved body reacted with violence to her nearness. He drew back for a moment, regaining a shaky control.

"Can—can we take this off?" His voice was rough with passion. Before she could answer, he found the hem of the garment and pulled it up and over her head. She didn't resist.

He wished he'd left the candle lit so he could see her. Her skin was satin smooth. He groaned with impatience as his trembling hands learned the shape of her, the gentle curve of hip, the hollow of concave stomach, the slight swell of breasts. He took a tender nipple in his mouth and suckled it, and she gasped.

Pleasure knotted inside of him, a sweet delight.

"I'm not hurting you, am I, Annie?" His voice sounded strangled, and his breath was coming in short bursts, as if he'd been running.

Bobby Hutchinson

"No. It doesn't hurt, it's—it's, ummmm, peculiar." It was little more than a breath of sound against his cheek.

Peculiar? He grinned and slid a hand down over her velvety stomach, his fingers discovering her silky mound. Soon she was hot, damp. With the last remnants of his control disappearing, he deftly positioned her beneath him, insinuating himself between her legs, trying not to hurry.

Her arms came around him, and her lips met his in shy, eager acceptance. She moved, clumsily, against him, and he gritted his teeth against the exquisite, driving urge to plunge into her.

He tried to make his entry smooth and slow, but the unbelievably hot, wet tightness of her passage combined with his own long abstinence undid him. At the last moment, when he knew without doubt that she was a virgin, he fought for control, but it was too late. With a strangled cry and an inner sense of despair at his impatience, he lunged, once, again, and at the final instant—

There must not be a child—there must never be a child of his again.

With superhuman effort, he pulled out of her, groaning as his seed spilled on her belly and legs and on the sheet beneath them.

He collapsed beside her, the swirling delight of release making his body seem boneless and light. In the aftermath of passion, he was ashamed of his haste.

"I'm sorry, Annie," he murmured. "Next time, it will be better for you, I promise." He gently disentangled their bodies and moved a careful distance away, so that no part of him touched her. Within moments, he slept.

Annie felt somehow bereft. She heard his breathing change, becoming deep and even. She

150

waited until the pattern was well established before groping for her nightdress and struggling into it, careful to keep her movements from waking him, conscious of his warm, wet stickiness on her belly and legs.

She lay on her back, scrupulously keeping the distance he'd drawn between them. She'd always slept with her sister, and having this man beside her was going to take getting used to.

Her private parts throbbed with the strangest mixture of pain and thwarted pleasure. She stared wide-eyed into the darkness, confused and a little frightened by this act that had changed her from spinster to married woman.

Elinora had done her best to explain it. "It's either heaven or hell, dearie, depending on the man," her landlady had said, but this hadn't been either one. There must be something between the two extremes that Elinora hadn't told her, Annie deduced.

Would it be possible to ask in a letter? Elinora had told her to write about anything at all and promised to do her best to answer honestly.

Dear, forthright Elinora. Tears filled Annie's eyes as she thought of the countless miles that now separated her from her best and only friend. The night before her proxy wedding, Annie's rotund little landlady had brewed a pot of ginger tea and spoken candidly to her about this entire aspect of marriage. "Some men are thoughtful, see. They try to pleasure their women. But there are others unskilled at such things, unaware, or just uncaring that women can enjoy the act as much as men. I was lucky in marrying Mr. Potts; he was one of the giving sort. I pray your Noah Ferguson is like him, pet."

Was he, Annie wondered? So far, Noah was a puzzle. One minute he was friendly, and the next there was this vast distance.

151

He'd been gentle at first, but then a madness she didn't wholly understand had taken him over. And just when the first, fierce pain inside her dwindled and another sensation began, he'd made that strangled sound and torn himself away and it was over.

At least she knew why he'd pulled back like that. Again, Elinora had explained. "You know about babies, pet, and how they're made. A clever girl like you doesn't work with a hundred others and not come by that information," she'd begun, going on to explain to an astonished Annie how men and women prevented them.

She'd described the technique Noah had just used, but she'd advised Annie not to rely on her husband in this matter.

"Out in that wilderness, he's likely to want a passel of young 'uns, so don't count on him being any help," she'd warned Annie. "Farmers need a big family to help with the work. But a woman don't last long when she carries a baby every year. You have to take care of yourself in such things, my girl. There are female preventatives you can use to make sure one child's well grown before another's planted, and if you're clever, he don't ever need to know."

Annie had cringed at the thought of still another deception. She'd already told so many lies that she could hardly remember all of them, and preventing babies seemed so unnecessary.

"I *want* babies, Elinora," she'd protested. "I want lots of babies."

"More fool you," Elinora had snorted. "Wait until you know for certain what sort of man he really is." And so, in Annie's trunk, hidden among her petticoats, was the device Elinora had given her, a sponge with a string attached, and directions for a vinegar solution.

It didn't look as if she'd need to make use of it,

however. If tonight was any indication, it seemed that Noah and Elinora were of one mind, whether they realized it or not. He wasn't taking any chance that she'd get with child, and it made her feel empty, diminished in some unexplainable fashion.

Gradually, Annie's weary body began to relax in the strange bed, beside the man who was now her husband in more than name.

Careful not to disturb him, she turned on her side and curled into a ball, sorely missing Bets's warm body close against her back.

A log fell in the heater, and outside the dog barked in response to a far-off, unearthly howling. Annie shivered, thinking of the miles of wilderness that surrounded this place, and how totally dependent she and Bets were on the strong man sleeping beside her.

She hated being dependent on anyone. She'd never felt as lonely in her entire life as she did at this moment, not even when her mother had died.

But she would get used to it, Annie told herself fiercely, trying to ignore the tears that trickled down her face and soaked the pillow. It was a chance for a different sort of life, the only chance she and her sister might ever have.

She'd gotten used to the factory, and she'd been only a little girl when she started there. She'd gotten used to taking care of her sick mother, to being solely responsible for Bets. She fished for her handkerchief, tucked under the pillow, and softly blew her nose.

She'd get used to this man. She'd get used to being his second wife, chosen not by love, but by necessity.

All she needed was time.

Chapter Five

March 26, 1886
Medicine Hat, Northwest Territories

Dear, dear Elinora,

Your first letter just reached me, and I'm so glad to have it, and am answering forthwith because I have many things to tell you and twice as many other troublesome matters for which I long for your assistance.

First, I shall try to answer your questions.

Yes, Bets is over the grippe, and although she still coughs a lot, she is much improved. As to the weather, there is still a great deal of snow on the ground, but some days are quite tolerable—one can now visit the outhouse without frostbite!

Lantern In The Window

You ask about the view, and I have to smile. There's a great deal of nothing at all, empty, rolling plains and vast sky and precious few trees. As I'm sure I mentioned in my first letter, the ranch is situated only a short distance from the South Saskatchewan River, and Noah says there are willows along it which turn quite green in summer, but for now, everything is white, although sunrise and sunset are quite wonderful on days when the sky is clear.

As for me, my health is good, as always, but oh, my dear Elinora, sometimes (at least a dozen times each day) I fear I'm not suited to this ranching life at all.

My first week here, Noah took me outside to show me what "chores" would be mine, and for the first time in my entire life, I encountered cows and chickens and pigs and horses. I was, and am still, utterly terrified of all of them, although I do my best not to appear so to Noah. He seems to find my ignorance amusing, at least outdoors, and the surprising thing is that Bets doesn't share any of my concerns. She is quite at home around the animals in the barnyard—Noah has even promised to teach her to ride a horse when spring comes, and he's given her a kitten whom she's named Tar.

With me, it's quite a different story. He's trying to teach me to milk, but the cow hates me and either slaps me across the face with her tail or deliberately puts her filthy foot in the pail.

One rooster with a terrible disposition lies in wait to chase me, jumping on my back and pecking every time I step out the door, and I now carry an empty pail so that I can drop it over him, putting a heavy stone on top, thereby trapping him until Noah comes and sets him

155

loose again. If only I had the stomach for it, I'd serve the beast up as Sunday dinner! (The rooster, not Noah.)

As for horses, I had no idea how large they are up close. And pigs—dear Elinora, is it true they have a tendency to eat their young, or is Noah having a joke at my expense? Jake, the old dog, is the only animal with whom I feel a true kinship.

Inside the house, things are not a whole lot better. Because you took such fine care of us and I worked so many years in the factory, there's a great deal I don't know about housewifery. I feel the ghost of Noah's first wife watching me with disapproval as I dust her house and scrub her floors and try to cook on her stove. (That reminds me, do you have a reliable recipe for making bread? I've tried, but the results of my efforts are not edible, to say the least. Even the chickens refused the last attempt, and as you probably know, chickens eat anything at all.)

I know all too well that Noah compares me to that other wife and finds me wanting. Last week, I rearranged some small items on the sideboard, and although he didn't say anything, he soon put them all back just the way she must have had them.

Enough of this whining. There is also good news. Elinora, I can hardly believe it myself. You remember my last letter was filled with the difficulties of caring for Noah's father? Well, a near miracle has occurred, and it's thanks to Bets. She's befriended the old man and is teaching him her sign language, and his disposition is improved beyond belief now that he can communicate. The two of them have endless games of checkers, and Bets is always able to understand what he needs and wants.

Taken altogether, my dear friend, I have been more than fortunate with this "adventure," as you label it. Noah is the most generous of husbands. He took me to town last week and insisted I buy warmer clothing for Bets and for myself, and he eats whatever I prepare without complaint and thanks me politely for my attentions to his father. If at times lonely tears drip into the dishwater and I long for the kind of romance I used to moon over in my beloved dime novels, I remind myself that Noah could have been fat and ugly, with warts on his chin, a bulbous nose, and a mean nature.

Instead, as I told you, he actually resembles those mythical old-fashioned heroes, tall and strong and handsome. And, unfortunately, silent most of the time. He's not a talker, and I needn't remind you, Elinora, that I am. He's kind, he's unfailingly polite, and he's unnaturally quiet. At times I even wish he'd lose his temper and rage at me, but he's far too controlled for such excess of emotion.

I can hear you telling me to count my blessings, and you're right, of course.

And now, enough of me. Are you well? Are the new girls behaving themselves? Is Fanny still with you? I know she doesn't read, or I would write to her. Give her my regards, and tell her that although I don't miss the factory, I do miss her.

I miss you too, dear Elinora, more than I can ever say. I feel so far away from you—I wonder, shall we ever again share a cup of tea and a wicked gossip?

Write soon. I love you.

*Your old friend with a new name,
Annie Ferguson.*

April arrived.

The weather improved, and one windy day in mid-month, Annie awoke with laundry on her mind. Blankets, sheets, curtains, clothing; she suddenly wanted everything clean for spring.

"After breakfast I'll need your help in getting your father up, Noah," she announced as soon as she opened her eyes. "So I can change those filthy sheets on his bed. I need to do a big wash. Could you help me bring water in from the well to fill the copper washtubs and set them to heating?" Inspired, she added, "Also, Mr. Ferguson sorely needs a bath, and he could also do with a haircut and a shave."

It was the beginning of a long, hard, satisfying day.

Alone in the bedroom late that night, Annie sank deeper into the old tin tub, letting the hot, soapy water soothe the ache in her arms and shoulders and ease the tension in her back from bending over a washboard hour after hour.

Ooohhh, this was heaven.

Her hands were raw from scrubbing, and the entire house smelled of soap powder and garments fresh from the clothesline.

Weary as she was, there was an enormous sense of accomplishment in what she'd done today—for once, everything had gone perfectly.

Every sheet, every towel, every sock in the house was clean and dry and folded. Next door, Zachary Ferguson slept in a fresh and sweet-smelling bed. He was bathed, shaved, trimmed, and wearing a fresh nightshirt, and he looked a different man.

She'd said as much to Noah and gotten a quiet nod in return.

158

There was a tap at the door, and she jerked upright in the tub and then hurriedly ducked beneath the suds again as Noah came into the room, carrying a kettle. The candle on the dresser flickered as the door closed behind him, sending long shadows up the walls. He towered over her, and instinctively she folded her arms across her naked breasts. She was still shy about having him see her unclothed.

"I thought you could do with some more hot water," he said matter of factly. "Pull your feet back and I'll pour it in."

She'd never felt as exposed in her life. She could feel her whole upper body flushing as she curled her legs up and he slowly poured the steaming water into the tub.

"Thank you," she said weakly, waiting for him to go back into the other room.

But he stayed, looking down at her with such raw, kindling passion in his dark eyes that her heart began to hammer against her ribs and her breath caught in her throat. Slowly, daringly, she let her arms fall into the water, leaving her pink-tipped breasts exposed to his view.

"I thought maybe you'd let me wash your back," he said, and now there was no coolness in his voice. Indeed, its rough warmth seemed to stroke over Annie's bare skin, leaving a tingling trail of anticipation in its wake.

She gave a tremulous nod, and deliberately, never taking his eyes from her, he rolled his sleeves up past the elbow and knelt on the braided rug.

Noah lathered the cloth. He started slowly, at her neck, where tendrils of curly red hair were escaping the untidy bun on the top of her head. Her skin was gold-tinged in the candlelight, the back of her neck as fragile as a flower stalk.

Damn it all. He'd struggled with himself, trying to

resist her these past weeks. He didn't want to desire her the way he did; he didn't want the thought of her to haunt him every waking moment. She wasn't the woman he loved—but he was forced to admit she was a woman he desired, a woman who intrigued and amused him with her quick-witted remarks, her contagious giggle, her endless energy and enthusiasm.

Why couldn't she have been older, colder, fatter, less appealing—why couldn't she be more like the stolid person he'd envisioned when he wrote that confounded advertisement and mailed it to the paper?

He drew the washrag down, his eyes registering the slender curve of shoulder, waist, hip, his body reacting with fierce need, against his will, to the look and smell and feel of her.

She smelled of soap and of some other essence that was singularly her own, that he'd come to recognize— a musky, warm odor that inflamed his senses.

"Ohhh, that feels so good, Noah. Do it again, please."

He was trembling as he rinsed the cloth, soaped it again, and resumed the long, sensual stroking. This time, his hand slid around to cup her small breast, and the nipple rose hard against his palm.

He groaned and lost whatever battle he was fighting.

"Annie." The word was wrung out of him, low and tortured.

He slid his hands under her arms, and in one smooth motion lifted her dripping from the tub. She made a small, startled sound and he gave her a rueful grin.

"I do believe you're quite clean enough," he said with a catch in his voice, snatching up the towel from a nearby chair and wrapping her in it, blotting her dry, loosening it to dab gently at a shoulder, a narrow hip, a long stretch of thigh.

He scooped her up and laid her on the bed. It was cool in the room, and he covered her naked form with the quilt until his own clothes were off and he could slide under the sheets.

The first contact with her warm, damp nakedness made him shudder. He gathered her close, wrapping his arms and legs around her, drunk with the feeling of skin against skin. He took her head in his hands and held it, kissing her lips and the long line of her throat, taking first one nipple and then the next into his mouth, moving down the satiny, narrow ribcage, nipping at prominent hipbones until at last his mouth found her center.

"Noah—" There was both shock and pleasure in her protest.

When she overcame shyness and relaxed, her body began to move instinctively, in a rhythm impossible for him to mistake. The small, desperate sounds she was making were more than he could bear. He slid up and in one long, steady motion, he entered her, half mad with wanting, but mindful that he mustn't hurt her.

Long, careful moments later, she exploded beneath him in a paroxysm of delight, and he muffled her cries with his mouth, delight taking hold of him until he lost all control.

His seed spilled and spilled, and he was too far beyond thought to pull away. She fell asleep in his arms and didn't wake when he gently untangled himself and got up to blow out the candle.

When he lay down beside her again, he made certain her bare shoulders were well covered, but he moved until there was the usual distance between them so that no part of her warm body was near enough to touch him.

Bobby Hutchinson

In the darkness, she awakened from a dream, knowing that she was falling in love with Noah.

His lovemaking had changed her, and she knew that her perceptions of herself were forever altered. Her body had depths and needs she'd never suspected, and in her heart was amazement and tenderness, gratitude to the husband who'd taught her these mysterious truths about herself.

But instead of lying warm in his embrace, she was facing his back. She slid one tentative arm up and around him, snuggling close and curling herself like a spoon to fit his sleeping shape.

He wasn't asleep. His body stiffened in her embrace, and after a moment he carefully lifted her arm and moved as far away as the bed would allow.

Annie's body stiffened with hurt. She swallowed, her face and body burning with humiliation. She stared into the darkness, fighting the tears that threatened.

It hurt. It hurt more than she would have believed possible, this constant, quiet rejection of her love. It told her more plainly than any words that Noah might succumb to the desires of his body—he'd even make very certain she, too, enjoyed the marriage bed—but anything beyond that coupling was not allowed between them.

Companionship, laughter, conversation—the elements she instinctively knew constituted deep and abiding love—those were things Noah was unwilling to share with her. Those were the things he'd shared with his Molly, and he guarded them jealously.

It felt to Annie as though the ghost woman of that first marriage even shared the bed now, lying between herself and Noah.

With one silent gesture, he'd made it clear that the wall he maintained around himself and his deepest feelings was firmly in place, and that although his

162

body might succumb to Annie, his heart would belong always to Molly.

Was this, too, something that she'd get used to as time passed?

As the slow, dark minutes of that night dragged into hours, and the beginnings of a new day drew closer, she could only pray that it might be so.

Chapter Six

It snowed again the following day, and it wasn't until early May that the mud began to dry and the first faint tinge of green appeared on the prairie.

Noah had gone to mend fences right after breakfast one sunny morning, and Annie, still unable to bake a loaf of bread that resembled anything but a rock, made up her mind once and for all that they'd just have to learn to live on biscuits forevermore.

She'd just taken a batch of popovers from the oven when Jake's frantic barking announced visitors.

"Hello, neighbor." Gladys Hopkins greeted Annie with a warm handshake and a wide smile, handing her a loaf of fresh bread as high as a haystack and a jar of dark red preserves.

"Set the dough last night, baked it first thing. That's some wild strawberry jam to go with. This here's my daughter Rose. She's been just dying to meet your little sister. She's been at me every day to come over, but we had to wait for the weather. Now where is that sister of yours? Feeling better than when she first arrived, I hope?"

"Bets is very well, thanks, Gladys. Pleased to meet you, Rose." Annie smiled at the plump little girl whose golden hair hung in careful ringlets down her back.

Annie was uncomfortably aware that neither Rose nor Gladys knew as yet that her sister was deaf.

"Bets is having a game of checkers with Mr. Ferguson. I'll get her." Annie, feeling flustered and more than a little apprehensive, hurried into Zachary's bedroom and signed to her sister and the old man that they had company. Neither was particularly pleased at the news—Betsy's face became anxious at the ordeal of meeting strangers, and Zachary scowled and slumped dejectedly into the pillows at this interruption.

Bets and Zachary had become the best of companions in the past weeks. By now there was a powerful bond between the young girl whose ears didn't work and the old man who'd lost the ability to speak.

Taking Bets's hand, Annie led her out and introduced her, adding an explanation of Bets's handicap as matter-of-factly as she could.

"She's—she's deef and dumb?" Gladys's eyes seemed almost to be popping out of her head as she studied Bets. "I never had the foggiest idea she was deaf and dumb."

"Deaf," Annie corrected firmly. "But she's certainly not dumb. Bets talks, but she does it with her hands. She'll be glad to show Rose how."

Rose was half hidden behind her mother's skirts, peering out at Bets as though expecting her to suddenly foam at the mouth or grow horns.

The violent hammering of Zachary's cane on the floor made them all jump, and Annie realized how seldom he'd banged it recently.

Bets felt the vibration, picked up her skirt, and flew in to see what he wanted. Annie knew the girl was relieved to escape the scrutiny of the Hopkins women.

Gladys whispered, "Ain't you scared he'll hammer her with that thing?"

Annie laughed and shook her head. "Those two are thick as thieves," she assured Gladys. "See, Bets has taught Mr. Ferguson to sign, and it's made the world of difference to him. He can let us know what he wants now, and he's much happier. Bets is awfully fond of him. He's like a grandpa to her. Come and sit and have some coffee, won't you?"

Annie sliced Gladys's bread, envious of the yeasty loaf. She put out some of her own popovers and set the butter crock and the preserves on the table.

Rose, with a dejected expression, slumped down across the table from the women, obviously prepared to be bored to death.

"Rose, would you be kind enough to take this bread and some coffee in to Mr. Ferguson?" Annie spread jam on a thick slice and thrust the plate and cup at the girl before she could refuse. "And then ask Bets to show you her cat. There's a new litter of kittens out in the shed, too. She'll take you to see them."

"But—but how can I ask her anything if she can't—" Rose's voice trailed off at a look from her mother.

"She can read a lot of what you say on your lips," Annie reassured her gently. "Just try."

Rose reluctantly did as she was asked. In a moment, she and Bets went silently out to the shed where the kittens were, and just as Annie hoped, it wasn't long before the two girls had brought the entire litter of kittens inside and were giggling together at their antics. Bets showed Rose her sign for cats, and slowly the two began to communicate.

Gladys watched them and then turned to Annie with a shamefaced expression. "You must excuse us, dearie. We don't mean no offense. It's just we ain't never seen a deaf and—a deef young'un before," she amended hastily. "How did she come to be that way?"

Annie explained, and in the process revealed a great deal of her and Betsy's background. In turn, Gladys told of coming in a covered wagon to Canada from Minnesota with her husband, Harold, when she was pregnant with Rose. Some of the light went out of her blue eyes and tears welled up when she confided that she'd lost three babies in succession after Rose was born.

"Looks like she'll be our only one," she said with a sigh. "It's a shame. My Harold would have liked a big family." She took a sip of her coffee and lathered her own preserves on one of Annie's biscuits, lowering her voice so Rose wouldn't hear.

"Easy for men to want more, ain't it? They don't go through it all. Why, I remember Noah sayin' he wanted a dozen more babies when Jeremy was born, and the look on poor Molly's face—"

She stopped suddenly, and her already rosy face turned magenta. "Oh, my. I am sorry. Me and my big mouth." She rammed the entire biscuit in and chewed ferociously, as if to prevent any further indiscretion.

Noah wanted a dozen more babies—Annie felt as if she'd been hit in the stomach. She thought of the nights when he made love to her—nearly every night, now—and of how careful he was to pull away from her body so that there'd be no babies.

Only that once had he ever lost control . . .

To hide the pain that she knew was mirrored on her face, she got up and shoved more wood into the

167

stove and filled their cups again with fresh coffee, coming to a decision.

Better the ghost you know—

When she sat down, she leaned across and put her chapped hand on Gladys's arm. "Gladys, I need a favor. I need you to tell me about Molly, please. Noah won't so much as say her name, and I need to know what kind of woman she was." She gestured at the room. "Every single thing here is hers. It feels like I'm living with a spirit I never even met."

Gladys looked uncertain. "Oh, I don't know. You sure it won't bother you none, hearin' about Noah's first wife?"

Doing the best acting job of her life, Annie shook her head vehemently and plastered on a smile. "Of course not. How silly. What did she look like?"

Gladys looked over her shoulder as if expecting Molly to materialize. Then she leaned forward in a confiding manner, resting her elbows on the table, her voice little more than a whisper. "Well, let's see. Molly was lots shorter than you are, and she—" Gladys made a motion that indicated Molly had possessed a good-sized bosom, narrow waist, and shapely hips. "She was real womanly," Gladys said discreetly.

Annie crossed her arms over her own meager bosom. Even though every single syllable Gladys uttered was a knife in her heart, she nodded encouragement and fixed the smile on her lips.

"She had pale, smooth hair, sorta like flax, long and braided up around her head like a crown. She had these dark blue eyes, and oh, my, she was so sweet. Gentle and sort of quiet. She had a real nice way with her, did Molly. And she could turn her hand to anything. Why, her piecrust was the best I've ever eaten—"

The eulogy went on and on, and Annie died by de-

grees, her smile feeling more and more like a grimace.

"How—how did Noah meet her, Gladys?"

"Oh, they lived in the Hat, her and her papa. Molly's father was a fine man, a preacher. When his wife
died back east, he came out west here to the prairies.
Molly was just seventeen. He set up the first church
in Medicine Hat. Poor man, he died last year himself.
It was his heart, but folks believe it was losing his
daughter and grandson the way he did." She shook
her head. "It hit us all right hard when he passed
away. He was well liked by all that knew him."

Annie thought of her own drunken father and shivered.

It didn't seem fair at all. It was as if the fates were
playing a joke on her, sending her here to be Noah's
second wife.

If Annie had set her mind to imagining her own
exact opposite, she supposed that Molly would have
been that image—and guess who any man in his
right mind would choose, given a choice? she
thought bitterly.

No wonder Noah loved Molly still, with no room
left over in his heart for Annie.

Chapter Seven

By mid-June, summer had come to the prairies.

One afternoon Annie looked at Bets and saw that she was blooming like one of the wild roses she'd just picked and put in a jar on the table. The good food and clean air had done exactly what Annie had prayed they would—the cough that had plagued Bets for more than two years was gone, and her painfully thin body was showing the first timid signs of a bosom and hips.

It was a busy time on the farm. Calves were being born, Noah was finishing the last of the spring planting, the early lettuce and radishes Annie had planted in the garden at the back of the house were up, and the kitchen door stood open to catch the fragrant evening breeze.

Annie drew in deep draughts of the warm, fresh air and prayed that she wouldn't throw up again.

"What is wrong with you?" Bets's hands flew, her brow furrowed with worry over her big sister. "Every day, sick, sick, all the time. Maybe you go to see doctor, yes? I worry over you," she added plaintively, wrapping her arms around Annie. "I love you," she added, pulling away enough so Annie could see the sign.

"I love you too." Annie returned the hug, fighting against the nausea that made her stomach churn. She was in the midst of making supper, and she'd had to run to the shed twice in the past hour.

It was a time of new beginnings, and for the past week, Annie had been fairly certain she was pregnant.

It had taken her a while to figure out what was wrong with her. What had confused her was that Elinora had written that the natural order of such things was to be sick in the morning and miss her monthly.

Instead, Annie had been fine every morning and miserably sick in the afternoons. Her monthly came for a day and went away, came for another and went away, in fits and starts.

She was going to have to tell Noah. Her hands knotted into fists. How would he react when he found out?

The thought of telling him weighed heavily on her. Not that she feared his temper, although she knew he had one. She'd seen him furiously angry at times—when a renegade wolf killed one of the best milk cows, and when the Medicine Hat Times reported some new insanity the politicians had decreed law.

She'd also witnessed the gentleness in him—with a sick newborn calf, and always with her sister. From the very first, he'd made a real effort to learn Bets's sign language. And with his father, Noah was unfailingly thoughtful and kind.

Annie knew also the depths of his passion and the intensity of his loving; not once had he taken her without thought of her pleasure. Indeed, he'd taught her to want him, to need as terribly as he that physical joining.

But he'd been most deliberate about preventing babies. Without ever saying a word, he made it clear each time they loved that he absolutely didn't want a child with her.

Well, he was about to have one anyway, Annie thought rebelliously, slamming down the oven door and reaching inside, forgetting that the towel she used as a potholder was threadbare.

"Owww! Lordie, owww!" She howled with pain and dropped the pot, spilling the entire stew all over the oven door and the floor. Noah would be in for his supper in a few moments, and now the meal was ruined.

Spill the stew, ruin the bread, get herself with child; couldn't she do anything right? Annie threw herself into a chair, put her head down on her arms, and burst into a storm of tears.

Bets patted her back and then quietly cleaned up the mess, wisely letting Annie cry for a while. Then the young girl made a vinegar poultice for Annie's burned fingers, brewed a pot of tea, poured two cups, and indicated that Annie should take one to Zachary.

"You go talk with Mr. Ferguson. I will make us eggs and bacon for dinner," she promised.

"There's no bread," Annie said miserably. "Today's batch was so bad I took it out and buried it behind the barn."

"I will make biscuits," Bets assured her. "Go, go." She pointed towards Zachary's room.

Well, the biscuits her little sister made would be lighter than hers, that was certain, Annie concluded dolefully as she blew her nose and made her way in to sit beside Zachary.

Zachary looked at her and gave her his crooked smile, and Annie did her best to return it. How strange it was that the old man who'd scared her half to death at first had become someone she liked to be with. She and Bets and Zachary had spent delightful moments together in the past months.

In short spurts, using his garbled speech and a lot of sign language, he'd laboriously told the sisters tales of his early life in eastern Canada, of how after his beloved Mary died, he and Noah, a young man by that time, had emigrated to the western plains and found this place on the South Saskatchewan River, building the cabin that eventually became this house and slowly building up their herd of cattle. He told of renegade Indians and drunken white men who'd threatened the Fergusons' very existence here, and of how he and Noah together had fought them off and won.

Listening, Annie had gained a greater understanding of Noah, of his quiet strength, his courage, the steely determination that made him the man he was.

The man she'd fallen in love with, she thought despairingly as she handed Zachary his tea and lowered herself wearily into the rocking chair Bets had moved beside his bed.

Lordie, why couldn't she have settled for just *liking* the man she'd married? Why in heaven did she have to *love* him to distraction?

Annie tilted her head back and closed her eyes. There were times when she could pretend that Noah loved her back—those rare moments when he smiled at her with affection, or walked with her along the river bank in the evening when they talked together of the day's happenings. And there were the nights, especially the nights, when he made such passionate love to her—but each time, afterwards, the distancing came again, the drawing away.

A sound from Zachary made her open her eyes. He was watching her, and the part of his face not affected by the paralysis was smiling, his dark eyes, so like Noah's, gentle and questioning.

"Tired?" His hand moved in question. He gestured at the burns on her palms. "Sore?"

173

"I spilled the damn stew all over the floor and burned my hands in the bargain." She tried for a smile, but the tears welled up again and rolled down her cheeks, and despair overwhelmed her.

"Oh, Zachary," she wailed. "Why can't I do anything right?" The words tumbled out of their own accord. "The bread I make is like rock, my piecrust isn't fit to eat, I burned that confounded roast last week to a cinder and—and now—" The words welled up in her and she couldn't stop them. "Oh, Zachary, I'm—I'm going to have a—a baby, and Noah—he doesn't—doesn't want babies." Tears dripped off her chin and wet the front of her dress.

Zachary groped under his pillow and handed her the clean handkerchief that Bets put there each morning.

"You want me to talk to Noah?" he asked.

Alarmed, Annie shook her head, mopped at her eyes, and tried to stop sobbing. She blew her nose hard and gulped. "No, thank you. I—I absolutely must tell him myself."

"He's a good man," Zachary signed with a sigh. "He loved his little son with all his heart."

"I know that. And I know he loved Molly that way too, and that he still misses her, and—and Jeremy, too."

Zachary nodded, his own sorrow for his lost grandson plain on his face.

"But that's over, Zachary. They're dead and gone, and nothing can bring them back." Her voice became passionate, and all the feelings she'd stifled for so long came pouring out in a torrent of words.

"I want him to be happy about *my* baby, I want him to love *this* baby and not always just brood over what he's lost," Annie went on, her voice filled with anger, not even caring that she was almost shouting. "So what if what Gladys said was

174

right and his blessed Molly was perfect and I'm—I'm not? This baby"—her hands cupped her still-flat abdomen—"this baby deserves a father just as much as Jeremy ever did. It's not my fault that Molly and Jeremy died, this new baby shouldn't have to pay just because—"

"That's quite enough."

Annie jumped and almost fell off her chair as Noah's voice thundered from directly behind her. She whirled to face him, feeling the blood drain out of her extremities, wondering how in heaven he'd managed to come in without her hearing him.

And Lord, how long had he been listening? He was in his stockinged feet; he must have taken off his muddy boots outside, and of course she'd forgotten the kitchen door was wide open.

Speechless now, she stared at him in horror, knowing that the guilt she felt was plainly written on her face. "Noah, I didn't mean—"

"Come with me." He reached down with both hands and grasped her arms, his fingers like iron bands digging into her flesh, almost lifting her off her feet.

In a moment they were in their own bedroom, and Noah had slammed the door shut so hard that it seemed the whole house shook.

Annie's knees were trembling, along with the rest of her. She whirled to face him when he released her arm.

Her breath caught at the fury on his face. His strong features were cold and hard, his jaw clenched with rage. His narrowed eyes weren't cold, however; they were like black pools of fire. He glared at her, and she felt as if his gaze had the power to sear her. His hands were planted low on his hips, and she could see that his huge fists were clenched tight enough to turn the knuckles white.

175

Bobby Hutchinson

"Noah," she began in a shaky voice. "I'm sorry, I never meant for you to hear—"

"To hear what?" he interrupted, his voice choked with fury. "To hear how you talk when my back's turned? To find out you're having a baby"—the word came out as a sneer—"and that I'm the last to know, after you've told my father and your sister and that Elinora woman you write to—and probably Gladys Hopkins, who'll delight in informing the whole of Medicine Hat?"

"Oh, phooey, I did not tell Bets or Gladys," she denied hotly, refusing to let him see that he frightened her. She plopped down on the bed before her legs gave out. "I didn't mean to tell your father, but I burned myself and ruined dinner and somehow it just came out. I *said* I was sorry." She swallowed back the nausea that rose in her throat.

"You will *never*"—his words were measured and he spoke very low, almost in a whisper—"*never* again speak of Molly or of Jeremy. Never, do you hear? They are not your business. They have nothing whatsoever to do with you. You didn't know them, and I will not have you tarnishing their memory."

Her mouth fell open and she gaped at him. "*Me?* Tarnish the memory of your first wife and child? How can you say such a thing?" The unfairness of the accusation overwhelmed her.

"And as for the unfortunate child you carry," he went on as if she hadn't spoken, "I wish to God it were otherwise. I wish it had never happened, but the blame is mine as much as your own, and I will do my duty by him, just as I have with you."

Unfortunate child? Duty?

In an instant, all Annie's remorse turned to outrage.

"Your—your duty?" she sputtered. "You—you pompous hypocrite, you. Is *duty* what you call what

176

goes on in this bed, then?" She thumped the bed-covers with both her doubled-up fists and sprang to her feet so he couldn't look down on her. "It was more than duty that started this baby, Noah, whatever you choose to believe." She spat the words at him and met his eyes fearlessly now, her chin held high. "You cling to the past as if your dead wife and child hold all the love and happiness life will ever offer you, and I'm sorry for you, because you can't see what's right under your nose. When I lie with you, I feel much more than duty." She struggled to keep her voice from trembling and failed. "God help me, I feel love for you, Noah Ferguson."

Chapter Eight

Annie could see some of Noah's righteous anger giving way to shocked disbelief.

"And as for the child," she went on, "the only thing unfortunate about our baby is that his father doesn't want him. Well, I'll make up for that, never fear, because already I love him with my whole heart and soul." She'd made it through without crying, and she was proud of that. But the turmoil in her stomach made the victory short-lived. She gagged suddenly, pressed a hand over her mouth, and ran as fast as she could for the outhouse.

Noah didn't move. Annie's words were like blows from a heavy fist that stunned him and held him immobile.

She'd said that she loved him.

Pain wrenched at his gut. He didn't want her love, he told himself savagely. He didn't want to love her

178

back, or care for the child he'd carelessly allowed to begin. He *couldn't* give that kind of love again, didn't she see that?

Sweat broke out on his forehead, and he shut his eyes tight, willing himself to remember.

For weeks now, he'd struggled to recall the exact shape of Molly's face, the precise sound of his son's baby voice calling him daddy. They were recollections Noah had believed to be engraved on his very soul, impossible ever to erase.

But fight it as he would, Noah's memories of them were fading. Now, in his dreams, it was more often than not Annie's husky voice he heard instead of Molly's softer, sweeter tones, and God knew that when he held Annie in his arms, in this room, in this bed, the sweet passion he'd awakened in her and the mad, bottomless hunger she stirred in him left no room for memories or thoughts of another.

Because, some traitorous part of him whispered, with Molly there had never been the sexual intensity he experienced with Annie. And he felt the foulest sort of traitor to acknowledge that there were days—even weeks—now, when he didn't think of his first wife at all.

The rest of June passed with excessive politeness and long silences between them.

July brought blistering heat and long hours of backbreaking work for Noah, and for Annie as well. Days started at four and ended only at full dark.

The words they'd hurled at each other remained between them.

In bed, they lay rigidly back to back, each achingly aware of the other's body, each longing for the lovemaking that had been their only meeting place. Feeling wretched, neither reached out for the other.

Annie, wounded by his rejection, couldn't, and Noah, wanting her more with every sultry, wasted night, wouldn't.

"Bets, I'll take the lunch out to Noah today." It was nearing the end of August, and he was clearing land that bordered the river, about a mile away from the house.

Annie usually sent Bets out with Noah's lunch every afternoon, but today she'd been busy making rhubarb jam all morning, and she was hot and thoroughly sick of being indoors.

The jam had turned out, though. She could hardly believe how impressive the row of jars with their pink contents looked lined up on the table. Even more amazing, she'd made good bread four times now—tall, golden loaves, crusty and delicious.

It was the most peculiar thing. She'd waited until Noah was out one day and then, feeling both guilty and defiant, she had ventured up to the attic to look at the beautifully carved cradle, setting it to rocking and wondering if the child she carried would ever sleep in it.

There, in a box behind the cradle, she'd found recipes that Molly must have written. Feeling like a thief in her own home, Annie brought them down and began trying them.

Unlike the ones Elinora had sent, these were easy to follow, and one after the other, she turned out perfect bread, piecrust, puddings, even a sponge cake.

And for the first time, Annie found herself whispering fervent thank-yous to the ghost who shared her house.

Exuberant with the success of the jam, she relished the long walk along the riverbank and through the fields to where Noah was working.

She saw him from a distance, using the team of heavy workhorses, Buck and Bright, to pull stumps.

His snug-fitting pants were tucked into high leather boots, and he'd taken his blue shirt off and hung it on a nearby bush. Brown suspenders rested on equally brown-bare skin, and he had a wide-brimmed straw hat on his head. The muscles in his arms and back bulged as he added his considerable strength to the efforts of the animals.

He didn't see her at first, and Annie's eyes traveled over his long, broad-shouldered body, sweat-sheened and powerful.

He was a beautiful-looking man. He was a man any woman would be proud to claim as her husband.

Slowly, torturously, the gigantic stump parted from the earth, and Noah threw his fists to the sky and hollered in triumph, unaware that she was watching.

It was a revelation to see him this way, exhilarated and noisy. "Hello, Noah. I brought you fresh water and some sandwiches," she called as she walked across the torn earth to hand him the bucket she'd packed the lunch in.

He actually smiled at her. His face was streaked with dirt, and sweat poured from him.

"Thanks, Annie. Whew, it's a scorcher today. I'm thirsty and hungry both." He took his hat off and mopped his face with a red checkered bandanna. "There's a shady spot over by the riverbank." He paused, and she could tell he was uncertain as he added, "Will you come sit and share this with me?"

Annie hadn't planned to linger, but for the first time since their quarrel, the tension between them seemed somewhat eased.

"I'd like that, Noah." She didn't know about him, but she was sick and tired of the strain between them. She'd never been good at holding grudges—what purpose did they serve? Life went right on.

Besides, the thought of sitting somewhere cool for a spell was appealing. Her dress was light cotton, but her long skirts were cumbersome. She'd shoved her sunbonnet back, and as usual curls had escaped from under her sunbonnet and were glued to her forehead and neck with sweat. A fresh crop of freckles were undoubtedly popping out like gooseberries on her nose and cheeks, and she didn't care.

Noah retrieved his shirt and handed it to her to carry while he took the team down to the water for a drink and then turned them free to graze. When they were settled, he led the way to a sheltered, grassy knoll among the willows that bordered the riverbank.

Annie plunked herself down, relishing the feel of the cool grass. A slight breeze came drifting from the water. Meadowlarks trilled from the bushes.

Noah sat down beside her and opened the fresh tea towel she'd wrapped around his sandwiches and held them out to her.

Good thing she'd packed extra. She accepted a thick chicken sandwich—she seemed always to be starving these days. The early sickness had passed, leaving a bottomless hunger in its place.

Her belly had begun to gently round, but she was also putting on extra weight all over her body—the first time in her life that she'd been more than skin and bone.

"I made a dozen jars of rhubarb jam, and they turned out," she remarked, still feeling pleased with herself.

"This bread is delicious, too, Annie." He bit into another sandwich and chewed appreciatively.

"I guess I've finally gotten the knack."

"I guess the chickens are relieved," he said, and Annie blinked. Was Noah actually *joking* with her?

She looked at him, and he was grinning. Another moment, and they were laughing together, the memory of her calamitous efforts at bread-making forming a bond between them.

They finished the lunch, munching on apples and chatting easily now about the field he was clearing, the new colt that had been born the week before, the latest gossip in the Medicine Hat Times.

It was growing even hotter. Annie fanned herself with the dish towel, looking at the water, and an irresistible idea began to form.

"I'm going wading." She sat up and began unlacing her boots.

Noah nodded in agreement. "Why not come for a swim? It's hot enough to melt bullets, and there's a backwater down there just made for swimming."

He stood and, without any hesitation, swiftly removed his boots, pants, and underdrawers. Pretending to be oblivious to her startled gaze, he calmly walked down the embankment stark naked and dove straight in, disappearing entirely for a heart-stopping moment before he surfaced a short distance away from the shore.

"It's fine," he hollered, sending droplets flying as he shook water out of his ears. "It's cool. Come on in."

She hesitated for only a split second. Then a kind of madness seized her. She shucked off her dress and stockings, her long petticoat, until all that was left was her white cotton chemise and underdrawers. She picked her way gingerly down to the water, aware that Noah, neck deep, was watching her every move.

The delicious coolness on her toes enchanted her. In a moment, she was up to her knees, and then her thighs.

"You tricked me," she gasped. "It's not just cool, it's downright freezing."

"Careful, the bottom drops off fast right about there." Noah swam over and stood, taking both of her hands in his.

"Can you swim, Annie?" Drops of water clung to his eyelashes, the whorls of dark hair on his chest glistened, and he smiled at her, lighthearted, boyish—and very bare.

The shock of the water and the sight of Noah's naked body was taking her breath away. "No, I can't swim," she gasped, clinging tight to his hands, laughing with the wonder of it all. "I've never done this before."

"Put your arms around my neck, but don't choke off my air."

He turned his back to her and she looped her arms around him, heart hammering at the feel of his skin against hers, and in one smooth movement, he sank down into the water with her half floating on his back.

She screamed in delight as the chill of the water reached her buttocks, her back, her breasts. She clung to him, laughing uncontrollably, drunk with the sensation of weightlessness, the naked male body pressing against her. He swam a few strokes, and she felt the power of his muscles as he stroked and kicked, easily supporting her.

Like carefree children, they splashed and teased and played, until all at once, laughing up at him in waist-deep water, Annie met his eyes and caught her breath.

The game had changed.

His arms slid further around her, and one hand cupped her breast. His mouth came down to claim hers, and with a groan, he scooped her up in his arms and carried her out of the water, up the bank to where the grass was soft.

He stripped her of dripping chemise and drawers, spread his shirt, and drew her down upon it.

Their loving was both easy and intense, because in this one thing they seemed to know instinctively what the other required.

The sun beat down upon them, the meadowlarks

sang, and the rushing of the river muffled the sounds they made.

"I've lost my hairpins, and I can't put my hair back up without them." Annie was searching the grass.

Noah, dressed again in trousers and the crumpled blue shirt they'd lain on, knelt obligingly beside her and combed the ground in search of them.

"Here's three, is that enough?" He couldn't help but grin at the picture she made kneeling there in disarray, scowling as she tried to control the wild red curls covering her shoulders and tumbling down her back. Her freckled face was golden from the sun, her body voluptuous.

He refused to dwell on the reason for that new lushness, the child that grew within her. Today he was at peace, with her and with himself. There'd be time later to come to terms with the child.

"Thank you, Noah." She stuck the pins in her mouth and smiled at him as she wrestled with her unruly hair.

Her eyes were as green as the grass they knelt on, as wide and clear as the pool where they'd been swimming. He leaned forward and pressed a kiss on her swollen lips, then regretted his impetuous gesture when her eyes shimmered with sudden tears.

But she gave him a wide smile and pulled her stockings up, teasing him with one last glimpse of shapely leg before she struggled to her feet.

"I have to get back. Bets and Zachary will think I've been taken by Indians. Do I look decent again?"

He pretended to study her. Her dress was creased beyond redemption, and there was grass in her hair. He reached over and took it out before she tied the sunbonnet on.

"You look just fine," he assured her, knowing that

anyone with half an eye could tell by the rich color in her cheeks and the slumberous look in her eyes that she'd been well and truly loved. But Bets was too young and innocent for such thoughts, and if Zachary should notice, well, Zachary would be overjoyed that the strain of the past weeks was over and done with.

"Let the past go," he'd communicated to Noah just the other night. Zachary had come to love Annie, and he made no secret that he blamed Noah for the problems between them.

Yes, his father would be delighted to see Annie like this.

Noah tucked the dish towel into the lunch pail and handed it to her, and he watched as she set off across the field. A hundred yards off she turned and waved, and he raised a hand in response, feeling happy and more at peace than he'd been in a long while.

She disappeared over the hill, and he walked toward the peacefully grazing horses. "C'mon, boys. Buck, Bright, time to get back to work."

He was whistling as he harnessed them and led them over to another stump, and he was still whistling half an hour later when he heard the frantic call.

"Noah—Noah."

His body stiffened as he caught sight of Annie and Bets, skirts held high, racing towards him over the uneven ground.

A terrible foreboding filled him as he ran to meet them.

Chapter Nine

Bets was sobbing, her face soaked with tears and sweat. Annie, too, was crying as Noah reached them, her flushed face contorted into lines of anguish.

"What is it? What's happened?" He grasped Annie by the shoulders. "Tell me, for God's sake."

"It's—it's Zachary. Bets was—she was coming—to get us," she gasped. "I met her on the trail, I ran back to the house with her, but it—it was too late. Oh, Noah—" She gulped and her voice broke. "He's gone. Zachary's dead." She pressed her hands against her mouth, trying to still the sobs so she could talk.

"Bets said she—she was playing checkers with him, and he had some sort of a seizure, just for a moment or two, and then—then he just fell back on the pillows—"

An absolute stillness seemed to surround Noah. He heard the words, but they came from a great distance. He turned and ran over to unhook the team. Then, with his hand on the harness, he paused and laid his forehead against Buck's rough, warm flank.

His father was dead.

Hurrying served no purpose, because Zachary was no longer there for him, the way he'd been through the whole of Noah's life.

His wife, his child, and now his father—fate had a way of taking everything he cared about. It was a reminder, a grim warning, not ever to let himself love without reservation.

November 14, 1886

My dear Elinora,

We're having the first real snowfall of the year, and it's still coming down like big, soft feathers. It's pretty, but it also makes me feel lonely and rather a prisoner. It's been over two months now, but Bets and I still can't seem to get through a day without crying for dear Zachary—we do miss him so very much. I find myself longing for the sound of that cursed cane of his banging the floor.

Thank you for the letter, and the parcel. You are altogether too generous, dear Elinora. The baby clothes are beautiful and much appreciated. Tell Fanny I shall treasure the shawl she knitted. And the book you sent, Advice to a Mother, *has cleared away many of my questions about the birth process. I note that it is written by an Englishwoman; surely the English are more enlightened than the rest of us, to publish so outspoken a volume.*

You ask when this blessed event will occur—I see Doctor Witherspoon each time we go to town, and he says about the third week in Jan-

uary. Although I hate the very thought, Noah is adamant that I go and stay with friends in Medicine Hat after Christmas so the doctor will be in attendance at the birth. Elinora, I can't help but feel in my heart that I'm being banished, even though my head tells me the idea is a sensible one—we are far from town, it's winter, and the doctor might not reach us in time.

Enough of my ranting! Truth to tell, I am in perfect health, although I grow to look more like a pumpkin every day. Gladys is quick to inform me that my rounded shape is going to get worse before it gets better. She and Rose came to visit again last week, the first time since the funeral. I think I told you that Zachary is buried in a spot near the river, alongside Noah's first wife and baby. I go there when the weather permits; I feel strangely close to all three of them.

Gladys has become a good friend, and Rose and Bets are as thick as thieves. Rose can sign almost as well as I can. We're planning a get-together for Christmas day. Gladys says her family will come here because of my "condition," and we'll all make Christmas dinner. Bets and I are busy making gifts—aprons and potpourri from wild roses for the women and socks for the men. I'm making Noah new mittens from scarlet yarn; his are full of holes.

You asked in your letter how Noah is doing with the death of his father, and I have to say I don't really know. You see, he won't talk to me, Elinora. I try, but it's as if he's far away. I did think, just before Zachary's death, that things had changed for the better, but it hasn't worked that way at all.

As always, he is kind and very thoughtful—

he brings all the water in and takes the slops out and warns me not to lift heavy things. He bought me two new (voluminous) dresses last trip to town, as nothing I have fits anymore, but he refuses to speak of the baby, which is what I need and want him to do. Every time I've brought it up, he gets up and walks away.

I love him with all my heart, Elinora, and I've come to realize I'm an all-or-nothing sort of person. If he can't see his way to loving me and this child equally, the day will come when I will have to leave.

Well, this is a sad excuse for a letter, but you told me always to write as I feel. Enclosed is a note from Bets—her penmanship is getting much better, isn't it? I make her do lessons every day. You wouldn't recognize her. She's grown a foot and put on weight and looks a different girl altogether. Coming here has been good for her, at least.

I hope you are well and not working too hard. Bets and I laughed over your story about the new boarder. I imagine you have her quite housebroken by now.

I hope to hear from you soon. Each time Noah goes to town, I pray for a letter.

> *Your loving, expectant friend,*
> *Annie.*

In mid-December, at Bets's urging, Noah cut a bushy willow tree and nailed it to a stand. The sisters decorated its stark branches with strings of cranberries, popcorn, and paper angels.

They tied suet to the outdoor clothesline for the birds and wrapped the gifts they'd made and stacked them under the tree. Noah bought extra sugar in town, and Annie made candy and baked cakes in preparation for Christmas.

The temperature dropped to 38 degrees below zero and stayed there for a week. Annie and Bets fretted over whether it would be too cold for their guests to travel, but on December 23, it suddenly warmed up again, to only 10 below.

All the Christmas preparations were finished, and the house was clean. Annie awoke that morning filled with energy, determined that the time had come to tidy Zachary's bedroom and turn it into a nursery for the baby. She'd been putting it off—Noah had shut the door to his father's room after the funeral, and it had remained closed. Now, for some reason, it was urgent to her that the room be in order before the next day, when the Hopkins family came over.

She told Noah that morning at breakfast what she was planning, and as usual these days, he didn't really answer her. He simply nodded in that distracted way he had, pulled on his heavy coat and hat, and disappeared out the door in the direction of the barn.

Half the time, she thought despondently, she didn't know whether he even heard what she said to him.

Annie enlisted Bets's help in dismantling Zachary's bed and setting it against the wall. They folded his clothing neatly into a box, dusted down the walls, and scrubbed the floor. Annie lined the dresser drawers with fresh paper and lovingly laid her meager collection of baby things there: flannel diapers and tiny dresses and knitted leggings that she was certain were too small to fit anything human.

In spite of the freezing temperature, Bets carried the rag rug out to the clothesline and gave it a vigorous beating.

Bobby Hutchinson

Noah had been out in the barn all morning, shoveling hay down from the loft to load on a sled to take out to the cattle in the south pasture, and when he came in at noon, Annie showed him what they'd done.

"Now we need your help in moving the bed and mattress to the attic," Annie told him, adding with her heart in her throat, "and Noah, do you think you could bring the cradle down?"

All morning, she'd worried over his reaction to that suggestion—she knew Noah had built the cradle before his son was born. Zachary had carved the angels and flowers and wood sprites into the satiny wood, and having it in plain view would be a painful reminder of both dead father and lost child.

The roof in the attic room was too low for him to stand upright. With Bets's help, Noah lowered the awkward mattress to a spot against the wall and, half crouching, forced himself to look around at the things he'd sworn never to look at again—Jeremy's cradle, his high chair, the soft blankets and shawls that had kept him warm, the trunk packed with his baby clothing, the wooden box Noah had fashioned to hold his son's toys.

Bets plucked a stuffed kitten, its tail gone, out of the toy box and stroked it. Then, with a nervous glance at him, she carefully put it back again.

Noah winced, remembering his sturdy, mischievous son pulling on that tail until it finally came loose from the toy. "Broke," he'd said matter-of-factly, handing it to Noah. "Da fix."

How he missed his little son. How he'd loved him, right from the moment Molly told him she was pregnant. He'd begun the cradle that very day. With pride and delight, he'd watched his wife's body changing, placing his hand on Molly's belly and laughing with awe and joy to feel their child moving. He'd rubbed her back and teased her and laced her boots each morning when she could no longer reach them.

And what had he done for Annie?

Nothing. Nothing at all, except make it plain in every way he could that he didn't want her child. He'd witnessed the anxiety in her eyes just now when she asked him to bring down the cradle.

She'd actually thought he would refuse her even the use of the cradle for the baby she carried.

He straightened suddenly and smacked his head on a rafter. He swore viciously, but the pain mirrored the sudden, shamed anguish in his heart.

He couldn't pretend he wanted this child, because he didn't.

But neither could he deny his feelings for Annie. In spite of himself, against every vow he'd made, he cared for Annie.

It was for her sake that he lifted the trunk that held Jeremy's baby clothing and carried it downstairs. It was like slowly plucking the scab from a deep, half-healed wound, but he returned for the cradle, the box of toys, and the high chair, setting everything in the room that Annie was preparing for the baby.

She watched wide-eyed as he brought down all of Jeremy's things. When he had finished, she came over to him and, without a word, locked her arms around his neck and pulled his head down to kiss him full on the lips.

"Thank you, Noah. I know it's difficult for you, and I thank you." Her green eyes shimmered with tears, and the gratitude and love on her face were more than he could bear.

God, she was beautiful. She'd spilled something brown down her front and she smelled of cooking, and her fiery hair rose like a nimbus around her head, curly and messy and wild, and it came to him that he loved her. He'd loved her for a long time, without being able to admit it to her or to himself.

Longing overwhelmed him, and he wrapped his arms around her and held her close against him, his eyes shut tight, his heart aching for release, imagining for a split second how it might have been with her if only . . .

But he could feel the mound of her belly pressing his, and the babe inside suddenly kicked hard against him.

Panic filled Noah at the emotion that contact created.

He jerked away from her embrace and blindly reached for his overcoat and hat. "I'm taking a load of hay out to the cattle this afternoon. I'll be home in time for supper."

His voice was harsh, because something was happening in his chest. A tight knot that he'd never allowed to unwind was stubbornly coming undone.

He fought with all his strength, but the sobs started when he was halfway across the yard, tearing, painful sobs that he'd denied when Molly was taken from him, when Jeremy died, when he lost his father.

He knew that strong men didn't cry, but he couldn't stop himself any longer. He stumbled into the barn and stood there, arms braced against a stall, tears raining down his face, the savage agony of all his losses bursting in his chest and erupting in an avalanche of grief that he couldn't force down anymore.

At first he fought the tears with all his strength, horrified, ashamed of such weakness, but their power overwhelmed him and at last he gave in, sinking to his knees on the hay and weeping until he was empty.

At last he staggered to his feet, mindful of his cattle needing to be fed. Still in a daze, he harnessed Buck to the loaded sleigh, not taking note that the wind had changed and was now blowing from the north, or that the western sky was bruised-looking and inky dark, heavy with stormclouds.

Instead, he looked toward the house. Smoke curled cheerfully from the chimney. It was a dark afternoon, and the lamp shone from the window. He imagined the little Christmas tree and thought he could hear Annie and Bets laughing together as they so often did over their work.

They were his family now, and he desperately wanted to tell them so. He needed the comfort that affirmation would provide, but he couldn't go in now, with red, shamefully swollen eyes. He'd only be gone two hours. He'd tell them when he returned.

When he came home, he'd take Annie in his arms and confess how wrong he'd been all these months. He'd beg her forgiveness, and because he knew her so well by now, he knew she'd give it freely, with all the fervor of her passionate, generous nature.

His chest filled with warmth and anticipation. At the last moment, he remembered the wolves that preyed on his cattle and went back to the barn for his rifle. Then he clucked to Buck and headed off across the snow-covered landscape.

Annie and Bets were totally engrossed by the pleasurable task of readying the baby's room. Bets wiped the cradle down and made it up with its tiny sheets and warm shawls. They smiled and made admiring faces at the wealth of meticulously hand-sewn shirts, knitted sweaters, and tiny flannel nightdresses in the trunk. Annie arranged some of the wooden toys on the dresser, only vaguely aware that the wind had gotten up and snow was beginning to fall outside.

At last Bets drew her attention to the window, and

Annie was shocked at the ferocity of the storm. A
flicker of uneasiness made her shiver as she caught
sight of the clock. "Lordie, Bets, we'd better hurry
supper. Noah must have come back hours ago. He'll
be hungry," she murmured, grunting as she bent
over the wood box to get a log for the cookstove. Her
huge belly made bending difficult, and her back had
been aching on and off all afternoon.

"You peel these potatoes, and I'll start some sau-
sage frying," she instructed her sister. "We'll open a
jar of crabapples; they'll do for dessert."

For the next half hour, she and Bets hurried to get
the meal prepared, anticipating Noah's arrival at any
second. But the minutes passed, and when all was
ready and she'd walked to the window a dozen times
to peer out, Annie tried to hide her growing concern
from Bets.

"Noah must have decided to do the milking early,
what with this blizzard," she said. "I'm just going to
walk over to the barn and see if I can help. It's getting
late."

But Bets grabbed her sister's arm. "You will not. I
will go. What if you fall on the ice?" She made a face
and a slicing motion across her throat. "Noah will
kill me if I let you outside in this." She grabbed an
old coat, tied a shawl over her head, and stuck her
feet into a pair of Zachary's boots.

Annie went with her to the door. When they opened
it, both were shocked at the force of the storm. A
maelstrom of wind and snow whirled around Bets as
she set off in the direction of the barn.

Annie shut the door and leaned back against it,
cupping her hands around her belly, trying to take
comfort in the restlessness of the child inside, trying
to still the fear that was making her heart hammer
and her hands tremble.

Where was Noah?

Chapter Ten

It seemed to Annie that an eternity went by before the kitchen door opened again and Bets was half blown in on a cloud of swirling snow and frigid air. What little daylight there had been was now entirely gone.

Bets tugged off her mitts, but even before her fingers flew with their message, the alarm on her sister's face told Annie what was wrong.

"Noah is not there. He's still gone with Buck and the hay sled."

They stared at one another, their eyes filled with horror.

Outside, the wind howled like a mad demon, and the snow blew thick and blinding. The windowpanes rattled, and even the stoves hissed as snow was driven down the chimney and hit the burning coals.

"Something's happened. Something awful's happened to him, Bets," Annie whispered. Inside her, fear and urgency combined with the most awful feeling of helplessness. A woman big with child, a half-grown girl, a raging blizzard; what in heaven could they do?

"I will ride to Hopkins and get help." Bets's fingers flew. "I will take Noah's horse, Sultan. I know how to saddle him. Noah showed me."

"Oh, sweetheart, you can't." Annie gave her brave sister a hug, then stood back so she could explain. "For one thing, it's storming far too hard to ride to the Hopkins place—you'd get lost—and for another, Noah's the only one who can ride Sultan. He's a demon—Noah says so himself."

Bets's bravado disappeared and she started to cry. "We must help. We must do something."

Annie reached out and wiped away the tears from her sister's face with a corner of her apron. "We will, but it's not going to help if we go out and get ourselves lost, so we'll wait until the worst of this storm stops and then we'll get on old Bright and go find him together. Bright can carry us both. And in the meantime, we'll light the extra lantern and put it in the window, so if Noah comes, he'll see the light from a distance and not lose his way in the storm."

Even as she signed the optimistic words, Annie knew that blizzards like this could last days and days, and that unless the storm abated soon, it would be too late.

She turned her head and gazed at the frost-covered window. If anything, the wind had increased.

"I love Noah," Bets signed in her forthright manner. "Always, he is good and kind to me. Never he makes me feel less because I am deaf."

Anguish and terror filled Annie's heart, and a low moan came from her throat. *Noah, my husband, where are you?*

With all the fierceness of her being, she willed him safe, but she knew that no one could survive long outside in these conditions.

Together, they found the lantern, filled and lit it.

They prepared an emergency bundle with food and dry clothes and a blanket, and they gathered their warmest clothes, ready to put on at a moment's notice.

But as the night deepened, the storm raged on. Bets finally fell asleep on the couch, but weary as she was, Annie couldn't rest.

She stoked the fires, one hand pressed to her aching back, and walked a million times to the window where the lantern burned, praying each time that the storm had lessened, that some miracle would bring Noah bursting through the door.

It didn't happen. It was a long time later when, half dozing beside Bets, the sudden silence brought Annie fully awake.

The wind had died. She lumbered to her feet and hurried to the window. The lantern, still shining bravely, had kept the pane clear of frost, and outside Annie could see snow falling heavily, but the worst of the blizzard was over. Her eyes flew to the clock.

Four A.M. It was Christmas Eve morning, and he'd been gone for more than twelve hours.

She sent up a desperate prayer, then went over and touched Bets.

"It's time to go for Noah," she signed when the girl's eyes opened.

He was within a mile of the cattle when the first of the blizzard hit, and Noah considered turning back, but he knew that if he did, many of his cattle in the south pasture would die; they were already short of feed, and unlike horses, they couldn't paw down to the frozen earth for sustenance.

He'd been allowing Buck to go along at his own speed, but now Noah hollered and used the reins to hurry the big animal onward.

Buck nickered in protest, but he responded, going from an ambling walk to a cumbersome trot. The sleigh where Noah rode atop the hay bounced along, but the wind and snow increased until Noah could hardly make out the horse's shape through the storm.

He drew his scarf up over his nose and mouth, thankful for his buffalo coat but cursing himself for a fool. Being out alone on the prairie in a blizzard was a hazardous thing, and if he'd had his wits about him, he would never have left the ranch.

At last he came upon the huddled shapes of the cattle. Using the pitchfork he'd brought along, Noah unloaded the hay as fast as he could. Driving pellets of snow and the howling wind snatched his breath away, blinding him and making his face and hands numb with cold. The cattle grouped themselves around the feed, backs to the wind.

He should stay here, he knew, waiting out the storm in the dubious protection of the cattle's warm bodies. It was the sensible thing to do, because the trip back would be treacherous.

But who knew how long the blizzard would last? Annie would be terrified at his absence, and she was close to her birthing time.

He needed to tell her how much he wanted their baby. . . .

He had to get home, even though by now he couldn't see a single foot in front of him, and all his usual good sense of direction was gone.

Buck would know where the ranch was. Animals were uncanny in that regard.

Swiftly undoing the harness, Noah abandoned the sleigh.

"Let's go home, old man." Rifle on his shoulder, Noah leaped up to the horse's broad back, noting that already there was no sign of the tracks they'd made; the blowing snow had obliterated everything.

The horse stood for a moment, getting his bearings, then began to move steadily ahead into what seemed a holocaust.

Time disappeared in the unholy force of the storm. Noah, lying almost flat along Buck's broad back, had no idea how long they'd been blundering through the knee-deep drifts when suddenly the big horse stumbled and Noah heard the horrifying crack of breaking bone and, in the next instant, his horse's awful scream of agony as Buck's broken foreleg crumpled beneath him.

Knowing he was in danger of being pinned beneath the huge animal's body, Noah tried to throw himself free.

He landed on a patch of frozen ground blown free of snow, and the impact stunned him, but he could hear Buck's unendurable screaming even over the roaring of the wind. It sickened him.

He knew what he had to do as he scrambled to his feet and searched frantically for his rifle. Finding it, he struggled against the might of the storm to reach Buck, nausea choking him.

"Easy, old friend, poor old friend . . ."

He cursed in a long, helpless stream. Then he tugged off his mittens, raised the rifle, laid it against Buck's head, and pulled the trigger.

The screaming stopped, and Noah retched into the snow. It was only when the sickness passed and reason returned that he was able to acknowledge that the animal's death almost certainly meant his own. Already, his fingers were numb, his toes aching with the cold. He crouched beside the still-warm carcass, his mind as chaotic as the storm that raged around him, and what he thought of first was Annie.

If he died here, he'd never have the chance to tell her that he loved her. He'd never see the baby they'd made together. He wouldn't be around to make sure that the

201

young men who came courting pretty Bets in a year or two were suitable.

Damnation, if he died, there'd soon be suitors lining up and fighting over Annie.

She was full of life, passionate, funny, endearing—in fact, Noah admitted, Annie was everything any man could ever want in a wife. And confound it, she was *his*.

The thought of those faceless men daring to come courting his wife sent a rush of jealousy and primitive anger through Noah, and with the anger came determination.

He wasn't going to die out here, damn it. There'd been enough tragedy in the Ferguson family. He refused to add to it.

He needed the chance to set things right, to tell Annie he loved her, to welcome his new son or daughter, to live out the rest of the years of his life unafraid of what fate might bring. He'd been a total fool this past year, but he was going to make up for it.

Like a light going on in the depths of his soul, Noah knew he was going to survive. He just had to figure out how.

His mind became very focused, very clear.

Setting off on foot in this howling storm would certainly get him lost. He'd wander in circles and finally freeze to death.

He had to stay where he was. His only chance lay in the hope that the storm would blow itself out before Buck's huge carcass began to grow cold. If the wind finally died, Noah knew that his sense of direction would unerringly tell him which way to go, but in the meantime, his only chance was to huddle close to the dead horse, using him as a shield against the storm.

With the image of Annie and all the things he had to say to her firmly lodged in his brain, Noah hunkered down beside Buck and waited, pressing himself against the warm horseflesh.

At last the wind lessened. It was still black-dark and snowing when he stood up. There was no guarantee that the storm was really over, but he was cold and dangerously sleepy.

Sending a silent thanks and a last good-bye to the old horse, Noah stamped feet that felt like blocks of solid ice and staggered off across the snow-covered landscape in the direction he prayed would lead him to the ranch.

Chapter Eleven

Annie and Bets gave the old workhorse his head, and Bright stoically waded through the drifts with the two of them perched on him.

Every few moments, Annie called Noah's name, but the sound was muffled by the heavy fall of snow. Her hands and feet grew numb with cold, and she was grateful for Bets's warm body pressing close against her aching back.

Her throat was hoarse from hollering when at last she thought she heard an answer, faint and far away.

"Whoa." She tugged on Bright's reins, afraid even to hope.

"Noah?" Her voice sounded lost in the icy darkness.

"Noooaah," she screamed, every ounce of her own desperation in the call, and this time she was certain she heard his voice respond. She urged Bright on, and soon a tall, snow-covered figure came staggering out of the darkness toward them.

"Noah." With a mixture of laughter and tears, Annie

slid down from Bright's back and into his half-frozen arms. "Oh, Noah, thank God you're all right. What happened? Where's Buck?"

In a few stark sentences, he told her, holding her close, his strong arms locked like a vise around her, her huge belly cradled against him. "I've been such a damned fool, Annie," he said in a hoarse whisper. "I love you, and I'll love this baby of ours when it comes. Now, let's hurry and get you home where it's warm. It's Christmas Eve, and we're going to celebrate—just the three of us."

She turned her face up to him, green eyes full of joyful wonder, hardly able to believe what she'd heard. And in that ecstatic moment, the first horrendous pain ripped through her abdomen.

"Owwww!"

Holding her, Noah felt her brace with the contraction, then fall against him, stunned at its intensity and duration.

A new and awful fear gripped him. He supported her until it was over, doing his best not to let her suspect the utter panic that he felt.

Was she about to have their baby in the middle of this snowstorm? "How long have you been having pains, Annie?"

She leaned on him, panting as the pain receded, her forehead damp with perspiration and snowflakes. "Only this one, but my back's been sore all day."

Noah swallowed hard. God willing, there'd be time to get her home, but the baby was undoubtedly coming, and the storm would make it impossible to bring the doctor. Even sending Bets for Gladys Hopkins was out of the question—it was too far and there was far too much snow.

He'd birthed animals, plenty of them, but Noah hadn't even been allowed in the room when Jeremy was born.

"Let's get you home, sweetheart." Catching Annie under the arms, he lifted her up on Bright's back. "We'll be there in a few minutes." He pulled a frozen mitten off and with a few rapid signs, told Bets what was happening. "Hold her tight, Bets," he signed.

A few moments before, struggling exhausted and alone through the darkness and the snow, Noah had thought with every single step that he couldn't force himself to take another.

Now, he took Bright's reins and ran easily beside the huge horse. They had to stop twice more as sharp pains gripped Annie, and giddy relief spilled through Noah when at last the lantern the women had lighted and left in the window became visible in the distance, shining through the snow, a beacon welcoming Noah and his family home.

Later, Annie remembered the haze of the lamplight as Noah gripped her hands in his strong ones and urged her to push out their child.

His sleeves were rolled up, and perspiration rolled down his face. He smiled and spoke loving words of encouragement, giving her not the slightest inkling that he was deathly afraid that he'd be unequal to the task ahead of him.

As soon as they had Annie warm and settled, Bets had brought him the book Elinora had sent, entitled *Advice to a Mother*.

Desperate for any small bit of assistance, Noah flipped through it. The book actually had illustrations that depicted the birth of a child, and he propped it on the bedroom dresser and dragged the dresser close to the bed. Referring to the instructions it contained, he and Bets lit lamps and found scissors and folded flannel into pads and filled the copper washtubs with water and set them to heating.

With Bets in charge of keeping the fires burning well and fetching anything he thought he needed, Noah stationed himself beside Annie, glancing more and more distractedly at the book as the hours passed, urging Bets to turn the pages back and forth, soundly cursing the volume's numerous omissions as the birth inevitably progressed in spite of him.

At ten past noon on December 24, 1886, with the able assistance of his young sister-in-law, Noah Ferguson successfully delivered his tiny daughter, Mary Elinora.

Annie and Bets survived the ordeal exceptionally well, but the first sound of his baby's outraged squalling so relieved her father that dizziness overcame him, and he had to sink down on the bed with her minute, naked body cradled awkwardly in his two huge hands.

He actually thought for the first time in his life that he was about to faint, and he had to draw deep breaths before he could really examine the child he held.

She was scrawny, but already he could sense Mary's enormous life force. The damp curls plastered against her minute skull were undeniably red, and when she opened her eyes and looked vaguely up at him, Noah saw an exact reflection of his own coal-dark gaze.

Annie was watching, and it was evident from the besotted expression on his face that in that first instant, Mary Elinora had captured her father's mighty heart in her tiny fist.

Annie and Bets looked at each other with tears in their eyes and giggled.

From their vantage point in a corner of the room, an old man and a young woman with a laughing little boy between them smiled angelic smiles and nodded at one another with the satisfaction of a job well done.

They alone could clearly see the magnificent golden glow that filled the room, the radiance of intense and lasting love, and at last they knew it was time for them, too, to leave, to go toward the light.

A CHRISTMAS MIRACLE

To all my readers who believe in the magic of Christmas.

Chapter One

New York City, October 1867

Megan Kelly's feet felt like clumps of ice as she dragged herself slowly back to her third-floor walk-up flat. She wasn't just cold and tired, but hungry as well. Frozen pellets of snow stung her ivory cheeks, bringing tears to her expressive violet eyes. She shivered beneath the meager protection of her thin coat and tried to ignore the biting pain of nearly frozen toes. The unusually cold October gave hint of the long winter yet to come, and Megan shivered with foreboding. Being penniless, friendless, and pregnant in New York City with winter coming on was excessively frightening.

Tucking her face into her raised collar, Megan hastened her steps. One flannel petticoat beneath a threadbare dress and shoes lined with damp newspaper offered scant protection against the howling wind whipping around buildings and through alley-ways.

The wind whistled through the deserted streets, picking up a discarded newspaper and blowing it up and over and around, spinning it into the air and depositing it at Megan's feet. Thinking it would make warm lining for her shoes, Megan picked the paper up and tucked it under her arm, intending to read it first. Her dwindling funds did not allow for luxuries such as newspapers.

Hampered by her advanced pregnancy, Megan trudged through the slush with slow, measured steps, fearful of falling and hurting her unborn child. Her stomach rumbled loudly, making known its displeasure. She had already consumed the one meal she allowed herself each day, and it wasn't enough to satisfy both her and her unborn child. But her slim hoard of coins could be stretched only so far. Megan had already missed two months' rent on her tiny flat and lived in fear of being evicted.

Each day Megan left early to look for work and returned late, cold, hungry, and without hope. No one was interested in hiring a woman far gone with child, and she couldn't blame them. If only Patrick hadn't died of a virulent fever on their voyage from Ireland. Megan sighed despondently. Together they could have surmounted hardships. But alone she had virtually no hope of surviving. After Patrick's death, she had cried enough tears to last a lifetime.

Megan had been stricken with morning sickness during the early weeks of her pregnancy and was unable to work. And once her pregnancy became noticeable, no one would hire her. For the past few months she had lived on the paltry savings she and Patrick had accumulated. Her money was nearly gone now, and she lived in fear of being thrown out on the streets to face death by freezing or starvation.

Unless she could find work, she and her innocent babe were doomed.

Megan trudged wearily up the stairs of the dingy gray building she'd called home since arriving in New York City four months ago and entered the foyer, grateful to be out of the driving sleet no matter how unwelcoming the dreary interior. Girding herself for the walk up to the third floor, Megan paused briefly at the foot of the stairwell.

"Mrs. Kelly, might I speak with you a moment?"

Megan's breath slammed against her chest. She knew what was coming, had expected it each time she returned home from her fruitless search for work. Being confronted by the landlord now only confirmed her darkest fears.

"Can it wait, Mr. Hemmingway? I'm too tired tonight to engage in conversation."

"Tired or not, this won't wait. I can't continue to keep you if you don't have the money to pay the rent. There are people waiting in line to rent your flat. You're two months behind on rent, and I'm not in business to support paupers. If you can't pay, you'll have to leave."

Megan swallowed painfully. "I have nowhere to go, Mr. Hemmingway."

Hemmingway sent her a shrewd look, almost insulting in its intensity. "Too bad you're in the family way. I have friends who would help a young beauty like you, if you catch my meaning. Come back to see me when you've gotten your figure back and maybe I can help you." He leered at her. "You Irish wenches are good for that kind of thing. Meanwhile, if you can't pay, you'll have to leave. I'm giving you twenty-four hours to vacate your flat, Mrs. Kelly, and I'm being generous. I've already allowed you to stay longer than most landlords would have."

Megan's violet eyes turned dark with indignation.

To her regret she had learned that most people treated Irish immigrants like dirt, but as long as she paid her rent on time, Mr. Hemmingway had kept his views to himself. Time and again she had faced the same kind of prejudice while looking for work. There were so many Irish immigrants in the city that they were looked upon as inferior beings. They were hired for the lowliest jobs at less than average wages. Megan couldn't count the times she was confronted with help-wanted signs that boldly stated: *No Irish need apply.*

"I don't have to stand here and take your insults, Mr. Hemmingway. I'm a decent woman and would never consent to what you're suggesting. You know I've been looking for work. If you could let me stay until . . ."

"I don't take in charity cases, Mrs. Kelly. Twenty-four hours." Turning abruptly, he walked briskly down the hall to his own apartment.

Megan watched until the door closed behind him, wondering what was to become of her. She had no friends, no money, and nowhere to turn for help. She could always appeal to Father Paddy for help, but the Catholic parish was a poor one and any help he could give would be fleeting at best. Most Irish immigrants were no better off than she, and most had too many mouths to feed to take in a pregnant woman.

Not one to give in to tears, Megan started up the stairs, her legs wooden, her head beginning to pound. By the time she reached the third floor, she was panting from exertion. She entered her dismal flat and shivered; the fire had gone out in the stove long ago and the cold settled around her like an icy blanket. She hurried to strike a fire and was dismayed to find only four lumps of coal remaining in the coal shuttle. She recalled the newspaper still tucked under her arm and decided it would be put to better use inside the stove. Her hands shook and her fingers were stiff as she began tearing the newspaper into strips.

Suddenly her gaze fell on the classified section and she ceased tearing. It wasn't often she had the opportunity to peruse the want ads, so she spread the pages out on the table and eagerly scanned the selection of jobs available. The offerings were meager, she noted, dashing her hopes of finding employment. Abruptly she came to the last item in the column. Mr. Grayson Petrie was in need of a woman to care for his house and two children. Since no Mrs. Petrie was mentioned, Megan supposed the poor man was a widower. For the space of a heartbeat, Megan's spirits soared—until she viewed herself as Mr. Petrie might.

Too young, too pregnant . . . and Irish.

What man in his right mind would employ a woman with no qualifications except having cared for her younger siblings while her parents worked from dawn to dusk to support them? It would take a special man to see past her youth and heavily pregnant body. She loved children and was very good with them. As for housekeeping skills, she had those aplenty. Nothing pleased her more than a clean, orderly house.

Cooking wasn't a skill she excelled at, but she was willing to learn. At home there had been little beyond oats and potatoes to fill their stomachs. That was one of the reasons she and Patrick had decided to marry and leave their native sod for America, the land of opportunity. Adventurous by nature, Patrick had so looked forward to America, the land of plenty. Unfortunately, Patrick had died before their dream of wealth could be realized.

That night Megan prayed fervently for acceptance

into the Petrie household. She had always been one to look on the bright side of things but of late it had been difficult to remain optimistic in the face of such overwhelming adversity. Being evicted had nearly defeated her, but finding the newspaper had been like an act of God. She could use all the help she could get.

With rapidly beating heart, Megan approached the impressive Petrie residence. Located in a prominent section of town, the house was large and sturdy, constructed of mellowed red brick. A frisson of apprehension slithered down her spine. If the job was already taken, or if Mr. Petrie didn't want her, she would probably die of starvation before her babe arrived. Megan hoped she looked presentable. She had donned her best dress, tamed her unruly dark hair with a brush until it shone with blue-black highlights and pinched her pale cheeks until they reddened. She could do nothing about her threadbare coat and worn-out shoes.

Taking a deep, steadying breath, Megan reached for the brass knocker attached to the ornately carved front door. Her hand had barely touched the knocker when the door flew open and a plump, gray-haired woman pushed past her.

"Mrs. Putnam, won't you reconsider?"

Megan heard the man's deep voice before she saw him. Low and vibrant, it held a note of panic tinged with desperation.

"I'm sorry, Mr. Petrie, but my daughter needs me. Her youngsters are more than she can handle, and her in the family way. I've given you two weeks notice, and today's my last day."

Grayson Petrie appeared in the doorway, filling it with the powerful width of his imposing frame. His massive shoulders stretched the fine cloth of his jacket and his tall, well-muscled body moved with easy grace as he rushed past Megan without giving her a second glance.

"I'll double your salary, Mrs. Putnam." He really did sound desperate, Megan thought. "The children are accustomed to you. You know I've had little luck securing a housekeeper the children would be comfortable with."

Mrs. Putnam stopped at the bottom of the stairs. "I'm getting on in years, Mr. Petrie, and my lumbago is giving me fits. I need my family around me in my last years. Your children are getting to be too much for an old woman to handle. If you want my advice," she said, sending him a stern look, "you'll spend more time with them. 'Tis a father they need, not a housekeeper. I'm sorry, Mr. Petrie, but you can't say I didn't give you sufficient notice."

The old woman turned and limped away, leaving Grayson looking decidedly uncomfortable. Megan studied him with open curiosity as he pleaded with Mrs. Putnam. There was inherent strength in his face, she decided, even if his expression was a bit strained. He had a generous mouth, an aquiline nose, and a straight forehead. His well-shaped head was covered with thick brown hair, tapering nearly to his collar. Megan stared in fascination as he lifted one large hand and dragged it though his hair, quite obviously irritated. Then he turned abruptly and charged toward the open door. Megan might as well have been invisible for all the attention he paid her.

When it became apparent that Mr. Petrie wasn't going to acknowledge her, she stepped boldly into his path.

"Mr. Petrie?"

Gray focused cool gray eyes on the young woman. "Yes? What do you want? I'm a busy man." His voice was fraught with impatience. His problems were many, and he had no idea how to solve them. His housekeeper had left, he couldn't leave the children alone, and he had an important meeting this morning.

Undaunted, Megan thrust the newspaper beneath his nose. For her, finding employment was the difference between life and death. She couldn't back down beneath Grayson Petrie's icy glare. "I've come in answer to your ad, sir. You did advertise for a housekeeper, did you not?"

A muscle twitched at the corner of Gray's mouth. "You? You're applying for the job? You're still a child yourself. How do you expect to handle my two?"

"I've had plenty of practice, sir," Megan said, thinking Grayson Petrie had to be the most arrogant man she'd ever met. And the coldest. "And I'm no child. I'm nearly twenty-one."

Gray stared at Megan, momentarily distracted by the lilting voice and pert features of the raven-haired woman. "You're Irish." He hadn't meant to sound gruff or insulting, but to Megan that was exactly how he appeared.

Drawing herself up to her full five-foot-two, Megan faced Gray squarely. "So what? 'Tis proud I am to be Irish. It seems to me that you're in desperate need of a housekeeper, Mr. Petrie, and beggars can't be choosers. Won't you at least give me a chance?"

An icy breeze whistled around the corner, setting Megan's teeth to chattering. Suddenly Gray noticed the threadbare condition of her coat and thoroughly wet shoes and cursed himself for a cad. The woman might be too young and inexperienced to hire, but he had no right to treat her so shabbily.

"This is no place to talk. Come inside, Miss . . . Miss . . ."

"It's Mrs. Mrs. Kelly." Megan followed him

through the door to the inviting warmth of the foyer, bumping into him when he stopped abruptly just inside the door.

"You're married?" Megan nodded. "I'm sorry, Mrs. Kelly, but this job is full-time. I often work late and need a woman to live in and look after the children." Gray was more than a little relieved to find a reason for not hiring the all-too-attractive Mrs. Kelly.

"I'm a widow," Megan replied. "Living in would be agreeable to me." More than agreeable, she thought but did not say.

Gray sighed, not wanting to be rude but convinced that this woman simply would not do. "Come into the parlor and warm yourself by the fire," he heard himself saying. "It's raw outside today. Everyone says we're in for a rough winter." He was rambling, he knew.

Megan accepted gratefully. There had to be something she could do or say to convince Mr. Petrie to hire her. The alternative was frightening.

The fire in the grate beckoned Megan, and she approached the fireplace eagerly, stretching her hands toward the cheery blaze. It would be heaven to be warm like this every day of her life. Gray followed Megan inside the room, puzzled by her awkward gait. She moved slowly, as if carrying a heavy burden, which seemed unusual in a healthy young woman. He found himself concerned when he didn't want to be. When she finally turned around to face him, Gray saw something he hadn't noticed before. Her coat barely buttoned around her bulging middle.

"My God! You're pregnant! And close to delivery, if I'm not mistaken. You should have mentioned it immediately, Mrs. Kelly. You're wasting both my time and yours. You won't do, won't do at all."

Megan felt as if the whole world had suddenly

turned against her. "Do you have something against motherhood, Mr. Petrie?"

Gray looked at her narrowly. "I thought you said you were a widow?"

"So I am. My husband died of fever aboard the ship carrying us to New York several months ago. I didn't know I was pregnant at the time."

Gray didn't know whether to believe her or not. In any case, it didn't matter. He needed a healthy woman strong enough to manage a household and two active children. "I'm sorry, Mrs. Kelly, you're not what I'm looking for."

Megan fought to subdue her rising panic. Somehow, some way she had to convince Grayson Petrie to hire her. "I'm strong, Mr. Petrie. I'll work hard. I love children and they love me. You need a housekeeper and I need the job. I've been evicted from my flat and will have my babe on the streets if I don't find work."

Gray muttered an obscenity beneath his breath, doing his best not to feel pity for the tragic creature who needed work so desperately. This day was going from bad to worse. First Mrs. Putnam walked out on him, and now this Irish baggage was trying to work on his sympathy. Too bad she had no way of knowing he had little sympathy where women were concerned. Lilith had taught him that women weren't to be trusted. Not even a pregnant woman was above conniving to get what she wanted. Yet when he looked into those appealing violet eyes, he could almost feel her desperation and something stirred inside him, something he hadn't felt in a very long time.

"Look, Mrs. Kelly, I appreciate your dilemma, but I have problems of my own. If I don't find a woman capable of caring for my children, I'll be forced to stay home and my business will suffer. I have an important meeting to attend this morning, and I still haven't found anyone to replace Mrs. Putnam. I can leave them with the cook, but that's only a temporary solution. I don't mean to seem heartless, but my time is valuable. I'll see you out."

Stubborn by nature, and desperate, Megan squared her shoulders and refused to budge. "Please don't turn me away, Mr. Petrie. You need someone to care for your children and I need work. Give me a chance. Hire me for today, and if it doesn't work out I'll leave and not bother you."

Annoyed, Gray stared at her. "You are persistent, aren't you, Mrs. Kelly? You win. I don't have the time to stand here and argue. I'm expected at the office. The children are in the nursery awaiting their tutor. Come upstairs and I'll introduce you." Megan's gratitude shook him more than he cared to admit, and her smile was so winsome that Gray nearly lost his train of thought. "But this is in no way a permanent arrangement," he stressed. "How close are you to delivery?"

Megan blushed and dropped her eyes. "December or January, I'm not sure."

"What does the doctor say?"

Megan stared at him as if he'd lost his mind. Did he think she was some rich nob? "I haven't the coin to consult a doctor."

Gray groaned, dismayed at the enormous responsibility he'd taken on. Whatever had possessed him? He should have turned the girl away before hearing her hard-luck story. After all, he wasn't noted for his soft heart. A man in his position couldn't afford to be taken in by a pair of wide violet eyes and a sad tale. For all he knew, the woman was a whore who had been thrown out by her madam when she became pregnant. And yet . . . Something about the young widow pulled at his heartstrings.

"Come along, Mrs. Kelly, my meeting won't wait."
He turned and started up the open staircase. Megan
hurried to catch up with him. She stumbled once,
and Gray caught hold of her elbow.

"Thank you," she said shyly. She hadn't had anything to eat since yesterday noon and was nearly
faint with hunger.

They reached the top of the stairs and turned left
into a wide corridor. Megan's eyes grew round at the
opulence of Grayson Petrie's home. Never had she
seen anything so grand. She heard the children before she saw them. Boisterous and lively, they
sounded like normal children to Megan.

Gray paused at the open door just outside the
nursery, a smile hovering at the corners of his lips.
Megan peeked into the room and saw a boy and girl
romping on the floor with a variety of toys the likes
of which she had never seen before. Suddenly the girl
looked up, saw her father, and froze.

The girl looked to be about eight or nine years old,
all legs and arms and eyes. She was blonde and
pretty and much too thin. The boy noticed his sister's
abrupt withdrawal and dropped what he was doing
to stare at his father. For some reason, his arrival
blunted the children's natural exuberance.

Gray entered the room, his smile wavering uncertainly as the children waited politely for him to
speak—almost too politely, Megan thought, puzzled
by the children's reaction to their father.

"This is Mrs. Kelly, children," Gray said. "She's going to stay with you today." He turned to Megan.
"Beth is nine years old and Alex is six."

"Good morning," Megan said brightly. "I'm sure
we'll get along famously."

Beth sent Megan a look that intimated just the opposite, while Alex scowled darkly and asked, "Where
is Mrs. Putnam?"

"She is no longer with us."

"What's wrong with Mrs. Kelly?" Beth asked, eyeing Megan's middle. "She's fat like Mommy was before she had Alex."

Gray groaned in dismay. He had known this was a mistake from the beginning. His daughter was far too astute not to notice the woman's condition.

Megan smiled and stepped forward, certain she could handle this better than Mr. Petrie. "I'm going to have a baby," Megan explained. "It's a natural state and nothing to be ashamed of."

"That's enough, Mrs. Kelly!" Gray thundered, appalled by Megan's unsolicited remarks. He didn't know much about children, but he didn't think people talked so frankly in front of them. "This is not the kind of subject I wish discussed in the children's presence."

Beth and Alex, unnaturally subdued by their father's appearance, withdrew even more during his rebuke. Megan noticed but was at a loss to explain the children's reticence toward their father. Gray seemed a loving and concerned father, but it appeared that he lacked the ability to relate to his own children.

"It's getting late," Gray muttered, glancing at his pocket watch. "I really have to leave. Are you certain you'll be all right, Mrs. Kelly?"

"The children and I will be fine," Megan assured him.

Gray hesitated. He was really taking a risk leaving his children with a virtual stranger. He couldn't understand his reckless behavior. Normally he'd demand references and check them out thoroughly before bringing a new employee into his home.

"The cook can be found in the kitchen. She's been with me a long time and can tell you anything you need to know. Mr. Seymore, the children's tutor, will arrive in one hour and remain until two this afternoon. The children eat lunch at noon and dinner at six. You may eat with them. You can occupy Mrs. Putnam's room for the time being. Beth can show you where it is."

"When will you be home, Mr. Petrie?"

"When I get here," Gray said curtly, already thinking about his upcoming meeting. "The children go to bed promptly at eight o'clock."

Megan watched him descend the stairs, her soft heart bleeding for the children who rarely saw and hardly knew their busy father. She wondered what had happened to their mother, and if their father knew how much they needed his warmth and love.

Chapter Two

Gray left the house feeling more than a little apprehensive. Whatever had possessed him to leave his precious children with a woman he knew nothing about? It was so unlike him to behave in such an unorthodox manner that he began to question his own sanity. Perhaps he'd been working so hard lately that he'd suffered a momentary lapse in judgment. Or maybe he'd felt a twinge of compassion for the woman whose violet eyes held such pain and desperation. Compassion was so foreign to him that he'd momentarily lost his head, but tonight he'd send the Irish baggage packing. He had enough on his mind without assuming responsibility for a pregnant woman barely out of the schoolroom.

It wasn't as if Gray had reached an advanced age, but at twenty-nine he'd seen sufficient pain and suffering to last a lifetime. He'd returned from the hellish war between North and South unscathed but for a minor wound, expecting to find his wife awaiting him with open arms. Instead he'd discovered her in bed with a strange man. He promptly sued for divorce. Lilith had been appalled at the scandal Gray had caused but offered little objection when he claimed the children before she fled to Europe with her lover. Gray suspected that he hadn't heard the last from Lilith, for he had subjected her to ridicule when he sought a divorce and Lilith was a vindictive woman. Socially prominent people did not divorce.

Gray had married Lilith because she was his social equal and he had been beguiled by her beauty. But after giving birth to two children, she had coolly informed him that they would no longer share the same bed because she feared becoming pregnant again and ruining her figure. Then the war took up the next four years of his life. He didn't have to enlist, but he'd felt it was his duty to fight for what he believed in. When he returned, he'd fully expected to make the best of his marriage for the children's sake, but finding her in bed with another man brought his world crashing down around his ears.

To Gray's dismay, the children hardly remembered the strange man who came back from war and took them from their mother. And he was having the devil's own time finding a way to gain their love. He worked long hours to make his export-import business successful and consequently had little time to devote to his children. They were too young to appreciate his efforts and grew remote and resentful in their dealings with him. He loved them so much, he wished desperately he could be more outgoing, but he had never been a demonstrative man. And on top of all his problems, he now had a pregnant Irish immigrant to deal with when he returned home tonight.

*   *   *

Megan eased herself into a chair to watch the children as they resumed their play. The moment their father left, they underwent a complete personality change. No longer subdued, they romped enthusiastically and with boundless energy. Megan thought it most puzzling and somewhat sad. Whatever had Grayson Petrie done to earn his children's disregard?

"Mrs. Kelly, are you going to be our new housekeeper?" Beth asked, fixing startling gray eyes on Megan.

"I . . . I don't know yet, Beth. I'm hoping your father will hire me."

"Are you really going to have a baby?"

"Yes, I really am."

"Then Papa won't hire you," Beth announced with certainty. "He doesn't like children."

Megan was stunned. "Who told you that?"

"If Papa liked children, he would stay home with us more," Alex argued. "He wouldn't have taken us away from Mama."

"Your mother is alive?" Megan was astounded as well as confused. She had been so certain Grayson Petrie was a widower. "Where is she?"

Beth shrugged. "Papa says she's traveling, but I think he sent her away. He doesn't like her much, either."

"Mama left us alone a lot, too," Alex ventured.

"I think your father loves you very much," Megan offered lamely. She couldn't help wondering about the kind of parents these poor children were saddled with.

"You're lying!" Beth insisted. Her little chin quivered as she stared defiantly at Megan. "You're mean to say that when it's not true. You don't even know Papa. But I don't care. I don't like Papa any better than he likes me. And I don't like you."

"I don't like you, either," Alex declared, echoing his sister's sentiments.

Megan felt such overwhelming compassion for these two children that she wanted to take them into her arms and hug them, but she knew they would object. It was almost with relief that she heard someone knocking on the front door.

"That must be your tutor," she said, rising clumsily. "I'll go down and let him in. I'll see you at lunch."

Rudyard Seymore was an earnest young man of medium height and unassuming looks. He was somewhat startled to see Megan but quickly recovered and introduced himself.

"I'm Mrs. Kelly," Megan informed him. "My charges are waiting upstairs for their lessons. I assume you know the way?"

Curious, Seymore peered over rimless spectacles at Megan. She was so lovely, she took his breath away. And so obviously pregnant that he couldn't imagine Mr. Petrie hiring her. "You're the new housekeeper? Mrs. Putnam told me she had given notice." He couldn't keep the admiration from creeping into his voice.

"I'm not sure," Megan said after a brief hesitation. "I hope to be hired permanently. Why don't you go upstairs to the children. I'm sure they're anxious to begin their lessons."

Seymore's face flamed. "You must think me rude, Mrs. Kelly. Forgive me. If you were my wife, I'd not let you care for other men's children."

"I'm a widow, Mr. Seymore."

Seymore was really flustered now, so much so that Megan took pity on him. "If you take lunch with the children, I'll see you then."

Taking the dismissal in stride, Seymore bounded up the stairs.

A few minutes later, Megan found her way to the

kitchen, where a large, sour-faced woman was peeling vegetables. She looked up at Megan and scowled. "Who are you? How did you get in the house?"

"I'm Megan Kelly. Mr. Petrie hired me to look after the children."

The stocky, raw-boned woman gave Megan a look that conveyed her skepticism about her employer's hiring an Irishwoman. "So Buella Putnam left. Mr. Petrie should have found someone when she first gave notice."

"I was fortunate enough to apply for the job before anyone else applied."

"What would Mr. Petrie want with the likes of you? Irish, ain't you? And pregnant to boot. Mr. Petrie ain't the kind to take pity on shanty Irish immigrants."

Megan's chin rose fractionally. "Mrs. Putnam left Mr. Petrie in a bind."

"She gave notice. She's been with the Petries since before the mister went away to war, but age caught up with her. Them brats were too much for her to handle after Mr. Petrie divorced their mother. Scandalous, I say. Gray Petrie always was a wild one. Never could understand why he came home from the war and divorced a sweet woman like Lilith."

Megan's mouth gaped open. "Divorce? Oh, my."

"Oh my, indeed," the cook agreed. "I'm Mrs. Hooper. Been cooking for the Petries since before old Cyrus Petrie and his wife moved to California and left his son the business. A word of advice—keep the children out of the kitchen. They disrupt my day."

"Don't you like children, Mrs. Hooper?"

"No more nor no less than the next person," Mrs. Hooper grumbled. "Why, even their own father don't cotton to them much. Speaking of children, Mrs. Kelly," she added, "when is yours due?" Her keen gaze settled knowingly on Megan's rounded middle. "December, I think."

"Then I guess you won't be hanging around here long. Let's hope Mr. Petrie will hire a proper house-keeper and you can go back to your husband."

"I . . . I don't have a husband. I'm a widow."

Mrs. Hooper hooted in disbelief. "Sure you are, dearie. More like you got yourself in the family way and are passing yourself off as a widow." She chuck-led. "Won't be the first time some poor girl used that excuse. Far be it from me to condemn. I've never been married yet, and I call myself Mrs. Hooper."

Megan decided that no reply was called for in view of the woman's hostility. Was the entire household at odds with one another? What was wrong? Could no one bridge the chasm between Mr. Petrie and his children?

"Can I help, Mrs. Hooper? The children are at their lessons, and I have nothing to do at the moment. It smells wonderful in here."

Megan's mouth watered and her stomach rum-bled. She was so hungry that the aroma from the fresh bread cooling on the table made her giddy. She swayed and caught hold of the counter to steady her-self.

"What's wrong with you, girl?" Mrs. Hooper asked. "You ain't sick, are you? It wouldn't do to bring sick-ness to those innocent children."

Megan bit back a smile. It appeared that Mrs. Hooper was more bark than bite. She'd hazard a guess that the woman was more tenderhearted than she let on.

"I'm not sick, Mrs. Hooper. Just hungry. I . . . I for-got to eat this morning."

Mrs. Hooper eyed Megan narrowly. "For pity's sake, girl, don't faint on me. Sit yourself down and have a slice of fresh bread."

Megan sank into the nearest chair, which happened to be at the well-scrubbed table, while the cook placed a generous slice of bread and a crock of creamy butter before her. Megan buttered the bread and stuffed nearly the entire slice into her mouth. When Mrs. Hooper returned with a glass of milk, she gasped in shock.

"For pity's sake, girl, don't gobble your food. There's plenty more where that came from. How long did you say it's been since you've eaten?"

"Too long," Megan admitted. "This is delicious bread." Another piece appeared before her, and that too disappeared in minutes. When Mrs. Hooper offered her another, Megan sat back and shook her head. "That will hold me till lunch. Mr. Petrie said I could eat with the children."

"If he said so, then I reckon you can," the cook allowed grudgingly. "Why don't you lie down and rest in Mrs. Putnam's old room until lunchtime. You look ready to drop. Go straight through the kitchen to the back hall. Second door on the right."

"I don't mind helping," Megan offered.

"I don't need help. Been cooking for this family without help since afore you were born. Off with you now."

Megan smiled to herself. The cook was a good woman at heart. Like the rest of this restrained family, she tried to hide her true feelings behind a facade of gruffness. Something was very wrong here. Starting with Mr. Grayson Petrie, who appeared cold and passionless, down to little Alex, each member of the household had a fear of showing affection. Such behavior had become so commonplace that even the cook responded in the same curt manner as the master. Accustomed to a large, boisterous, happy brood, Megan felt overwhelming pity for the family and wished she could help in some small way.

*   *   *

Gray was distracted during the long day, so much so that even his assistant remarked on it. "Aren't you feeling well today, Gray?" Robert Proud asked. "You seem out of sorts."

"My housekeeper left this morning. She had given notice, but I expected her to stay until I replaced her. I had to leave the children with a virtual stranger. I really should leave early and stop at the employment agency to hire someone on a permanent basis. We can both use an early night, Rob."

"Thank God. My wife and children were beginning to feel neglected. I'll bet your children feel the same. It'll be good to join my family for supper for a change."

Gray stared at Rob. He hadn't realized just what a slave driver he'd been until Rob voiced his pleasure at being given an early night. Guilt brought a flush to his face. He'd become too immersed in his flourishing business and spent too little time getting to know his own children. He loved them beyond reason but had difficulty expressing it. They had been so tiny when he'd left for war, they hardly remembered him when he returned. There had been no time to win their love before he took them from their faithless mother.

"Perhaps we should skip these late-night sessions," Gray suggested. "At least until after the holidays."

Rob smiled his agreement. "Suits me, Gray. I'm off, then. See you in the morning."

Gray let himself into the house at the unheard-of hour of six o'clock. He couldn't recall when he'd been home early enough to see the children before they were tucked into bed. He smiled when he envisioned their surprise at seeing him so early. His smile faltered when he recalled that he must somehow dismiss the very pregnant Mrs. Kelly before the new housekeeper arrived in the morning.

Gray hung his coat and hat on the hall tree and strode into the dining room. He paused at the doorway, strangely moved by the sight of his smiling children seated around the table with Mrs. Kelly. He felt like an interloper in his own home. He sincerely wished he could achieve that kind of intimacy with his children.

Beth's fork halted midway to her mouth when she noticed her father standing in the doorway. "Papa! What are you doing home?" Her outburst brought Mrs. Hooper from the kitchen.

"Please set a place for me, Mrs. Hooper. I'll join the children and Mrs. Kelly for dinner."

"Will wonders never cease," the cook muttered as she banged down a plate and silver. Obviously the crusty old woman held no fear of losing her job, for she offered her opinion with impunity.

"How did the day go, Mrs. Kelly?" Gray asked Megan. "I hope the children weren't too difficult."

"The children are no more difficult than any other children their age. We got along fine."

Beth sent Megan a defiant look, as if challenging her remark.

"How did your lessons go?" Gray wondered as he looked from Beth to Alex.

"Mr. Seymore made me memorize the Preamble to the Constitution," Beth complained.

"And he made me do the multiplication tables to five," Alex objected.

"Mr. Seymore seems a competent young man," Megan remarked. "I think he's very good for the children. They are too much alone."

Gray took the remark personally. "Are you criticizing my ability to raise my children, Mrs. Kelly? I

233

do the best I can. My business takes a great deal of my time."

"Oh, no sir," Megan denied hastily, "I'd never do that. 'Tis sorry I am for presuming to interfere."

Megan looked so stricken that Gray chastised himself for rounding on her. He wasn't comfortable with his decision concerning the woman, but he had no desire to take on another dependent, which he would be doing if he allowed the Irish widow to stay on as housekeeper.

"After you finish eating, Mrs. Kelly, I'll see you home," Gray said, pretending great interest in the food on his plate. "You'll be amply reimbursed for staying with the children today."

Megan's fork clattered against her plate. "You're sending me away?" Her stricken expression gave Gray a moment of distress, which he promptly ignored. He had the children's well-being to consider.

"I told you this morning you weren't what I was looking for. I allowed you to remain for the day because I hadn't the time to hire a proper housekeeper. I had an important business meeting to attend and was desperate. But I took care of hiring Mrs. Putnam's replacement before coming home tonight. The new housekeeper will arrive tomorrow morning."

"We don't want a new housekeeper!" Beth cried, turning her chair over as she leaped to her feet. "Alex and I can take care of ourselves."

"Sit down, Beth," Gray said quietly. "You are too young to know what you want."

"Are not!" Alex said rebelliously. "We know what we want."

"What *do* you want?" Gray genuinely wanted to know.

Beth answered for both of them. "We don't want

234

a housekeeper. We want a mother, and brothers and sisters."

Gray looked abashed. "You want to live with your mother?"

Beth looked at her brother, and they shook their heads in unison. "Mama doesn't want us, either. We want a mother who will pay attention to us when you're too busy for us."

Gray felt their need keenly, yet he feared he could never trust another woman enough to remarry. It would have to be a special woman, one capable of lavishing love and affection on his children. The love and affection he didn't know how to give them. He had failed them and it made him sad.

"For the time being," Gray temporized, "a housekeeper will suffice. Now, do you think you can entertain yourselves while I take Mrs. Kelly home? I'll ask Mrs. Hooper to stay late tonight to keep an eye on you."

"I don't care if Mrs. Kelly does leave," Beth lied. "I don't like her anyway."

"I don't like her, either," Alex echoed.

"You're excused, children," Gray said sternly. After they trooped up the stairs, Gray turned to Megan. "You'll have to forgive them. I told you they were a handful."

Megan's eyes remained fixed to her plate as a large tear slid down her cheek. What was she going to do now? Where would she go? She was so hoping Mr. Petrie would allow her to stay on. Counting on it, in fact. Her prospects for the future were growing dimmer and dimmer.

"There is nothing to forgive, Mr. Petrie. Your children lack affection. They've been hurt; lashing out at others is a way of expressing themselves."

Unwilling to lay bare his family problems before a stranger, Gray rose abruptly. "My children are my

problem. I'll take you home if you're ready to leave."
He felt like a hard-hearted cad but he had to consider
his children's welfare.

"No need, I can see myself home."

"I wouldn't hear of it. It's freezing outside. I left
the carriage out front."

Megan rose awkwardly, wondering if she still had
a home. More likely she'd be locked out of her flat
and forced to huddle in a doorway tonight, trying to
keep from freezing to death.

Chapter Three

"You live here?" Gray asked, grimacing in distaste. The crumbling old tenement wasn't fit to be occupied, he thought as he lifted Megan down from the carriage.

"Thank you, Mr. Petrie, I'll be perfectly fine now." Megan feared Mr. Hemmingway's reaction when she tried to enter her flat and couldn't bear to have the wealthy Grayson Petrie witness her embarrassment.

"Indeed not, Mrs. Kelly, I'll see you to your door. The sidewalks are glazed with ice, and I'd never forgive myself if you fell."

As if giving credence to his warning, Megan's feet slid from beneath her and she made a desperate grab for Gray. Gray grasped her shoulders and held her steady, keeping a tight grip on her as they climbed the stairs to the door. Megan was stunned at how safe she felt in Grayson Petrie's strong arms. She knew instinctively that he would protect her even if his own safety was in jeopardy. He was that kind of man.

"On what floor is your flat?" Gray asked once they were inside and faced with several flights of stairs.

"Third floor." Gray sent her a startled look but withheld comment. "Come along, then." Megan was grateful he hadn't removed his arm from her shoulders, for she desperately needed his strength.

"Well, well, if it isn't the little widow." Hemmingway appeared from the shadows, as if he had been waiting for her. "I see you took my advice and found yourself a protector."

Gray stiffened, subduing the urge to strike the smirking man. "Who are you?"

"I'm the landlord. And before you go up to the lady's room for a bit of fun, I suggest you pay her back rent. You arrived just in time. I was about to change the lock on the door. Got a new tenant coming tomorrow."

"How much does Mrs. Kelly owe?"

Hemmingway named an amount that seemed outrageous to Gray, considering the condition of the building. It was probably swarming with rats and vermin. Nevertheless, he dug in his pocket for the amount and thrust it at the landlord.

"My, you are eager, aren't you? Don't know how you'll get past her big belly, but that's your problem." Hemmingway looked at the money in his hand, then back at Gray. "This is enough for the back rent, but it doesn't cover this month's."

So great was Megan's misery, she wanted to melt into the woodwork. Never had she suffered such acute embarrassment.

A muscle in Gray's jaw twitched. It took tremendous effort to keep from pounding the man into the ground. He was so angry that he blurted out something he had no intention of saying and would probably regret later. "Mrs. Kelly will no longer require the flat." He shoved the man aside. "Get out of the way. I'm taking Mrs. Kelly upstairs to gather her belongings."

Hemmingway smiled knowingly. "Why not set your doxy up here? I can let you have a better flat on the second floor for a small difference in rent."

Megan gasped in outrage and stepped from the protection of Gray's arms to confront Hemmingway squarely. "You're a despicable toad, Mr. Hemmingway. Mr. Petrie is a gentleman and has been nothing but kind to me." Her eyes blazed with fury, and Gray felt reluctant admiration as she vented her Irish temper upon the landlord. At that moment he thought her the most captivating woman he'd ever known.

"See here," Hemmingway sputtered, "you've no cause to insult me. You're nothing but Irish trash. You just proved it by bringing home a man. And in your condition, too. You ought to be ashamed of yourself. Go on, get your belongings. You're no longer welcome here."

"Come along, Mrs. Kelly," Gray urged, grasping her arm and pulling her gently up the stairs. "Don't waste your breath on this scum." What he didn't say was that he intended to notify the building inspector first thing in the morning about the pitiful condition of the tenement.

"Aye, you're right," Megan agreed, "but I shouldn't have lost my temper. He might have allowed me to stay until I found work." She gave Gray a wobbly smile. "I'll pay you back, Mr. Petrie, as soon as I get back on my feet."

"We'll worry about that later," Gray muttered, thinking he was out of his mind to shoulder this kind of responsibility.

I might be dead later, Megan thought but did not say. "You're a kind man, Mr. Petrie."

Gray gave a snort of laughter. "Few people would agree with you."

The hallway reeked of rotten cabbage, and Gray wrinkled his nose in disgust. Garbage littered the floor, and they had to maneuver around it to reach Megan's flat. Gray took the key from her hand, opened the door, and followed her inside. He quickly found a lamp and struck a light.

"It's freezing in here." Gray walked to the coal shuttle, found it empty, and cursed beneath his breath. "Hurry before you catch your death."

While Megan packed her meager belongings in a canvas bag, Gray allowed his gaze to wander around the shabby apartment. It consisted of two rooms—a combination living room and bedroom, and a tiny space that served as a kitchen. There was no indication that Megan kept or cooked food in her flat.

"I'm ready," Megan said when she noted Gray's distraction.

"Let's go, this place depresses me." Taking her bag in one hand and her elbow in the other, they started the long trek down the rickety stairs.

When they reached the carriage, Megan stopped abruptly. "You've been more than kind, Mr. Petrie, but I can't allow you to put yourself out for me. Go home to your children. They need you."

Gray searched her face, seeing beyond the beauty of her features to something far deeper. He saw strength and determination and pride. And hopelessness. It was that very hopelessness that brought Gray to a decision. "Where will you go, Mrs. Kelly? Do you have relatives living in the city?"

"All my relatives are in Ireland, Mr. Petrie. But don't worry, I'll be just fine. I have the money you gave me for taking care of the children today."

Gray snorted in derision. "How long will that last? Get into the carriage, Mrs. Kelly."

When Megan balked, he picked her up bodily and thrust her inside. He was surprised at how light she was despite the added weight of her pregnancy. Had she been starving herself? he wondered. While he was making money hand over fist, this poor woman was slowly starving, and there probably were plenty of others like her living in the city. The least he could do was make sure this brave woman had a warm bed and food. He no longer cared if she was a widow or something other than she pretended. All he saw was someone in desperate need of help. This Irishwoman was an enigma to him. Until he met her, he'd only known women like Lilith, women who thought only of themselves and their own selfish needs.

"Where are you taking me?" Megan asked warily. "I refuse to go to the workhouse."

"I'm taking you home."

"Home?"

"My home. I've changed my mind. I want you for my housekeeper. The children will appreciate someone younger in the house. You'll find the pay generous, and you can have Sundays off."

Megan's face lit up. "Housekeeper? You mean it? Oh, Mr. Petrie, you don't know how grateful I am."

"I think I do."

Suddenly her smile wobbled. "But the baby . . ."

"We'll face that when we come to it."

"Then I accept gladly, and thank you. I'll care for your children as if they were my very own. I'm already fond of them."

Megan settled down in the comfortable bed that once belonged to Mrs. Putnam and dreamed pleasant dreams. She awoke the next morning to the rattle of pots in the kitchen. Afraid she'd overslept, she rose quickly, washed in icy-cold water, threw on her shabby dress, and hurried into the kitchen. Mrs. Hooper greeted her with surprise.

"You still here? Will wonders never cease!"

Megan gave her a broad smile. "Mr. Petrie asked me to stay on as housekeeper."

Mrs. Hooper's gaze settled on Megan's bulging stomach. "Far be it from me to pass judgment. I ain't the boss here. Well, if you're going to stay, you may as well call me Clara."

"And I'm Megan. What time do the children arise? I'll go awaken them."

"Seven o'clock, but the mister usually gets them up before he comes down to breakfast. If you want to make yourself useful, you can set the table."

Megan complied gladly, even humming as she applied herself to the pleasing task of placing spotless china and gleaming silver on the long dining room table. Handling such fine things brought her a kind of satisfaction she had never known before or ever expected to know. She and Patrick would never have been rich or had such beautiful things, for Patrick had been a fun-loving soul who tended to squander money.

Gray entered the dining room in a state of agitation. He had overslept and was anxious to get to the office. Sleep had eluded him until the wee hours of the morning, when he'd finally dozed off. He couldn't imagine why thoughts of Mrs. Kelly—hell, he didn't even know her first name—should keep him awake. He feared he had acted rashly last night, adding another burden to those he already shouldered. He kept thinking about the child the woman carried and wondered how the household would react to a newborn babe. How *he* would react. Lord, he hadn't even been around when his own children were tiny.

"Good morning," Gray said, walking past Megan to take his place at the head of the table.

"Good morning, Mr. Petrie. I'll see if Mrs. Hooper has your breakfast ready."

"Have you had your own breakfast?"

"No, not yet. I'll eat when everyone is through."

"You'll be busy with the children then. Tell Clara to fix your breakfast so you can join us."

Megan looked dubious. "I don't think . . ."

"I am your employer, aren't I?"

"Oh, aye, most assuredly."

"Then set yourself a place and eat with us. I didn't hire you to wait on us. You're here to see that the household is run efficiently and that the children are clean and moderately well-behaved."

"What about the cleaning, washing, and ironing and such? Surely Mrs. Hooper doesn't perform those chores."

Gray laughed. "Mrs. Hooper cooks and cleans up the kitchen, period. A maid comes in three times a week to clean. And the wash is sent out once a week."

Megan's mouth dropped open. "But that must cost a fortune. I thought a housekeeper did all those chores."

"Not my housekeeper. Especially not one in your condition. See that my children are happy, Mrs. Kelly, and I'll be happy."

Megan opened her mouth to reply that everyone would be happier if they'd learn to show affection, but the children trooped into the dining room just then, forestalling her answer. Beth saw Megan and stopped abruptly. Alex plowed into her and fell flat on his little behind. Gray leaped from his chair and helped him up.

"Mrs. Kelly! What are you doing here? I thought . . . Papa said . . ."

"I know what I said, sweetheart, but a man is entitled to change his mind."

"Is Mrs. Kelly going to stay with us?" Alex wanted to know.

"I hired her last night. I'll stop by the employment

agency on my way to the office and let them know I've already filled the position. Does that please you?"

Beth shrugged, displaying neither pleasure nor displeasure, but her eyes held a glow Gray hadn't noticed before. Alex, following his big sister's lead, merely scowled.

"Since I hear no objection, I'll take that as an endorsement," Gray said, digging into the food Mrs. Hooper placed before him. "Eat, children, for I'm sure you have a busy day ahead of you. Sit down and join us, Mrs. Kelly. No one in this house goes hungry. And by the way," he added as an afterthought, "I'll be home in time to take dinner with you tonight."

After Gray left for work, Megan asked Beth to give her a tour of the house. Complying with alacrity, Beth led her from room to room, shyly proud of being treated in such an adult manner. They ended up in the nursery, and Megan suggested a game she had often played with her brothers and sisters. At first the children were reluctant to give their trust, but after a while they lost their reserve and joined in the game wholeheartedly. Though Megan could not romp with them, she derived great enjoyment from watching.

Try as she might, Megan could not help pondering the unacceptable situation between Grayson Petrie and his children. Was Mr. Petrie one of those men who could neither show nor receive love? she wondered curiously. Why had he divorced his wife? It was all so confusing, but no matter how much she might wish it otherwise, it was not Megan's place to approve or disapprove. Oh, how she wished she could change things! Didn't the man know how much his children needed him?

"Papa said he's going to be home early again tonight," Beth said when Megan called a halt to the game so the children could calm down before the tutor arrived.

"Aye, won't that be wonderful?" Megan replied enthusiastically.

"Why would he come home early twice in a row?" Alex wondered. "He never had time for us before."

"Neither did Mama," Beth added with such overwhelming sadness that Megan dismissed her reservations and vowed to do something about it.

"I think your father misses you," Megan argued. "What do you say we do something special tonight for dinner?"

"Something special? Whatever do you mean?" Beth asked.

"We could have a picnic. That would be different."

"It's too cold," Alex said plaintively.

"We've never been on a picnic," Beth said wistfully.

"Never?" Megan couldn't believe her ears. She and her siblings had always loved picnics and went on many during the summer months. Even Patrick had loved picnics. After they wed, he had taken her on one every Sunday, weather permitting. "Mary preserve us. If you've never been on a picnic, then 'tis about time you did. We'll have our picnic tonight on the parlor floor."

"Papa won't like it," Beth predicted. "He'll think it's silly."

Megan was inclined to agree but kept her thoughts to herself. "I'll speak with Mrs. Hooper. Why don't you get out your books and go over your lessons? Mr. Seymore will be here shortly."

"Are you daft, girl?" Clara Hooper asked. "Only a fool would expect a man like Gray Petrie to sit on the floor to eat."

"I'll accept responsibility, Clara, if you prepare the food. Something simple that the children can eat with a minimum of utensils and mess. I'll take care of everything else."

"You're headed for disappointment, Megan, but you'll find that out for yourself. If you're thinking to change things, I suggest you mind your own business. I've been here longer than you and have the sense to know when things are hopeless."

"Nothing is ever hopeless," Megan said softly.

Megan wasn't just thinking of Gray Petrie and his children, but of her own situation. Fate had intervened just when things looked the bleakest. She'd had nearly a year of marriage to her childhood sweetheart before Patrick died and cast her adrift without friends or money. For her child's sake, she had pulled herself together and faced the fact that life went on no matter how desperately she missed Patrick. She had almost surrendered to defeat when she was evicted, but then fate had stepped in and brought the Petrie family into her life. Perhaps God had placed her here for a purpose.

Gray's steps were surprisingly light as he entered the house shortly before six o'clock that evening. The weather had moderated somewhat but was still raw and blustery for late October. The moment he stepped inside the door, he noted a marked difference. The atmosphere seemed warmer somehow, almost welcoming. He would have given the world if the children were on hand to greet him with hugs, but he knew how unlikely that was. He was a stranger to his own children, and he didn't know how to remedy the situation.

Gray stopped just inside the foyer, sensing something, something he couldn't put his finger on.

Unconsciously he found himself looking for Mrs. Kelly's pert face and gently rounded body. She was one of those rare women whose natural beauty was enhanced by impending motherhood.

As if his thoughts had conjured her up, Megan entered the foyer. Gray thought she appeared nervous and hoped the children hadn't been too much for her to handle. The twinkle in her eye soon put his mind at ease.

"I hope you're hungry, Mr. Petrie. The children and I have a surprise for you tonight."

Gray frowned. He didn't like surprises. "That depends. What have you cooked up? Today has been exceptionally tiring."

"A picnic," Megan said brightly. For the children's sake, she hoped he didn't object too strenuously.

Gray's shapely brows rose sharply. "Have you looked out the window lately? I'm not about to freeze to death for anyone."

"It's a picnic in the parlor, Papa!" Beth exclaimed, skipping into the foyer. "We've never been on a picnic."

Gray groaned in dismay. Inadequate would hardly describe how he felt, knowing that his own children had never sampled one of life's simple pleasures. It took a poor, homeless immigrant to show him how little was required to make a child happy. Beth was grinning and jumping up and down, and Alex could hardly contain his excitement.

"Megan said a picnic would be fun," Alex declared. "We're having it on the parlor floor. Come on, Papa." He grasped Gray's hand and tugged with all his might. When Gray appeared rooted to the spot, Beth grasped his other hand and together they pulled him into the parlor.

Megan, Gray thought. So that was her first name. Somehow it fit. But it wasn't proper for the children

247

to address her so familiarly. "I'm sure Mrs. Kelly would prefer that you address her properly, children."

"I asked them to call me Megan," Megan said. "In fact, I prefer it."

"Here we are, Papa. What do you think?"

Gray stared at the large spot in the center of the parlor floor where the furniture had been shoved aside. A white tablecloth had been spread with plates and silver, and a huge picnic basket rested at its center. "It . . . it's quite nice," he said, at a loss for words.

"It will be such fun!" Beth cried. "Sit down, everyone."

Gray lowered his tall frame to the floor and was happily surprised when Alex threw his little arms around his neck and hugged him tightly. It was the first time either of the children had voluntarily offered affection, and his eyes grew misty. When he looked up at Megan in wonder, her radiant smile warmed his soul.

Chapter Four

The breakthrough in Gray's relationship with his children didn't happen overnight as Megan hoped. The children remained cool and unreceptive to Gray's overtures after the picnic on the parlor floor, and Gray seemed preoccupied and remote. October slipped into November with little fanfare. One evening, Gray returned home after the children had been put to bed and made straight for the liquor cabinet. Since Mrs. Hooper had already left for the night, Megan waited for Gray in the parlor, ready to serve him dinner should he want it.

Gray didn't notice Megan as he poured himself a generous measure of brandy and downed it in one gulp. His hand shook as he poured another. It was the first time Megan had seen him drink.

"Is something wrong, Mr. Petrie?"

The glass fell from Gray's hand and shattered on the floor. "Must you creep up on people like that, Mrs. Kelly?"

"I've been here all along. You just didn't see me." She rose from the chair and approached him gingerly. She could tell by the white line around his lips that something was desperately wrong. "I've kept dinner warm for you."

"I'll eat if you join me," Gray said, feeling an unaccountable need for Megan's company.

"I've already eaten with the children."

"Then sit and keep me company, unless you're too tired."

His need seemed so great that Megan didn't have the heart to refuse. "I'm not too tired. I'll join you if you wish. I could use a glass of warm milk before retiring."

Gray picked at his food with little appetite while Megan watched him with increasing alarm. Despite his request for her company, he seemed disinclined to talk.

"Perhaps you would feel better if you told me what is bothering you," Megan suggested shyly. She didn't want to intrude on something that was none of her business, but she was beginning to feel like a part of this family.

Gray lifted his gaze from his plate and searched her face, genuinely surprised by her concern. "I never thought that bitch would do this to me." The venom in his voice sent chills racing down Megan's spine.

"Who are you talking about?"

"Lilith, my ex-wife. Or she will be my ex-wife in a very short time. The divorce won't actually be final until a year after filing, which is the last day of November. Lilith returned from Europe without her lover and is seeking permanent custody of the children. When I took them from her, she didn't contest my taking custody. All she cared about was leaving the country with her lover to escape scandal."

Megan was stunned. "What changed her mind?"

"Damned if I know, but you can bet it has something to do with money. God, Megan, I can't bear to lose my children. They mean everything to me."

Megan was startled by Gray's use of her first name, but somehow it sounded right coming from his lips. "What are you going to do about it?"

"I've already discussed it with my lawyer. I'm going to fight it, of course. It shouldn't be difficult to prove Lilith an unfit mother. I have a feeling it isn't the children she wants but something else. I suspect I'll learn very soon."

Suddenly Gray noticed the pained look on Megan's face and realized that he was burdening her with problems that didn't concern her. She looked tired, as if these last weeks of pregnancy were weighing her down. "Why don't you go to bed, Megan? You look exhausted." With a start he realized that he had addressed her by her first name and that it felt natural and right. "I'm sorry," he apologized. "I hope I didn't offend you. You have a beautiful name."

"I don't mind," Megan said softly. "The children call me Megan, and so should you."

"Only if you call me Gray."

"Oh, but it's . . ."

"Perfectly all right. I'd feel more comfortable using your first name if you used mine."

"Very well." She sent him a tentative smile. "I think I will retire, Mr. . . . Gray." His name tasted sweet on her tongue. "Good night."

"Oh, Megan, before you leave, I forgot to tell you I visited Doctor Dunbar earlier today. He's agreed to examine you in his office tomorrow morning at ten o'clock. The children will be having their lessons with Mr. Seymore, so you won't be missed. I've arranged for a carriage and driver to pick you up. And on the way home, you're to stop at the dressmaker and pick up the dresses I ordered made for you."

Megan's mouth dropped open in shock. "You want me to see a doctor? As you can see, I'm perfectly healthy."

"We can't be too safe now, can we? There's a child's life at stake. If everything is normal, Doctor Dunbar will arrange for a midwife for your lying-in."

"You know I can't pay."

"Consider it part of your benefits. You will do as I say, won't you?"

Megan found it surprising that Gray had taken time to think of her with the problems confronting him. The least she could do was comply with his wishes. "Aye, if you wish."

Gray smiled, erasing the worry lines between his eyes and making him seem young and vulnerable. "You won't forget the dressmaker, will you?"

"Why? Why are you doing this?"

"I've noticed that your dresses are straining at the seams." She blushed furiously. "You need something comfortable to wear these last weeks. I instructed the dressmaker to make up the dresses in soft pastels. Nothing black. I know you're still in mourning, but I'd prefer you to wear something cheerful around the children."

"I don't like black either. And Patrick wouldn't like me wearing it. He loved seeing me wear bright colors."

"A wise man," Gray said. "Off to bed with you."

"Will you be all right, Gray?" She worried about him excessively and wondered about the kind of woman he had married and then divorced. What had she done to warrant such treatment?

Gray felt a melting sensation in the vicinity of his heart. He couldn't recall the last time anyone had been concerned about him. "I'm fine, Megan. Good night."

"When is your baby coming, Megan?" Beth asked excitedly as Megan prepared for her visit to the doctor's office. "I love babies. Will you let me hold it?"

"Of course."

"Will the baby be our sister or brother?" Alex wanted to know.

"Silly goose," Beth chided. "Papa would have to marry Megan to make her baby our brother or sister."

Alex's face lit up. Megan thought he looked just like his father when he smiled. "Then he *should* marry her. Maybe he will if we ask him."

Megan was mortified. What would Gray Petrie want with the likes of her? If he remarried, it would be to someone of his own class. She was surprised that a handsome, obviously virile man like Gray didn't have a string of women waiting in line for his favors. But in the weeks she'd lived in the Petrie household, she saw no sign of another woman in his life.

"Oh, no, you mustn't mention it to your father! 'Tisn't right to even suggest such a thing. Be good for Mr. Seymore. I'll be back soon."

After an embarrassing examination and some pointed questions, the doctor pronounced Megan somewhat underweight but in good health and saw no reason a midwife couldn't deliver the babe. He told Megan he would arrange everything and let her employer know where the woman could be reached when her time arrived, which should be sometime in January. He couldn't be sure of the exact date because Megan had been so vague about her missed woman's time. Thanks to Grayson Petrie, she could now look forward to a brighter future than she'd anticipated a few weeks ago. She worried that Gray would change his mind about keeping her on as housekeeper after her child was born but tried to put it from her mind.

A stop at the dressmaker proved enlightening. Megan found three dresses waiting for her. They had been fashioned of material she never could have afforded and were in muted colors suitable for a widow—soft mauve, light gray, and pale blue. They were fashioned to play down her pregnancy while allowing for comfort. The dress she wore now was indeed straining at the seams, and she had let it out repeatedly until there was no more material left to use. Included with the dresses were petticoats, stockings and undergarments. And a coat trimmed in fur. Everything was so beautiful that Megan cried all the way home. She had never met a kinder, gentler man than Gray Petrie. She searched her mind for a way to convince his children of his worth as a father.

Megan waited eagerly for Gray to come home that night so she could show off her new dress. The children were upstairs playing, and she hoped he'd arrive in time to share dinner with them. Her patience was rewarded when she heard him at the front door. Moving awkwardly, she met him as he stepped into the foyer. He looked worried, and she wondered if he'd solved any of his problems with his ex-wife since they'd discussed it a few nights ago. He looked up, saw her, and smiled.

"You look quite fetching, Megan. Do you like the dresses?"

"Aye, and everything else you bought. It's too much, Gray, I'll never be able to repay you."

"Many employers buy uniforms for their employees. Consider the clothing another benefit. After the babe is born, we'll see about having something appropriate made for your slimmer figure. Are the children upstairs? I'm not too late to join them for dinner, am I?"

"Your timing is perfect. I'll call them."

They left the foyer together but stopped abruptly at the sound of vigorous rapping on the front door. "I'll get it," Gray said. "You go fetch the children."

Megan turned and climbed slowly up the stairs. Gray watched her clumsy gait, feeling as if the warmth had suddenly left the room. The woman was pregnant with another man's child, yet he couldn't recall when he'd seen anyone more beautiful. She was also wise beyond her years. For someone so young, Megan seemed to know how to make his little family come alive. He hadn't known women like that existed. His children were growing more than fond of her. Even crusty Mrs. Hooper was protective of her, and he . . . well, she made him feel things that had nothing to do with protectiveness, although that was there too.

The annoying rapping on the door brought Gray's wayward thoughts to a halt, and he crossed the foyer to admit his visitor.

"Hello, Gray, surprised to see me?"

"Lilith, what in the hell are you doing here?"

"Did you receive notice of my suit to gain custody of the children?"

"I received it. You know damn well you don't want the children. You never wanted them. Where is your lover?"

"May I come in?"

Gray opened the door. "Suit yourself, as long as you don't stay long." She walked into the parlor and sat down with great aplomb.

Connie Mason

Gray followed but remained standing. "Why are you here?"

Lilith, a delicate blonde with cornflower-blue eyes, wet her bottom lip with the tip of her tongue and gave Gray a coy smile. "I suppose you know our divorce will be final at the end of the month."

"I know. So what?"

"According to law, we can reverse the divorce if we decide to live together as man and wife."

Dumbfounded, Gray stared at her. "Why would we want to do that? What about your lover? Have you grown tired of him already?"

Lilith laughed, the sound harsh and derisive. "After he spent every cent of the settlement you gave me, he disappeared. I had to make my way back to New York alone. I'm broke, Gray. You owe me after putting me through the embarrassment of a public divorce. If we cancel this divorce, my self-respect will be restored and we can raise the children together. If you refuse, I'll retaliate by going through with the custody hearing. If I gain custody of the children, you'll have to pay me a generous monthly stipend for their support."

"You heartless bitch!" Gray spat. "All you care about is money, not the children's welfare. Nothing will ever convince me to take you back as my wife."

She shrugged expansively. "A woman has to look out for herself. You're forcing my hand."

"I'm not going to let you have the children. I'll fight you every step of the way and spend every cent I have to keep them."

"Mama! When did you get back? Papa told us you were traveling." Beth entered the parlor, saw her mother, and rushed over to greet her. Alex hung back, unsure of his feelings where his mother was concerned.

"Hello, dear," Lilith said, offering a cool cheek to

256

her daughter. "How would you like to live with me?"

"Over my dead body," Gray gritted from between clenched teeth.

"Are you and Papa going to live in the same house again?"

"It's a possibility," Lilith conceded.

"No! That's completely out of the question."

"Gray, dinner's ready. Mrs. Hooper says . . . Oh, I'm sorry, I didn't know you had company." Spying Lilith, Megan stopped abruptly, wobbling unsteadily and losing her balance. Gray reached out to steady her.

Lilith's gaze swept over Megan with insulting scrutiny. "My word, who is that? You didn't waste any time bringing your whore into the house, did you? You're a potent bastard, I'll give you that. I wonder what the judge will say about this development?"

"Megan's going to have a baby, Mama," Beth announced grandly.

"So I see. And soon, from the looks of her. My, my, Gray, whatever possessed you to take someone so common when you could have me?"

"Children, go tell Mrs. Hooper to serve your dinner. Megan and I will join you shortly. Your mother can have a longer visit with you before she leaves."

The children trooped out, relieved to be leaving the tense situation behind. Once they were out of earshot, Gray said, "Megan is my housekeeper."

"Surely you can make up something better than that," Lilith scoffed.

"'Tis true, Mrs. Petrie, I am Gray's—er, Mr. Petrie's housekeeper."

"You're nothing but Irish trash. From the looks of you, you're not long off the boat. Give me some credit. Gray would never hire someone like you to care for the children. He got you with child and feels responsible for you. When he and I get back together, I'll see that you are paid off and sent packing. If Gray doesn't have the guts to do it, I do."

"My God, Lilith, you haven't changed one bit. Regardless of what Megan is to me, you have no right to talk to her like that. As for you and I getting back together, you can forget it. It will never happen. And you can forget about taking the children from me. You may have a short visit with them if you wish and be on your way. I'll see you in court."

"I've already seen the children," Lilith said, rising gracefully and making a grand exit. "Tell them Mama will see them soon," she threw over her shoulder. "I'll withhold the custody suit until the end of the month. That should give you time to change your mind about us getting back together. And Gray, do send an announcement when your little bastard is born."

"Get out, Lilith—get the hell out of here! You always were an unnatural mother. Hell will freeze over before we get back together."

"I wouldn't have been a mother at all if you hadn't forced your children on me," she shot back in parting. "Don't bother coming to the door, I can let myself out."

Pale and shaken, Megan hung onto the mantel for support. Never had she encountered a woman like Gray's ex-wife. Cruel and heartless, she appeared to care for no one but herself. Megan felt justified in saying she loved Gray's children more than their own mother did.

Gray's mouth hardened as Lilith let herself out of the house. His fisted hands moved restlessly at his sides, fighting the urge to punish the woman for hurting an innocent like Megan. He turned to Megan, her stricken features tugging at his heartstrings. He walked to where she stood, small and fragile, and carefully took her into his arms. Her head fit beneath his chin as if it belonged there.

"Pay her no heed, Megan. Lilith is a vindictive woman who enjoys hurting people."

"How could you marry a woman like that?" The moment the words left her mouth, she wished them back. Gray's past was none of her business.

Absently, Gray stroked Megan's shiny black hair. "Lilith and I came from the same background. We met at a social function. We were both young, not yet twenty. She was beautiful and witty and I fell under her spell. My mother pushed for marriage, and Lilith eagerly accepted my proposal. Unfortunately, trouble began almost immediately. I learned that Lilith cared more about her social-climbing friends than having a family."

"She is the mother of your children," Megan reminded him.

"That was more my doing than hers. I was the one who wanted children. Now I feel guilty for bringing them into the world. I've failed them miserably. Lilith didn't want me to go off to war, but I wanted to fight for what I believed in. Alex was still a baby when I left, and Beth was three. My children were strangers when I returned, and I had no one to blame but myself. I abandoned them to go to war and lost them."

"And Lilith? Was she a stranger, too?"

Gray gave a bitter laugh. "That's another story. One I don't care to discuss."

"I didn't mean to pry. Perhaps we should join the children in the dining room."

Strangely, Gray was loathe to release her. Megan was like a refreshing breeze after Lilith's corruption. She felt right in his arms, even though he knew she had loved her departed husband dearly.

Megan started to move away, and the babe inside her lurched in her womb, making its presence known in the most basic way. Gray felt it and froze, looking down at Megan in wonder.

"Your babe is going to be as strong as his mother. I've never felt a babe move inside his mother before. It's quite . . ." He searched for the right word. ". . . extraordinary. No," he amended, "more than that. Miraculous."

"Did you never feel your own children move in their mother's womb?"

"You've met Lilith. Does she look like a woman who enjoyed being reminded of impending motherhood? Lilith isn't like you, Megan."

Abruptly he released her. "Come along, the children are waiting. Perhaps we can have another one of those picnics Sunday. Do you think they'd like that?"

"They'd love it, Gray. Children respond spontaneously to love, giving it freely in return. You didn't fail your children. You just don't know how to show your love."

"How did you get so wise, Megan?"

Megan lost the ability to speak when she saw Gray's eyes kindle with affection.

Patrick, help me, she silently implored. *I didn't expect this to happen but I can't seem to help myself.*

Chapter Five

"I tell you, Cantwell, I can't lose the children," Gray insisted with a hint of despair. "Lilith wants them merely to punish me for divorcing her. What kind of life could she give them, hopping from lover to lover? You're my lawyer; I'm depending on you to see that it doesn't happen. This is December. Our divorce is final, and Lilith knows now that we will never be together as husband and wife."

"Calm yourself, Gray," Mason Cantwell said. "I intend to do everything I can to see that the children stay with you. I have to warn you, though, some judges aren't favorably disposed to single fathers, and I can't predict which judge we'll get. I've been informed that Lilith's lawyer has filed the custody suit. I strongly advise that you marry before the hearing is scheduled, which will probably be shortly after the new year."

"Marry?" Gray repeated dumbly. "I'm not even romantically involved with anyone."

Connie Mason

"Come, come, Gray, surely there are one or two young women of your acquaintance eager for a husband. You're considered quite a catch. Think about it and let me know what you decide. Meanwhile I'll prepare our case on the facts you've given me concerning Lilith's numerous infidelities."

"Truthfully, Cantwell, I don't feel comfortable airing our problems in public. I don't want to hurt the children by revealing scandalous secrets about their mother. We'll use that as a last resort."

"Then I strongly advise you to persuade Lilith to drop her request for custody."

Gray gave a snort of laughter. "You don't know Lilith. I'll certainly give your suggestion careful consideration, but I don't hold out much hope for Lilith's capitulation."

"Then find a wife, Gray. At least that will impress the judge favorably." Mason Cantwell coughed discreetly. "As much as I hate to bring up the subject, keeping a pregnant woman in your home won't help your case. I don't know what she is to you and I don't care, but if you're serious about retaining custody of your children, get rid of her. Pay her off if you must."

Gray stiffened visibly. "Megan Kelly is my housekeeper. She is . . . I can't just turn her out."

"Your housekeeper. Of course," Cantwell repeated evenly. Gray could tell the lawyer didn't believe a word he said.

"Who told you about Megan?"

"Lilith's lawyer. He called on me yesterday and mentioned that your—er, housekeeper is living with you and that Lilith doesn't want the children subjected to that kind of situation."

"What a hypocrite," Gray bit out.

"It's the judge you need to convince, Gray. I'm telling you this merely to warn you that Lilith is prepared to dig up any kind of dirt she can against you.

I've tendered my advice. It's up to you to act on it."

Gray left Cantwell's office in a daze. How could he dismiss Megan when the children were beginning to care for her? She had made a difference in their lives in the short time she had been with them. She had no place to go, no one to turn to. He could give her a generous severance, but eventually that would run out, leaving her destitute. But if dismissing Megan meant the difference between losing or keeping his children, he would have no choice. With a heavy heart, he slowly made his way home.

Each day Megan moved a little more slowly as she approached the last weeks of her pregnancy. Climbing the stairs became a chore, and the children helped by not demanding it of her. The day was brisk and the fire comforting and Megan hummed happily as she sat in the parlor sewing a tiny garment for her baby while the children were at their lessons. She'd bought the material with her very first pay and had still been able to put a small amount aside against the day she was no longer needed in the Petrie household. She didn't delude herself. Gray Petrie was a handsome man. One day he would remarry and have no further need of her. She envied the woman who would share Gray's life and hoped she would love his children as much as Megan did.

Megan had tried not to become intimately involved with the family, but somehow Gray and his adorable children had found a permanent place in her heart. It was not that she had forgotten Patrick. On the contrary. She spoke to him each night, telling him about their child, somehow knowing that he heard. But no matter how hard she pretended, she knew Patrick was dead and would never answer her.

Megan's humming stopped abruptly when she

sensed Gray's presence. She looked up from her sewing, smiling when she saw him standing in the doorway, his hair dusted with white and his cheeks red.

"You're home early, Gray," she greeted him. "Isn't the snow beautiful? Christmas is just around the corner. Have you made special plans for the children? They've admired the decorated store windows and are eagerly looking forward to the holidays."

Gray walked into the room, hating what he had to do. "Truth to tell, I haven't given Christmas much thought." He sounded distracted, and Megan set her sewing aside, sensing his need to talk.

"If you have decorations put away somewhere, I'd like to put them up—with the children's help, of course. And a tree!" She clapped her hands excitedly. "Oh, Gray, we have to have a tree. We can put it up Christmas Eve and afterward pop corn and sing Christmas carols. The children will love it. I hope you don't mind that I've bought them a little something. It isn't much, of course, but I wanted to do it."

"Megan, you're going too fast for me," Gray said, dropping into a nearby chair. "First of all, you shouldn't spend your money on my children. You should save for your future. There might come a day when you'll have to depend on your own resources."

What was Gray trying to tell her? Megan wondered. Fear clutched her heart. He sounded as if he intended to dismiss her. Had she done something to anger him? Try as she might, she could think of nothing she'd done to upset Gray or the children.

Gray's long fingers tunneled distractedly through his damp hair. Megan sensed his agitation and was frightened by it. She had never seen him so upset. "Have I done something to annoy you, Gray? If I have I'm . . ."

"You've done nothing, Megan." God, he hated this,

Gray thought as Megan's eyes widened in apprehension. "I spoke with my lawyer today and he advised me to . . . to . . ." He swallowed convulsively.

"To what, Gray? What did your lawyer say to do?"

"For one thing, he advised me to marry."

Megan tried to keep her dismay from showing. "That makes sense. Do . . . do you have anyone in mind?"

"There are several possibilities."

"I understand. Once you marry, you'll no longer need a housekeeper. No matter what happens, I'll always be in your debt for coming to my rescue." She rose awkwardly and gathered up her sewing. "Do you want me to leave now or after you marry?"

Gray surged to his feet. "Dammit, Megan, I don't want you to leave at all! I want . . ." He paused dramatically, then blurted out, "I want you to marry me."

Gray couldn't believe he'd just proposed to Megan. She wasn't appropriate. Not appropriate at all. She wouldn't know how to act with his friends and certainly couldn't be expected to move comfortably in his social circle. However, because she needed a home, she offered the least threat to his freedom and privacy.

Megan swayed dizzily and Gray reached out, gently pulling her against him. "Gray, please, don't say anything you'll regret later. I know you're desperate to keep your children, but I'm not the wife for you. Find someone from your own social class. I'm sure there are women who would be thrilled to marry you."

"What about you, Megan? Do you hate the idea so much? I know you loved your husband and you're still in mourning, but he is dead. I'll be a good father to your baby for as long as we remain married. As soon as I gain permanent custody of the children, you can have an annulment."

"Marrying me will hurt your cause."

"I beg to differ with you. I need a wife, Megan, and I have damn little time to find one. The children have grown accustomed to you."

Megan didn't delude herself into thinking Gray cared for her. He was desperate, and she was handy.

"It will be a marriage of convenience, of course." He laughed nervously. "I realize that's all it could be until you recover from childbirth, but I won't pressure you even then."

God, he was digging himself deeper and deeper into a hole. He knew he lacked the willpower necessary to keep marriage to Megan strictly platonic if they remained together after her child was born. Even pregnant, Megan was a desirable woman, whose beauty glowed both inside and out. He had grown to depend on her. Somehow his freedom looked less attractive compared to the possibility of having Megan as a wife. Yet something deep and frightening prevented him from showing the growing affection he felt for Megan. He had failed his own children because of his inability to display love, and it hurt. Why couldn't he express his feelings like normal men?

Megan leaned her head against Gray's broad chest, confused and beset with doubt. Patrick had been dead less than a year, and at times she felt his presence keenly. But it was never an angry presence. Instead, he seemed pleased with the direction her life had taken. If only she could be sure.

"I need time to think, Gray. I don't know if it's the right thing to do. I'm so confused."

Gray kissed Megan's forehead, then lowered his head and placed a tender kiss on her lips. She tasted incredibly sweet, her lips lush and pliant beneath his. But he didn't want to frighten her, so he ended the kiss before he was ready and stepped away.

"Think about it, Megan. I'm going upstairs to visit the children before dinner. Perhaps they'll give me a hint of what they want for Christmas. And in answer to your question earlier—yes, there are Christmas decorations in the attic. I'll bring them down so you can sort through them. When the time comes, I'll find us the biggest tree in the city."

Touching her lips softly, Megan watched Gray walk away, mentally comparing him to Patrick. Patrick had been a boy, cheerful and happy by nature. It had been impossible to make Patrick take life seriously. He loved to laugh and play tricks on people. He was like an overgrown puppy who craved constant attention. She had loved every one of his flaws because his goodness made them easy to ignore. But Megan knew that in the fullness of time, Patrick would not have changed. He would have remained a small boy at heart while she grew and matured. Maybe, as time passed, she would have outgrown him.

During the past few weeks, Megan had learned that Gray was a man who accepted responsibility easily. There was nothing boyish about him. He was mature and kind and generous. And handsome in a way that made carrot-topped Patrick's cocky looks seem almost clownish. Gray had a capacity for loving that he hadn't totally explored, while Patrick had loved exuberantly, vocally, with little finesse. Gray would never give her cause to regret marrying him. And she cared deeply for Gray Petrie. Maybe not in the same carefree way she had loved Patrick, but she was not the same carefree girl who had once thought coming to America was a grand adventure.

Still confused, Megan realized that she needed to seek the advice of a higher authority. If she hurried, she could walk to Saint Matthew's and return before dinner. Her decision made, she went through the kitchen to her room to retrieve her coat.

"You're not going out now, are you, girl?" Clara Hooper asked when she saw Megan with her coat on. "Dinner will be ready soon. Was that the mister I heard coming home?"

"Aye, he's upstairs with the children. I thought I'd walk over to the church before dinner, Clara. I . . . there is something on my mind, and church is the best place I know to get the answers I need."

"Be careful, Megan. The sidewalks are treacherous. There will be a half foot of snow by morning. Beginning to look like Christmas."

"Don't worry, Clara, I'll be careful. Saint Matthew's isn't far."

An overwhelming sense of peace flowed over Megan when she entered the neighborhood church a short time later. Her steps were surprisingly light as she walked slowly down the aisle between rows of deserted pews. She genuflected before the altar, then eased into the front pew, reciting prayers as she gazed lovingly at the nativity scene and surrounding statues.

"Tell me what to do, God," she prayed aloud. "Should I marry a man who doesn't love me for the security he will give me and my child?"

No answer was forthcoming. She repeated her question, half expecting the answer to come from the stone walls surrounding her. Still nothing. Sighing in disappointment, she leaned her head back against the pew and closed her eyes, allowing weariness to claim her.

"*Acushla*."

The Gaelic endearment flowed over her like sweet, warm honey, and her eyes flew open. Patrick had always called her *acushla*."

"You are troubled, *acushla*."

Megan's eyes widened as her gaze took in the man sitting next to her. Surrounded by muted light, his cocky smile was as endearing as she remembered. Even the tiny laugh lines around his green eyes were the same. The unruly hank of brash red hair that fell across his forehead made her itch to push it out of his eyes.

"I've missed you, Patrick," Megan said softly, not really surprised to see him.

"I've not left you, *acushla*. I couldn't. Not until I knew you and our child were taken care of."

"I've sensed your presence. There were times when I could have sworn you were with me. I was so frightened after you . . . you left me, Patrick."

"I know."

"The lowest point in my life came when Mr. Hemmingway evicted me from my flat and I realized I was totally alone. I didn't know what to do, where to turn. I needed you so."

"I was there, *acushla*. Do you remember the newspaper that landed at your feet that night? The one with Mr. Petrie's ad?"

"Aye. But what . . ." She inhaled sharply. "You mean you . . . But how?"

"Aye, 'twas me. Mr. Petrie needed you, and you needed him."

"Then you know he's asked me to marry him. I'm so confused, Patrick. I'm beginning to care for him, but that seems so unfair to you."

"Ah, *acushla*, when I was alive, you loved me well. 'Tis time to let me go. I will always be a part of you, but you've the whole future ahead of you. I want you to be happy."

"Then you think I should marry Gray Petrie? You must know he wants me because he needs me, not because he loves me."

"The man deserves more credit than you're giving

him. Search your heart, *acushla*. You already know the answer."

Megan stared at him, memorizing his dear, familiar features. Even in death he seemed happy. "Are you a ghost, Patrick?"

"If that's what you think I am. I prefer being thought of as a happy memory."

"Will I see you again?"

"Only if you need me. But I don't think you will need me if you marry Gray Petrie. Life is sweet, Megan—enjoy it to the fullest. I always did. Mr. Petrie is a good man. He will be good to you and our child."

Megan smiled wistfully. "I'll always wonder what life would have been like had you not . . . died."

"No you won't. Not if you open your heart to a new love."

"Is that what you really want for me, Patrick?"

"You will have a better life than I could have given you."

"I already love Gray's children. But I want Gray to love me for myself, not because he needs me. And once married, I don't want an annulment, unless he presses for one."

Patrick gave her a crooked smile that brought sweet memories washing over her. "How could he not love you?"

"Thank you, Patrick. I'm so glad we had this chance to talk. There was so little time before you . . . you left me. I prayed for an answer to my dilemma, and God sent you to me. Even though I love Gray, you'll always hold a special place in my heart."

"I know. I have to go, *acushla*."

Crushing sadness brought tears to her eyes. "Can't you stay a little longer?"

"You no longer need me. I think you realize that now. Close your eyes, *acushla*."

Megan didn't want to close her eyes, knowing that Patrick would disappear if she did, but they grew so heavy that she could no longer keep them open. Resting her head against the pew, her eyelids fluttered shut. An instant later she felt a whisper-soft tingling against her mouth and let out a trembling sigh. The kiss lingered sweetly on her lips, and she smiled in perfect contentment.

Gray didn't even bother with his coat as he rushed out of the house. Stunned when Mrs. Hooper told him Megan had walked to church, he tore out of the door as if the devil were after him. In his mind he pictured Megan losing her footing on the slippery sidewalk and lying on the cold ground. Relief shuddered through him when the church came into sight and he saw nothing to indicate that Megan wasn't inside. Snow fell in solid white sheets, and darkness hovered on the horizon as Gray pushed open the church door and peered into the candlelit interior.

The church was deserted save for a lone figure sitting in the front pew. A sense of peace reached inside Gray's soul as he walked down the narrow aisle toward Megan. It had been a very long time since he'd been inside a church, and he wondered why he had stayed away so long. When he reached the front row, he slid into the pew beside Megan. Her head was tilted back and she appeared to be sleeping. She looked so serene, so beautiful that Gray could not resist placing a tender kiss on her lips. The kiss was a mere whisper across her mouth, but sweeter than any Gray had ever tasted. Megan must have thought so too, for the corners of her mouth turned up in an enchanting smile and her eyes opened slowly.

"Megan. I was terrified when I learned you left the house alone in such vile weather."

Connie Mason

Megan's gaze focused on Gray with difficulty. What had happened to Patrick? Just moments ago, Patrick was sitting next to her. He had kissed her . . . Her hand flew to her lips. She could still feel the lingering sweetness of his kiss.

"I didn't mean to startle you, Megan. Forgive me, I couldn't help kissing you."

"You kissed me? I thought . . ." Her head swiveled slowly, as if searching for something or someone.

"Are you looking for someone? You were alone when I arrived." He frowned and glanced behind him when Megan continued to stare past him.

"No . . ." She fell silent, recalling vividly the conversation she'd had with Patrick. It couldn't have been her imagination. Every word, every smile, every gesture remained clear and coherent in her mind. Patrick had been here; she could still feel his presence. She had sought an answer to her dilemma and Patrick had responded.

"Megan, are you all right? You look strange."

"I'm fine, Gray, truly. My answer is yes."

For a moment Gray looked confused. Then his brow cleared, and a warm glow kindled in his gray eyes. "Are you saying what I think you are?"

"I'll marry you, Gray. It's what Patrick would want."

"I'd rather it was what you wanted."

Megan searched his face, wondering if he'd forgotten about the annulment he'd promised her. When she married again, she wanted it to be forever.

Chapter Six

"Is Megan going to live here forever?" Alex asked when told of the impending marriage between Megan and his father.

"Perhaps," Gray replied, recalling his rash promise to have their marriage annulled.

"What will Mama say? I don't think she'll like it," Beth mused thoughtfully.

"Your mother and I are no longer married. We are each free to live our lives as we see fit. I want to keep you and Alex with me, and marrying Megan will help my cause."

Megan winced at Gray's frankness. She knew he didn't love her, but hearing it put so bluntly still hurt.

"Papa, I just thought of something!" Beth exclaimed excitedly. "I'm going to have a baby brother or sister."

"When are you and Megan getting married?" Alex wanted to know.

Gray laughed. "One question at a time, children.

273

Megan and I are getting married next week. We'll be a family before Christmas. And yes, Megan's baby will be your brother or sister, in a manner of speaking. The correct term is stepsister or stepbrother."

Beth stared at Megan's belly with a mixture of awe and curiosity. "Can I feel the baby move sometime, Megan?"

Megan smiled at the child, grasped her hand, and placed it on her protruding stomach. "The baby kicks nearly all the time now."

"Me too," Alex piped up, raising his little hand. Megan took it and placed it next to Beth's.

After a brief hesitation, Gray asked, "What about me?"

Startled, Megan nodded shyly. When Gray's large hand joined those of Beth and Alex, the baby gave a healthy kick. The children squealed in delight, and Gray assumed such a blissful look that Megan lost the ability to speak. If she'd ever doubted her decision to marry Gray, the expression on his face cast all doubt aside.

The day of Megan's wedding dawned cold and clear. A weak sun shone through the clouds, and Megan took it as a sign of Patrick's blessing upon her marriage. The wedding was to take place at three o'clock in the afternoon in the sacristy of St. Matthew's church. Gray had spoken to Father Sean O'Reilly, and he had happily agreed to perform the marriage ceremony. Gray had asked his assistant, Robert Proud, to be his best man and Robert's wife was to be Megan's attendant. Of course the children would be present, along with Mrs. Hooper and Gray's lawyer, Mason Cantwell.

Megan trembled nervously as Gail Proud, who had arrived early to assist her, helped her into the beautiful pale-violet gown Gray had purchased for her. Megan glanced at her thick waist and wished the wedding could have waited until she had regained her figure, but she understood Gray's haste. The gown was lovely, but it was much too late to disguise her pregnancy beneath billows of lace and ruffles.

"You're going to be a beautiful bride," Gail Proud said, trying to hide her dismay over Megan's advanced state of pregnancy. Her husband had told her Gray's wife was in the family way, but she'd had no idea how near the birth was. "You're getting a good man. We've known Gray a long time and want him to be happy. Lord knows Lilith didn't make him happy, although some people consider Gray a cold fish and don't blame Lilith for seeking comfort elsewhere." She stared fixedly at Megan's belly, as if to say that Gray must have sought his pleasure elsewhere, too.

Megan blinked but said nothing. She hadn't known Gail long enough to speak freely. Gray might be reticent about expressing his feelings, but he certainly wasn't a cold fish. He was warm and thoughtful and caring. He had taken her in and shown her nothing but kindness. She loved him for every one of those qualities and hoped he found qualities worth loving in her.

Gail prattled on, unaware or uncaring that Megan paid her little heed. After straightening Megan's dress one last time, she stepped back to survey her work.

"There, you look lovely. Are you ready to go? Robert has a carriage waiting outside to take us to the church. Gray has already left with the children and Mrs. Hooper."

Megan tried to tell herself that everything would be all right, that she was doing what was best for both her and Gray, but doubts still assailed her as she and Gray stood side by side before Father Sean. When it came time to repeat her vows, she hesitated for the space of several heartbeats. But when she looked at Gray and saw his smile of encouragement, all her reservations melted. Then, from the corner of her eye, she saw a shadowy figure hovering at Gray's shoulder. She felt the comfort of Patrick's ghostly presence and smiled.

The priest repeated his question, and Megan became aware that Gray was staring at her strangely. When she realized that he was waiting for her to speak her vows, she glanced at Patrick and saw him nod his approval. Returning her gaze to Gray, she stared into his eyes and vowed to take him as her lawful husband till death parted them. When she looked up, Patrick was no longer there.

A small reception at the house followed the ceremony. Clara Hooper had outdone herself cooking for the guests, and Megan truly enjoyed herself. But she tired easily. After the meal, Gray made it clear that Megan had to rest and the guests left. Megan fidgeted nervously as Gray bade them good-bye. When he had closed the door on the last guest, he kissed Megan's cheek and said, "It's time for a rest, sweetheart. It's been a long day."

Megan agreed, and when she turned to go to her room beyond the kitchen, Gray swept her from her feet and carried her up the stairs. "You don't belong in the housekeeper's room. I've had your things carried upstairs to the spare bedroom. It's a cheerful room. I think you'll like it. And as soon as I find someone, I'll hire you a maid."

A maid. Imagine that. "You're a wonderful man, Gray Petrie," Megan sighed contentedly. "And strong. I'm no lightweight. Sometimes I can hardly drag my own weight around."

"Pregnancy becomes you. You're all rosy and

round and soft. It makes me wonder what you'll look like when the babe is in your arms instead of in your belly." Color stained his cheeks when he realized what he'd said.

Gray didn't release Megan until they stood inside her room. Then he set her carefully on her feet. "I'll wake you in time for dinner. Turn around and I'll unfasten your dress. All those tiny hooks look complicated, but I think I can manage."

One by one the hooks parted, and Gray stared in fascination at the smooth, creamy flesh he'd bared. He swallowed convulsively and looked away. He had married Megan for convenience, he tried to tell himself, yet it would be so easy to love her, so easy to *make* love to her. His breath caught painfully in his throat when he recalled offering to annul their marriage once he gained custody of the children. It frightened him to think Megan might actually desire the annulment he had promised simply because he couldn't express what was becoming increasingly clear to him. He cared a great deal about Megan.

"Gray, I know this isn't the kind of wedding night a man like you deserves, but . . ."

He placed a finger across her lips. "Let's not speak of wedding nights. Just concentrate on delivering a healthy child. There will be plenty of time afterwards to decide which direction our marriage will take, or . . . or if we want to stay married. We haven't known each other long, and I don't want to supplant your dead husband in your heart, but I hope . . . that is . . . dammit, Megan, I'm no good at this. I can't even express myself to my own children; how can I expect you to understand how I feel?" Spinning on his heel, he made a hasty exit.

Gray was wrong, Megan thought. He was beginning to express himself to his children just fine, and they were opening up to him. In the weeks she'd lived

Connie Mason

in the Petrie household, she'd noticed a gradual easing of the tension between Gray and his children. He was much more open with them now, able to accept their shy overtures of affection without feeling inadequate. They rarely mentioned their mother, except to comment now and again on her neglect of them throughout the years. If the children could express their feelings to the judge, Megan felt certain they would voice a preference to remain with their father. But to Gray's credit, he felt they were too vulnerable to scandal and refused to allow them to be questioned.

Gray will win, Megan thought as she drifted easily into sleep, feeling secure and protected for the first time in many months. She no longer feared for her child's future. Her only fear was that Gray would demand an annulment once he was awarded permanent custody of the children.

Two days later, Gray sat in his office poring over a report, unable to concentrate on business. Everywhere he looked he saw Megan's beautiful image. He loved the sprinkle of freckles scattered across the bridge of her nose, and the way her thickly lashed violet eyes tilted upward at the corners. Her lilting laugh never failed to enchant him, and her Irish brogue was most provocative. He worried about her excessively. Her body seemed too small to accommodate the child she was carrying.

Suddenly the door was flung open, and Lilith burst inside without being announced. She sent Gray a provocative look and flounced into a chair without being invited.

"Sit down, Lilith," Gray said with a hint of sarcasm. "To what do I owe this pleasure?"

"Politeness won't work, Gray, you ought to know

that by now. I heard about your marriage. What did you expect to accomplish by marrying your mistress? Such a plain little thing, too. Whatever do you see in her?"

"You wouldn't understand, Lilith. What is it you want?"

She sent him an impudent grin. "Just to tell you you're not the only one getting married."

A crushing pain began behind Gray's eyes. He didn't give a fig if Lilith remarried. What worried him was the impact it might have on the custody hearing. Lilith with a husband was a greater threat than Lilith without a husband.

"Am I to assume you no longer want custody of the children?" he asked hopefully. He should have known better.

Lilith laughed shrilly. "You *are* naive. Taking the children away from you is the best way I know of punishing you. I'll never forgive you for the humiliation I suffered when you divorced me. It just isn't done in our circle. It's no longer a matter of money; the man I'm marrying is a rich Texan. I'll be taking the children to Texas as soon as I'm granted custody."

"*If* you're granted custody," Gray corrected. "May I ask who you are marrying? Rather sudden, isn't it?"

"No more sudden than your marriage. Perhaps you know him. His name is P.J. Simpson, and he's in town seeking backing for his railroad. We met at a party. It was love at first sight."

"P.J. Simpson?" Gray knew Simpson. He had called on Gray a few weeks ago soliciting backing for his railroad, but Gray hadn't been interested. "My God, he's twice your age! Being wealthy has its rewards. Somehow I can't picture Simpson raising a second family. Is he aware that you intend taking the children to Texas?"

"He will be as soon as I tell him." Lilith rose regally, dismissing Gray with a wave of her hand. "I just dropped by to tell you my good news. I must be off. I have to buy a trousseau. Have a nice Christmas."

"Do you want to see the children during the holidays?"

Lilith frowned. "I'll see them every day after the hearing. There are so many parties and social events planned during the holidays, I doubt I'll have time for them. I'll send gifts around. P.J. is a very wealthy man, and generous."

"When is the wedding?"

"I didn't think you were interested. We're to be married tomorrow at city hall." On that note, she swept out of the room with the aplomb of a reigning queen.

"Damn, damn, double damn!" Gray swore, slapping the desk with the flat of his hand. Just when he thought things were looking up, something came along to knock him back down. Leave it to Lilith to make sure she held the winning hand. With P.J. Simpson's money and influence behind her, she had a very good chance of taking the children away from him.

Gray assumed a thoughtful look. He wondered how badly P.J. needed backing for his railroad and how anxious he was to bring small children into his life at a time when his own were grown. A slow smile curved his lips. If Lilith wanted to play dirty, she was tangling with the wrong person.

"Come in, the door is open."

Gray turned the knob and entered the lavish hotel suite occupied by P.J. Simpson. P.J. himself sat on the sofa with papers spread out all around him.

"Well, what is it?" P.J. asked, not bothering to look up.

"I hope I'm not intruding, P.J."

P.J. glanced at Gray and smiled. "Well, well, Gray Petrie. To what do I owe this pleasure? Have you changed your mind about investing in my railroad?" His eyes narrowed speculatively. "Or have you come to talk about Lilith? Lilith told me your divorce was final and you've remarried."

"What I have to say concerns both Lilith and your railroad."

"Sit down, man, sit down. Speak your piece. I'm a plain-speaking man myself."

Gray took a chair opposite P.J., looking totally at ease despite his reservations about P.J.'s reception to his proposal.

"Are you still looking for backing for your railroad? Or have you already found all the money you need?"

"I'm still fifteen thousand shy," P.J. grumbled. "I'd hoped to be back in Texas before the beginning of the year. But one good thing came of the delay—I met Lilith."

Gray choked back a bark of laughter. "You wouldn't be able to leave in any case until after the hearing."

P.J. frowned. "Hearing? What in the hell are you talking about?"

"The custody hearing. Lilith is suing for custody of our children."

"You have children? Somehow Lilith forgot to mention the fact that she had children. Where have they been all this time?"

"With me. And I intend to keep them. Lilith is suing for custody. I didn't know you were so anxious to have small children underfoot after raising your own brood."

281

"Small children? How old?"

"Nine and six, and a more boisterous pair you won't find."

P.J. surged to his feet, his florid face growing even redder. He removed an immaculate handkerchief from his pocket and mopped his face, then tunneled thick fingers through his unruly thatch of white hair. He appeared agitated and began pacing. Gray felt heartened and pressed on, his voice low and confidential, "If you're agreeable, we could help one another enormously."

P.J. stared at him. "We could? How do you figure that?"

"I assume you're anxious to get back to Texas."

"Damn right. But I can't leave until I get all the backing I need for my railroad."

"What would you say if I invested in your venture? I'll give you the last fifteen thousand you need so you and Lilith can leave town without delay. I'm prepared to write a bank draft today in the amount you need."

"My God, man, you turned me down once! I'm no fool. What is it you want from me?"

"Very little," Gray said calmly, "except to convince Lilith to drop her custody suit. She hasn't been a mother to the children for many years. She could live very well without them, whereas I can't bear to lose them."

P.J.'s keen gaze settled disconcertingly on Gray as he mulled over Gray's words. The silence stretched painfully, until Gray feared he would explode with the suspense.

"You know Lilith better than I, Gray, but I would have to agree that she seems unsuited for motherhood. So much so that she hasn't even mentioned her children to me. Of course I knew she was once married to you and that you were divorced, but it didn't matter to me. Dammit, Gray, I want Lilith. She makes me feel younger than I have in years. I've been a widower too long. But young children are another thing."

"Lilith is no fool, P.J. She appreciates money and all that it brings. Convince her to drop the custody hearing and leave immediately for Texas, and I'll write out the bank draft here and now. Given an ultimatum, Lilith will do what is best for herself."

"I'm a father myself, Gray, and I love my children dearly. I'm impressed that you would go to such lengths to keep them. Ordinarily I'd say the mother should be granted custody, but were I in your shoes, I'd fight just as you're doing. Besides, I really don't want to raise another family, and Lilith is a social butterfly. I agree they'd be better off with you. And," he added with a twinkle, "I need your backing. I hate New York City. I want to go home to Texas."

Gray could hardly contain his excitement. "Then you'll do it? You'll convince Lilith to drop her suit?"

"I'll do it. I'm selfish enough to want Lilith to myself during my declining years, though Lord knows I've got a lot of life in me yet. Make that draft out to Simpson Enterprises." P.J. pushed an inkwell and pen toward Gray.

Gray felt more optimistic about his chances of keeping the children than he had in weeks. P.J. was a sensible man, and an honest one. He'd made no bones about wanting Lilith, or about his reluctance to raise a second family at his age. Gray couldn't wait to tell Megan his good news.

Megan. His wife. The words had a nice ring. The little Irish immigrant had taught him more about expressing his innermost feelings than he'd thought possible. The children were beginning to open up to him, to trust him, despite his absence during their early years. His heart told him he'd have no problems accepting Megan's babe as his own. He'd even begun fantasizing about having Megan in his bed regardless of his offer to seek an annulment once he gained permanent custody of the children. Originally he'd offered marriage because he supposed Megan would be so grateful for a home, she'd make no demands upon him. His freedom and privacy would remain intact.

Little did he imagine the feisty Irish beauty would become so thoroughly indispensable to his life that the thought of giving her an annulment would become too painful to contemplate. Would he ever be able to tell her how he felt? Gray wondered.

Gray's steps slowed when he passed a street corner where Christmas trees were being sold. He recalled Megan's words about decorating a tree on Christmas Eve. He spotted the perfect tree leaning against a building and approached the seller. Within minutes, a deal was struck and Gray made arrangements to have the tree delivered that evening.

Happier than he could ever recall being, Gray turned the corner and hummed the rest of the way home.

Chapter Seven

With eager anticipation, Megan sorted through the box of Christmas decorations Gray had retrieved from the attic. Some were very old, having belonged to Gray's parents, who had moved to California to be close to Gray's only sister.

"Are we going to hang decorations, Megan?" Beth asked excitedly as she fingered a large red bow.

"Let's surprise Papa and do it before he gets home," Alex urged. "The house will look ever so nice decorated."

"That's a good idea, children," Megan said enthusiastically. She felt like a youngster revisiting the excitement of Christmas with her exuberant family. "We can set aside the tree decorations until we get a tree."

Alex's face screwed up into a worried frown. "We're going to have a tree, aren't we?"

"Of course," Beth answered, not at all sure but wanting to reassure her little brother. "Papa wouldn't forget a tree."

"He certainly wouldn't," Megan agreed. "Now, help me separate the tree ornaments from the rest; then we'll decide where to hang them."

After everything was sorted, Megan surprised the children by bringing in holly that had been delivered earlier that day. With a squeal of delight, the children decorated the mantel, tables, and stair railing. When Clara brought in a huge bowl of popcorn, thread, and needles, Megan showed them how to string popcorn and holly berries for the Christmas tree.

"While you're stringing popcorn, I'll place red bows on the railing and hang a few from the chandelier," Megan said, gathering up an armful of bows.

Megan felt as light as a feather despite her girth as she tripped up the stairs. She couldn't recall when she'd had such fun. Christmas had always been special. The holiness of the season and the wonderful feelings it generated among people brought her a sense of joy and peace. Since it was a special time to Megan, she wanted it to be special to those she loved. And Gray and his children certainly fell within that category. Her heart overflowed with love for them.

Standing on the landing, Megan tilted her head and surveyed her handiwork. The red bows provided the finishing touches to the holly trailing down the staircase. Now for the chandelier. Spying a stool standing against the wall in the foyer, Megan dragged it beneath the chandelier, wondering if she'd be tall enough to reach the fixture if she stood on it. The children were so engrossed in their popcorn stringing, they didn't see Megan climb atop the stool with a red bow held tightly in her hand.

Stretching to her full height, Megan raised her arms, disappointed that they fell a few inches short of reaching the elusive chandelier. Rising to her tiptoes, Megan stretched again, almost within reach this time. Balanced precariously on her toes, Megan felt the stool begin to tilt when her weight shifted to one side. Immediately she tried to correct her balance but instead over-corrected. The stool listed to the right, poised a breathless moment on two legs, then crashed to the floor, sending Megan tumbling. The children heard her scream and came running.

"Megan, what happened? Are you all right?" Beth asked anxiously.

Unable to speak, Megan blinked repeatedly as pain radiated through her body. The breath slammed against her chest and lodged in her throat, making speech and breathing difficult. She clutched her stomach, trying to shield her child from harm as pain ripped her apart. Then she felt wetness between her legs, and alarm shuddered through her.

Clara Hooper heard the commotion and rushed from the kitchen. "What is it? What happened?" She spied Megan lying on the floor, her face contorted in agony, and Clara cried out in panic. "Oh Lord, oh lord, oh lord!"

"Megan fell, Mrs. Hooper," Beth said as she dropped to her knees beside Megan and began stroking her arm. "Do something. I think she hurt herself."

His head filled with happy thoughts, Gray let himself into the house—and entered a scene straight from his worst nightmare. Mrs. Hooper stood over a moaning, writhing Megan, wringing her hands and flapping her apron. Alex was sobbing, and Beth had left off stroking Megan's arm and was trying to lift her.

"What's going on? Is it Megan's time? Why haven't you summoned the midwife, Mrs. Hooper? What in the hell is Megan doing on the floor?" Then he saw the overturned stool and scattered bows, and his heart lurched up into his mouth.

"Megan fell, Papa," Beth said, her gaze never wavering from Megan's pale face. "She was trying to hang a bow from the chandelier. I think she's hurt."

Gray had but to look at Megan to know she was hurt. She seemed barely aware of what was going on around her as she clutched her stomach and rolled with the pain.

"She needs a doctor," Gray muttered, distraught. "I'll go as soon as I get her to bed." He eased his arms beneath Megan and lifted her carefully. Megan stiffened and moaned but said nothing.

"I'll go for the doctor. It isn't far," Clara Hooper said. "You stay with your wife."

Gray silently blessed the woman as he started up the stairs with Megan. When the children made as if to follow, Gray told them to continue with what they had been doing, that they couldn't help Megan now. He could see they wanted to protest, but something in his manner must have gotten through to them, for they obediently returned to their popcorn, though their hearts were no longer in it.

Gray placed Megan carefully on the bed and began undoing the buttons on her dress. When he noted the blood on her skirt, he clenched his fists and spat out a curse.

"My baby," Megan said between spasms of pain. "Don't let anything happen to my baby." She clutched Gray's hand in silent desperation, and Gray had never felt more helpless.

"Your baby—our baby," he amended, "is going to be just fine. Lie still, sweetheart, and try to relax." He didn't want to scold her while she was in pain, but he couldn't imagine what had possessed her to climb that stool in her condition. Although he was deeply concerned about her unborn child, he didn't want to alarm her in any way. "I've sent for the doctor."

When he slid the dress down her hips, he folded it so the blood wouldn't show and tossed it into a corner. Then he covered her with a blanket, eased down beside her, and held her hand. It was all he knew how to do.

"Gray, if anything should happen to me . . ."

"Nothing's going to happen."

"But if it does, and my baby lives . . ."

"Don't worry, sweetheart, you're not going to die. I won't let you. The children and I need you. In any case, don't worry about the baby. I accepted responsibility for your child when we married."

Another pain brought a moan to Megan's white lips, and she had to wait for it to pass before she could speak. "Have you heard anything about the custody hearing? Once you gain permanent custody of the children, you'll want an annulment and my child and I will no longer be part of your lives." She was rambling, she knew, but pain was making her giddy. She had no idea what she was saying.

Gray's heart sank. He wondered how badly Megan wanted an annulment. "This is no time to speak of an annulment. I won't go back on my word. Everything in its own time. Just concentrate on having a healthy baby. Beth and Alex are ecstatic about the baby, you know."

Suddenly Megan arched upward, her eyes unfocused, her breath hissing past her teeth in a hoarse cry. She didn't want an annulment. Didn't Gray know she didn't want one? She gripped Gray's hand so tightly that he winced in pain but did not let go.

"It's too early," Megan said once the pain settled down to clenching spasms. "The baby isn't due for a month."

"I'm sure it's not too early," Gray soothed. "You were very close to delivery. Damn, where is that doctor?"

Twenty minutes later, Doctor Dunbar bustled into the room, rolling up his sleeves and calling for hot water, soap, and plenty of clean towels. Then he ordered Gray out of the room. The moment Gray's hand withdrew from hers, Megan felt the loss keenly. She wanted to ask him to stay but knew it wasn't proper. She had to bite her tongue to keep from telling him how frightened she was, how alone she felt, how much she had come to depend on him.

Gray didn't want to leave Megan but supposed the doctor knew best. He and Megan were almost strangers, and perhaps she'd feel embarrassed to have him witness so intimate a moment. He wasn't the baby's father, though he might feel like it in his heart. He wished he could tell her how much she had come to mean to him, how possessive he'd become of her baby, wishing it were his, but he couldn't find the words. Instead, he squeezed her hand and gently withdrew it from hers.

"I'll be downstairs with the children if you need me, sweetheart," he said as he paused just inside the door. Megan couldn't muster the energy to answer, though she appreciated his concern. The way he called her sweetheart made her feel like a real wife instead of someone he had married out of necessity.

Gray and the children ate a silent supper. Mrs. Hooper had agreed to spend the night in the event she was needed to assist the doctor, and she put the children to bed at eight o'clock despite their protests. When Gray went to tuck them in, he found them in tears. He couldn't bear it. He had never seen them cry before, nor felt so close to them.

He sat on Alex's bed, and after hesitating a brief moment, held out his arms. For the first time in his memory, Alex scrambled onto his lap voluntarily and hugged him tightly. Wanting the same kind of closeness shared by father and son, Beth joined them, throwing her arms around Gray's neck and burying her face in his shirt front.

"Is Megan going to be all right, Papa? What about our baby brother or sister?"

"I'm sure Megan is going to be just fine, children," Gray said with less assurance than he felt. "And so will the baby. You love Megan very much, don't you?"

"Oh yes, Papa." Beth's answer sufficed for both her and her brother.

"Things are different since Megan came to us," Alex said innocently. "We know she's not our real mama, but she feels like it. I don't think our real mama loves us as much as Megan."

"You're even different, Papa," Beth said with an astuteness that belied her nine years. "Before Megan came, you didn't have time for us. You never talked to us. Mama didn't want us and neither did you."

Gray felt like crying. He realized how much his children had suffered because of his inability to show affection and it made him sad. "I've always wanted you. I love you." Lord, how easily those three words came since a little Irish immigrant had taught him that his children needed more than food and shelter to survive. They needed a father who could express his love. Megan had loved his children right from the first, showering them with affection when he could not.

"Why do you think I'm fighting your mother for permanent custody? Why do you think I married Megan? I can't bear the thought of losing either of you. Your mother wants to take you to Texas after she remarries. It would break my heart."

"We don't want to go to Texas," Beth wailed. "We want to stay here with you and Megan and the baby. Oh Papa, do you really love us? Alex and I have always loved you, but you seemed so fierce we feared telling you. Until Megan came, we didn't think anyone loved us. She told us we had to be patient with you, that love would come and we'd be a real family."

"Forgive me, children. I didn't know how to be a father, but I've always loved you. Before Megan came into our lives I never could have sat down and talked with you like this. It's like a miracle. You'll never know how many times I wanted to hug you, but you always seemed unwilling to have me do so. I feared that you blamed me for divorcing your mother."

"Do we have to go to Texas, Papa?" Alex asked, getting to the crux of the issue. "Will Mama's husband be our new papa? Is Megan going to be with us forever?"

"You're not going to Texas if I have anything to say about it. And I'm counting on Lilith's new husband to talk her out of suing for custody. He's not an unreasonable man."

"What about Megan?" Beth persisted.

Gray thought about his promise to annul the marriage once he gained custody of the children and hoped Megan wouldn't hold him to his promise. He wanted Megan to be a real wife to him. He wanted to protect her and her child. He wanted . . .

He wanted Megan. In his home, his life, and his bed. Was that what love felt like?

Much later, Gray paced the parlor, glancing at the mantel clock as the hours ticked by. How long had the doctor been upstairs? Two hours, three, four? It seemed forever. Gray started up the stairs, determined to find out what was happening. Earlier Mrs. Hooper had carried a tray of food to the doctor and returned silent and grim-faced. Since he didn't want to alarm the children, he said nothing, waiting until he could learn for himself how the birth was progressing.

Gray had just reached the top of the stairs when the doctor came out of Megan's room. He frowned when he saw Gray, more than a little distracted.

Gray's heart plummeted down to his toes.

"What is it, doctor? What's happening?"

"Mr. Petrie, I wish to speak with you. Your wife is very weak. The fall damaged Mrs. Petrie's insides, and the baby is lodged in the birth canal. The fetus is large despite being somewhat early, and that's complicating matters. And one more thing . . ."

Gray waited impatiently for the doctor to continue. "Yes, what is it?"

"Mrs. Petrie seems worried about something. It's interfering with her concentration. Do you know what's bothering her?"

"Er . . . ours is an unusual marriage. We haven't known one another very long."

"Long enough to get her pregnant," the doctor said tartly. "Nonetheless, the danger exists that neither she nor the baby will survive. I thought I'd best warn you."

Gray's face went white. "Not survive! My God, man, you can't let either one of them die. That baby is everything to Megan. I couldn't bear it, and the children will be devastated."

A scream from behind the closed door sent the doctor rushing back into Megan's room.

"Doctor, wait! I want to see Megan."

"I'm afraid that's not possible. I don't want her upset. Maybe later."

"Later, hell!" Gray said, striding past the harried doctor to Megan's bedside.

"A few minutes, then, no more," Doctor Dunbar warned as he busied himself with his array of instruments.

Gray knelt beside the bed, taking Megan's hand and bringing it to his lips. "Megan, can you hear me?"

Megan whimpered, clutching Gray's hand as if he'd just offered her a lifeline. "I hurt, Gray. I hadn't expected this kind of pain."

"Can't you give her something?" Gray hissed in an aside to the doctor.

Doctor Dunbar shook his head. "Anything I give her will harm the babe. She needs all her wits about her to bring this child into the world."

"You have to be brave, Megan," Gray said, wishing he could suffer in her place. "Think how wonderful it will be holding your child in your arms."

She gasped and shuddered through another agonizing spasm, and Gray felt compelled to take her into his arms. She was his wife; she needed his support. He wanted to be with her, to comfort her, to let her know he cared. She had given him back his children.

"Don't leave me," Megan gasped. "I feel so alone."

"I'll not leave you, Megan. Not now, not ever. And you're not alone. Patrick is with you. In spirit if not in body. And I'm here for you. I didn't get a chance to tell you earlier, but it's quite possible Lilith will drop the custody suit. She's getting married to a rich Texan who isn't crazy about raising another family. He's much older than Lilith."

Megan clutched Gray's hand. "Oh, Gray, I'm so happy for you. You should have waited. You married me for nothing. I . . . I suppose you'll want an annulment as soon as possible."

Gray searched her face. "I know I promised you your freedom, and I rarely go back on my word, but I hope you won't insist on an annulment."

"You don't want one? I thought . . ."

"Without your gentle prodding, I'd be forever treading on eggshells around the children, afraid of baring my heart, fearing they'd reject me just as Lilith rejected me. If not for you, they would never know how much I love them. I was finally able to open up to them."

He smiled at her. "You brought meaning into our lives. You taught me that physical attraction, which was what brought Lilith and me together, is a shallow kind of love. I've not touched you as a husband and what I feel for you cannot be described in physical terms, but you've become dear to me nevertheless. To all of us. Too dear to part with. I don't want an annulment, Megan. I want to love and cherish you and your child forever. I want you to love me in return. I promise to be a good father."

Nearly delirious with pain, Megan managed a weak smile before her face contorted with renewed agony.

The doctor was beside Megan instantly. "You'd better leave now, Mr. Petrie, and let me tend to my patient. I've got a baby to deliver."

"I'm not going anywhere," Gray said stubbornly. "Megan is my wife and she needs me. I can't recall when anyone has truly needed me."

"I've found that fathers aren't particularly suited to watching this kind of thing. You'll only get in the way."

"No, please, let him stay," Megan said weakly.

Gray gave her a brilliant smile. "Squeeze my hand all you want. I'm not going anywhere. Not until this baby is born."

"Have it your way," the doctor said, "just don't faint on me."

Hours passed and Gray began to fear for Megan's life. She grew weaker with each passing minute, too weak to push her child into the world. Gray consulted frantically with the doctor, whose brow seemed furrowed into a permanent frown.

"The baby's turned wrong," the doctor announced after examining his patient. "I'm going to turn it. Hold your wife, Mr. Petrie, while I do what must be done. If it doesn't work, I'll attempt a cesarean section. The procedure isn't performed often and the complications are numerous, but it may be our only chance to save mother and child."

Gray swallowed convulsively and nodded, holding Megan firmly in his strong arms while the doctor turned the child inside her womb. She screamed once, then went limp. A few minutes later, her eyes flew open and her mouth worked in a silent scream.

"Thank God," the doctor said. A moment ago he'd seemed defeated, but now he was bustling with renewed energy. "It looks like we're going to have a baby. It's time to push, Megan. Let's bring this baby into the world."

Chapter Eight

Megan opened her eyes slowly, her hands flying immediately to her flat stomach. The pain of childbirth was still with her, but she managed a weak smile as she recalled holding her child in her arms after he made his belated appearance. Though her memory was hazy about certain things, she remembered quite clearly Gray's strong arms around her, holding her, murmuring words of encouragement as the doctor toiled to bring her son into the world.

A son. She rolled the word around on her tongue and savored the sweetness of it. He was tiny but healthy, the doctor had said. He had all the required number of fingers and toes and was all pink and wrinkled and so beautiful that looking at him was pure joy. Gray had agreed and told her so as he gazed down at the babe resting peacefully in her arms. Gray had left then, returning a short time later with a cradle he'd brought down from the attic and placed beside the bed within reach.

Megan was alone now. The light of a new day brightened the room. She wondered how long she'd slept. She'd been given something to drink—laudanum, she suspected—after the difficult birth and had fallen asleep. Upon awakening she found she hurt in so many places, she doubted she'd ever be the same. Her gaze settled lovingly on the cradle holding her sleeping babe. He lay on his side, facing away from her, swaddled in one of the gowns she had sewn for him.

Grateful for the miracle of her tiny son, Megan was overcome with the need to touch him and reached out toward the cradle. She gasped and drew her hand back in surprise when she saw Patrick's image materialize beside the cradle. He was smiling down on his son with such overwhelming tenderness that it brought tears to Megan's eyes.

"Patrick, you've come back."

"Aye, *acushla*, I couldn't leave until I saw my son. You're both going to be fine, Megan."

"You don't mind if Gray helps me raise our son?"

"I counted on you to follow your heart and do what's best for you and our babe. You're going to be a fine mother, Megan, and Gray Petrie will be a fine father to our son. Probably better than I. My faults were many. Though I loved you dearly, I was selfish and self-centered. I could never have given you the kind of life you deserve. I would always have remained a free spirit, shunning responsibility instead of becoming a man."

"I loved you no matter your faults, Patrick."

Suddenly the door opened, and Gray stuck his head through the opening. "You're awake." He glanced around the room, saw it was empty, and said, "I thought I heard you talking to someone."

Megan glanced at Patrick and was startled to see his image growing dimmer. "No, don't go!"

"I wasn't going anywhere," Gray said, stepping into the room. "The children want to see the baby. Is it all right to let them in? Do you feel well enough for visitors?"

"I'm well enough to see you and the children," Megan said by way of invitation.

"Come in, children," Gray called through the open door.

Their faces glowing with excitement, the children trooped into the room behind Gray. Megan watched with amazement as they filed past Patrick without seeing him. With rapt attention the children stared at the babe, thrilled with their baby brother. After a sufficient time had passed, Gray sent them from the room and sat down on the bed beside Megan.

"Our son is beautiful, Megan. And so are you." He bent down and placed a gentle kiss on her lips. "What are you going to name him?"

"Daniel," Megan replied promptly. "It's my father's name."

"How about Daniel Kelly Petrie," Gray suggested.

Megan glanced at Patrick and saw that he was nodding his approval. "It's perfect."

Gray grew apprehensive at the way Megan kept looking over his shoulder and turned his head slowly in the direction of her gaze. He saw nothing but the cradle, which for some unexplained reason was rocking gently back and forth. "What are you looking at?"

Startled by his question, Megan brought her gaze back to Gray. "You wouldn't believe me if I told you."

He stared deeply into the violet depths of her eyes and suddenly didn't want to know. "Keep your secret, sweetheart. Your past is yours to savor. All I ask is that you share the future with me."

Megan's gaze wandered toward the cradle, crying out in dismay when she saw Patrick's image fading,

fading, until only the dim outline of his face remained. Moments before he disappeared entirely, he gave her a playful wink and a jaunty wave of his hand. Then he was gone.

"What's wrong?" Gray asked fearfully when he heard her cry out. "Do you hurt somewhere? Should I summon the doctor? You gave us a scare, you know. I was never more frightened in my life. I thought I might lose you and the baby."

"I'm fine," Megan replied, sending him a reassuring smile. She knew instinctively that Patrick would not return. He might live in her heart, but she'd never see or speak to him again. He had kept vigil over her, given his approval to this marriage, and urged her to devote her life and love to another man. He had even picked out the man for her.

"You're tired. I should leave," Gray said, rising reluctantly. "Is there anything you need, anything at all?"

"Just one thing. I need to hear you say you aren't going to pursue an annulment. I remember you saying something like that, but I was in so much pain that I could have imagined it."

"Your memory is quite right, sweetheart. I want us to be a real family. In the short time we've known you, you've become indispensable to us. I've never felt this way about a woman before. Especially a woman I've never laid a hand on." He smiled ruefully. "But I hope to change that when you're fully recovered from childbirth. I want to be your husband in every way. I want you in my life, in my home, and in my bed. I know you loved Patrick, but he's dead and I'm alive. I intend to make you happy, if you'll let me."

Megan blushed and looked away. Patrick had made love to her with lighthearted gaiety. He had been a clumsy but exuberant lover, making up in spontaneity what he lacked in finesse. She imagined that making love with Gray would be different, more refined but supremely satisfying. Loving Gray seemed right. All his wonderful qualities made him so easy to love.

"I want to make you happy, too, Gray. We've shared something special, the birth of a child. You were with me during the entire ordeal. I want to be your wife. In every way. I did love Patrick, but I feel sure that he would be happy knowing I've found another man to love."

She sighed wistfully and shot a quick glance at the place where she'd last seen Patrick. She imagined she could still see his cocky grin, and she sent him an answering smile.

"Might I hope that smile is for me?"

"Yes, Gray, it's for you; it will always be for you."

He kissed her again and rose to leave. "Get some rest."

"Wait! What day is it?"

"Christmas Eve."

"Oh, Gray, the Christmas tree! I promised the children we would decorate it tonight. I have to get up."

"Not on your life. The doctor said you had to remain in bed at least a week. He's sending a nurse over to take care of you. The children and I can trim the tree. I don't believe we've ever done that together. I'll carry you downstairs to see it after it's decorated."

"What about gifts? I have a few things but . . ."

"Taken care of, sweetheart. Would I forget my own children?"

Later that day, Megan awakened to squeals of delight as Gray brought in the tree and the children made a game of trimming it. Later, Mrs. Hooper stole upstairs and described the scene to Megan,

Connie Mason

shaking her head in amazement.

"I can't believe this is the same family I've known for years. Mr. Petrie is acting as foolish as the children. I've never seen him like this before. What did you do to him, Megan?"

"Nothing, really," Megan said, reaching for her son and putting him to her breast. "He cared for me when I had no one and taught me there were good people in the world."

"And Megan showed me how to relate to my children," Gray said, striding into the room. "I was losing them until Megan came into our lives and brought us together."

Mrs. Hooper nodded her head and ducked out the door, feeling like an interloper.

"Do you feel like going downstairs for a few minutes if I carry you?" Gray asked, staring fixedly at little Danny nuzzling Megan's plump breast. "The children want you to see their handiwork. They spent the entire afternoon trimming the tree."

"I'd love to see the tree. Will you put Danny back in his cradle?"

Gray swallowed convulsively. "Me? I . . . I don't know much about babies."

"Then it's about time you learned." Lifting Danny from her breast, Megan carefully placed him in Gray's arms, showing him how to support his head.

"My God, but he's tiny! I don't want to hurt him."

"You won't. I trust you, Gray."

Trust. It was an awesome burden, one that Gray prayed he could live up to. He placed Danny in his cradle without mishap and turned for Megan, watching in silent appreciation as she pulled her nightgown together. Gray handed her a robe and helped her into it. Then he gathered her into his arms and carried her downstairs.

"Surprise!"

Bursting with enthusiasm, the children danced around Megan and Gray.

"Look at the tree, Megan," Beth said, unable to contain her excitement. "Papa helped us. Isn't it beautiful?"

"I put the angel on the top," Alex proudly informed her.

"It's lovely," Megan said, brushing a tear from her eye. "I couldn't have done better myself."

"Can Megan stay downstairs, Papa?" Beth asked.

"No, she's going right back to bed. Perhaps Mrs. Hooper will fix us a picnic so we can eat together in Megan's room."

"Like the picnic we had on the parlor floor?" Alex asked.

"Would you like that? You'd have to promise to be good and not tire Megan."

"Oh, yes, Papa," the children chimed in unison. "We'll be very good, you'll see."

"Go tell Mrs. Hooper while I carry Megan back to bed."

The children ran off to the kitchen, and Gray turned toward the stairs. He hadn't taken two steps when he heard someone pounding on the front door.

"Who in the world could that be?" he wondered aloud.

Not wanting to answer the door with Megan in his arms, he carefully lowered her into a chair, telling her he'd only be a moment.

Gray was more than a little surprised to find his lawyer at the door. "I'm sorry to intrude, Gray, but my news can't wait."

"Cantwell, come in. What is so important to take you away from your family on Christmas Eve?"

"Good news, Gray, very good news indeed. Lilith's lawyer called on me earlier today and told me Lilith has decided to drop her custody suit. She and her

Connie Mason

new husband are already on their way to Texas. Lilith's only request was that she be allowed to see the children whenever she visits New York."

"Granted," Gray replied promptly.

"Then I'll take my leave so you and your family can celebrate Christmas."

"There's been an addition to the family since I last spoke with you," Gray said proudly. "Megan and I have a new son."

"Well, well, there is indeed much to celebrate this year. Congratulations again, Gray."

"Did you hear, Megan?" Gray asked when he returned to the parlor. "I feel as if a burden has been lifted from my shoulders. As long as P.J. keeps Lilith happy by showering her with gifts and affection, she'll not bother us again. He's quite taken with her youth and beauty and cares enough about her to keep her from straying."

"I'm so happy for you, Gray," Megan said sincerely.

"For us, sweetheart. From now on we're a family. You and your child have brought a Christmas miracle to our lives. I've never seen the children this content, and I've never been happier. Thank you, sweetheart. Now put your arms around my neck and I'll carry you back to bed."

Sighing in contentment, Megan wound her arms around her husband's neck and laid her head on his chest. Chancing to glance over Gray's shoulder, Megan swore she saw Patrick standing beside the Christmas tree smiling at her. Closing one eye, she sent him a sassy wink.

THE TREASURE

For my beloved husband, Rob

Chapter One

"She's dead. What the hell do we do with the baby?"

Trader Elijah Bolls glared down at the Indian woman who had just given birth, then died. A chill winter wind fluttered her hair and blew black strands across the naked, squirming body of her baby boy as if to keep him warm even in her death.

"No husband neither," answered Jesse Planke. "Why'd she have to go and die?"

"Just makes more trouble for us," complained Bolls. "Ah geez, look at that. What's he doin'? It's gettin' all over."

The two traders stood shaking their heads in disgust. Bolls, the older one, was a stout man. His deep-set blue eyes peered out of a weathered face covered in gray stubble. Planke, leaner and taller, hunched his shoulders to the wind and pushed a scrap of lank

307

brown hair out of his eyes. Both men wore leather tunics and trousers and floppy leather hats.

One of the packhorses snorted. "Let's go," said Bolls. "I want to reach Fort McCraig by nightfall."

"Aw, let's have a wee drinkie first," said Planke.

Obligingly, Bolls walked over to the closest packhorse and fished around in the saddlebag. Triumphantly he withdrew a flask of whiskey and waved it aloft. "A baby. This calls for a celebration!"

"No, it don't," replied Planke. "Dead woman. Baby. Nothing to celebrate about that."

Bolls took a long draught of the whiskey. "Ye're right," he agreed.

The baby gave a little cough, the first sound he'd made since both men arrived.

The traders' eyes were drawn to him. Bolls said, "Guess we better bury the woman."

"Why?"

Bolls shrugged. "That's the proper thing to do, ain't it? Coyotes or wolves will get her otherwise."

Planke glanced around. "It *is* gettin' dark," he allowed. "Guess it wouldn't hurt. That way no wolves will get *us*."

Bolls laughed and took another swig from the flask. "Want some? Grave diggin' is hard work."

Planke took a swig and then the two traders set to digging. Once the grave was finished, they walked back to the woman.

"That baby still alive?" asked Bolls in some surprise.

"Yep, sure looks like it," agreed Planke.

Both men stared at the baby, whose fists were waving. "Take him off her," said Bolls.

Planke bent and cut the umbilical cord with his hunting knife. Then he gingerly lifted the baby off the mother. "Sure is tiny," he observed. "Cold, too."

"Won't last long in this wind," said Bolls. He took

a step closer and peered at the baby in Planke's hands. "Say, I just thought o' somethin'."

"Yeah? What?"

"I bet ol' Factor Hayes at Fort McCraig would pay a good chunk of gold for this here baby," said Bolls thoughtfully.

"You think so?" Planke's grey eyes lit up with greed.

"I heard tell he's been wantin' a son."

Planke chuckled. "Well now, just maybe we got the son for him."

Both men laughed. Bolls took another swig of whiskey. He held the flask to Planke's lips so he could drink while he held the baby. "To celebrate," explained Bolls. "We just found ourselves a gold mine."

The traders built their campfire next to the freshly mounded grave.

"This baby stinks," observed Planke.

"He shore do. It's your turn to wash him in the crick."

"I did it last time. It's yourn."

"'Tis not."

"Well, hell. If you don't wash him, and I don't wash him, he's gonna stink worse."

"That's so," agreed Planke. "Tell you what. You wash him in the crick, and I'll milk ol' nanny goat."

Bolls grimaced and said, "If it weren't for old man Hayes payin' us so much gold for this here baby, why, I'd—"

"Aw, he's gonna pay us. He's gonna pay us good," said Planke. "I feel it in my bones."

That brought a grimace to Bolls's lips. "I seem to remember your bones bein' wrong a time or two."

"Not this time," argued Planke. "This time, I know we gonna be rich!"

"Oh, all right, I'll wash him." Clumsily, Bolls picked

Theresa Scott

up the baby and staggered to the creek. Afterwards, he wrapped the infant in a narrow strip of green, red, white, yellow, and cream-colored Hudson's Bay blanket. "Gimme some more of that blanket."

Planke took out his hunting knife and sliced off another piece of blanket. "What we gonna do when we run out of blanket?"

"Dunno. Cut up another one, I guess. This here baby is costing us blankets." Bolls frowned. "If we had some of them cotton cloths—diapers—we wouldn't have to use blankets."

"Well, it won't be our problem for long. We'll get to the fort and ol' man Hayes will want this baby. We'll be rolling in gold then. Or maybe beaver furs."

"Yeah, soft gold," chortled Bolls.

When Planke came back with the goat, Bolls said, "This baby whines, you notice?"

"Yeah. Here's some milk." Planke worked the goat's udder and squirted some warm milk into the baby's mouth. "He's sure thirsty."

"Greedy, pure and simple, that's what he is," said Bolls. "Here, you hold him. You got lousy aim. I got milk all over my leather shirt. It's my turn to squirt."

When they'd finished feeding the baby, Planke said, "Aw, look! Now he's gone and pissed the blanket again."

"Your turn to go to the crick," said Bolls.

"Hand me a piece of that blanket." Planke gave him a dark look. "We gotta start dryin' these things or we're gonna go through our whole stock of Hudson's Bay blankets. And they ain't cheap."

Later, the traders rolled themselves in their blankets beside the fire. "Hope he ain't one of them cryin' babies," said Bolls.

"Just you keep thinkin' about all them furs and gold ol' man Hayes gonna give us," answered Planke. "We gonna be rich."

310

Chapter Two

Gentle Fawn crouched beside the mound of dirt. Under that mound she'd laid her baby, dead at birth.

She tried to swallow the tears, but they kept coming. She clenched her fists, fighting back the pain and the memories. She remembered that when she'd been giving birth to this child, her heart had soared with joy. At long last a child would be born to her and Hawk Catcher!

She'd had a powerful dream one night, when the babe was but half-grown in her womb. In her dream she'd held her son. He'd nestled his dark head against hers, and her heart had filled with hope and love for him.

For so many years she'd waited for the happy day. Five of her babies had died, and she'd buried each one of them. She'd cried hot tears each time until she thought she had no more tears left. Why couldn't she grow a baby?

But this time, with this baby, she'd been so certain

311

her child would live. Her dream had told her so. And this time had been her last hope.

When her babe was born dead, his tiny body as blue as her other babies', she'd stared at him out of dull, hopeless eyes. There would be no son for her, no child for Hawk Catcher.

She wept as she remembered. He'd been beautiful. Her heart and arms still cried out to hold him. But she did not hold him. The earth did.

Gentle Fawn sank down on the newly churned earth and wept. Finally, when she could weep no more, she stood up and faced the bitter winter wind. The wind was her friend. It dried her tears.

She did not need to look at her beloved husband's handsome face. She knew the wind had dried his tears too.

The wind had dried their tears six times.

She felt Hawk Catcher's arm draw around her shoulders, and she flinched. Even now, after this last, terrible loss, he was kind to her. How could she love a man so much and fail him so miserably?

She met his deeply sad, dark eyes. "It is no good, my husband. We have lost another child."

"Yes," he agreed. "Come, let us return to our home. It is cold out here and you need to rest."

She bowed her head, and the cold wind ruffled her ragged black hair, which barely reached her shoulders now; she'd chopped it off in grief and mourning for her babe.

Slowly she followed Hawk Catcher back to their tepee. She entered its familiar warmth, hardly noticing the furs laid out for them to lie upon, the herbs hanging from the poles, the baskets of dried meat and berries and roots. It was their home. But how much longer could she share it with him?

She refused to look at the baby's papoose she had sewn. Hawk Catcher had brought her a beautiful

The Treasure

doeskin, and she had tanned it until it was as soft as duck's down. She had stretched the leather on the willow frame that Hawk Catcher had made and then sewn a design of beads on the leather. Together, they had made this papoose for the child they so longed for. But now she could not bear to gaze upon it, at the promise it once held, at its haunting reminder.

She yearned for a child. Hawk Catcher yearned for a child. But how much longer could she ask him to wait? She released a long sigh.

How she wanted a son or a daughter. A child in their tepee would be the greatest gift the Great Spirit could ever give them. Hawk Catcher would teach a son to hunt; Gentle Fawn would teach a daughter to tan hides, to cook, to sew.

She brushed away a tear, turning away from Hawk Catcher lest he see that she still mourned. She did not want to remind him of his own sadness.

"Rest, my wife," he said gently. "We will rest and gather our strength for the new day."

She gazed at the embers of the fire. "What new day, my husband?" she asked and she could hear the hopelessness in her own voice. "Our children are all dead. They died at birth, one by one. There will be no new day for us."

"Do not talk so, my wife." He patted her shoulder.

She touched his hand, wanting desperately to be consoled. She met his piercing black eyes. His handsome face was drawn, his cheeks hollow from his own grief. Yet his eyes were full of love. Her heart sank. She would give her very heart, her soul, anything she possessed, to give her husband a child. He had waited so long, and she so loved him. How much longer could she deny him his heart's desire? He was getting older. They both were. He needed a son to help him hunt. To be a companion. To bring joy to his life.

313

She needed a son or daughter to love, to guide, to give herself to.

Carefully, she removed her hand from his, afraid lest he read her very thoughts.

But he would not let her go so easily. He took her hand back and held it, warm between his own. He had known her since her girlhood, this man who had met and faced with her the most terrible grief of their lives. And he would not let go of her hand, even now.

She met his eyes, her own tearing. "I love you," she whispered softly.

Chapter Three

Planke was humming as they entered the wide wooden gates of Fort McCraig. He ignored the two cannons pointing at them from the corner bastions and the two men on sentry duty, flintlocks loaded, who slouched against the stockade up on the high walkway. On the western side of the fort were the men's quarters. On the eastern side was a corral and a garden.

"Stop that hummin'," said Bolls. "Ol' factor Hayes will get suspicious if we're too happy."

"Pshaw. Ol' man Hayes don't know nothin'." Planke continued his humming. "He'll want this baby, I tell you."

Bolls shot him a dark look. "Don't you go ruinin' this trade," he warned. Then he glanced back at the mule. "Think the little beaver's all right?"

Planke kept humming.

Bolls swore and handed Planke the reins to the chestnut packhorse. "Here, wait here." Bolls marched back to the mule and looked into a large basket on one side of the animal. He marched back to Bolls. "Baby's fine," he said. "Still stinks, though."

"It was your turn to clean him," said Planke self-righteously. "I did it yesterday."

Bolls growled at him and snatched the packhorse's reins out of his hands. "Let's go," he said.

Planke hunched his shoulders and started walking toward the factor's house. He resumed humming.

They reached the large wooden house that was set midway between the two bastions in the middle of the western wall.

Planke held the horse and mule while Bolls shuffled up the two steps and pounded on the heavy wooden door.

It opened.

"Mr. Hayes in?" demanded Bolls.

"Yes," came a disdainful feminine voice.

Bolls waited. "I want to talk to him."

"Wait." The heavy door slammed in Bolls's face.

Planke hummed louder and grinned at his partner. Bolls grimaced and glanced at the basket on the mule.

After a five-minute wait, the door opened once again and a heavyset white man strode out.

"Mr. Hayes, sir," said Bolls, touching his floppy leather hat brim.

"Bolls." Frederick Hayes stopped and rocked back and forth on his heels. "What do you free traders have for me? Are you bringing me some furs you traded from the Indians?"

"Better than that." Bolls rubbed his hands gleefully.

"What can be better than furs?" muttered Hayes.

"You'll see." Bolls led the Factor over to the mule. "Show him, Planke."

Planke whipped the ragged blanket off the basket. "Look."

Hayes frowned at the two traders, then cautiously approached the basket as if he thought it would bite him.

"See!" crowed Planke.

Hayes peered into the basket. "A baby?" he asked, incredulous.

"A baby," Bolls assured him. "Want to buy him?"

Hayes drew back as though he had been bitten. "I—I don't know. Let me talk to my wife."

"Oh, Mrs. Hayes, she'll want this baby. Look at him." Grinning, Bolls strode over and beamed at the basket. "A boy. That's what she's been wanting, isn't it?"

"Mrs. Hayes," said Frederick Hayes with a distasteful grimace, "has not conveyed to me her wishes in the matter of children." His look said he doubted she'd conveyed them to Bolls, either.

"What do you mean?" demanded Bolls. "Why, everyone knows she's been wantin' a baby and can't have one—"

"Bolls! You forget yourself!" warned Hayes, his face growing florid. "You speak of my wife!"

"Yeah, sure," agreed Bolls. "That's who I'm talkin' about. Mrs. Hayes."

Frederick Hayes turned on his heel and re-entered his house. The heavy door slammed once more upon Bolls and Planke.

Bolls and Planke grinned at each other. "I can feel that gold already," crowed Planke.

"I'm gonna buy me two casks of whiskey and a chaw of tabaccy!" promised Bolls, a look of rapture on his face.

The baby cried.

"Go see what he wants," urged Bolls.

Planke tiptoed over to the baby. "You be quiet," he

warned in a loud voice. "Don't you go cryin' and queerin' the deal."

The baby subsided to a whimper.

"Maybe he's hungry," said Bolls.

"Naw. I fed him when we had our whiskey at breakfast. That was"—Planke squinted at the sun—"oh, about five hours past, I reckon. That baby can't be hungry," said Planke confidently.

"I don't know," said Bolls. "That baby's always hungry, seems to me." He glanced at the basket, then shrugged. "Let Hayes feed him after he buys him."

Planke nodded vigorous agreement to that.

The door opened and Hayes came out.

"Well?" Bolls beamed and rubbed his hands. "How much you gonna give us?"

"I don't want the baby," said Hayes.

Frozen, Bolls and Planke stared at him, jaws dropped. Planke paled. Suddenly Bolls came to life. "What do you mean?" he screeched. He ran up to Hayes and seized him by the throat. "What do you mean, you don't want this baby? He's a boy, ain't he? Your wife wants a boy! Everyone knows—"

"Bolls," warned Hayes, tearing at the trader's skinny fingers, which were closing around his windpipe. "Cease this instant!" He shook the trader off the way a dog shakes a rat.

Bolls landed hard on the ground.

"My wife," snarled Hayes, "does not want an Indian baby."

Bolls glanced at Planke. "Why, he's no Indian baby," said Bolls hastily. "No sir, he sure ain't. White baby, that one."

"His hair is black," observed Hayes pointedly.

"Heh, heh, it is, it is," agreed Bolls. "But that's because he, uh—"

"His mama had black hair," said Planke helpfully.

"Real black. White woman with black hair, that's all."

"Yeah," continued Bolls. "That's all. His mama had black hair. She's white, I tell ya."

"Where is his mother?"

Boll glanced at Planke.

"Dead," said Planke.

"Dead," echoed Bolls.

Hayes shrugged. "Well, it doesn't much matter. He looks Indian and my wife doesn't want him."

"You gonna let her tell you what to do?" demanded Bolls desperately. "Here you been wantin' a son for years, and now you gonna let your wife tell you—"

"My wife," said Hayes, "is entitled to decide."

"But everyone knows that she wants a baby," whined Bolls.

The door opened once more, and a young woman walked down the steps. Her red hair shone in the winter sun; her mouth scrunched up when she saw the two traders.

Bolls and Planke stared at her.

"My dear." Hayes smiled, taking her hand. "This is Bolls and Planke. Meet my wife."

"Your wife?" squeaked Bolls.

"Certainly my wife," answered Hayes.

"But—but I saw your wife. She's old. She's gray."

"That was my dear, departed Ruth," said Hayes unctuously. "She died this past summer. Then I married the lovely Sally Beaufort."

He smiled at the pretty red-headed woman. The lovely Sally Beaufort turned up her nose at Bolls and Planke.

Bolls glared at Hayes. "What the hell did you go and marry *her* for?" he demanded.

"I beg your pardon?" Hayes glared back at the traders. "Peddle your wares somewhere else."

Bolls gritted his teeth. He glowered at Hayes and

Sally Beaufort. Then he snapped, "Come on, Planke. Let's get the hell out of here."

The disgruntled Bolls seized his packhorse's bridle and led the animal off, trade items tinkling. Planke spat on the ground, wheeled the mule's head around, and followed after Bolls.

"What perfectly awful men," observed Sally.

"You're so right, dear," murmured Hayes. "Let's go inside, shall we?" He held open the door and Sally sailed into the house.

"Damn!" snarled Planke. "What do we do now?"

"Damned if I know," answered Bolls.

They walked towards the corral. "Let's get these animals bedded down. Then we can decide what to do."

Just as they reached the corral, Bolls seized Planke's arm and pointed. "Look, ain't that Mrs. What's-Her-Name?"

"Who? Who?" Planke's head swiveled around.

"Her, you fool."

"Oh. Mrs. Pritchard."

"Yeah. Her husband is Chief Clerk here, ain't he?" Bolls smiled meaningfully at Planke.

Slowly Planke grinned back. "Yeah, Chief Clerk." He paused. "Say, you reckon she'll want a baby?"

"You're readin' my mind, boy," chortled Bolls. "Chief Clerk could pay and pay well for a babe."

The two ambled over to a tired-looking woman with a two-year-old child on one hip and a three-year-old child on the other.

Bolls elbowed Planke. "She likes children," he whispered, encouraged.

"Yeah," grinned Planke in excitement. "I bet she's the one's gonna buy this baby!"

"Mornin' ma'am," said Bolls, touching his floppy leather-brimmed hat.

The two-year-old started crying.

"Hush," said the mother. "You stop it now."

"Would you like to buy a baby, Mrs. Pritchard, ma'am?"

"What?" The woman stared at them. Her dress was loose, and her hair looked as if she'd put it in a bun only yesterday. The three-year-old perched on her hip said, "Want to get down, Mama. Want to get down. Want to get down."

"Hush, son," she said. "What baby?"

Proudly, Bolls led her over to the basket. "This one," he crowed. "Fine-looking baby, ma'am."

The woman peered into the basket. She frowned and looked at Bolls. "When did you change this baby last?"

Bolls shrugged. "Yesterday?"

"For sure," volunteered Planke. "Yesterday!"

"Oh," moaned the woman, clucking at the infant. "You poor little dear," she cooed.

"Want to see, want to see, want to see," chanted the three-year-old.

The woman let him down. "You stay by Mama," she warned, taking her son's hand. She glanced into the basket again. "Hello, little one," she said. "My, you are a good little thing, aren't you?"

"Damn fine baby, ma'am."

"We'll sell him to you," added Planke eagerly.

The woman pushed a stringy lock of hair out of her face and looked at the traders. "You won't get anything for him unless you clean him up," she said.

Bolls glanced around. "Hard to find water, ma'am," he muttered.

"Bring him to my house," she said. "I have water heating." She sighed wearily. "I always have water heating. We'll change him there."

"Yes, ma'am!" beamed Bolls, winking at Planke. Gold!

Theresa Scott

They went to her small cabin near the southwestern corner.

"There!" said the woman, after her ministrations. Her own children played quietly on the floor. "Now he's all clean again." She gave the baby a smile and was rewarded with a tiny gurgle. "He's very sweet," she said. "And he's so quiet!"

"Yes, ma'am," said Bolls. He would agree with anything she said, if only she'd buy the baby.

"How much are you gonna pay us for the baby?" asked Planke, unable to restrain himself any longer.

She glanced at him in surprise. "Why, I'm not going to pay you anything."

"You're not?" Both traders' jaws dropped.

"Why, no." She waved a hand around the room. "I have five children already." She patted her stomach. "And another due next month."

Bolls groaned and rolled his eyes.

Planke cursed under his breath.

They stomped out of the cabin.

"Now what?" asked Planke.

"Let me think," snapped Bolls. After a moment, he said, disgust in his voice, "We can't sell him. No one wants him. Hell, let's leave the baby out overnight. He'll freeze."

Chapter Four

Bolls took a swig from his whiskey flask. "Aaah, that tastes good," he murmured and passed the flask to Planke.

Planke threw back his head and drank until Bolls snatched the flask away. "That's enough," the older trader snapped, tucking the flask back inside his saddlebag. "Damn fool, you'll drink all my whiskey."

Planke rubbed his hands together and shivered. "It's cold out," he complained. "I need something to warm me up."

"Yeah? Well, cuddle up to Taos Lightning there." Bolls chuckled, pleased with his joke. Taos Lightning was the nickname given to one of the most potent liquors on the frontier. It was also the name of Planke's mule.

They plodded on. Fort McCraig was behind them. They'd managed to leave just before the heavy wooden gates were closed for the night. Though it was dark, the moon was full and they could see enough to follow the rocky trail. "Too bad we had to leave at night," complained Planke, flapping his arms to warm himself.

"Yeah. Well, we can't be there when the baby's found. What'll folks think?"

"Who cares about a baby?" asked Planke indifferently. "No one will blame us. No one will even care."

Bolls was silent for a while. "You're probably right," he agreed. "No one cares what happens to a baby. He was just a nuisance anyway."

"Yeah," agreed Planke. "All that pissin' and everythin'."

They plodded on. Then Bolls said, "Maybe we better go back to the fort and check."

"Check what?" asked Planke.

"Just check."

"Check what?"

"Just check, that's all. Stop askin' so many beaverdam questions!" said Bolls in irritation. He swung the packhorse around.

"What the hell are we supposed to check?" muttered Planke. He flapped his arms again to warm himself. "Wonder how the little beaver's doin'? Awful cold tonight."

Bolls halted his packhorse in mid-stride. "What's that sound?" He peered ahead into the night.

"I didn't hear nothing," answered Planke.

"Quiet. I hear something." Bolls listened. "There it is again."

"Mr. Bolls!" came a distant cry.

"Beaverdam!" said Bolls. "Someone's following us."

"Mr. Bolls," came the cry, a little closer this time.

"Can't be Indians," observed Planke. "They don't call your name all polite-like. They just jump out and ambush you." He glanced around nervously.

They waited, the mule nosing some sagebrush, the

packhorse snorting restively.

Out of the darkness arrived a woman, riding a mare. A goat trotted amiably at her side. "Mr. Bolls," she said and leaned over. He could see it was awkward for her. She was very pregnant.

"Miz' Pritchard!" he exclaimed. "What are you doing out here?"

"Mr. Bolls." She sounded out of breath. "I had to catch you. The baby—you left the baby. One of my daughters found him."

"Ah, geez." Bolls spat halfheartedly on the ground.

"I thank you, ma'am," said Planke, rolling his eyes at Bolls. "Don't know how we forgot him."

"I cleaned him for you," she said. "And I'm giving you some cotton rags for diapering, as many as I can spare." She lifted the basket that was tied to the saddle. She smiled down into the basket. "Why, you little sweet baby, you never cry, do you?" she cooed.

Bolls glanced at Planke and grimaced.

Mrs. Pritchard handed the basket to Bolls. "Here you go, Mr. Bolls," she said. "He's all clean and fed." She gestured with the goat's lead rope. "You forgot the goat too."

"Thank you, ma'am," said Bolls in feigned humbleness.

"Mr. Bolls," she said, and her voice was stern. "You have not been changing this baby often enough! He has a very bad rash on his bottom!"

"Well, uh, I, that is—"

"I've included an ointment of fat and herbs. Use it, Mr. Bolls! On his bottom. Six times a day. He'll do much better, I assure you! Poor little infant."

"Thank you, ma'am," gritted Bolls.

"You're welcome," she answered, but the sternness did not leave her voice. "I expect you to change that baby. Every time he wets, he needs clean diapering!"

Her voice became severe. "And certainly you must change him after he defecates!" She glared at them. "How often have you been changing him?"

"Er, uh, well, that is—" stammered Bolls.

"Whenever we thought of it," whined Planke. "We'd change him just that often."

"Think of him more often then!" she exclaimed and her voice sounded like a high mountain blizzard. "If I didn't already have five children with a sixth on the way, I'd take that child, let me tell you! But the good Lord has put enough on my plate."

With that, she handed the rope lead for the goat to Planke and wheeled the mare around. "Good night," she called over her shoulder. "And take better care of that child, do you hear?" She disappeared into the night.

"Take better care of that child," mimicked Bolls, making a face over the basket.

A little fist waved at him. He sighed. "What do we do now?" he asked Planke.

Planke shrugged. "Make camp and some new plans?" he suggested.

"Oh, all right," sighed Bolls. They hobbled the animals and made a fire. Bolls set the basket near the fire's warmth and the baby slept.

"What we gonna do with the little papoose?" asked Planke. "Our plans to freeze him didn't work so good."

"No, they didn't," snapped Bolls. He took a long draught on his whiskey flask. "Say," he said thoughtfully, wiping his mouth with the back of his hand. "I know a preacher hereabouts. . . . "

Planke warmed his hands over the orange flames and looked hungrily at the whiskey flask. "Preacher?" he echoed.

Bolls took another draught. "Man named Witberg," he mumbled. "The right Reverend Witberg."

Planke reached for the flask. Bolls slapped his hand away.

"He want a baby?" asked Planke, properly chastened.

"He might," allowed Bolls. "He's got money."

"A reverend? Money?"

"Yeah," answered Bolls. "You know someone better?" he added angrily.

"Not me," said Planke, eyeing the flask. "Give me some," he pleaded.

Bolls stared at him, dangling the flask casually. "I dunno," he said. "You ain't doin' much to help me in this here search for gold."

"I did!" protested Planke.

"You gonna change that baby?" The flask dangled. Planke glared sullenly at his tormentor.

Bolls grinned. "You change that baby. All night. Every time he pisses." He watched Planke and then took a long, satisfying swig. "Ah, beaverdam, that tastes good," he crowed.

"All right, all right," muttered Planke. "I'll change the little pup. Just give me the whiskey."

With a triumphant cackle, Bolls handed over the flask.

Planke took a long draught. "Hey! This is empty," he cried.

"Too bad," chuckled Bolls.

Planke threw the flask down and it made a dull clank on the gravel.

Bolls retrieved it. "Tsk, tsk," he chortled. "That's no way to behave. Not when we're goin' callin' on the right Reverend Witberg tomorrow!"

Chapter Five

The sky was a gray bowl above Gentle Fawn's head. "It will snow soon, my husband," she said.

Hawk Catcher nodded. "We have enough time to get the beaver pelts," he said. "We will return to our home soon."

She smiled. Hawk Catcher was a good hunter and trapper—a fine provider. Already they had twenty thick beaver pelts in their tepee. Soon they would travel to Fort McCraig and trade the furs for more winter provisions of flour and some of the white man's molasses and even some tobacco for Hawk Catcher. They would weather the winter very well, because Hawk Catcher was an industrious and thrifty man.

It was good to be working, to feel the skinning knife beneath her fingers. Work helped her to forget. . . .

They walked for a time until they came to the next trap on the trapline. Hawk Catcher waded out and retrieved the body of a plump beaver. He laid the fifty-pound beaver on the ground and Gentle Fawn skinned it, careful to avoid slicing the castor musk sacs that could ruin the fur.

Hawk Catcher reset the trap in the river. Then they followed the river trail in the direction of the next trap.

They approached a bend in the river. Willow trees and greasewood trees bordered the water. A small cabin was set in the woods, on the opposite bank. Hawk Catcher pointed. "I know the white man who lives there."

Gentle Fawn had been on this trapline route with Hawk Catcher two times already, and she had noticed the cabin before. Knowing it belonged to a white man, she had shown no curiosity, preferring to stay away from the strangers. More and more of them appeared in Nez Perce lands every season. She, for one, was not curious about them. Or so she told herself.

"He is a good white man," said her husband.

"Hunh," she grunted, not wanting to contradict him openly.

"It's true." Hawk Catcher sounded amused, as if he knew she did not believe him. He stopped and pointed at the small cabin. Gray smoke curled from the stone and dried-mud chimney. "He is at home," observed Hawk Catcher. "Would you like to visit him?"

"No."

"He has a woman," continued Hawk Catcher. "They are both old. Too old for children."

Gentle Fawn turned away, hurt by the reminder of children.

"I do not seek to hurt you, wife," said Hawk Catcher, catching her chin and bringing her around to face him. "My words were careless."

She met his eyes and saw the bleak look therein. *He suffers too*, she thought. "I understand," she murmured and smiled tremulously.

He kissed her lips. "Though the cold of winter stalks our trail, I took you with me on this trapline," he said, "to get you away from your pain, not to further burden you."

She nodded and brushed her hair to the side, the touch consoling her. "What is the white man's name?" If her husband wished that she take an interest in these strangers, then perhaps she could at least show more curiosity.

"Rev-ren Wit-berg," he pronounced the strange name carefully. "He is a white man who always talks about his god. His god is different from the Great Spirit."

"How?"

"He talks about his god as a baby."

"A baby?" she frowned.

"Yes. His god is a baby. Je-sus."

"How odd," she murmured. "Our Great Spirit is fully grown, I believe. Not an infant."

He kissed her and chuckled. "I think so, too. I don't think a child could be a god. But Rev-ren Wit-berg says it is true. I listen and nod. He believes what he will."

She nodded and they trekked on. The talk of babies caused roiling feelings inside her. She wondered if she should ask the Great Spirit for a child one more time. Her dream had not left her. No, she had not imagined pressing his dark head to her breast. That dream had been real and strong—almost a vision. And yet her baby son was born dead. Oh, what did it all mean?

She glanced at her husband, wondering what he would say if she told him her confusion about her dream. Hawk Catcher had probably forgotten about the dream, it had happened so long ago. Perhaps she was wrong to take it as a promise from the Great Spirit. Perhaps the dream meant she would hold the child to her and then have to let it go.

She shook her head. No—that interpretation did not seem right. In the dream she'd felt love and hope. Not death and despair. Yet that was what her life was full of now. Death and despair.

She trudged on, forgetting where they were, forgetting all but her own torturous thoughts.

They came to the next trap. Hawk Catcher waded into the cold water and brought out another big fat beaver. "Ho!" he said when he reached the bank where she stood. "Another one for you to tan, wife. You will be busy all winter."

She tried to smile. "Yes," she assured him. "I like to tan the beaver hides." It kept her occupied and she didn't have to think. About her dead babies.

But there was something that nagged at her as she met Hawk Catcher's sparkling black eyes. Something she hadn't told him. Something that would cause him despair too.

She forced out an exclamation of delight and glanced away, as if impressed with the size of the beaver. "His pelt is thick," she assured Hawk Catcher. "And he is big. We will get much for him at the fort's trading post."

"We will." Hawk Catcher grinned. "And," he added, wading back into the river, "there is another beaver trapped too."

"Ah!" she exclaimed. "A good catch."

Hawk Catcher looked pleased. But he would not look so pleased if he knew the truth, she thought guiltily. If he knew what her old aunt, the tribe's medicine woman, had said.

Her aunt's words rang in Gentle Fawn's ears even now. The old medicine woman had taken Gentle

Fawn aside, after the baby died.

"There is something I must tell you, daughter," the old woman had said kindly. "I am sad to tell you this, Gentle Fawn, but it is better that you know. I have seen that most of your babies have been born a strange blue color. Something is hurt deep inside your womb and it makes your babies die. I must tell you: you will never be able to give birth to a child again."

Chapter Six

"This where he lives?" asked Planke.

"Yeah." Bolls dismounted and tied the packhorse and his own bay horse to a small pine tree. "Smoke is comin' out of the chimney. Reverend Witberg is home!"

Planke excitedly grabbed the basket off the mule. The baby gave a cry at the jostling. "Can't wait to get rid of this baby," exclaimed Planke. "Can't wait for all that gold, either."

Bolls chuckled, in good humor. He walked up and stopped several feet from the door. "Hallooo, the Reverend!" he called.

No answer.

"Halloo, the Reverend!"

"Maybe he ain't home, after all," said a disappointed Planke.

"He can't have gone far," objected Bolls. "That smoke is still comin' out the chimney."

He went up and knocked on the heavy door. He

tried pushing it to see if it would open. It didn't.

"Who's there?" quavered a feminine voice from behind the locked wooden door.

"Elijah Bolls and Jesse Planke," answered Bolls. He whispered to Planke, "Only the old woman is at home."

"Maybe she wants the baby," Planke hissed back. "Women love babies."

"Yeah?" answered Bolls nastily. "Then how come Sally Beaufort didn't?"

Before Planke could reply, the door opened and a woman's gray head poked out.

"Mr. Bolls? Mr. Planke? Are you friends of my husband?" She glanced toward the river and trees nervously.

"Friends? Oh yes, ma'am," answered Bolls, touching the brim of his leather hat. "Know him real well, I do."

"Oh," she said, opening the door a little wider. "You must be good Christian gentlemen then."

"Oh, we are," Bolls assured her. Planke giggled and Bolls elbowed him in the gut.

"Please, do come inside," the woman said, and the two sauntered into the cabin.

The woman touched her graying hair. Her plump body was encased in a red-and-white calico dress and she wore a yellow-and red-striped Hudson's Bay blanket over her shoulders as a shawl. A fire burned in the fireplace at one end of the room. The one-room cabin was very warm.

The woman held out her hand and said graciously, "My name is Rachel Witberg. Welcome to my home."

Bolls took her hand but didn't know what to do with it so he let it drop. "Thank ye, ma'am. We're right glad to be here. Uh, is the Reverend about?"

"I'm so sorry, but no. Though I do expect him back at any time. He's two days overdue already." She smiled. "He's out doing God's work: converting the heathens and ministering unto the poor in spirit." She spied the basket. "And what do you have in the basket?"

Planke cleared his throat. "It's a baby, ma'am. We thought you and your husband might like to buy him."

Her hand went to her heart. "Buy?" she gasped. "A baby?"

"Yes, ma'am," said Bolls. "We thought maybe your husband would need help in his uh, misery, I mean ministry. This little one will grow up and be right handy-like in helpin' convert the heathens and such, ma'am."

She peered into the basket. "I'm sure you're right," she answered dubiously. "But—a baby?"

Planke lifted the basket closer so she could see. He winked at Bolls.

"Let's put the basket on the table where I can see a little better," she murmured.

Planke obliged.

"Oh," exclaimed Mrs. Witberg. "What a lovely wee bairn!" She ducked her head closer and cooed, "Aren't you a lovely little thing? Oh, yes, you are! So pretty, so dainty—"

"Uh, ma'am?" interrupted Bolls. "That there's a boy."

"Oh." Then she ducked down to see the baby and continued, "Such a big boy you are, too. So handsome . . ."

Bolls grinned at Planke. Gold!

When she was done cooing at the baby, Mrs. Witberg lifted her head. Her face was flushed and her eyes shone.

Bolls grinned broadly at her.

"I'm so glad you brought this baby to me," she exclaimed. Her hands fluttered. "But oh, what would I do with him? A baby! All the feedings, changing his diapering cloths, and those sleepless nights! I just don't know . . ."

"Oh, ma'am, nothin' to it," said Bolls encouragingly. "Me and my partner here, why, we been takin' care of him. It's easy."

She frowned. "That's not how I remember it." She glanced at them uncertainly, then at the infant. "He is very little," she said. "But he is oh-so-sweet."

"Yeah, ma'am," said Planke. "Quiet. Good as gold."
Bolls elbowed him in the gut again.

"I—I could—Oh, what should I do? Mr. Witberg does need a helper in his ministry. Oh, and this baby is a sweet delight." She smiled and nodded at the baby. "I will take the baby."

Bolls's grin nearly split his face. Planke did a little dance on the wooden floor.

"But first, before we talk about money," said the reverend's wife crisply, "this baby needs a good bath!"

She hummed as she poured water into a big iron pot beside the fireplace. "There. This will soon heat," she said.

"Did you know, gentlemen," she said conversationally while she bustled around the cabin, "I have already raised my family. Two strapping boys!" She found some calico and began tearing it into strips for diaper cloths.

"No!" said Bolls, rolling his bloodshot eyes. "A delicate woman like you?"

She giggled. "It's true. Two strapping boys. I thought I was all done with child rearing!" She laughed.

Bolls laughed with her.

The water was steaming when she brought a pan over to the table. She carefully picked up the baby. "Oh, you little sweetie, how are you? Come to Rachel." She buried her nose near his neck. She jerked her head right back up. "Oh dear," she said.

"What's wrong?" asked Bolls in alarm.

"He smells terribly. When was the last time you cleaned him?"

"This morning," lied Planke.

Mrs. Witberg swiftly disrobed the baby. "Well, we'll take care of you now," she cooed at the baby. She kissed the air above his head. "We'll get you all cleaned and—oh, what is this?"

"What?" chorused Bolls and Planke.

"What?" added Bolls. Perplexed, he leaned forward to see what she was staring at so transfixedly.

"This—this rash! Why, I've never seen such a bad case."

"Heh, heh, yes ma'am," chuckled Bolls. "We been puttin' ointment on it. Yes, we have—ain't we, Planke?"

"Huh?" Planke was staring at the rifle above the fireplace. Bolls elbowed him in the stomach.

"Oh, yes, we sure have," volunteered Planke, holding his stomach.

"Good baby," said Bolls, trying to imitate Mrs. Witberg's manner with the child.

"I see you like to talk to the babe too," she observed. "Babies need to be talked to, you know."

"Talk to him every day," said Bolls.

Planke was staring at a small box on the mantle. "Must be where they keep their money," he whispered to Bolls. Bolls nodded.

When the baby was cleaned and Mrs. Witberg was holding him, she asked, "How have you been feeding the child?"

"We got a goat," explained Bolls. "Nanny goat does the feeding."

"Very good, Mr. Bolls. Let's feed him now." She handed Bolls a tin cup.

He handed it to Planke. "Go milk the nanny," he told Planke.

Planke took his wistful eyes off the box on the mantle and sauntered out the door.

He returned soon with warm milk in the cup.

"Let me feed him," demanded Mrs. Witberg.

"Please do," answered Bolls, rolling his eyes at Planke.

She sat down in an old rocker near the fireplace. She sat and rocked and fed the baby and talked to him the whole while. Planke was fidgeting, bored.

"Uh, Mrs. Witberg?" Bolls asked politely.

"—such a sweet, sweet little suckling, aren't you? Oh my, yes, you are," she was saying. "Poor, poor little thing. But when you're a big, big boy I'll bake you cookies and—"

"Uh, Mrs. Witberg." Bolls was firmer this time. "We gotta go."

"Oh, heavens, my, yes!" she exclaimed. "You go right ahead. Thank you so much for the baby!"

"You're right welcome, ma'am," grinned Bolls. Then his grin vanished. "We want our money."

"Money?"

"For the baby, ma'am. He ain't free."

"Oh. Money." She struggled to get out of the rocker, baby in her arms. "It's been a long time," she muttered, "since I had such a tiny one around. . . ." Finally, she managed to rise from the rocker. She shuffled over to the box that Planke had been staring at so longingly. He grinned at Bolls.

Bolls merely lifted an eyebrow. They heard the clink of coins and then he smiled and opened his palm.

She shuffled over. "Here you go," she said and plunked two coins into his hand.

There was no trace of his grin now. "Two pennies!" he exclaimed. "Is that all you got?"

The Treasure

She stared at him. "Why, yes, it is, Mr. Bolls. My husband has more money—"

"Where is it?" demanded Bolls.

"Why, with him, of course," answered Mrs. Witberg in a reasonable voice. "He should be back soon. Any day . . ."

Bolls snatched the baby out of her arms.

"Mr. Bolls! Give me back my baby!"

"I will *not*, madam! Not until he's been paid for!"

"I'll pay for him," answered Mrs. Witberg, her eyes round in surprise. "I just can't pay you until my husband returns."

"We'll come back then!" thundered Bolls.

Mrs. Witberg held out her arms. "But my baby—"

"He's not yourn!" cried Planke. "Not until you pay for him!"

"I'll pay! I'll pay!" cried Mrs. Witberg. "Only give him back to me!"

"No!" yelled Bolls. "Infernal woman! You tricked us!"

"I did not!" she screamed. "I'll pay you!"

The baby started to cry.

"Now look what you done," yelled Bolls. "You woke the beaverdam baby!"

"Oh, no," she moaned. "Poor, poor little sweetie—" She reached for the infant.

Bolls stepped back, the baby just out of her reach. "That does it!" he cried. "Planke, get the basket. We're leaving!" Planke dashed for the basket still on the table.

"Don't go!" cried Mrs. Witberg. "My husband will be back—"

"Glad to hear it, Mrs. Witberg, glad to hear it," muttered Bolls, backing out the door with the baby. Planke inserted himself between the distraught woman and Bolls. She tried to lunge around him to get at the squirming infant, but he neatly intercepted her. "Back, Mrs. Witberg, back!" Planke warned.

"My baby!" she cried. "Bring me back my baby!"

"You get the beaverdam money!" cried Bolls. "Then you can have the beaverdam baby!"

He and Planke seized the reins of their horses and marched down the trail.

Mrs. Witberg ran after them. "My baby—!" she cried.

"Get back to your cabin, woman!" blazed Bolls. "You'll get the damn baby when we get the damn money!"

"Soon, soon!" she cried. "Only bring him back to me! Please!"

"Infernal woman," muttered Bolls as they left her farther back on the trail behind them. He stuffed the baby in the basket.

"Two pennies! What's wrong with that woman's head that she thinks she can buy a baby for two lousy pennies!" demanded Bolls.

"Dunno," answered Planke. They walked along for a while and then he asked, "We gonna come back and get the money from her husband?"

"Yeah," snarled Bolls. "We'll come back. But I tell you, Planke, if I get a better offer, I'm gonna take it! Infernal woman and her two lousy pennies!"

Chapter Seven

Gentle Fawn walked hand in hand with Hawk Catcher. The winter day was cool, and snow still threatened. A feeling of warm companionship swept over her as she held Hawk Catcher's hand. Time with him was precious as they walked the beaver trapline. She loved him so much.

They stopped to rest, and she removed the load of beaver skins she carried on her back. Suddenly she bent down and stared at the ground. "What animal made these tracks, husband?"

Hawk Catcher knelt to look. "Three horses, a mule . . ." He gently touched one of the prints and shook his head. "I do not know these tracks, Gentle Fawn. It looks like some kind of small deer. But very tiny."

"A small deer? Walking alongside horses?" she asked. "That is odd."

He agreed.

They both rose and stood gazing at the tracks.

"Very odd," she muttered, intrigued by the prints.

"Come," said her husband. "Let us find the last beaver trap on the line, then we can return to our home."

Gentle Fawn did not move. Though she feared disturbing the tranquility between them, she knew their peace was a false one. A secret lay between them.

"My husband, there is something I must tell you." Dread filled her. She had held her aunt's words inside her for a long time. Now it was time to let them out to the light of day, to tell her beloved Hawk Catcher the truth.

He waited.

She took a breath. "After I gave birth to our—our son—" She hesitated. Perhaps he did not need to know this. Perhaps she was foolish to speak of it. *But he does need to know this*, she thought. *He wants a child as badly as I do. He needs to know!*

He watched her calmly; his dark eyes held hers, and she found her courage again.

"My aunt, the medicine woman, told me that I could bear no more children. She told me that something inside me had been hurt by the birth." Gentle Fawn expelled her breath, waiting . . . For what, she did not know.

Hawk Catcher's dark eyes looked tortured. "You can bear no more children?"

Gentle Fawn shook her head. "I cannot grow babies. The medicine woman told me they will all die." She bowed her head, grief overtaking her heart. She stared at the ground through her blurred tears.

Hawk Catcher lifted her chin. "Can we still—"

She nodded hastily. "I can still be wife to you," she murmured. "The medicine woman gave me an herb so that no more little ones shall grow in my womb. I cannot bear to go through another birth—and death. And no little baby should suffer so." She could not meet his eyes. "It weighs upon my heart too much to lose another child, and now my body cannot bear it either."

He was silent.

"I can still sleep with you in our bedrobes," she assured him. "But if I grow a baby, it will die." Despairingly, she met his eyes.

She started to weep at the sorrow she saw in his eyes. "I—I—" She stopped and wiped her tears. In all fairness to him, she should tell him that she understood if he wanted to set her aside, or take another wife. But truly, though she could understand it, her heart did not want it to happen, not yet. Not ever.

Hawk Catcher looked stunned. He did not meet her eyes now, only stared at the river. But she saw his jaw muscles tighten, and she knew that what she'd told him hurt.

"I must have time," he said at last, "time to think about this."

Her heart fell. It was the beginning of the end of their marriage. She knew it. Bravely, she choked back her tears and said, "I will give you time, my husband. I will go to the mountain and pray."

He met her eyes then and he looked dazed, uncomprehending. "Yes," he answered at last. "That is wise."

Never, not in all the seasons of their marriage, had he let her go off alone. The land held dangers: wolves, cougars, bear . . . And man. It was his deep grief that clouded his wisdom, she said to herself.

She picked up the beaver skins and tied them and slung them on her back. Then she took a step away. Then another step. At every step she expected him to call her back. But he did not.

Through her tears she saw the strange small deer hoofprints. "I will follow these," she thought. Her life

343

with Hawk Catcher was dying, and there was nothing more she could do.

She followed the tiny tracks. They led in the direction of the mountain where her people went to pray. The mountain was a half day's journey away. Perhaps the little tracks would guide her.

But the tracks ran out after she had only gone a short distance. She brushed aside her tears and continued on. She would go to the mountain. She would pray to the Great Spirit.

Hawk Catcher shook himself out of his dazed state. He had been staring at the river for a long time.

It was growing dark. Where was Gentle Fawn? Then he remembered. She had said she was going to the mountain to pray. He vaguely remembered telling her it was wise. But when he glanced around at the darkening land, he realized that he should not have let her go alone. *He* had not been wise.

He bent and touched one of the tiny hoof tracks. Gentle Fawn had followed them. He easily followed her trail, but then the small deer prints and her footprints disappeared.

He glanced around. It was dark. She was alone out there. He cast around in small circles, trying to find her tracks again, but he could not.

Distraught, he made a fire and decided to wait until dawn. He would find her then.

Chapter Eight

"She wanted that baby," mused Planke. "You saw it. Miz Witberg wanted him. Bad."

Bolls wouldn't answer. All day he'd refused even to speak of "that infernal woman," as he called Mrs. Witberg. Planke had tried all day to draw him out.

Finally the silence got to Planke. He walked up to Bolls's packhorse and rummaged in the saddlebag. "Aha!" he crowed and dragged out the whiskey flask.

He shook it, unscrewed the lid, and peered inside. "Beaverdam!" he swore. "It's empty."

Bolls snickered.

Planke glanced at him. "You think it's funny when your partner's so thirsty he'd drink beaver piss?" he demanded.

"Like to see that," answered Bolls.

"You won't." Still holding the flask, Planke sidled around the mule to the other side. He pulled out the little cork on the side of the big wooden whiskey cask and filled up the flask. Then he took a long, hearty draught.

Theresa Scott

"Hey!"

The flask was snatched out of his hand. Bolls's red face glared at him. "What do you think you're doin', drinkin' my whiskey?"

"It's ourn," answered Planke coolly. "I bought it with you. You just think it's yourn."

Bolls wiped off the top of the flask with a dirty hand and tipped his head back. He drank for a long time. When he was done, he eyed Planke challengingly and said, "Ahhhhh, that tasted good!"

Planke reached for the flask. When Bolls wouldn't give it to him, he walked over to the mule, pulled out the little cork and put his mouth under the steady stream of whiskey.

"Get away from that!" yelled Bolls, running over. He kicked Planke in the butt and Planke went sprawling. Bolls shoved the cork back into the wooden cask.

The baby started to cry.

"Now look what you done," protested Planke. "You woke the baby!"

Hearing those dreaded words, Bolls froze. "Beaverdam!"

They tiptoed over and looked inside the basket. "He's wet," said Bolls. "It's your turn."

"It's yourn," Planke snorted.

"You do it," slurred Bolls, "and I'll let you have a wee drinkie."

Planke's narrowed gaze went from the baby to his trading partner and back again. "No," he muttered. "Last time you tricked me."

Bolls laughed. "No tricks. You change the baby, I'll give you a wee drinkie."

"I'll do it," Planke said. He picked up the baby and walked to the cold creek. He took off the wet diaper and splashed water on the baby. The child cried louder.

346

"What are you doin' to him?" demanded Bolls. "You let anything happen to that pup and you're in a heap of trouble. That pup's worth money and don't you forget it!"

Planke was smiling when he returned with the baby. He wrapped a clean calico cloth around the slippery, kicking little body and grinned at Bolls. "Her husband is goin' to pay us gold for this baby, I tell you. I can feel it in my bones."

"You can take your bones and stuff 'em in a beaver trap for all I care," snapped Bolls.

"Yeah? You're just jealous 'cause it was my idea to keep the baby," said Planke.

"It was *my* idea!" Bolls glowered at his companion.

Planke dropped the babe back in the basket. "Now see here," he said, drawing himself up to his full lanky height. "I had the idea to trade this little trapper! It's thanks to me we're gonna be rich men!"

"Yeah? We ain't gonna be nothin' less'n you get that little trapper to stop cryin'."

"Hell," muttered Planke, "babies always cry."

"Yeah? How come you know so much about babies?" needled Bolls.

"I take good care of this baby, you just see if I don't."

"Hmmph, not as good as I do." Bolls thumped his chest with a thick thumb.

"When's the last time you fed him then?" demanded Planke belligerently.

"Just this morning." Bolls grinned in triumph.

Planke squinted at the sun. "Well, it's noon now and you ain't done nothin'! That little trapper's starving."

"Naw, he ain't," said Bolls in surprise.

"He is," said Planke. "And Mrs. Witberg ain't gonna want to buy a skinny baby. She wants a fat one."

"You think so?" asked Bolls, rubbing his chin. He

took another drink from the flask. "Maybe we better feed him," he acknowledged. "Don't want no skinny baby."

"The right Reverend Witberg probably don't neither," Planke reminded him.

They got the nanny goat and baby in position and squeezed the goat's udder until the thin white stream fell onto the baby's lips. "Come on, eat, little beaver," said Planke awkwardly.

"You ain't cooin' like old Mrs. Witberg," complained Bolls. "Cooin' makes the baby want to eat. Hey, I got an idea." He pulled a tin cup out of his saddlebag and poured a long stream of whiskey in it. Then he drank a gulp of the whiskey.

Planke stared at him.

"Remember when that infernal woman fed him? From a cup like this?" Bolls downed another gulp of whiskey from the cup.

"Yeah."

"Well, let's feed him from this tin cup, then," ordered Bolls. He held the cup near the nanny goat's udder. "Squirt some milk into the cup."

"With that whiskey still in it?" asked Planke.

"Sure. Nothin' wrong with a little whiskey."

"I don't think I should," said Planke uncertainly. "Might make the baby sick."

"You think so?" asked Bolls. He rubbed his chin in thought. "I think the whiskey's good. Make him grow." He laughed.

Planke eyed him balefully. "Naw. I ain't gonna feed him whiskey. If he gets sick, then the Reverend Witberg won't pay no gold for him."

Bolls frowned. "You're right." He drank the dregs of whiskey from the cup. "*Now* will you squirt?"

Planke milked the nanny goat, the white stream shooting into the cup. When the cup was half full, they fed the baby.

"Now he's wet again," observed Planke. "It's your turn."

"Ah, geez," said Bolls. "You just changed him!"

Planke shrugged. "I never knew there was so much to takin' care of a baby. We're never gonna get where we're goin' like this."

Bolls grumbled the whole time he washed the baby; his grumbles were loud enough to drown out the little one's cries.

Planke waved at Bolls. Then he took a long drink from the flask. Bolls glared at him over the crying baby.

"Now he's ready," Bolls announced. He put the baby in the basket and strapped it on the mule. "Let's get the hell out of here. Maybe we can find someone else to sell this baby to."

"I thought we was goin' to sell to him to Reverend Witberg?" said Planke.

"This here's a fine baby," retorted Bolls. "Reverend Witberg might pay a lot of gold for him, but then he might not. Maybe someone else is gonna pay us even *more* gold."

"Might be," said Planke thoughtfully.

They rode along for some time until they came to a river. A grizzled trapper stood on shore near some greasewood trees. He'd just finished hiding his canoe under the low branches.

Bolls hailed him. "Where you goin'?" he asked in a friendly fashion.

"I'm goin' to visit a woman," said the trapper. He was a middle-aged man with a long beard and long gray hair down the shoulders of his leather tunic. He carried a thick bundle in one hand and his rifle in the other.

"Ooowhee," answered Bolls. "You headin' for a good time, then?"

Planke laughed. "You tell us where that friendly

Theresa Scott

woman is, and we'll have some fun too," he chortled.

The trapper didn't laugh. He leaned on his rifle and tipped his leather hat back.

Bolls watched him. "You want some tabaccy?" offered Bolls finally.

"Yeah," answered the trapper.

Bolls cut off a tiny portion of the tobacco he carried for trade. "No sense in wasting good tabaccy," he whispered to Planke as he passed him. "Just enough to be sociable-like."

Planke grinned.

They talked with the trapper awhile, asking about the beaver pelts he'd taken and asking if he knew of any rich men in the area. The trapper shook his head.

The trapper was clearly anxious to get to the woman, so Bolls and Planke bade him farewell. Just as he was walking past him, Bolls glanced at the bundle. It was a book. "That's a mighty thick book," he observed.

"Yeah," grunted the trapper. "I'm taking it to the lady."

"Givin' her presents?" Bolls grinned suggestively.

"Naw," answered the trapper. "Some bad Injuns attacked her husband. Hit him on the head. Then he fell in the river. He almost froze up solid. They stole his horse, his money, left nothin' but this here Bible."

"Too bad, too bad," murmured Bolls insincerely.

"Yeah. Some good Injuns takin' care of him now. I'm takin' this Bible to his wife. Gotta get her over to the Injun village to help him. He's awful close to dyin'." The trapper opened the first page of the book. "It's got some family names in here," he said. "Since I knowed him, I thought I'd better take it to his wife."

Bolls went still. "Say," he said slowly. "What might the injured man's name be?"

The trapper cleared his throat. "His name's the right Reverend Josiah Witberg. You knowed him?"

350

Chapter Nine

Relief flooded through him when Hawk Catcher spotted Gentle Fawn in the distance. He moved closer, knowing she had wanted to be alone, but he could not help himself. He had to see her, to know she was safe. He crept forward quietly. She had keen hearing and he did not want to scare her.

The sharp cry of a raven rasped high over his head, and he glanced up. He scanned the thick gray clouds above. The raven warned that snow would come soon, perhaps even before they returned to their tepee. But Hawk Catcher would not let his beloved be caught in the snow alone. He would stay and watch over her.

Gentle Fawn sat on a rock, staring at the river. Behind her towered the scarred black stone height of the mountain. She had sought out this place before, when her heart had sorely troubled her. Now she sought it once again, sought it for its wild beauty, for its peace, for the river's murmuring—and yes, for the raven's raucous cry overhead.

"Great Spirit," she began aloud. Her voice trembled, but she forced herself onward. "I come to you with troubled heart. I know not what to do anymore. My life is—" She took a breath. Is what? she wondered. Destroyed? Full of despair? She bowed her head in her hands and cried. When she could cry no more tears, she lifted her head. "All those children," she cried out angrily. "My babies. Dead. Why? Why?" Her voice rose in anguish.

Only silence answered. The raven wheeled overhead, his cries stilled for the nonce.

"I do not know why," she said at last. "Unless you tell me, I will never know." She stared at the water. "It comes to me now that even if I knew why my babies died, it would not help me. It has been too sorrowful, this life of mine. I cannot go on bearing children only to see them die—only to send them back to the cold earth." She started to cry again. "Please, oh please, help me. In my dream, did you not promise me a child? Why then, did you take back your promise? I know not what you want of me."

She put her hands over her face. "I cannot go on hoping for a child. Hope for a child has no place in my life any longer. I—I—" Sobs tore from her throat. "I cannot hope; hope has died too."

The sounds of her sobs drowned out the river's murmurings. When at last she raised her head, she glanced around. The river water still rushed past her. Above her the raven still wheeled. Pine trees still sat on the mountainside. And she still grieved.

She took a breath. Now came the most difficult part. The Great Spirit must be told what she had decided. "Great Spirit," she said again. "It is about my husband, Hawk Catcher. I love him. I have loved him since I was a young girl. He has been a good husband to me, brave and kind. I thank you for him." She bowed her head. "But we both know I cannot give him a child. Nor can I trap him with my love, or hold him in the snare of it. No. I must set him free so that he may find a new wife—a new wife who will give him what I cannot. Therefore, I ask"—she took a breath—"I ask that you—" The words would not come, no matter how she forced them. "I—I—"

The raven cried out overhead. She looked up. He wheeled in circles far above her. "What is it you say, messenger of the Great Spirit?" she asked. "Have you been sent to strengthen me, to give me courage?" The raven's hoarse cry rang out again.

Gentle Fawn watched the raven coast in one large arc and then fly off to the west. She took new courage from the raven. "I must go on with my prayer," she told herself.

She took a breath. "I ask you, Great Spirit, you who know how deep my love is for my husband. I ask that you take all the love that I have in my heart and pour it into another woman's heart. I ask that you find a woman who can love Hawk Catcher as I do—a woman who can bear his children!"

She slumped on the rock. The words, the request, had taken every feeling of life from her. She touched her chest; that her heart still pounded within surprised her. She should have nothing left. No life at all. Because to give up Hawk Catcher was to die.

Hawk Catcher heard her words. He bowed his head and wept.

Chapter Ten

"Say, trapper," said Bolls. "What'd you say your name was?"

"I didn't," replied the trapper. He looked weary. "I shouldn't be standin' here a-socializin'. I should be takin' this book to the woman. Her husband's hurt bad."

Bolls and Planke were silent.

"My name's Archibald McKay," said the trapper at last.

Bolls and Planke gave their names.

"Do much trappin' hereabouts?" probed Bolls.

McKay shrugged and turned away, evidently not much interested in lively conversation.

Bolls hastened after him. "Say, McKay, you look like a man who needs a baby."

The trapper halted and whipped around to stare at Bolls and Planke. "Now why," he answered slowly, eyes wide, "would I need a baby?"

Bolls shrugged and grinned. "Never can tell. A man

needs a baby for any number o' things. Some men need them for sons." He eyed McKay keenly. "Bet you don't have no son."

"I don't," acknowledged McKay.

"Well," said Bolls expansively. "You need one. Who else gonna carry on the McKay name?"

McKay shrugged.

"We got a baby," said Planke. "Right fine baby. Doesn't cry. Don't have to change him much. We even got a nanny goat so's he'll have plenty o' milk."

"Nanny goat?" McKay stroked his beard thoughtfully.

Seeing his interest, Bolls said, " 'Course we can't sell him to just anyone," said Bolls. "This here baby, why he has a right royal history. Don't he, Planke?"

Planke nodded. He went over and untied the basket from the mule. He brought it back. "Have a look-see," he urged.

McKay peered into the basket. "Why, you do have a baby in there!" he exclaimed.

"Sure do," answered Planke.

"We been offered bales and bales o' furs for this here little beaver, ain't we, Planke?" said Bolls.

Planke gaped at Bolls. Bolls glared at him.

"Yeah," muttered Planke.

"We been offered, oh, a hunnerd furs by one factor who wanted this baby. Factor of a big, important fort. But we said no, didn't we, Planke?"

Planke looked wary. "Yeah."

"We're not goin' to give this baby to no factor for a measly one hunnerd furs. No sir! Not when this here little trapper is royalty, that's what he is."

Planke took a few steps backward, glancing around nervously, as if he wanted to depart the scene.

"Right, Planke?" menaced Bolls.

"Right."

"And royalty deserves more than one hunnerd furs! That's what we think!"

McKay eyed Bolls. "This baby's royalty?" He shook his head in disbelief.

"Sure is," crowed Bolls. "Why his daddy is Lord Howard, that's who."

"Who's Lord Howard?" asked McKay.

Bolls started to laugh. "He don't know who Lord Howard is, Planke! Fancy that! Why, Lord Howard, he's the only son of William and Mary, you know."

McKay looked blank.

"William and Mary Harvard. Or was it Yale?" Bolls didn't wait for Planke's helpless shrug. "One o' those royal families anyway."

McKay frowned. "I don't like you laughin' at me."

"Now, now," said Bolls hastily, not wanting to put his quarry off. "Perhaps a dedicated trapper like yourself hasn't heard. That's it. You was out trappin', working like a dog gettin' those beaver pelts, and no one tol' you about royal Lord Howard travelin' through the land, drawin' pictures, pickin' plants, cookin' up deer skulls and meetin' with the Indians and all that."

McKay shook his head. "No, didn't hear none o' that," he agreed, mollified. And interested.

Bolls leaned closer confidentially. "Well, one o' them meetings Lord Howard had was with a lovely Indian princess. They had a night o' love. And this here baby is the result!" Bolls threw his arm wide, as though presenting the baby.

"Geez," muttered McKay. "You say he was cookin' up deer skulls, too?"

"Not during the night o' love, o' course," assured Bolls. "But other times he did. Said it was a *scientific* expedition. Said he was shippin' the skulls back to England from whence he came."

"Geez." McKay scratched his head thoughtfully.

" 'Course we know a trapper like you would take good care of a baby," said Bolls, anxious now to make the sale. "Nothin' to it, anyway."

"It's easy," assured Planke, just as anxiously.

"I don't know," said McKay slowly, still scratching his head.

"Did I tell you we turned down a offer of a year's supply of furs?" said Bolls.

"No, you didn't tell me that," said McKay. He stared at the basket, at the goat, at the mule, and at the packhorses. "How much—"

"Well, for you," said Bolls in relief, "we'll not expect a year's supply of furs. No sir. From a fine, up-standing man like yourself why, we want only fifty furs."

"Fifty?" echoed Planke and McKay.

Bolls frowned at Planke. "Just to get the biddin' goin'," he said to McKay.

"I dunno," said McKay doubtfully.

"For a English lord's child?" exclaimed Bolls in mock horror. "Fifty furs is a bargain, sir! A bargain!"

"Why, me and my partner wouldn't be askin' so little, but we knowed you to be a good man," interjected Planke helpfully.

"You knowed that?" said McKay. "How'd you know that?"

"Why, by lookin' at you, sir," said Bolls desperately.

"That's it," nodded Planke enthusiastically. "By lookin' at you."

McKay smiled. "Well, that's right fine to know," he said and scratched his head. He glanced at the basket and the line of pack animals. His smile grew larger. "Tell you what—"

Bolls and Planke leaned forward expectantly. Bolls licked his lips.

"I don't want no baby," said McKay. "But—"

"You don't?" chorused Bolls and Planke, stunned.

"Hell, no. But I'll give you one pelt for the nanny goat. What do you say?"

Chapter Eleven

"We gotta get to Miz Witberg's before Trapper McKay does! Once Miz Witberg finds out Reverend Witberg's ailin', she's gonna forget all about babies," muttered Bolls. "Lucky I thought to tell McKay o' that 'shortcut' to the right Reverend's cabin."

Planke was still angry. "I thought he was goin' to buy the baby. I just knowed he was!"

"Yeah? Well, he didn't. So quit your bellyachin'." Bolls hurried on. "Come on, it's gettin' dark. We gotta get there before McKay."

"Gettin' dark?" exclaimed Planke after a while. "Why, it's startin' to snow!"

"Hurry!" cried Bolls. "Once McKay gets there, we won't have a chance to sell the baby to her. She'll be whinin' and cryin' over that injured husband of hers."

"What's the big hurry?" complained Planke. "She don't have no money."

"She got a Hudson's Bay blanket for a shawl, don't

she? She got a iron pot, don't she? She's probably got some old heirloom her great-great granny give her, too. Why, she's probably got gold hidden in that cabin! We'll take whatever we can sweet-talk her out of, I tell ya." Bolls grimaced at his partner. "Geez, sometimes you are so dumb!"

"Yeah?" snarled Planke. "Well, who's the smart one here? You? I don't see it myself. Tryin' to sell a baby to a old trapper who wants a goat!"

"Shut up!" roared Bolls. "Just you shut up!" He rifled through the saddlebags until he found the whiskey flask. He took a long swig. "Ah," he exclaimed. "That sure tastes good!"

"Don't it, though," sneered Planke. "You better give me some."

"Not likely," snarled Bolls.

"Give me some!" yelled Planke.

The baby started to cry.

"Now look what you done!" cried an infuriated Bolls. "You woke the baby!"

"That beaverdam baby's the cause o' all this!" cried Planke. "I'm cold, I'm wet, I'm thirsty, and that baby is squallin'. It ain't right!" He headed for the basket.

Bolls hurried after him. "Oh no, you don't," he cried. "You don't touch that baby. He's gonna mean *gold* for us yet. We need them heirlooms, remember? You leave him alone!"

Planke glared at Bolls. Bolls glared back at Planke. The baby wailed. Planke reached for the basket.

Bolls brought the whiskey flask down smartly on Planke's fingers.

"Owwww!"

"You stay away from that baby!"

Planke shook his fingers and then held his wounded hand. "That baby stinks."

"He always stinks!" said Bolls. "You leave him alone. You hear?"

"I hear," said Planke sullenly, nursing his sore hand.

"Good," said Bolls, tucking the whiskey flask into the mule's saddlebag. He peeked into the basket. "There, there," he muttered awkwardly. "Go to sleep, baby."

The child's cries gradually quieted.

"There," said Bolls in satisfaction. "Nothin' to it."

"Yeah," said a sullen Planke.

"Aw, don't take it so hard," consoled Bolls. "We'll be rid o' him soon."

"Not soon enough for my likin'," complained Planke.

"Come on," said Bolls, "we gotta get to Miz Witberg's cabin."

They tramped on. The snow came down harder and harder.

"Hey, Elijah?" cried Planke. "I can't see where in the hell we're goin. Can you?"

Bolls felt his way back along the pack train of animals. "Naw, I can't either. We're lost. This snow's comin' down so hard it's a blizzard!"

The baby cried.

"Put another blanket over it, or it'll freeze," directed Bolls. "Then we'll try and find our way. I'll lead."

They traveled blindly through the storm. There was no trail to follow. There was nothing but white wherever they looked. Soon they were hopelessly lost.

"What in the beaver balls is this?" muttered Bolls, bumping into something. His forehead hurt from striking the object. "Is it a tree?" He called back to his partner. "Planke? What the hell is this?"

Planke came forward, feeling his way along the pack animals' sides to guide him to Bolls. He felt the strange thing. "A tepee," he cried. "It's a damn tepee! We landed ourselves in a beaverdam Indian village!"

* * *

Huge flakes of snow drifted down outside the small cave that Hawk Catcher had found. Gentle Fawn snuggled further into his arms. A small fire at the cave's entrance kept them warm.

"It is good fortune we found this cave," she murmured. *And good fortune we were caught in a blizzard,* she thought guiltily.

It meant that she could stay just a little longer with Hawk Catcher. Soon enough she must tell him about finding another wife. But for now there were only the two of them and the fire and the silence of the blanketing snow.

Somehow she found peace. Perhaps it was simply knowing that he had cared enough to find her. The peace would be enough to keep her through the long night.

Chapter Twelve

The next morning, Planke and Bolls straggled out of the empty tepee they'd slept in and glanced around the Indian village. Several tepees were clustered in a circle. Smoke drifted out of the conical tops.

"Wonder if we should trade with these Injuns or if we should just move on to Miz Witberg's?" muttered Planke. "Snow's stopped. We could make good time."

"Ah, let's trade a few trinkets to them," answered Bolls. "We'll probably do better at the Witbergs', but why not pick up a fur or two here?"

"Might be some more money hidden around the cabin that Miz Witberg didn't tell us about," said Planke.

Bolls smiled at a young girl and held up a dangling blue bead necklace. "Come and get this, pretty girl," he coaxed. "What do you want to trade for it?"

Planke elbowed him. "We ain't got no time for playin' with no squaws."

"I ain't playin'," snapped Bolls. "Can't you tell when a man is tradin'?"

"Yeah." Planke sounded unconvinced.

The baby started to cry. An old woman wandered up and stared at the mule. The basket tied to the mule's back shifted and creaked. She pointed at it and said something.

"What the hell is she sayin'?" demanded Planke.

Bolls shrugged. The young girl walked away, placing the blue bead necklace over her head. With a grimace, Bolls strutted over to Planke and stuffed a beautifully beaded leather bag into the mule's saddlebag. "More beadwork," he sighed. "We got enough beadwork. I don't need more of it." He glanced at the elderly woman. "She wants to know about the baby," he explained.

He turned to the Indian woman and said, "Baby not for trade, you old beaver."

"She understand you?" asked Planke. "She might not like you callin' her a old beaver."

"Naw, she can't understand much, can you, you old beaver?" He grinned at her.

The woman grinned back.

"Lookit them front teeth," Bolls chortled. "Chisel teeth just like a beaver."

The woman said in her language, "I would not laugh so hard if I were you, fool. At least I have teeth! And," she added, pointing at the baby, "you are not caring well for that baby!"

"Look, I told you." Bolls held up his hands as if to ward off her stream of words. "No trading for the baby. No! None!" To Planke he said, "We can get a hell of a better deal from old Miz Witberg. All these Injuns got is beadwork. I got enough of that. Why, Miz Witberg's probably got coins hidden around that cabin. Probably lied to us."

"A *reverend's* wife?" asked Planke. "*Lie?*"

"Sure, why not? All women are liars, aren't they, old beaver?" He grinned at the elderly woman and

364

then glanced around. "It's time to get goin'," he said. "We still gotta beat McKay to the cabin, though the blizzard probably held him up too."

They led the pack train out of the village. The baby bounced along in the basket. "Maybe we'll come back here and trade, after we get the money from Miz Witberg," mused Bolls. "That Injun girl was right pretty. Maybe her papa will take a fur or two in exchange for her."

"You want a wife?" Planke sounded incredulous.

"Sure, why not? She's prettier than you. Probably cooks better than you do, too." Bolls dug in the saddlebag and pulled out his whiskey flask. He tipped it up and took a long draught, then wiped it off with a dirty hand. "Here," he said generously to the jealous, sullen Planke. "Have a wee drinkie."

Planke looked as if he was so angry he'd refuse, but he snatched the flask out of Bolls's grip and tilted it upward.

"Hey, that's enough!" cried Bolls, grabbing for the flask. "I said a drink, not the whole beaverdam flask!"

Planke grinned at him, his good humor fully restored.

"What's so funny?" demanded Bolls.

"You. Thanks for the drink."

"Your turn to change the baby," snarled Bolls. "That's all that drink was for. So's you'd change the baby."

Planke cursed all the way back to the mule.

"And you can feed him, too!" cried Bolls.

Gentle Fawn halted on the side of the hill in the snow. She and Hawk Catcher were still some distance from their village, but they would probably reach it by mid-afternoon. "What is that?" She pointed to a line of pack animals lurching through the snow. The wind blew a tiny cry to her, and suddenly she stiffened. "Do you hear it?"

"Hear what?" Hawk Catcher frowned. "I hear nothing."

Gentle Fawn trembled. Hawk Catcher was an excellent hunter. He could hear deer walking on the rocky trails. If he couldn't hear this tiny cry—like a baby's—then it must be supernatural. Her dead baby was crying out for her! She shuddered and drew closer to Hawk Catcher.

"What is it, wife?" He touched her shoulder. His warm touch calmed her and she smiled up at him. "I—I thought I heard—There! I hear it again!" The cry came from the line of pack animals. "It comes again!"

He shook his head. "I hear nothing."

"Oh, Hawk Catcher," she cried. "It is our baby. The one that died. He calls out to me! Oh, my baby, my baby!"

She ran, floundering through the deep snow and down the hill towards the line of pack animals. Hawk Catcher ran after her and pulled her back. "Gentle Fawn! I hear it this time too," he confirmed.

She halted and swung to face him. "You do?"

"Yes. It is not a ghost baby," he said. "It is something else." He indicated the pack train. "It comes from those animals."

She stared longingly at the passing train. "I must go to them," she muttered. "I must find out why a baby cries for me—"

"Wife," he counseled in a stern voice. "Do not do this. We do not know those men." He nodded at the two figures bent against the wind. "They are white men. White men do not take babies with them. We must let them go their way."

She hesitated. At last she admitted, "You give good advice, husband. I know not what troubled me. The

366

baby's cries—" She touched her forehead. "For a short time I thought it was our son."

Hawk Catcher enfolded her in his arms and kissed her on the top of her head. "I know you mourn our son's loss," he said. "As do I. But running after a line of horses is not going to help us. It will only cause us more grief."

"Yes, husband." They watched the pack train until it disappeared behind a hill. There were three horses and a mule, two men, and a black-and-white, dog-sized animal trotting beside the mule.

Gentle Fawn fell into step behind Hawk Catcher. Her heart still pounded from her scare. Even if her baby had been a ghost, she would have run to him. That was how desperately she wanted him back. And all wise Indians fled from ghosts.

When they reached the bottom of the hill, she walked over to look at the tracks. "See, husband!" she exclaimed. "The little tiny deer tracks. That must be the line of horses we tracked before."

Hawk Catcher stared at the tracks. "It is the little black-and-white animal that made the tracks," he marveled. "Very strange."

She agreed. "It did not look like a deer."

"No, not a deer."

They continued on their way back to their village. As they walked among the tepees, Gentle Fawn tried to keep her spirits up. But all too soon she must tell Hawk Catcher of her decision.

It was selfishness that made her want to hold on to him longer. If she truly loved him—and she did, deeply—then she must set him free to find a loving woman who could bear him his son. There was no other trail for her to take.

Chapter Thirteen

Gentle Fawn and Hawk Catcher stored the fresh beaver pelts and ate a meal. "It is good to be back in our village," observed Gentle Fawn, sitting beside the warm fire. Her sadness at what she must tell Hawk Catcher tinged her voice.

He glanced at her. "What ails you, wife?"

She shook her head, not ready to tell him. Not yet. Let her have a few more days with him . . . even a few more heartbeats.

"Gentle Fawn! Come out and see what I am wearing," cried a voice outside the tepee.

In relief, Gentle Fawn rose to her feet. "I must see why my sister's daughter calls me," she said quietly to Hawk Catcher. She avoided his intent black eyes and hurried out the doorway.

"Oh see, aunt!" cried her niece. "I have a lovely necklace." She lifted the blue beaded necklace she wore around her neck and held it out to Gentle Fawn. "See!"

The Treasure

"It is beautiful," agreed Gentle Fawn. She touched the blue glass beads. "Very beautiful."

"I got it from the traders," chortled her niece.

"Traders?"

"The two white men who stopped here during the blizzard." The girl's brown eyes danced. "I would have traded for more, but they left so swiftly. They had bracelets and armbands and kettles and thimbles and—"

"Did they have three horses and a mule?" asked Gentle Fawn.

"And a strange little black-and-white deer," added her niece.

"Yes, that was the line of horses I saw," mused Gentle Fawn. She smiled indulgently at her niece. "That necklace truly enhances your beauty."

Her niece nodded happily and skipped off. Gentle Fawn watched her go, wondering if she herself had ever been so carefree. No, she decided, shaking her head, she never had.

She had just ducked to re-enter her tepee when her old aunt, her father's sister, hailed her. "Gentle Fawn! Wait."

Gentle Fawn paused. This old aunt was the medicine woman who had delivered the sad news to Gentle Fawn that she would never be able to birth a healthy child. Warily, Gentle Fawn watched her aunt approach, wondering if she brought more bad tidings.

"What is it, Aunt?" Gentle Fawn asked guardedly.

Her aunt's wrinkled face broke into a smile and she touched Gentle Fawn's face with work-hardened fingers. Gentle Fawn met the older woman's gaze steadily.

"You were gone during the blizzard. I was concerned for you."

"I was with my husband," answered Gentle Fawn.

"We walked the beaver trapline and when the blizzard came, we waited in a cave."

"Very good," replied the older woman. She rubbed her lower back. "I did much walking. Before the blizzard I was visiting my husband's people. They are caring for an injured white man. He has a bad head wound, but I think he will get better now."

Gentle Fawn nodded. Her aunt was frequently sought out by neighboring tribes for her medical skills.

"Are you going to invite me into your home?" asked her aunt.

"Yes, Aunt," Gentle Fawn answered and entered the tepee. The old woman followed.

"Fine furs," grunted the old woman admiringly as she spied the beaver furs. Gentle Fawn nodded and helped her sit down. What did her aunt want?

Hawk Catcher nodded politely to her aunt, then rose. "I must see to my two horses," he said. "They will be hungry after this snowfall and will need more grass."

"I am surprised to hear that," noted Gentle Fawn's old aunt. "I did not think you ever fed them. They are so scrawny!"

Gentle Fawn heard the humor in her aunt's voice and so did Hawk Catcher.

"They may be scrawny," he agreed, "but they are well-trained."

"Hunh," grunted the old aunt. "They will not let me ride them."

"They are smart, too," said Hawk Catcher as he stepped outside.

"Hunh," grunted her aunt. She grinned at Gentle Fawn. "He is a good husband," she said approvingly.

Gentle Fawn stared at the swept dirt of her floor and nodded. She brushed away her tears when her aunt was not looking.

Her aunt spoke of the village, of the blizzard, of her days as a girl. She accepted some dried deer meat mixed with berries and fat and smacked her lips as she ate.

Gentle Fawn waited politely for her aunt to tell her why she had come to visit.

At last her aunt stopped speaking and sat silently. Gentle Fawn waited.

Finally the old woman said, "Two white traders visited our village this morning."

"I heard that," answered Gentle Fawn. "My niece traded for a pretty necklace."

"Those traders are fools," snapped her aunt.

Gentle Fawn wondered at the disapproval in her aunt's voice. She waited.

"They have a baby."

Gentle Fawn started. "I—I heard a baby's cries," she admitted. "I thought perhaps it was one of their animals crying."

"I do not think it is *their* baby!" Her aunt glanced at her sharply.

"Not their baby?" asked Gentle Fawn cautiously. "Did—did they offer to trade the baby?"

Her aunt shook her head. "They refused to trade the baby. But they do not treat the baby well. The baby was smelly and dirty."

"Perhaps they do not want the baby!" cried Gentle Fawn. Hope leaped in her heart.

Her aunt met her eyes. The wrinkled face looked thoughtful. "Perhaps."

Gentle Fawn stared at the fire, struggling with the warmth that turned her cheeks to flames. She remembered how the baby had cried out to her. She remembered how she had run through the snow to try and find the baby. Only Hawk Catcher had held her back. Excitement swept through her.

"I must speak with my husband," Gentle Fawn

said, rising to her feet. Her old aunt tried to rise also, but she was old and slow and she could not get up. Gentle Fawn helped her to her feet.

"I will go now," said the old aunt. She tottered out the door.

Gentle Fawn left the tepee and ran down the path to the corral where the horses were penned. "Hawk Catcher! Hawk Catcher!" she called. Breathless when she reached him, she tried desperately to regain her breathing before she spoke. "Traders!" she gasped. "Two traders! Baby!"

"What are you saying, wife?" demanded Hawk Catcher sternly.

She took a deep breath and slowed her breathing. "My old aunt told me that the traders who visited here *did* have a baby. They have a baby!"

He shrugged and turned back to feeding one of his mares. It was a chestnut, so thin her ribs showed.

"Hawk Catcher," said Gentle Fawn urgently. "We must go and trade for that baby!"

Hawk Catcher scraped with his moccasined foot at the snow underfoot and uncovered some more grass. He bent and picked it and gave it to the mare.

Gentle Fawn listened to the horse crunching the grass. "We must go, Hawk Catcher," she implored. "We can trade for the baby!"

At last he looked at her. His obsidian eyes were sad. "We know nothing about that baby," he said. "It may be sick. It may be that the baby is a son or daughter of one of the traders and they have no wish to trade him. . . . "

"My aunt said they refused to trade," admitted Gentle Fawn. She grasped his arm. "But we can try!" She met his eyes, her own desperate. "Please, Hawk Catcher. Let us go and offer for that baby!"

He stared into her eyes, as if trying to read into her very soul.

"Please?" she whispered. "It is my only chance. . . ."

"Hush," he said. He took a breath. "Very well," he answered at last. "We will go and find them. We will make our offer."

"Oh, Hawk Catcher!" She kissed him. "Oh, I am so happy!"

Excitedly she ran back to their tepee and began gathering up everything she thought she could offer for the baby: the twenty beaver furs that she had already tanned, the beadwork she had spent so many winter evenings sewing on a leather tunic, both of her biggest woven baskets, and a pair of moccasins she was saving to give to Hawk Catcher. She spied the papoose and hesitated. She stroked the soft leather hopefully, then she set it aside. She put on her buffalo robe and tied on her snowshoes. As she was heading out the doorway, she snatched up the last basket of dried strips of deer meat.

Hawk Catcher appeared, leading the two mares, the chestnut and the bay. "Did you get all the furs?" he asked, as he lifted the saddle and put it on the bay.

"Yes."

When he had loaded up the bay, he turned to saddle the chestnut. He tied the two bales of beaver pelts onto the chestnut. "These are our best furs," he said grimly.

"They are beautiful," she answered excitedly, stroking one of the furs. "The traders will want them."

He smiled at the confidence in her voice. "Let us ask your aunt which way they went," he said. "Perhaps she knows their destination."

Gentle Fawn nodded and ran off to ask her aunt.

"Oh, yes," answered the old woman, her face crinkling. "They wanted to go to the cabin of the white

man who lives near the fort—it is the white man who
speaks always of his god. I told the traders how to
get there." A satisfied smile crept across her face.
"But I told them the long way."

"Aunt," scolded Gentle Fawn. "You sent them the
long way?"

"I did," confirmed her aunt. "They are not good
men."

A shiver went through Gentle Fawn then as she
thought of the little baby with such men, but she did
not linger to say any more. She ran back to join
Hawk Catcher.

"We must journey towards the white man's cabin,"
she said. "There we will meet the traders!"

Chapter Fourteen

Gentle Fawn did not like the look of the traders. There was something about them that made her uneasy.

She watched Hawk Catcher approach them as they waited, stamping their feet in the snow.

"What do you want, Injun?" asked the shorter, burly one. He lifted a metal flask to his lips and took a long drink. Then he staggered as he handed it to his partner.

"Hurry up with it, Injun. You better have a good reason for stoppin' us. These horses are tired and we got somewhere we gotta be. Soon."

The other trader grinned at him, then took a draught from the flask. "Real soon."

Gentle Fawn understood a little of their language and she saw from their manner that they were rude. Not a good start to a trade.

Gentle Fawn led the mares up and stood behind Hawk Catcher. The wind blew sharply. The sky overhead was gray and heavy with clouds. Beneath her snowshoes, the snow's cold crept into her feet. She was thankful for the warm buffalo robes that she and Hawk Catcher wore.

She glanced at the mule. On one side of the mule's saddle balanced a big wooden cask. On the other side of the saddle was tied a large basket. The bitter wind tore at a tattered blanket covering the basket.

"Want to trade," said Hawk Catcher.

"Yeah?" The burly trader pushed his leather hat brim off his forehead. "And what might you be wantin' to trade?" He said to his partner, "Let's get rid of this Injun quick, Planke. I want to get to Miz Witberg's before that beaverdam trapper does."

"Want to trade for baby." Hawk Catcher's face was impassive as though he did not care one way or the other what the traders answered.

"Baby?" Bolls drew back, surprised.

"Well, now, this *is* mighty unusual," he said, stepping closer. "The baby, huh?" He rubbed his graying beard thoughtfully and glanced at the basket.

"Well, now," continued Bolls thoughtfully, "what are you prepared to trade?" He glanced at Gentle Fawn and grinned. "How 'bout the woman?"

Planke guffawed.

Hawk Catcher looked grim. Gentle Fawn moved closer to him. Small whimpers came from the basket on the mule. Her heartbeat quickened.

Hawk Catcher lifted his arm and swept it through the air, presenting the pelts that were tied on the bay mare's saddle. "Offer beaver furs."

"Furs," mused Bolls. He looked dubiously at his partner.

"Let's take a look-see," said Planke eagerly.

The two traders tromped through the snow and peered at the furs. "How many?"

Hawk Catcher held up ten fingers, closed them and

opened them again. Twenty.

Bolls glanced at the furs. His little eyes darted to his partner's and back to Hawk Catcher. "Not bad," he said laconically. "But I've seen better."

"Where?" asked Planke, fingering a thick pelt.

"I have, I tell you." Bolls glared at him. "Gimme that flask." He grabbed the flask from Planke's hand.

"Hey." Planke's mouth turned down in disappointment.

Hawk Catcher and Gentle Fawn waited. Gentle Fawn's excitement began to fade. The burly trader, the one she sensed was the chief, did not look pleased with the offer.

"Got anything else?" said Bolls, his eyes fastened greedily on the chestnut's load.

Gentle Fawn stepped over to the mare and pulled out her beadwork. She'd beaded a cowl of tiny green, white, red, and yellow beads on the breast of a soft leather tunic. It was her best work and she felt proud to offer it.

"Beads!" growled Bolls and turned away.

Gentle Fawn's eyes widened at this rejection of her work.

Next she showed him the two large baskets she'd woven.

"Baskets?" Bolls spat.

With trembling fingers, Gentle Fawn brought out the dried deer meat she'd preserved.

"Pemmican," said Bolls indifferently. "We got enough dried meat."

Hawk Catcher said, "Want baby."

"Too bad," said Bolls. "We got a better offer."

"Do you think Miz Witberg *can* offer better?" asked Planke uncertainly.

"Yeah," answered Bolls easily. "She's gotta have some gold hidden in that cabin." He glanced at the heavily clouded sky. "Let's go." To Hawk Catcher he said, "No trade, chief." He shook his head. "Not enough."

When she understood his words, despair flooded Gentle Fawn's heart. Not enough!

She met Hawk Catcher's eyes. His black eyes snapped with anger.

Bolls took the mule's lead. "See ya, chief."

He and Planke slowly walked away, leading their horses and mule through the snow. The little black-and-white goat gave a stuttering cry as she tried to jump through the knee-high drifts behind the mule.

With great sadness, Gentle Fawn watched the mule depart, the basket swaying. She bowed her head while despair engulfed her.

"White man!" called Hawk Catcher.

Bolls paused. He turned. "What?"

Hawk Catcher gestured at the chestnut mare, one of his precious horses, the star of his herd. "Offer horse."

Bolls came tramping back. "Which one?"

Hawk Catcher indicated the chestnut. "Good horse."

Bolls eyed the mare consideringly. "Too skinny," he said, but there was a light in his eye now. "Wouldn't even take both horses," he said. "They look like too much trouble. I'd need too much hay to fatten them up just so's they could carry a regular load."

The basket on the mule stirred and Gentle Fawn heard a tiny cry. Her heart constricted. The baby! How she wanted the baby! She took a step towards the basket. A baby to hold, to love, to take care of . . . and to give to Hawk Catcher. *Please, Great Spirit,* she prayed. *Please!*

"Naw. Sure is a shame you don't have enough, though." Bolls sauntered back to join his partner.

Gentle Fawn watched them as the horses pawed a trail through the snow once more.

Hawk Catcher bowed his head.

Gentle Fawn refused to give up. She ran after the burly trader.

"White man!" she dared to call, her voice high and piercing on the wind.

Bolls turned.

She ran across the snow, awkward in her snow-shoes. Her breath panted steam into the air. She took off her buffalo robe and handed it to him. "Here."

He threw it back at her. "Naw, not enough."

Then he laughed and walked away.

Chapter Fifteen

Snow drifted down from the heavy gray sky.

Hawk Catcher, his face grim, stalked after the traders. Gentle Fawn held a breath. As he passed her, she whispered, "It will do no good, Hawk Catcher. These traders but play with us."

"They know we want the baby," said Hawk Catcher grimly. "They will take everything from us."

He strode after the pack train. "Trader!" he thundered.

"Yeah?" Bolls turned, his face screwed tight against the white of the snow. "What you want, Injun?"

Hawk Catcher, face stony, took off his buffalo robe and threw it in the snow at the trader's feet.

Bolls slowly bent and picked up the robe. A beatific smile wreathed his face. "Well now, chief, I suppose I can take your buffalo robe. Yer horses are skinny, but I suppose they'll do. I'd say we got a deal!" The smile disappeared. "I want all your furs, all your woman's trinkets, both horses, and both buffalo robes. What do you say?"

"Give me baby," Hawk Catcher's face was impassive.

"Yeah, sure, chief." Bolls took a swig of his whiskey.

"I thought we were gonna trade the baby to Miz Witberg," said Planke, scratching his head in befuddlement.

"Naw." Bolls gave him a withering glance. "That trapper probably reached her by now." He glanced at the sky. "It's cold out, snowin', and this here is a firm offer, ain't it, chief?" He grinned at Hawk Catcher, then tottered over to the mule.

Gentle Fawn was already there, reaching for the basket.

"Well now, mama," chortled Bolls, pushing her aside, "you want this baby, huh? Real bad, don't you?" He lowered his face and looked her right in the eye.

She reeled back from the gust of his breath, but it mattered not. Her heart, her hands, trembled with hope.

He untied the basket and lifted it off the mule, then he lifted the blanket and peered in. Weak whimpers came from inside.

He peeled off the tattered blanket and took the baby out. Her eyes followed his every move. He handed her the baby. "Here."

Heart pounding like a drum, she reached for the tiny baby. "Ohhhhh," she moaned, drawing the tiny one close. "You are so precious," she whispered in his ear. "You are so sweet. I love you!"

He weighed little in her arms. He was so small and thin, but he was her baby. A welling of love pooled in her heart. She met Hawk Catcher's gaze over the top of the baby's head. She smiled and he smiled back.

Her eyes full of grateful tears, she bent and closed them as she kissed the baby on top of his little head. Her heart soared.

Suddenly she paused; the baby smelled very bad. She opened her eyes and glared at Bolls, disgusted that he would let such a thing happen.

He grinned at her.

The baby shivered and whimpered. She reached for the tattered blanket on the basket so she could wrap him and keep him warm.

"Oh no, you don't," said Bolls, snatching the blanket out of her reach. "A deal's a deal. No one said nothin' about no blanket in this deal." He chuckled. "You're lucky I'm letting you keep the diaper."

She turned away from him and bumped into Hawk Catcher's broad chest. Her eyes met his. "How can I feed him?" she asked, her stomach clenched in fear. "I have no milk." Had they come so far only to be defeated?

"How you feed baby?" demanded Hawk Catcher of Bolls.

Bolls jerked his thumb at the goat. "Squirt him the milk from the goat."

"Goat? Want goat then." Hawk Catcher glared at Bolls.

Bolls stared at him, considering. At last he sighed, "I guess you need the goat to feed the baby. Tell you what." Bolls looked suddenly pleased with himself. "You give me that there fine flintlock rifle you got, and I'll give you the goat."

"No. Need rifle. Shoot deer." Hawk Catcher's eyes were cold.

"But will the rifle be enough to keep us from starving?" wondered Gentle Fawn. "And how will we keep warm in the snows?"

Hawk Catcher still argued with the trader.

"Enough. Give goat." Hawk Catcher's fists clenched on the barrel of the flintlock.

"Oh, all right, chief," muttered Bolls. "Take the beaverdam goat. Can't do nothin' with it anyway."

Hawk Catcher walked over and untied the goat's lead rein from the mule's saddle. Then he whispered farewell to each one of the mares.

The baby shivered in Gentle Fawn's arms. He was naked from the waist up and wore only a torn rag around his little hips. "He is cold," she told Hawk Catcher. She cuddled the baby close to her breast in an attempt to warm him.

Hawk Catcher glared at Bolls.

Bolls ignored him and said, "Come on, Planke. Let's go."

"Go where?" asked Planke. "No sense goin' to Miz Witberg's cabin now. Where should we go?"

"Since it's snowin'," said Bolls, "we'll go to Fort McCraig." He grinned at his partner. "The fort's close by and, after all, it *is* Christmas Eve."

Planke scratched his chin and his face brightened. "Christmas Eve? It is?"

"Time to celebrate," said Bolls, taking another drink from the flask. He handed the flask to Planke. "Here. Have a drink. We done a good day's tradin', thanks to chief and mama here."

They took one last swig of whiskey each, then headed off in the direction of Fort McCraig.

Hawk Catcher peeled off his leather shirt and wrapped it, still warm from his own body, around the baby. Gentle Fawn thanked him with her eyes. "I love you," she whispered to him.

He gave a grim smile. "Let us return to our tepee. We must get our baby to a warm fireside. We must hurry. I fear for you in this cold."

She clutched her precious baby tightly. "Do not fear for me, husband. I have much to keep me warm," she said and followed him into the darkening night.

Chapter Sixteen

Fort McCraig
Christmas Eve night, 1825

"Look at that," said Bolls as they approached Fort McCraig. "They didn't close the gates yet."

"It's after dark," slurred Planke. "They should've closed 'em by now."

"Listen to all that singing," said Bolls. "Sounds like a whooping good party to me!"

"Who goes there?" yelled a voice out of the gloom.

"Elijah Bolls and Jesse Planke. Free traders!" Bolls teetered as he snatched the flask from Planke. "And mighty fine traders we are, I might add!"

A trapper tottered up. "Unload your animals there," he said, jerking his thumb in the direction of some sheds. "And then come on over to the big party we're having at the men's quarters!"

"Sounds good to me," said Bolls.

They walked the mules and their three horses and

thc two scrawny Indian horses over to the corral.

"Aw," complained Planke. "It's gonna take too long to unload these horses."

Bolls glanced at the pack train. "Yeah," he agreed. "Say, I have an idee. These horses ain't goin' nowhere. Why don't we unload 'em later? That way, we can go over now and have a wee drinkie with the boys."

"Yeah," said Planke.

Bolls walked over to the mule and filled up the whiskey flask. Then he tucked it inside his shirt and patted it protectively.

Just as they reached the men's quarters, it began to snow harder. "Sure glad we beat the snow," Planke said, shivering.

They entered the low-ceilinged quarters. The small rooms, linked by open doorways, were crowded. Four men sat on a narrow wooden bunk. Two were crowded onto a top bunk. More men sat on the floor, anywhere they could find a place to squeeze in. Blue smoke hung in the lantern light, and a fire burned at the far end of the quarters.

"Let me tell you about this trade I made tonight," chuckled Bolls to the listening men. "Me and my partner here, we got furs, we got horses, we are rich men!" He roared his delight and slapped his leg for emphasis.

"Yahoo!" cried a man. "Let's drink to that!"

Planke grinned at Bolls. "This is a hell of a lot better 'n dragging a baby around."

"Sure is," agreed Bolls happily.

"Ooooooh," moaned Bolls. "I don't feel so good."

Planke snored at his side. All around them on the rough wooden floor lay men passed out from all the drinking and partying in the night.

The Treasure

"Wake up, Planke." Bolls elbowed his partner.

"Huh?" Planke blinked and tried to sit up.

"I said 'wake up' for beaversakes," said Bolls. "I don't feel so good."

"Yeah? What can *I* do about it?" yawned Planke.

"You can listen to me, for one thing," complained Bolls.

"I'm listenin'." Planke yawned again.

"I had a bad dream," said Bolls.

"Tell me about it later," whined Planke. "I want to sleep."

"Well, that's too beaverdam bad," snarled Bolls. "You listen to my dream!"

"Oh, all right. What was it?" Planke lay back down and closed his eyes.

"I—I, oh, it was a bad dream, Jesse. I dreamt I traded away a treasure."

Planke grunted unsympathetically in response.

"It was a bad trade too," worried Bolls. "I traded away a sack of gold for two piles of dirt and two worthless rocks." He blinked. "Can you see me makin' such a trade, Planke? Can you?" He muttered to himself. "Not me, not me."

Planke had fallen asleep.

"Wake up, you beaver!" prodded Bolls, irritated that his audience had fallen asleep. When Planke was awake again, Bolls explained his dream once more.

"Sounds like you made a bad trade," acknowledged Planke. "Real bad. You're usually a better trader than that!"

Bolls said sourly, "I didn't really make the trade, you fool! I *dreamt* it."

"Yeah? Oh."

"I sure don't feel good about it, though," continued Bolls. "I feel like I done lost a treasure. . . ."

Chapter Seventeen

Dawn's light crept through the doorway of the tepee. Gentle Fawn woke from her dream to find her baby still in her arms. She kissed the top of his head. Beside her, Hawk Catcher stirred, and she leaned back against his warm chest. The goat slept at their feet, keeping them warm in the night. "I am so happy," she murmured. "I have my husband, I have my baby. . . . "

"He smells better, too," said Hawk Catcher's deep voice.

She turned and smiled at him. "I thought you still slept," she said.

"I, too, am excited," he answered.

"About the baby?"

He nodded and his eyes twinkled. He kissed her lips. "And about you," he whispered.

She smiled. "Our son liked his bath last night."

"He should," said Hawk Catcher. "It was probably the first good cleaning he ever had."

The Treasure

She brought the baby out from the bedrobes and checked his diaper.

"The bear fat and healing herbs that I put on his bottom are healing his skin," she observed. "His skin looks much better." She kissed the baby.

He gurgled and she murmured to him, "I love you, little one. I am so glad you have come to live with my husband and me."

There was a little tinkling sound outside the tepee. Hawk Catcher rose to see what it was, but Gentle Fawn's hand on his arm stopped him. "I had a dream last night, husband," she said.

He sank back down beside her. "What was it?" He leaned over and sniffed the baby's head. He skimmed a finger over the baby's soft arm.

"It was a beautiful dream." Gentle Fawn sighed happily. "I dreamt our son was a grown man. He was loved by our people. From far and near, people came to speak with him and to learn from his wisdom." She glanced down at the baby she held in her arms. "In my dream the young man, our son, was named Treasure."

"Treasure." Hawk Catcher rolled the sound around on his tongue. "It sounds good," he said thoughtfully. "Let us call him that."

"He will be a great hunter, too," continued Gentle Fawn. "In my dream, our tepee never lacked for meat."

"Were we old in your dream?" asked Hawk Catcher curiously.

"Yes. And you were still handsome." She smiled dreamily at him.

Again came the tinkling sound.

"I will go and see what makes that noise." Hawk Catcher moved aside a blanket from the doorway and poked his head outside the tepee.

"Gentle Fawn," he said softly. "Look."

389

"What is it?" She crawled out of the blankets, carrying the baby with her. She would hold on to her baby!

She poked her head out of the tepee and stared in awe at the sight that greeted her eyes.

In the snow stood five fully laden horses and a mule. They were all tied together by a lead rein that now dragged in the snow. The lead horse was Hawk Catcher's scrawny, well-trained chestnut mare.

"Wha—what?" she gasped. "How did this happen?"

Hawk Catcher shook his head in disbelief. "It is the traders' horses and their mule. And all the trading goods they owned!"

"And our furs," she added excitedly. "And my beadwork!"

Hawk Catcher started to laugh. "The horses must have broken free from the traders, and my chestnut mare guided them back to our village." He glanced at Gentle Fawn. "I told you they were smart horses."

"You did, husband," she said slowly. "This is a wonderful gift for our son," she proclaimed.

In the tepee behind them, the goat gave a soft *baa*. Hawk Catcher put his arm around Gentle Fawn and kissed her. "Now we will survive the winter very well."

Gentle Fawn gave a long, happy sigh. "We will," she confirmed. "I have you to love. I have our son. I am truly blessed among women."

And as they turned and went back into the warmth of their tepee, snow began to fall softly. Soon the horses' tracks were hidden under a blanket of white.

AUTHOR'S NOTE

I hope you enjoyed reading "The Treasure" as much as I enjoyed writing it!

If you want to read more about the fur trade days, watch for my next novel, *Captive Legacy*. It is a Leisure release and will be available in January, 1996.

REFERENCES

Brown, Jennifer S.H. (1980) *Strangers in Blood: Fur Trade Company Families in Indian Country*. The University of British Columbia Press. Vancouver, B.C., Canada.

Combes, John D. (1964) *Excavations at Spokane House—Fort Spokane Historic Site 1962–1963*. Washington State University. Pullman, WA.

Garth, Thomas R. (1952) "Archeological Excavations at Fort Walla Walla." *Pacific Northwest Quarterly*, Vol. 43, pp. 27–50.

Stern, Theodore. (1993) *Chiefs and Chief Traders: Indian Relations at Fort Nez Perces, 1818–1855*. Oregon State University Press. Corvallis, OR.

Their First Noel

DON'T MISS THESE FOUR HISTORICAL ROMANCE STORIES THAT CELEBRATE THE JOY OF CHRISTMAS AND THE MIRACLE OF BIRTH.

LEIGH GREENWOOD
"Father Christmas"

Arizona Territory, 1880. Delivering a young widow's baby during the holiday season transforms the heart of a lonely drifter.

BOBBY HUTCHINSON
"Lantern In The Window"

Alberta, 1886. After losing his wife and infant son, a bereaved farmer vows not to love again—until a fiery beauty helps him bury the ghosts of Christmases past.

CONNIE MASON
"A Christmas Miracle"

New York, 1867. A Yuletide birth brings a wealthy businessman and a penniless immigrant the happiness they have always desired.

THERESA SCOTT
"The Treasure"

Washington Territory, 1825. A childless Indian couple receives the greatest gift of all: the son they never thought they'd have.

__3865-X**(Four Christmas stories in one volume)**$5.99 US/$7.99 CAN

Dorchester Publishing Co., Inc.
65 Commerce Road
Stamford, CT 06902

Please add $1.75 for shipping and handling for the first book and $.50 for each book thereafter. NY, NYC, PA and CT residents, please add appropriate sales tax. No cash, stamps, or C.O.D.s. All orders shipped within 6 weeks via postal service book rate. Canadian orders require $2.00 extra postage and must be paid in U.S. dollars through a U.S. banking facility.

Name_____
Address _____
City _____ State_____Zip_____
I have enclosed $_____in payment for the checked book(s).
Payment <u>must</u> accompany all orders.☐ Please send a free catalog.

TIMESWEPT

Christmas Carol *FLORA SPEER*

Bestselling Author of *A Love Beyond Time*

Bah! Humbug! That is what Carol Simmons says to the holidays, mistletoe, and the ghost in her room. But the mysterious specter has come to save the heartless spinster from a loveless life. Soon Carol is traveling through the ages to three different London Yuletides—and into the arms of a trio of dashing suitors. From Christmas past to Christmas future, the passionate caresses of the one man meant for her teach Carol that the season is about a lot more than Christmas presents.

_51986-0 $4.99 US/$5.99 CAN

WINTER LOVE

NORAH HESS

"Norah Hess overwhelms you with characters who seem to be breathing right next to you!"
—Romantic Times

Winter Love. As fresh and enchanting as a new snowfall, Laura has always adored Fletcher Thomas. Yet she fears she will never win the trapper's heart—until one passion-filled night in his father's barn. Lost in his heated caresses, the innocent beauty succumbs to a desire as strong and unpredictable as a Michigan blizzard. But Laura barely clears her head of Fletch's musky scent and the sweet smell of hay before circumstances separate them and threaten to end their winter love.

__3864-1 $5.99 US/$7.99 CAN